A Tessa & Weston Collection

SNAP SHOTS OF SUN LIGHT

ABBIE EMMONS

www.abbieemmonsauthor.com
www.100daysofsunlight.com

ISBN: 978-1-7339733-8-0

For Mum,
without whom I would not be a writer.
You are my sunlight.

TABLE OF CONTENTS

THE JOB

A Weston Story

WESTON

THEY SAY YOU NEVER FORGET YOUR FIRST JOB. THE
hard, honest day's work, the smell of dollar bills as you cash your
first paycheck, the expensive dates you take your girl on because
you're a working man now, and that means you can blow your
money on anything you like.

At least, that's how I always imagined my first job would be.
A cliché to live up to my childhood dreams of the struggle for the
legal tender. Sweat and pain. Demanding bosses. Coming home
at night and grumbling about work like a grownup.

And by "work," I don't mean *The Rockford Chronicle.* By
"demanding bosses," I don't mean my dad (although he can be
demanding sometimes). My weekly summer visits to help at the
newspaper felt less like work and more like a get-out-of-jail-free
card for something else I didn't want to do. It was fun to see where
my father spent his days, toiling over ad copy and problematic
margins and editors' editorials that still needed editing.

When I was a kid, my dad seemed larger than life—the

William Randolph Hearst of upstate New York. A visionary, a dreamer, a legend who would occasionally put his hand on my shoulder and say, "One day, Weston, you'll be the boss of this entire operation."

I always knew the job was mine if I wanted it.

But when you're seventeen, working for your dad isn't exactly what you call *a job*. For one thing, you can't complain about it to anyone at home unless you want to trigger Armageddon.

For another thing, it doesn't feel earned.

It feels handed to you on a silver platter with your name on it.

Call it pride, call it ego, call it whatever you like—I don't want a favor.

I want a job.

A real, hard-earned job.

A job I have to impress someone to get and work my ass off to keep.

Like every other seventeen-year-old before me.

And that's why I stop dead in my tracks halfway down Main Street at six forty-five p.m. It's an ordinary late-spring night—cold enough for jeans and a hoodie, but warm enough to make the crickets scream extra loud. I'm headed for Anthony's on the corner, to pick up a pizza and bring it back to Tessa's house, but everything slams to a stop when I see the sign.

HELP WANTED

Taped to the window of Bruiser's Boxing Gym.

Surprisingly, I've never been to this place before. It's one of those pay-to-be-a-member deals, which automatically disqualifies any guy without a steady income who has a girlfriend to keep happy with what little savings he's accumulated from odd jobs.

I've always wanted to train at Bruiser's. There's something about those rows of scuffed-up heavy bags, those shiny wood floors, those walls dripping with MMA posters and boxing memorabilia. You can almost smell the sweat and blood and victory, just looking through the windows into the lit-up gym. It's closing time, and there's only one person left in the place: the owner, mopping down the floors.

I recognize him because I've seen his truck parked on the street outside the gym—a beast of a lifted Chevy pickup with US Marine stickers all over the back window. The guy himself is like a human version of a lifted pickup: boulder shoulders, tattooed biceps the size of Everest, a ferocious buzz cut, and a permanent frown carved onto his face.

Not exactly the most approachable dude in the world. I can see why they call him Bruiser. But I'm not scared of the guy. What's the worst that could happen?

I decide to try my luck.

He's got his back to me when I step inside, setting off the door chime. "We're closed," he mutters in a gruff New York accent, aggressively pushing the mop back and forth.

"I know," I holler back over the '80s rock music blasting from the radio. "I'm not here to train. I… wanted to ask about the job."

That's when Mr. Bruiser finally turns around to look at me. He squints, giving me a once-over, and I'm suddenly glad I wore pants instead of shorts tonight. At first glance, I look like just an average high school grad in red Jordans and a UFC hoodie.

"I'm Weston," I say, because now seems like a good time to get on first-name terms.

Mr. Bruiser apparently doesn't share this opinion. He sets the mop aside and walks over to the radio, cranking the volume down low.

"You got any experience in boxing, Weston?"

"Yes, sir. I've done a lot of training over the past five or six years. Sparring with friends, that kinda thing."

"Where'd you learn?"

"Uh…" I shrug, rubbing the back of my neck. "I just picked it up, you know? I watch a lot of fights and try to learn technique. Practice on my best friend until he gets sick of getting his ass handed to him."

Bruiser grunts a dry laugh. I'm well aware of how unqualified I sound—an amateur enthusiast at best, talking up to a guy who was probably a heavyweight champion back in the day. I try to ignore the glint of trophies tucked in a glass case beside the benches. The guy's military tats are intimidating enough.

"Look, sir, I know I might not be the most qualified person for the job, whatever it is. But I love fighting. I love just… being in a place like this. And I'm a quick learner. I could do anything you want. Mopping the floor, for one thing. Uh, fixing stuff, cleaning up, keeping the equipment straight—"

"I don't need a janitor, kid." Bruiser cuts me off with a hard look in my direction. "I need an instructor."

My eyebrows rise. "An instructor?"

"That's right. Business has been picking up lately. I lead the classes, but it's been tough to keep up with everyone. The more students I've got in a class, the less time I can spend with each one of them. I need an assistant—a right-hand man who can do exactly what I would do without me having to train *him*, too. You catch my drift?"

I nod. "Yes, sir. And I think I could do that."

"You do, huh?"

"Yeah."

The way he squints at me makes my palms sweat. "How the hell old are you, kid?"

"I'll be eighteen in September."

A half-amused smirk twitches one side of his mouth. He's either about to laugh at me, or he's about to say, "You got the job."

But to my surprise, he doesn't do either of those things. He just steps up to me and taps his chest with one hand.

"Throw a punch."

I hesitate.

Throw a punch? At this dude who's twice my size?

Somehow, it's not the job interview I was expecting. In my imagination, there was going to be a civilized discussion with résumés and weak coffee and questions about dedication and work ethic. But there's only one way to respond to an ex-Marine boxer called Bruiser who tells you to throw a punch.

I throw a punch.

And God, the pecs on this guy. It's like hitting a rock wall.

He doesn't flinch.

"Come on, that's all you got? *Throw a punch.*"

I try again, driving my full weight into it.

BAM.

No flinch.

No response.

He just shakes his head and mutters under his breath, "Pansy-ass."

Okay, *that* pisses me off.

Who does this guy think he is, calling me pansy-ass?

He has no idea who I am.

This time, I *throw.* Hard.

But before my fist hits that iron chest, his hand shoots up

and blocks my punch. Bone-on-bone—*ouch*. A sizzle of pain numbs my forearm. I flow with it, ducking to miss his jab at my face, upper-blocking to knock off his right hook. I don't think about what I'm doing. It's all instinct, primal. In one fluid motion, I lurch forward and uppercut him in the stomach as hard as I can.

This time, he grunts—jerking back a step and rubbing his rock-hard abdomen where I landed my shot. His gaze is cold as ice as he stares at me, wordless, muscles wound tight.

Ohhhhh shit.

I stagger backwards, my life flashing before my eyes. I think about Tessa, how I'll never get to eat that pizza with her tonight. How I'll never get to make out with her again. Will she be at my funeral? Or will this guy dump my body in the woods to be eaten by vultures?

That's when he takes me by surprise, cracking a grin. "Not bad, kid."

I'm speechless. "Really?"

"Come back tomorrow morning before we open. I'll run you through a few drills and see what else you've got. Then we'll talk about the job."

It's impossible to keep the grin off my face. "Sounds great. Thank you, sir. I-I appreciate it."

The civil thing to do at this point is to reach out for a handshake, right? I go for it, but Bruiser doesn't move. Just stands there looking at me like I'm the world's biggest idiot for thinking I could shake his hand.

I clear my throat, hands retreating to my pockets. A nervous laugh stutters out of me as I walk back to the door. "I'll… uh… see you tomorrow morning."

Tessa looks like a dream come true when she swings open her front door and finds me standing on the porch. She's wearing one of my T-shirts, which is way too big for her, but somehow, it's the sexiest outfit I've ever seen.

"Pizza delivery," I say, extending the boxes.

She smiles, taking them and stepping back into the house. "Thank you, delivery boy." She pushes the door shut, but I stick my foot in the crack at the last second.

"OW! OW, MY FOOT! YOU JUST BROKE MY FOOT!"

Tessa gasps and whips the door open, her eyes wide. It usually takes her a moment to get jokes like that, which is amusing for me because my brothers don't fall for my fake-outs anymore.

Tessa bursts into laughter when she sees me laughing. Next thing I know, she's pulling me inside and kissing me, ditching the pizza boxes on a side table. I twirl her around, pushing her back against the closed door and squeezing her hips as I kiss her deep and slow, kiss her like a guy who just won the lottery.

"Mmm, you smell so good," I murmur against the curve of her neck, pulling her into a full-body hug. "You *feel* so good."

"Weston, my mom is here." She hisses it like a warning, so I back off. Her cheeks are all pink, and her shirt is rumpled, but she straightens up primly for her mother, who wanders into the foyer at the smell of pizza.

"Tessa, are you making out with the delivery boy again?" Heather jokes with a knowing smirk at her daughter.

Tessa says, "No," at the same time I say, "Yes."

Her grandparents are out with friends tonight, so it's just the three of us. Rather, just the two of us, because Heather takes her pizza to the couch and watches *Real Housewives* reruns while Tessa and I stuff our faces in the kitchen.

"Is something going on?" Tessa questions me halfway through dinner. "You're acting so… jaunty."

"Jaunty? What does that mean? Why do you always use these words I don't understand?"

"Chipper," she clarifies. "Lively, cheerful."

"I hope I'm always lively and cheerful."

"You are… you just… seem different tonight." She tilts her head, studying me like a psychic trying to draw out my secrets. "Has something happened?"

I shrug one shoulder, trying to keep the grin off my face. "Something *might* be happening. I applied for a job. Well, sort of."

"Really? Where?"

"The boxing gym downtown."

Tessa's eyebrows shoot up. "Really? What kind of work is it?"

"Assistant instructor. Helping out with classes, that kinda thing."

"Wow. That's awesome, Wes. When do you find out if you got the job?"

"Uh, tomorrow morning, I think. The owner, Bruiser, wants me to go there in the morning and do some boxing drills and stuff."

Tessa frowns. "Bruiser? What kind of name is that?"

"I don't know. A badass name?"

"What's he like?"

I tilt my head, not sure how to put him into words. "He's… an ex-Marine. Jacked as hell, man. He made me punch him, and he's, like, a hundred percent steel. I almost broke my knuckles."

"He made you *punch* him?"

"Yeah. It was no big deal." I lean back in my chair, feeling smug as I fold my hands behind my head. "I think he was impressed by how fast I was to react."

Tessa looks slightly appalled by the idea of using physical violence to qualify for a job, but she smiles lovingly across the table at me. "I'm happy for you, Wes. I hope it turns out well."

"Yeah. I hope so, too."

She narrows her eyes. "What is it?"

"What is what?"

"That look."

"What look?"

She leans her elbows on the table, peering at me like a psychic again. "*That* look I just saw two seconds ago. Are you... nervous about something?"

God, how can she see right through me like that? See the feelings I try to shove away before *I* even acknowledge what I'm feeling?

"I'm not nervous. I just..." I look down at the tabletop, running my fingertip over the lines in the wood. "He doesn't know. Yet."

There's no need to say *what* he doesn't know. Tessa understands. She nods slowly but says nothing, giving me space to spill my guts.

"It just didn't come up, and I didn't see the point in mentioning it, you know? I was afraid if he *did* know, he might assume... he might not give me a chance to prove what I can do." I glance back up at Tessa, who watches me with big blue eyes full of understanding. "I just wanted to be treated like any other guy who walked into that place looking for a job."

"That makes sense," Tessa says quietly. "So, what are you going to do tomorrow?"

I shrug one shoulder. "I don't know. I was thinking I could… hide it for a little while. You can't really tell when I'm wearing sweatpants. He doesn't have to know. Not right away."

Tessa reaches across the table and slides her warm, soft hand into mine. "That doesn't sound like the confident, devil-may-care Weston Ludovico I know."

I grunt a tired laugh.

"You know what I think you should do?" Tessa says.

"What?"

"Be yourself." She smiles, squeezing my fingers. "Don't feel you have to hide. It's nothing to be ashamed of. I know you want to impress this Bruiser guy, but… you shouldn't have to put on a mask to do that. If he's not impressed by you being *exactly* who you are, then he's not worth your time."

She's right.

I know she's right.

So why do I feel a knot in my stomach when I think about *being myself?*

I wake up at six o'clock the next morning, put on my prosthetic legs, and brush my teeth. Then I stand in front of my dresser for about fifteen minutes, trying to decide whether I should wear sweats or basketball shorts.

Standard workout clothes are shorts and a T-shirt, always. Eventually I rip off the T-shirt too when I get drenched in sweat. And boxing drills always mean lots and lots of sweat. *Sweat every-*

where, especially in my prosthetic socks, which make my stumps feel like they're swimming in liquid fire.

The last thing I want to do is wear pants.

But then I remember the way Bruiser looked at me last night—sizing me up in one quick glance. A high school kid, looking for work. Nothing more. Nothing less.

Throw a punch.

I had a feeling he'd said that to a million other kids before me. Those pecs of steel were used to getting blitzed by try-hard boxers in the making. That's what I want him to see when he looks at me.

A fighter.

Not an amputee.

So I shove my basketball shorts back into the drawer and slide it shut. It's not until I'm pulling up my pants that I remember Tessa's words from last night. The way she looked at me from across the table, her hand in mine.

Be yourself. Don't feel you have to hide.

She had a point. Bruiser is going to find out eventually, so why keep it from him now? If he changes his mind about me because of my legs, what does that say about the kind of guy he is?

I shouldn't care about this so much.

Why do I care about this so much?

Why am I so nervous?

"Pansy-ass," I mutter under my breath, shoving my sweats back in the drawer and taking out my basketball shorts instead.

———————

Bruiser is in the back office when I arrive at the boxing gym. I can't see him, but I hear him holler, "I'll be right there, kid!" as soon as I walk through the front door. The place looks different in the daylight. Less warm and welcoming, more cold and aggressive. While waiting for my potential future boss to show his face, I wander around the gym and check out the memorabilia covering the walls.

Vintage posters, sports magazines, boxing gloves autographed by all the greats: Muhammad Ali, Mike Tyson, Joe Louis, on and on it goes. There's a lot of MMA stuff mixed in with it, proving Bruiser to be a mutt like me—not a ride-or-die purebred boxer. I wonder where he first learned how to throw a punch. I wonder if he used to have brotherly fistfights with his best friend, like Rudy and I do.

My gaze catches on a framed photo that seems out of place among all the sports collectibles. It's a group shot of four Marines in full gear, standing in front of a Humvee in the desert. They're all grinning, faces shiny with sweat. It must have been a hundred degrees when this picture was taken, but they don't seem to care. Their smiles are reckless and immortal. One of them is making a "rock on" sign; another one is flipping his middle finger at the camera.

I recognize a much younger Bruiser on the left side, his arm slung around the shoulders of the rock-on guy. He looks so different, but that resting grumpy face is unmistakable. Somehow, even when he's smiling, he looks ready to kill someone. Or maybe that's just the sniper rifle he's got slung under his free arm.

"Alright, kid, let's see what you can—"

"Where was this picture taken?" The question pops out before I can think twice about it. When Bruiser doesn't reply, I turn around to look at him—half afraid I've shot my mouth off already.

But that's not the reason he's standing frozen two steps outside the office, his face pale and his gaze stuck on my legs.

Oh, right.

I almost forgot.

It's funny how, even after four years of walking around on prosthetic legs, the Reaction still hits me like a sucker punch. I feel it all the way to my guts. I tell people I've gotten used to it, and that's true—I *have* gotten used to it. Kind of like how Houdini got used to people slugging him in the stomach. Until one day, it killed him.

I'm not sure what I was expecting Bruiser's reaction to be— I hardly know the guy, after all. Given his gruff attitude and sleeve-ripper biceps, I was betting on either a stiff shot of tough-luck sympathy or total avoidance of the topic.

What I didn't predict was for him to drop his coffee cup on the floor.

It happens in a split second: He looks at my prosthetic legs, freezes up like he's just seen a ghost, then—

SMASH.

The cup shatters.

It's a first.

We both just stand there looking at each other for a painfully awkward moment, unsure of what to say. I *had* prepared a speech for this moment, but now there's a puddle of coffee on the floor and a broken ceramic cup and, somehow, what I was about to say doesn't seem to fit the mood.

All I can think is: *Why the hell didn't I wear the stupid sweatpants?*

Bruiser clears his throat, shaking himself out of his stunned daze. He doesn't seem to notice the mess on the floor, but he sure as hell notices the way my face has gone red all the way to my ears.

It's not embarrassment, not shame or insecurity.

It's something more like… *jealousy.*

I'm jealous of the Weston I was last night.

"I wasn't sure how to tell you, so I just…" The rest of that sentence dies in my throat as I look down at the broken coffee cup on the floor. When I start again, my voice is quiet but ironclad. "I know what you're thinking right now. But I want you to test me just like you were going to before. I want to show you what I'm capable of, and then you can decide if I'm the right guy for the job. Okay?"

Bruiser gives a single nod, his jaw hardening. "Okay." He looks a little sick to his stomach, which really helps to boost my confidence. I try to remember what Tessa said last night, her voice so strong and sure. Something about being myself… It's all a flickering shadow behind a dense haze.

I could leave right now. I could walk out that door and forget about this idea. I could find a job somewhere else, anywhere else.

No. That's a pansy-ass move.

So I suck it up and get to work, shoving the whole awkward incident to the back of my mind. I force myself to not think about it. To be myself.

Confident. Devil-may-care. That's what Tessa says I am.

So screw it. That's what I'll be.

Bruiser tells me to start with shadowboxing, facing the mirror. While he turns on some Black Sabbath, I get in the zone—checking my form in the reflection, throwing easy jabs as I move lightly on my feet. It's a showdown between me and myself, in more ways than one.

Once I'm sufficiently warmed up (aka sweating), Bruiser has me move on to the heavy bag, giving me the option to wear boxing gloves if I want to. I refuse, going bare-fisted instead (if only to prove I'm not a pansy-ass). It's brutal to work combos on an unfamiliar bag. I don't know any of the soft spots, but I remind myself, *This is good. Show him what you're capable of.*

Bruiser stands by with a stopwatch, watching with his shredded arms crossed over his chest. As each round gets longer, each break gets shorter. Three minutes on. One minute off. Four minutes on. Thirty seconds off. Five minutes on. Ten seconds off.

"Breathe, kid." He says it like he's about to push me into the deep end. Or maybe he just says it because I'm gasping for air like I'm going to pass out. "Five… four… three… two… go, go, go, don't stop!"

I flurry the bag like my life depends on it, fists blurring in front of my face, heart thundering in my ears. I don't realize my knuckles have split open until I see my blood smearing the bag.

I guess I should have taken the gloves.

"Slow down, kid. Give me combos of five. No repeats or you'll be doing knuckle pushups afterwards."

I grit my teeth and push through the pain, racking my brain for unique combos of five.

Jab, straight right, left hook, right hook, uppercut.

Jab, jab, left hook, straight right, uppercut.

Jab, left hook, jab, uppercut, straight right.

I try to mix up every combo, making sure I don't throw any of them twice in the same order. But that's not a simple task when you're in the middle of dying.

Bruiser calls me out whenever I slip up with a sharp, "Saw that!" or "Don't you dare!" He stands on the other side of the bag, watching me pour it all out, stony-faced. I embrace the agony, the sweat in my eyes, the fire licking over my skin.

I tell myself, *I want this. I love this.*

But honestly, I can't wait for him to stop that damn watch.

"Ten seconds—come on. Hands up. Go harder, harder, *harder*—"

I brutalize the bag like it's a monster who's trying to kill Tessa. Stupidly enough, that's exactly what I need to think about to survive until the end of the round.

"Time."

I collapse against the heavy bag, gasping and heaving so hard I feel like I might throw up. For a few minutes, I can't talk. All I can do is stand there with my forehead against the blood-smeared bag, my arms burning, my lungs shuddering.

When I step back, Bruiser is looking at the face of his stopwatch. "How long do you think that last round was?"

"I don't know. Five minutes?"

"Ten."

No wonder I almost collapsed.

I've never gone so hard for a ten-minute round in my life.

"How many times did you repeat your combos?"

I look down at my knuckles, which are split open and oozing blood.

"I'm not sure."

"Thirty-six."

My heart drops. "I guess you want me to give you thirty-six knuckle pushups, then."

Bruiser shrugs one massive shoulder. "You didn't want me to go easy on you, kid."

"That's right," I fire back, dropping into a plank on the floor.

I don't give him thirty-six knuckle pushups.

I give him a hundred.

My arms are shaking by the time I finish, but I don't care if he sees me weak, gasping for air, gritting my teeth, and swallowing back moans of pain.

I want him to see everything I have.

I want to leave it all on the floor at his feet and let *that* be what he remembers about me. Even if he never sees me again.

I push off my knuckles and stand up, leaving the floor smeared with my blood.

"Need a break?"

I shake my head. "I'm fine. What's next?"

Bruiser narrows his dark eyes at me, a smirk twitching at his mouth. For a second, he looks like he did in that picture on the wall—sadistic, indestructible.

"You tell me, kid."

I wipe the sweat off my brow. "What?"

"Looks like you really want this job."

"Yes, sir. I do."

"Well, you have good form. Endurance. Willingness to go beyond the call of duty." He eyes the smear of blood I left on the floor. "It'd be kinda dirty of me not to let you give it a shot."

"Are you saying I've got the job?"

Bruiser cocks his head to one side. "You're on trial, kid. Don't get too excited. Come back tonight, six to eight. Night classes are the busiest. You can keep an eye on the younger students. If I'm happy with your work by the end of the week… well, then we'll talk about the job."

It's not exactly as satisfying as hearing the words "you're hired," but after pouring out my blood and sweat all over the boxing gym floor, I'll take it. What's more, I reach out for a handshake—because I'm not a guy who learns from his mistakes the first time. To my surprise, Bruiser takes my sweaty, bloody hand in his and gives it a bone-crushing shake.

"See you tonight, kid."

———————

This time, I wear sweatpants. The hardest part is over, Bruiser knows, and he doesn't seem to care. Aside from that awkward cup-smash reaction, he was surprisingly mum about the whole thing. No staring, no questions about how I lost my legs. It was like a commercial break had interrupted our otherwise professional and uncomplicated relationship. A blip of raw, weird emotion—there and gone.

At first, I was worried he might go easy on me. But it's becoming obvious that Bruiser doesn't go easy on anyone. It's not in his blood. He pushed me through boxing drills like I was just your average cocky seventeen-year-old with a point to prove.

Tessa was right—being exactly who I am was enough to impress the guy. Now he knows what I'm capable of, and how hard I'm willing to push myself to win. He won't go easy on me.

He's different.

At least, that's what I think when I show up at the boxing gym that night, fifteen minutes to six.

"Playing it close, kid," Bruiser mutters, frowning at the face of his watch. "How you feeling?"

"Never been better," comes my automatic reply.

He grunts. "Good answer."

A small group of students stretch on the floor, talking as they warm up. Should I go over and join them? Strike up a conversation and be one of the guys? Or should I hang back and be intimidating, set apart in the instructor zone with Bruiser? I haven't earned my place as his right-hand man, but I'm also not part of the class.

While the rest of the students arrive, I ask Bruiser to talk me through the structure of the class, and he gives me the low-down. Warmup, focus mitts, shadowboxing drills, heavy bag combos, back to focus mitts, then whatever torture he feels like putting us through until the hour is up.

"You can choose a partner when we work in pairs, but don't choose the same partner twice. Do what the class does. Don't talk to me unless I talk to you first. And if you need a break, just take it, okay, kid?"

"I won't need a break," I say, chin up as I meet his stony gaze. "I can do anything the rest of the class can do."

Bruiser nods slowly, looking me up and down. It's impossible to tell what he's thinking, but I have a pretty good guess. I've seen that look before.

I thought this morning was my test, but now, as the rest of the class gathers in a circle to begin warmups, I realize *this is the real test*.

Can I keep up when there's competition?

Of course I can.

In fact, I'll do more than just *keep up*. I'll outdo every single one of them without breaking a sweat. I'll show Bruiser just how much endurance I'm capable of. How willing I am to go beyond the call of duty. Everyone will ask Bruiser after class, "Where did you find this guy? He's incredible! Superhuman! You should give him a job for life."

There are fifteen students in total—mostly twenty- and thirty-somethings, at least one guy in his forties, and a handful of teenagers. Bruiser introduces me to the class, but doesn't exactly describe what my role is. He just says, "Weston will be helping out this week. You can ask him anything you'd ask me. Or you can ask him anything you're too scared to ask me."

A murmur of dry laughter ripples through the class. Bruiser turns up the music, claps his hands, and tells everyone to get busy.

Game on.

"Welcome to the Jungle" starts playing from the bass-boosted speakers as we start our warmup drills. Three minutes of skipping rope. Three minutes of burpees. Three minutes of shadowboxing. I breeze through it all without breaking a sweat.

Then the buzzer rings, and Bruiser shouts, "Okay, give me a sprint around the block! Last one out the door will be doing knuckle pushups on the cement!"

In a flash, the entire class makes a beeline for the door and takes off, running down the street.

Shit. Didn't see that coming.

I'm the last one out the door, but knuckle pushups are the last thing on my mind right now.

"Uh, sir?"

Bruiser stops short just outside the gym entrance, watching the last student vanish around the corner of the block. He casts me a glance, seeming to understand why I'm standing here like an idiot instead of sprinting with the rest of the class.

"You can sit this one out, kid."

Something about the way he says it makes my jaw twitch. "It's not that I can't run, sir. I can—pretty damn fast, actually. But I need to wear my blades."

"Don't worry about it. Just stay here." With that, he takes off jogging in the other direction—to meet the class halfway and cheer them on. Although, to be honest, Bruiser's idea of *cheering* is more like *jeering*. I can hear his voice booming from down the street: "Come on, my grandmother runs faster than that! Get your hands up! Are we sprinting or strolling? MOVE IT!"

I sigh, leaning back against the wall and crossing my arms over my chest. It kills me to sit out a sprint—especially when I know I could outrun all the students in this class. Maybe tomorrow I can bring my running blades in my backpack and switch prostheses in the bathroom. But when would I have a spare few minutes to do that? Sprinting is part of the warmup. There's no time to change. Besides, I can't wear long pants with my blades— they get in the way.

I curse under my breath, tipping my head back against the wall.

There's no way around it. I'm doomed to the sidelines.

But I refuse to let this setback bring me down. So what? I can't sprint around the block. I can do everything else.

Moments later, the runners return—out of breath and glistening with sweat. I offer each one of them a congrats and a high-five as they file back through the door into the gym. All except one—a guy around my age wearing a cutoff hoodie and an irritated frown.

"How'd *you* get off the hook?" he challenges, slitting his eyes at me.

"I didn't," I fire back with a shit-eating grin. "Guess I just ran so fast, you didn't see me."

He scoffs and shakes his head, trudging inside. That's when I see the back of his hoodie, which is emblazoned with the emblem for Sawyer-Simms Academy. Ah, good old S&S, the prep school outside Rockford where every student drives a Tesla or a BMW, depending on how environmentally conscious their bankroller parents are.

I guess that explains the entitled scowl on his face.

"Never mind Devon. He's always like that."

I turn around at the sound of a girl's voice and immediately get a sensory overload of *pink*. Pink sneakers, pink leggings, pink sports bra. Thankfully, her hair isn't pink, but raven black—woven into double boxer braids that snake down to her waist. She looks like she's dressed for a *Sports Illustrated* photoshoot, not a brutal workout.

Even her boxing gloves are pink—and covered in glitter—which just intensifies the visual overload as I hold the focus mitts for her during the first set. Bruiser has us working one-two combos, switching back and forth.

"I didn't catch your name." I speak up between jabs. "Was it… Leah?"

"Leia," she corrects, sparkly gloves flying.

"Ohhh, okay, like Princess Leia." I grin and add in a silly, overly dramatic whine, "Help me, Obi-Wan Kenobi—you're my only hope!"

She bursts into a fit of giggles, losing her form. "Oh my god, that was uncanny."

"Thanks. I'm going to audition for the next *Star Wars* movie if this whole boxing thing doesn't work out."

Now Leia is laughing too much to throw a decent punch. I glance up to catch Devon shooting daggers at us from down the row.

"Hey, don't drop your hands, princess." I tap her shoulder with the focus mitt. "Bruiser will punish me with knuckle pushups for making you laugh. He's allergic to humor."

That's when the bell rings and Bruiser calls for a break—which doesn't involve *resting*, but doing as many sit-ups as we can in sixty seconds. After that, we switch partners, and I wind up working with the smallest kid in the class. He looks like he's eleven but must be at least thirteen, because that's the minimum age requirement to train with the adults.

He reminds me of Henry, with those sad brown eyes and zipped-tight lips. Like a turtle with his head pulled deep inside his shell. He has ruddy brown hair and a dull bruise on his left cheek, a battle scar that proves he's tougher than he looks.

"Hey, big guy," I say, dropping down on one knee and pretending to retie my shoelace—just so he can feel tall for a minute. "What's your name?"

"Steve."

My eyes widen, and I lean closer to whisper conspiratorially in his ear, "Any relation to Steve Rogers?"

That makes him laugh.

Mission accomplished.

"How old are you, Steve?"

"Thirteen."

I nod to his shiner and say, "You get that here?"

He shakes his head.

"School?"

Steve shrugs uneasily, which is as good as a *yes* in shy-eighth-grader language. Learning how to throw a punch is the best education this kid will get in his life.

I slide my hands into the focus mitts and straighten up. "Well, Cap, I'm new here—so you gotta go easy on me, okay?"

Steve grins, smacking his gloves together. "Okay."

By the end of our ten-minute round, he's throwing jabs like a mini Bruce Lee—taking all my corrections with an eager nod and a determined frown. When the bell rings and we move on to shadowboxing, he stays glued to my side, watching my combos and copying them.

It feels kind of awesome to have a student looking to *me* and not Bruiser for direction—even if said student is a tiny eighth grader I could bench-press with one hand tied behind my back.

Eventually, the bell rings again, and Bruiser calls my name, waving me over. I guess we must be demonstrating something.

"Remember, everyone, you need to keep your hands up," Bruiser says to the class, fists up and elbows tucked in. He turns to me. "Throw a jab."

I do. He swats it away like a mosquito.

"Again."

I jab. He blocks.

"Now, pay attention." He raises his voice for the class to hear. "If my elbows are up here, what am I leaving exposed?" His gaze swerves back to me. "Show me what you would throw next."

I swing a left hook at his lower ribs.

"The liver shot is one of the most vicious, painful hits you'll ever take. The worst thing you can do is stand there and absorb it.

Don't be so busy up here that you give your opponent an easy target on your body—got it?"

He's not kidding. I've never actually taken a liver shot, but I've watched enough knockout compilation videos to know the effect a spot-on body shot can have, even for pro boxers. One minute they're locked and loaded; then *wham*, they're curled up in the fetal position on the floor, cradling their sides.

Bruiser uses me to demonstrate a few more blocking techniques, then tells everyone to pick a heavy bag and start working the same combos, tagging a block onto the end of each one.

We go hard for five rounds, three minutes each, pausing to take exactly two breaths before the bell rings again and Bruiser is yelling at us to move our asses. I can't help but feel like I'm just another student in the group, sweating bullets and pounding sand. Aside from playing the dummy for that blocking demonstration, I don't seem to be "helping" much at all.

Is this a job or a free ticket to boxing class?

When we return to focus mitts for the last fifteen minutes, fate brings Devon and me together as partners. The guy was huffing and puffing until he realized he was going to face off with me. Now he seems to have caught a second wind—hissing through his teeth as he pounds the piss out of my focus mitts.

"Quit lunging for me, dude," I tell him. "I'll meet your shots halfway."

Devon scowls, rolling his shoulders back. "I'm not lunging."

"Yeah, you are. It's throwing off your stance. See, your heel is coming way off the ground every time you throw—"

"If I want your opinion, I'll ask for it."

I shrug. "Just trying to help."

"Well, I don't *need* your help."

"Switch!" Bruiser calls out.

The sound of ripping Velcro fills the gym as we swap gloves with our partners. Princess Leia tosses her glitter bombs to the woman she's working with and sneaks me a loaded glance. It's impossible to miss the sympathetic smile on her lips. Did she hear what Devon just said to me?

As I watch my delightful partner jam his sweaty hands into the focus mitts, I realize he deserves a movie character nickname, too. But try as I might, I can't think of a good Hollywood comparison—except maybe a Rodent of Unusual Size.

For two grueling, glorious hours, I pour my sweat out on the floor of Bruiser's Boxing Gym. The first class disperses at seven, and a new group shows up, at which point my boss-for-now pulls me aside and says, "Why don't you take a break during this warmup?"

"I don't need a break," I argue, and it's true—I don't. I may be sore as hell, and my stumps may be sweaty and throbbing inside the sockets of my prosthetic legs, but I'm not going to take a break.

I can't.

Not if I want to prove I'm strong enough for this job.

So I suck it up and go hard for the next hour, blocking out everything else and just focusing on the work.

That's all there is.

The next round.

The next combination.

The next '80s rock song, motivating me to keep moving.

By the time eight o'clock rolls around, Bruiser looks about ready to kick me out of his gym. It's just the two of us, cleaning up the scattered equipment and boxing gloves.

This is the part where he's supposed to launch into a heartfelt speech about how impressed he is with my dedication and hard work. Just like in sports movies, that iconic scene between coach and athletic hero where the lights are dim and emotional violin music plays softly in the background and the tough-to-impress coach slaps the athlete's shoulder and says, "I didn't think you had it in you, kid. I was wrong. You're destined for greatness."

Instead, I get a curt finger-snap and a "Hand me that last pair of gloves, will ya?"

I do as I'm told, shoving the sports-movie fantasy to the back of my mind.

Real life isn't like the movies.

The guy who tries the hardest never wins first place.

Bruiser takes the gloves from me and says, "Good work tonight, kid. Go home and sleep it off."

I could have handled more, I want to say. *I could have done anything you asked. Is this how it's going to be all week? You urging me to take a break every twenty minutes? Me blending in with the rest of the class? You pulling me out once in a while to act as a demo dummy? I don't want a free membership to your boxing club. I want a job.*

Those words burn on my tongue. I want to unleash them all and see how Bruiser reacts. See what he says. But something tells me it wouldn't be the smartest idea to explode into a whiney tirade about working conditions on my very first day.

So instead, I grab my water bottle from the floor. "See you tomorrow, sir."

———————————

"So, how was your first day? I want to hear all about it." Tessa's beautiful face is a sight for sore eyes (sore *everything*) as we Face-Time each other at ten o'clock that night. I'm lying on my bed, my hair still wet from the shower, and Tessa is painting her fingernails with her phone propped up on her desk.

"It was… immobilizing. I am immobilized." To prove my point, I swivel my phone and show her my disembodied prosthetic legs on the floor.

She laughs. "Aww, you poor thing. I wish I were there to cuddle you."

"I wish you were here, too. Not just to cuddle, but to get stuff for me."

"Get stuff?"

"Yeah, I could really go for a glass of milk right now, but there's no way I'm putting those things back on tonight."

Tessa pouts. "I could ask my mom to drive me over there so I can give you a glass of milk."

"You would do that? For me?"

"I would do that. For you." She gives me an air-kiss through the phone.

I give her one back. "You're going to make such an amazing wife one day."

She balks at the idea, but in a cute way. "I wonder who the lucky guy will be."

"Ouch."

We both burst out laughing, which makes Tessa smudge her nail polish and blame me for it.

"Okay, seriously, I want to know how it went!"

I blow out a sigh, dragging one hand over my face. "It…

went. Nonstop for two hours. Killer workout, man. I thought I was gonna puke at one point."

"Didn't your boss let you take a break?"

"He told me I could, but I didn't want to. If I'm going to keep this job, I've gotta prove that I can do everything he can do."

"Okay. Just don't hurt yourself—"

"I won't. I'm not some pansy-ass who needs special treatment."

Tessa frowns, surprised by my rough tone. "That's not what I meant, Wes. I only said it because I love you, and I don't want you getting hurt."

"I know. I'm sorry." I shut my eyes, rolling onto my side and resting the phone against my pillow. "I just felt like that's how Bruiser was treating me tonight. Like I wasn't up to par."

"Why? Just because he offered you a break?"

"No, that wasn't the only reason. I felt like I could have been doing more to help. I mean, he used me for a couple of demonstrations, but other than that, I was basically just another student. I offered advice to the kids I partnered with. Some took it well. Others… not so much." I sigh, massaging my achy shoulders. "I guess I was just expecting Bruiser to give me more responsibility. It's almost like he's already decided he's not going to give me the job, but he's letting me have this trial week so he doesn't feel guilty about saying no."

Tessa thinks about it all for a minute, painting her nails in silence. "It was only your first day, Wes. Maybe he just wanted you to learn the ropes. I wouldn't assume the worst yet." She smirks, tilting her head in a way that makes me wish I could kiss the side of her neck. "Where's my ray of obnoxiously optimistic sunshine?"

God, how does she always manage to light me up with a single glance? It's like there's a switch inside me that only she can throw. One smile and boom, everything goes from black-and-white to technicolor. Like that moment in *The Wizard of Oz* when Dorothy opens the door, and she's not in Kansas anymore.

Life without Tessa is basically sepia Kansas.

"You're right. I don't know what's gotten into me."

"I do. You're tired." Tessa leans closer to the camera, her hair glowing in the light from the desk lamp. "Get some sleep. And next time, just try to enjoy it. Don't be so hard on yourself. Okay?"

"Okay," I whisper. "Are your nails dry?"

She checks them. "Almost. Why?"

"Because I'm still waiting for that glass of milk."

If at first you don't succeed in blowing your boss's mind and making him want to hire you for life, try, try again. That's the motto I take with me into the boxing gym on my second day of "work."

Bruiser is still sticking to that "Don't speak to me unless I speak to you" rule, which leaves me guessing my way through the entire class. I tell myself, *Maybe it's better this way.* After all, Bruiser told me he didn't want to have to train his assistant—he just wanted someone who instinctively *knows* what to do.

So I pay close attention to him all night, watching the way he interacts with students, talks them through every offense and defense, helps them to truly *get it*. Then, halfway through class, I make the disastrous mistake of following in his footsteps.

We're in the middle of working combos on the heavy bags,

paired up in twos so that one person can hold the bag still while the other person throws punches. Incidentally, I end up holding the bag for Princess Leia—who is dressed in an overload of purple tonight. Purple sneakers, purple leggings, purple sports bra (this one even more low-cut than the pink one. Not that I'm looking. But it's kind of impossible to *not* look).

She keeps throwing the same combination—jab, straight right, left hook—and losing her balance on the last shot. That's when I decide to step in and offer a bit of friendly advice.

"Try twisting your hips to your right on the hook. It'll keep you grounded instead of throwing off your weight."

Leia frowns, puzzled. "Wait, what?"

"Like this." I set myself up in front of the bag and throw the same combo in slow motion. *Jab. Straight right. Left hook.* On the hook, I snap my hips to the right, driving twice as much force into the bag and making it sway on its chain. "See how my feet stay on the ground? You try."

I step back and watch as Leia attempts to copy my movements, but she fails miserably and tips her head back, groaning in frustration. "Ugh, I don't think I'm doing it right. Maybe you can… move my hips for me. As I punch."

"Uh, sure." I awkwardly shuffle closer, positioning myself behind her and placing my hands on those blindingly purple hips. That's when I realize this is probably not a good idea. It's different for a guy like Bruiser—he's more beast than man, devoid of all human emotion, treating every student like another slab of fresh meat to brutalize.

That's not what I see when I put my hands on Leia. I see… a woman.

Dear god, I have my hands on a foreign woman's body. It

feels like a betrayal to Tessa somehow—and I immediately want to get away from her. But I've already crossed the point of no return. Contact has been made, and it cannot be unmade. Not without looking like a total weirdo.

Leia throws her jab, straight right, and hook. At the last second, I twist her hips toward the front of the gym and help her land her best shot of the night.

"That felt better," Leia murmurs, turning to give me a long look over her shoulder. "You're an excellent teacher."

I just stand there, frozen like a deer in headlights. It's not until a few seconds later that I realize my hands are still stuck to her hips.

DISENGAGE CONTACT.

I step back with a jolt, almost crashing into the neighboring heavy bag. "Uh, sure. No problem. Just… keep throwing like that. You're doing good."

Princess Leia smirks and continues pounding on the bag, boxer braids flailing.

I don't pay for my crimes until the end of class when everyone is dispersing, water bottles and car keys in hand. That's when Devon the R.O.U.S. pulls me aside, murder in his eyes.

"If I catch you touching my girlfriend like that again, I'll make you sorry you ever met me, punk."

I almost choke. "Your girlfriend?"

"Leia," he seethes, stepping closer and lowering his voice. "Didn't think anyone saw you grabbing her ass earlier?"

"First of all, I was nowhere *near* her ass. Secondly, she asked me to do it. She wanted to know how to move her hips to throw a hook. It was nothing more than that, I swear to God—"

"I know exactly what you're up to," Devon snarls, jabbing a

finger at me. "And I'm telling you to stay the hell away from her, or else there will be serious consequences. Got it, punk?"

Serious consequences. Do all prep school kids threaten this eloquently? It's almost comical. *Punk.* Who even uses that word anymore? I get the feeling he's learned all his dirty slang from 1950s mafia movies.

"I have a girlfriend, okay? I'm not interested in yours. Punk."

Devon doesn't respond to this perfectly logical comeback. He just shoots daggers at me and loops his snobby sweat towel over his shoulders, marching out the door and meeting Leia on the sidewalk, where she leans against a black BMW, looking disgustingly pleased with herself.

Thankfully, Bruiser didn't overhear any of that exchange (although I'm sure he would side with me concerning the hand-to-ass proximity). He'd vanished into the back room a few minutes earlier with a check that one of the students gave him.

I knock on the open door as I lean into the crowded little office. "Sir? You busy?"

"No," he mutters, scribbling something in a logbook. "What's on your mind, kid?"

It sounds like a friendly invitation to spill my guts, and maybe that's exactly what I'd do if Bruiser was a trusty uncle who visited me at Thanksgiving and told me war stories on the back porch—but he's not. He's my boss. And gut spillages don't happen in your boss's office.

"Uh, nothing, really." I lean one shoulder against the doorjamb. "I just wanted to say I straightened up the mitts and gloves. And I wiped down the heavy bags. Do you want me to mop the floor?"

"Nah, I've got it. You can go now. You must be tired."

"I'm fine." I straighten up, in case the leaning posture is making me look like a weak pansy-ass who can't stand upright. "It was a great class. I think everyone enjoyed it."

Bruiser grunts. "Well, that's disappointing. I don't want them to enjoy it. I want to make them suffer."

"Oh, they did suffer. But… I mean… I think they had a good time suffering."

Bruiser falls silent, studying something in the logbook. He's not even listening anymore. This conversation isn't exactly going how I expected. God, diplomacy is torture. I wish I could come right out and ask him what I *want* to ask him.

Did I do a good job tonight?

Am I doing something wrong?

Do I even have a shot at being an instructor, or are you just waiting for the week to be over so you can put someone else on trial?

"Saw you working with Steve earlier," Bruiser says out of nowhere, muttering more to his fist than me. "That kid really responds to you."

It's not the compliment I was expecting (or fishing for), but it still makes something light up in my chest. "He reminds me of my little brother. I have three of them, so I'm used to working with younger kids."

Bruiser nods absently. "That's good. He could use a big brother."

And that, apparently, is all my boss has left to say to me. He rises from the desk and trudges to the broom closet, grabbing the mop and pail to finish cleaning up the gym.

"Next night class is Thursday. Guess I'll see you then."

"Guess so," I murmur, my gaze drifting to the clutter of frames on the wall. More boxing and MMA stuff, but also a few

military photos scattered throughout. I see at least two more pictures of Bruiser the Younger standing next to the rock-on guy from
the shot in the other room. They must have been pretty good
friends to take up this much real estate on his walls.

"You never told me where that picture was taken," I say.

Bruiser glances over his shoulder at me, like he's surprised I
haven't left yet. "What picture?"

"The one out there of you with some guys in front of a Humvee. This one looks like it was taken in the same place." I point to
the framed shot of him and Mr. Rock-on, geared up and looking
badass with their shades and rifles, a beastly helicopter looming in
the background.

Bruiser knows which one I mean without looking. "Ramadi,"
he answers.

When it becomes obvious from my facial expression that I
have no idea where Ramadi is, he clarifies, "Iraq."

I nod slowly, wondering if I should shut my mouth now and
go home. But, as usual, my curiosity gets the better of me. I can't
help asking, "What was it like over there?"

Bruiser grunts, kicking the closet door shut. "Hot."

I can tell that's as much of a war story as I'm going to get out
of him.

"Well, I guess I'll see you Thursday, sir."

"See you, kid."

On Thursday, I don't make the mistake of touching Princess Leia.
In fact, I do my level best to avoid her like a highly contagious

plague—I don't speak to her, don't look at her, don't acknowledge her existence in any way, shape, or form.

Unfortunately, she notices my sudden case of Leiaphobia and hunts me down during one of Bruiser's no-rest breaks. He has us all on the floor doing pushup punches, and somehow Leia manages to teleport herself across the room and materialize right beside me.

"Why are you avoiding me tonight?" she asks between push-ups, shooting me an accusatory pout over her shoulder.

"I'm not… avoiding you. I just don't want to cause any trouble."

She grunts, pressing up into a plank and throwing a punch toward the mirror. "What did Devon say to you?"

"Nothing. He just… He told me you guys are dating."

"Yeah, we are. So what?"

"So he doesn't want me working one-on-one with you."

"Is that what he said? Verbatim?"

God, she's a sucker for detail, isn't she? I blast through the final twenty seconds of pushup punches, then straighten up and meet her gaze—keeping my voice low in case the R.O.U.S. has ears as sharp as his radar vision.

"He said there would be serious consequences if I didn't stay the hell away from you. He also called me 'punk.' Verbatim."

Leia rolls her eyes, but she's smirking like she's not at all surprised. Like she *wanted* this to happen. "He's such a dickwad."

"He's your boyfriend."

"So? That doesn't mean he *owns* me. It was *his* stupid idea to even sign up for this boxing class. If I'm not going to be allowed to speak to whomever I want while I'm here, then I'll quit."

Bruiser claps his hands and calls for the next round of drills on the focus mitts. It's the perfect opportunity to evacuate this conversation, but before I can turn away, Leia grabs my elbow—claws out.

"You'll be my partner for this round, Weston."

I stiffen, glancing down the row at Devon in his obnoxious S&S hoodie. "I don't think that's a good idea."

"Why? Are you afraid of him?" Her gaze roams over my shoulders and arms. "Because, honestly, you look like you could handle him in a fight."

"I'm not afraid of him, Leia. I just don't want to lose my job over a stupid misunderstanding."

"Cut the chitchat," Bruiser interrupts, thrusting a pair of focus mitts at me. "Get busy."

In one last-ditch effort to escape, I scan the gym to see if anyone is missing a partner—but unfortunately, the odds are not in my favor. The odds are... even. And that leaves me stuck with Princess Leia.

She smiles wickedly, shoving her hands into her boxing gloves and extending her arms toward me. "Help me with the straps, would you?"

Begrudgingly, I tighten the Velcro around her wrists, then step back to put some space between us.

I guess it won't hurt to work with her for this one round. It's just part of the job. That's what I tell myself. *What would Bruiser do?* More importantly, *What will Bruiser think of me if I shy away from working with a student just because I don't want to piss off her sweat-towel-wearing boyfriend?*

I think I know the answer.

So for the rest of the night, I do my job and keep Leia at arm's length, hoping she'll get sick of my one-word responses to her questions and give up this game of cat-and-mouse she's playing. Or maybe it's a game of mouse-and-mousetrap. Devon being the mousetrap. Leia being the cheese.

Does she think I'm dumb enough to bite?

I'm not. Even if I *wanted* to bite. Even if I were single and desperate for love and she and I hit it off and I started fantasizing about what our future children would look like, I would *still* not bite because I know how the game of mouse-and-mousetrap ends.

With a broken neck.

Still, I have to give the girl an A for effort. She shadows me all night, staging eerily coincidental encounters. When the class scrambles around the gym between each set of drills, Leia's orbit just happens to intersect with mine. Not once, not twice, but seven times. At one point, Bruiser tells me to go get some sparring gear from the storage room in the back, and Leia pops up right behind me like an unwanted imaginary friend.

"Can I help carry anything?"

I politely refuse and stagger clumsily away from her, my arms full of gear. The R.O.U.S. is watching my every move. I catch him glaring at me when I come out of the storage room, fleeing from his girlfriend. I hope he realizes that *she's* the one stalking *me*, not the other way around. Anyone with half a brain could see that. But I'm not sure Devon *has* half a brain. Possibly three-eighths of a brain.

We do some light sparring for the last fifteen minutes of class, and by complete accident (of course), the stars align to bring me into some friendly hand-to-hand combat with none other than Princess Leia.

I'm regretting ever calling her that silly nickname.

I'm regretting ever making her laugh.

But it's okay. I'm safe because I'm in a crowded, sweaty gym, and it's plain to see that through no fault of my own, this girl is stuck on me. Literally *stuck*. Like a piece of tape on my fingers, I can't seem to shake her off.

When eight o'clock rolls around, everyone parts ways. Devon and Leia walk out hand in hand, her glancing over her shoulder at me as I tidy up the gym. As soon as that door swings shut, I feel my whole body relax. One more class tomorrow night, and then I won't have to see her for the entire weekend. Maybe by then she'll be over her game of mouse-and-mousetrap.

I feel hopeful for the future as I finish wiping down the heavy bags and stick my head in Bruiser's office. As usual, I ask him if there's anything else I can help with.

As usual, he answers no and then folds his brawny hands on the desk, giving me his full attention. "You okay, kid?"

I hesitate. "Yeah... why?"

"You disappeared into the back during the second warmup. Just wanted to make sure you weren't..." He shrugs. "Wanted to make sure you're okay."

I was hoping he'd been too busy brutalizing everyone to care about where I went. But I guess a guy like Bruiser notices everything. I don't want to tell him what I was doing. I don't want to tell him I have blisters coming on my stumps from working out for two hours straight in sweat-drenched socks. I don't want to tell him how good it felt to take off my prostheses and towel-dry my legs, to just sit there for a few minutes in the privacy of the storage room and let myself breathe.

I don't want to tell him—not because words like *stumps* and *blisters* and *sweat* are too gross for him to handle, but because the whole thing is proof that I'm not like the rest of them.

I'm not like *him*.

"Oh, that…" I clear my throat, forking a hand through my hair. "I was fine. I was just… avoiding someone."

Bruiser nods slowly, like he doesn't trust me as far as he can throw me. Or maybe that's an inappropriate metaphor in this case, because he could probably throw me across a football field.

"Leia Cooper?" he guesses.

"Yeah. You probably noticed how she kept trying to pair up with me."

Bruiser nods. "Try not to encourage any favoritism, kid. It'll get you in more hot water than you can handle."

"Hey, I'm not the one who's—" I freeze mid-sentence when my boss cuts me a stern glance as if to say, *You'd better stop there.* It's a look that makes me feel three inches tall.

"We've got a six and seven tomorrow," he says, glancing at the class schedule on his desk. "The first class will be the usual, but for the second I want to go heavy into sparring. So if you'd rather sit that one out, I understand."

I cross my arms over my chest, irritation prickling at the back of my neck. "Why? Were you not happy with my sparring to-night?"

"Tomorrow we'll be going harder. We'll be in the ring." Bruiser slides his gaze to me, that stone-cold brow unflinching. "I'm just giving you a heads-up. Making sure you know what you're getting into."

Would you be giving me a heads-up if I didn't have a disability?

That's what I want to say. But there's no need to ask a question I already know the answer to.

"I've been in plenty of fights," I say, my voice flexing with confidence. "Without boxing gloves. Without headgear or a ref to break things up if it gets too ugly."

Bruiser cocks his head to the side and shrugs. "It's your choice, kid."

But it's not my choice. I can tell by the look in his eyes, the tone of his voice. He doesn't want me to come tomorrow. He doesn't want to push me, punish me, cause me pain. All because of my stupid legs.

What's gotten into you? I want to yell. That first day, Bruiser was as tough as a drill sergeant—even after he knew I was an amputee, he put me to the test. He pushed me to the breaking point and watched me bleed, sweat, and grit my teeth through the pain. He didn't care.

What the hell has changed?

All throughout this trial week, he's gone softer and softer on me. Encouraging me to go home early, take a break, sit this one out, etc. Does he think I'm stupid? Does he think I don't know why he's suddenly being so nice to me? I've had plenty of people give me the easy treatment before. I've had plenty of people underestimate me. And I hate it.

But anger has a funny chemical reaction in my body. It never makes me want to lash out or start a fight or smash something.

It makes me want to prove a point.

Prove *myself.*

"I'll see you tomorrow," I say, and walk out.

If Bruiser thinks he's doing me a favor by putting me in timeout, he's dead wrong. There's nothing I like better than a challenge.

Outside, it's the golden hour—Tessa's favorite time of day. The whole street is lacquered in shades of pink and orange as I make my way towards the spot where I parallel-parked my mom's car. I toss my gym bag into the backseat, swing the door shut, and *boom.*

There she is.

Standing on the sidewalk right behind me.

I reel back a step, surprised.

"Sorry," Leia says with an amused smirk. "I didn't mean to startle you."

My mouth runs dry as I stare at her, the car key clutched in my hand. "I... thought you left. With Devon."

"Oh, he wanted to grab something from the liquor store before we head back."

I frown, trying to figure out how Devon can be old enough to buy booze at a liquor store. Maybe I miscalculated his age, and he's actually a twenty-one-year-old with an unfortunate baby face?

Leia sees me trying to puzzle it out and explains, "His dad plays golf with the owner."

Ah, now it all makes sense. Who needs an ID when you have friends in high places?

Better question: What is Princess Leia doing stalking me and not hanging out with her premature-drinker boyfriend?

"I wanted to catch you before you left," she begins, stepping closer. It takes all my self-control not to retreat. "About what I said earlier... I hope it didn't come across sounding petty. I wasn't hanging out with you because I wanted to spite Devon or some-thing."

"I understand." I nod quickly, spinning my keychain, glanc-ing up and down the street, trying to think of the most tactful way to X out of this conversation. "Don't worry about it. I know you were just trying to train and—"

"I like you, Weston."

It's hard to describe the gut reaction that happens when she says those words. Similar to the feeling you might get if someone stopped you on the sidewalk and said, *I have a gun. Don't move.*

"What?"

"I said I like you." Leia smiles sweetly, eerily, taking another step closer. "From the moment I first met you, I felt like there was something special between us."

The only thing between us is *not enough space.*

"I don't like you, Leia," I blurt out. Plain and simple, just how I prefer hurting girls' feelings. It's the only way to send a clear message. "There's nothing between us, okay? I have a girlfriend."

"So?" She hums a smoky laugh under her breath, drawing even closer. Warning alarms start firing off in my brain, like a car's backup camera when you get too close to running over your neighbor's dog. "You have a girlfriend. I have a boyfriend. That doesn't mean we can't have a little fun together."

Dear God, she's *touching* me now. She has her hand on my chest, but I can't move. It's like my feet are cemented to the sidewalk.

At last, I croak, "I… don't want to have fun."

And that's when she grabs my neck, pulls me down to her level, and kisses me. My knee-jerk reaction is to lurch backwards and get away from her—these are not Tessa's lips, and they do not belong on mine.

But then her tongue is in my mouth.

My keys slip out of my hand and crash to the cement.

I jolt away from Leia, breaking the kiss. My heart is hammering, and my face is blazing hot. I want to undo what just happened.

"I told you I don't like you," I bite out, trying to lay down the law once and for all. But my voice is shaky, cracking like I'm on the cusp of puberty.

Leia only grins and quirks one eyebrow. "Your girlfriend doesn't kiss you like that, does she? Hm. What a shame."

I clench my jaw, bending to snatch my fallen keys. "It's none of your damn business how my girlfriend kisses me. I don't know what kind of game you're playing, but I'm not gonna be a part of it. So just… knock it off."

With that, I unfreeze my feet from the sidewalk and storm around the car, diving into the driver's seat and locking all the doors in case she's crazy enough to jump in with me.

By the time I pull out onto the street, she's just a smudge in the rearview mirror—walking back towards the liquor store.

I'm still reeling, as if I just had a near-death experience. My heart is racing, and my mouth tastes like peppermint even though I haven't been chewing gum.

She was.

I lean into the gas, driving away as fast as legally possible.

A few minutes later, I'm in Tessa's driveway, texting her to ask if she's around and if she would come out on the porch for a minute. She messages me back with "Be right out!!" and even has time to send me a heart emoji with it.

I'm sitting on the porch steps when she swings open the front door. "Wes! I didn't think I'd be seeing you tonight. Did you just get out of work?"

"Yeah. Sorry I'm sweaty and gross. I just had to see you."

Call it guilt. Call it absolution. Call it the kissing equivalent of washing your mouth out with soap.

Sometimes a guy's gotta do what a guy's gotta do.

I pat the step beside me and say, "Can you sit down for a minute?"

Tessa sweeps over in her pretty little sundress and plops down next to me. She doesn't even need to be asked or prompted—she just leans in and kisses me softly on the lips.

It's perfect.

Tessa draws back to look at me in the faded pink light of sunset. "Something's wrong."

My heart backflips into my stomach. "What?"

Dear God, does she know? Can she taste a foreign woman on my lips?

"You just seem like something's bothering you." Tessa looks down, taking my hand in hers. Brushing her silky-soft thumb over my rough, split knuckles. "Ever since you started that job, you seem… I don't know. Stressed out. Do you want to talk about it?"

"About what?"

"Work. Whatever is happening at that boxing gym every night."

I look down at the cracks in the wood. There are a thousand things I could tell her—about Leia, about Devon, about Bruiser, about the way I keep running into this wall of self-doubt, afraid to speak my mind, afraid of what might happen if I don't.

Some part of me wants to tell her all of it. Cut open my chest and let her see the mess I'm keeping locked up inside.

Maybe I would feel better if I just let it all out.

But sitting here with Tessa, who looks so beautiful in the hazy, rose-tinted light, I don't want to think about what happens at that boxing gym. I just want to sit beside her. Feel her in my arms. Listen to her breathe. Be overwhelmed by the fact that she loves me.

"I don't want to talk about it," I whisper, squeezing her hand. "Why don't you tell me about your day instead?"

She smiles and gives an easy shrug. "My day was… inconsequential."

"I have no idea what that word means."

"It means—"

I kiss her again, rudely interrupting the Merriam-Webster definition that she was about to rattle off, which would probably make me feel like I have the reading comprehension of a third grader.

Instead, we do something better. We kiss, silent and slow. Then Tessa slides closer and rests her head on my shoulder, and I put my arm around her and lean my cheek against her strawberry-scented hair. We watch the sunset fade together. We say everything we need to, with no words at all.

And it's much better than washing my mouth out with soap.

———————

"Okay, here's how this is going down." Bruiser stands in front of the class, his tattooed arms crossed over his chest, his voice as solemn and diehard as a military general leading his men into battle. The boxing ring looms behind him, hungry for a sparring match. "I want two of you in the ring at a time. You're going to put together everything we've been working on this week. Whoever lands five points first stays in; loser steps out. We'll keep rotating until you all get three rounds in. Understood?"

We all nod and murmur our acknowledgment; then Leia's hand pops up with a question. I don't look in her direction. In fact, I haven't looked at her once since last night when she tried to seduce me on the sidewalk. *Stay away from me*, I warned her. But that door swings both ways—so tonight I'm doing my best to pretend she doesn't exist.

Bruiser grants her permission to speak, and she asks, "Will girls have to spar with the boys? Because that wouldn't be very fair."

This seems to amuse Bruiser for about 0.2 seconds. "No. You'll be splitting into two groups—ladies and gentlemen. Ladies, drill your combos on the bags while I work the gents in the ring. If you don't know whether you're a lady or a gent… there's the door." He claps. "Let's get busy."

As we put on our boxing gloves and headgear, I can't help but notice Devon shooting daggers at me. What is this guy's problem? I wouldn't touch his girlfriend with a ten-foot pole, especially after…

Oh. Shit.

The realization hits me like a ton of bricks.

He knows.

Last night when Leia kissed me on the sidewalk, she said Devon was at the liquor store—but he must not have been in there the whole time. He must have walked out at the worst possible moment and seen me and his girlfriend lip-locked down the street. From that distance, he wouldn't be able to tell who had initiated the kiss. He would only have seen *us*. Together. Her hands on my neck. My keys on the ground.

It was nothing. But Devon doesn't know that. And now he's

looking at me like he can't wait to get me in the ring so he can bust my balls.

But to be honest, the R.O.U.S. is the least of my worries. I don't care who I'm going up against. I need to fight hard, fight smart, fight my absolute best. I need to prove that I belong here. I deserve to be here—not because someone's doing me a favor or feeling bad for me, but because I'm a good boxer.

Bruiser set the stakes last night when he looked me in the eye and said, *I want to make sure you know what you're getting into.* He thinks that when push comes to shove, I won't have what it takes.

Tonight, I'm determined to prove him wrong.

He's in the ring now, acting as ref while two guys go at each other—Gaines and Robinson. I've worked with them both over the past week and seen their strengths and weaknesses up close. Now they circle each other in the ring, trying to land a point, while Bruiser shouts at them to "Move it! Keep your hands up. Come on, let's work!"

I warm up with some shadowboxing on the sidelines as I watch the sparring match and note what combos these guys are throwing. Robinson keeps going for the head—jab, jab, hook. Favors the left. Dips to the right. Gaines is a taker. He'll stand there all day and swat away punches until his opponent is panting and tired. That's when he moves in and lands a solid uppercut to the chest.

"Five!" Bruiser calls out, hand up to signal the end of the round. He gives Robinson a reassuring smack on the shoulder. "Step in; step out."

I'm ready to come on his command, but to my annoyance, Devon goes first. Something in me bristles as I watch Bruiser waving over the R.O.U.S., lifting the rope so he can step into the ring.

No big deal, I tell myself. *My turn will come.*

In the meantime, I study Devon's fighting style. Sure, I've been watching him all week and resisting the urge to correct his form—but shit is different when you're facing off with another person whose goal is to end you.

Devon is a doer. I guessed that from the moment I first met him, but now he proves it by blasting Gaines like a punching bag—going as hard as he can and landing two points in the first minute. But when his opponent comes back with a body shot, Devon retreats with surprise, like he's never been hit so hard in his life.

Pansy-ass.

I'm waiting for Gaines to control the fight like he did in his first round—sticking to defense and waiting until his opponent is good and tired before popping back. But Devon has better technique than I gave him credit for. He's not just aggressive, he's lightning fast, nailing shots before Gaines can react to block.

A few minutes into it, Bruiser calls, "Four-two!"

And then Devon lunges forward, landing a hook to Gaines's ribs.

"Five!" Bruiser taps Gaines's sweat-soaked shoulder. "Step out." He turns and locks eyes with me. "Weston, you're in."

Well, how's that for luck?

Out of all the students I could spar with tonight, it would have to be the one guy who wants to kill me. Maybe I shouldn't be happy about that. Maybe a normal person would be reluctant to step into that ring, scared of the bodily injury that could occur when facing a homicidal prep school brat who caught you kissing his girlfriend the night before.

But, ever the optimist, my first thought is, *Perfect.*

Devon will try his best to destroy me. And I'll give just as good as I get. And if that doesn't convince Bruiser I can take the heat, nothing will.

As I duck under the rope and step into the ring, I feel like this is the most important fight of my life. Like somehow, every single moment has led up to *this*. Sure, I've been in a lot of sparring matches—but most of them have been with my best friend, and I've had nothing to lose.

This is different.

This means something. To all three of us.

Bruiser shouts, "Come on, let's work!"

Devon snaps into action—driving forward with a jab, straight right, uppercut. I swat his shots away like flies, moving around the ring, positioning him where I want him.

Get your anger out now, punk.

Some boxers would dodge out of range, but that's not how I fight. Blame it on the prosthetic legs—they make me slower on my feet than most fighters, but I've learned to use it to my advantage. I've become a brawler—leaning into the danger zone, rolling with punches instead of darting away from them. I may have slow feet, but at least I've got fast reflexes.

I block, block, block while Devon hits, hits, hits. He's a machine, mad as hell. I'm a punching bag with arms. And who expects a punching bag to fight back? Devon doesn't. My defense makes him cocky, and he puts his hands down. Rookie error. When I finally throw something real, he's not ready. And I nail him right in the chest.

"One-zero!" Bruiser calls.

Devon apparently doesn't like being *zero*. He unleashes another combination, but I dip out of the way before his hook can score. I pop back with a headshot of my own and land it—knocking him off balance for a split second.

"Two-zero!"

If Devon wasn't homicidal before, he sure as hell is now. I see a flash of rage flare in his eyes as he straightens up, moving in for the kill.

Suddenly my back is against the ropes, and Devon's gloves are hammering me in the face. Jab, jab, jab, hook. My hands shoot up to block, and he uppercuts me in the stomach.

"Two-one!" Bruiser calls his point.

Devon doesn't back off—he keeps me pinned to the ropes, gloves blurring as he flurries me like a madman.

"Break, break, break!" Bruiser rushes over to pry us apart. Devon backs off, hands up, fury in his eyes. "Two-one, go!"

I surge forward, adrenaline coursing through my whole body as I throw a hard jab and nail him in the headgear, then follow it with a straight right.

"Three-one!" Bruiser calls.

And that's when I make a mistake.

I get cocky.

I think to myself, *I'm going to beat this pansy-ass.*

And at first, it feels damn good. To know I'm blowing Bruiser's mind right now—proving I have the guts and skill to do this. I can already imagine the conversation we'll have tonight in his office after everyone goes home.

I didn't think you had it in you, kid. I was wrong. The job's yours.

I move in with another combination, but Devon back-steps out of range. Maybe he's catching on at this point. Maybe it's finally dawned on him that I'm not going to shy away from his hits. I could stand here and take it all day, while he bounces around gasping for air like a fish out of water.

When I step forward, he steps back—retreating toward the ropes.

I close in, pinning him in the corner to give him a taste of his own medicine. It might not be the smartest move, but I'm hungry for those last two points. Hungry for victory. Hungry to make Bruiser proud.

I drive forward with a jab-hook combo. Devon drops into a crouch and ducks out of the way, spinning me around. In a flash, we swap positions—and now I'm the one blocked in the corner.

He blitzes me with a flurry of jabs to the face. So fast, I can't do anything but brace my hands up to block. I'm all defense, and he's all *jab, jab, jab, jab, jab,* then—*wham.*

He hooks me in the side with a liver shot.

At first, it doesn't feel like much. I tell myself to roll with it. But then the pain comes, in a flash of white-hot hell—a tsunami wave of fire swallowing me up, radiating from the lower right side of my torso. It feels kind of like getting kicked in the balls— because it doesn't just hurt where he landed the punch. It hurts *everywhere,* all at once.

My vision wavers, and I crash to my knees, my whole body dropping like a deadweight. Next thing I know, I'm curled up on the floor, gripping my side.

I can't breathe.

I can't breathe.

Bruiser crouches beside me, shaking my shoulder. "You okay, kid? Come on, talk to me."

I can't talk, not without moaning in pain. I just nod, blinking back tears. *Dammit.* I spit out my mouth guard, pressing my forehead into the floor as another wave of excruciating pain grips me from the inside.

God almighty, it hurts.

But after a moment, I force myself to swallow back the agony and straighten up. "I'm fine, Bruiser. I'm fine."

And it's true—the pain is nothing compared to the flames of humiliation burning me alive. I can't look at Devon as he ducks out of the ring on Bruiser's command and struts off to see his girlfriend. I can't look at any of the other students. I can't even look at Bruiser.

"Can you stand?" he asks.

And maybe he would have said it to anyone who just got their ass handed to them.

But saying it to *me* feels like another knockout.

"Yes," I bite out through clenched teeth. "Of course I can *stand.*"

Bruiser doesn't help me up. He watches as I climb to my feet and steady myself on the ropes.

"Take a timeout, kid. Catch your breath. I'll come check on you in a minute."

As I make my way over to the benches at one side of the gym, I can feel gazes following me. I can feel my self-respect withering up and dying in the pit of my stomach.

I tear off my gear, sit down on the bench, and grab my water bottle. For a second, I wonder if Leia is going to make a big deal out of this. If she's going to come over and pretend to feel sorry for me, offer to bandage me up and give me another slobbery kiss to make me feel better.

But then I spot her by the heavy bags, talking to Devon—caressing his sweaty face like he's some knight in shining armor who just slew the dragon who was out to get her.

I guess her game is over.

I sit out the rest of class, doing light stretches and maintaining my tough face so I don't look like a pansy-ass. When eight o'clock rolls around and the students disperse, Bruiser pulls Devon aside. I can't hear their conversation from this far away, but I can see the severe glint in Bruiser's eyes as he speaks, nodding in my direction.

Devon glances over his shoulder and sees me sitting on the bench, leaning forward on my knees. His gaze lowers to my shoes. And I could swear I catch a look of *regret* in his eyes.

Bruiser didn't tell him, did he? No. He wouldn't.

But then Devon walks across the room and stops in front of me, his gaze still stuck on my shoes.

"I'm… sorry, for what I did earlier. It was wrong of me to go that hard on you."

A knot of embarrassment and anger twists in my stomach. But I try not to let it show on my face. Instead, I just shrug and say, "I can handle it."

Devon nods stiffly, not looking me in the eye. "Well, Bruiser told me…" He clears his throat, abandoning the rest of that sentence. "Never mind. Let's just forget about what happened, okay?"

"Okay," I say.

But I'm boiling inside.

Bruiser told me… you're an amputee. That's what he was going to say. *Bruiser told me I shouldn't have hit you; I should feel bad for you. I should treat you differently because you're not like the rest of us.*

Devon didn't say any of those things, but I know how to read between the lines. I know what pity looks like. I know why some people can't look me in the face once they know.

Bruiser had no right to tell him things I deliberately kept private.

He had no goddamn right.

When the rest of the students leave, Bruiser calls me into his office. I swallow back my simmering anger and follow him, determined to speak my mind this time—to hell with the consequences. I'm sick of slipping and dodging the truth.

Bruiser sits behind his desk, pushing papers around in search of something. "You okay, kid? Got hit pretty hard back there."

"I'm feeling better now," I lie, taking my hand away from my side, which still feels like it got smashed by a battering ram. "It just surprised me, that's all."

"Surprised me too," Bruiser admits, adding insult to injury by saying, "That was one hell of a knockout. Didn't think Devon had it in him."

A muscle in my jaw twitches. "He had a score to settle with me."

Bruiser nods, like he already knew that. "And you had a score to settle with *him*, by the looks of it."

"No. I wasn't… That's not what it was about."

"What was it about, then?"

I stand there like an idiot with my mouth hanging open, unsure what to tell him. The truth? *I wanted to impress you. I wanted you to see that I have what it takes. I wanted to prove that I'm good enough for this job.*

But I can't say all that.

It would feel too much like… I don't know. Like carving my chest open and letting him see something I don't want him to see.

After a long silence, Bruiser sighs, looking down at an envelope in his hands. "You're a straight-shooter, Weston. So I'm going to be straight with you, too. Okay?"

I swallow, a twinge of dread taking root in my stomach. Somehow, I know exactly what's in that envelope. And I don't want him to hand it to me.

But he does.

"I don't think this is the right time for you to be working here, kid." He doesn't look me in the eye when he says it. "But I appreciate you giving it a fair shot. Here's a week's pay."

I take the envelope, my fingers stiffening around the corners. I don't want the money. I never wanted the money—I wanted this job. I *loved* this job. And I was good at it, too.

Now, I'm getting fired.

And I know the reason.

Still, I have to ask, "What did I do wrong?"

Bruiser shakes his head, looking down at the desk. "I didn't say you did something wrong. I just said it's not the right time—"

"When *will* be the right time? When my legs grow back?"

His steely eyes lock on mine. "It'll be the right time when you change your attitude, kid."

"My attitude?"

"You started out fine on your first day," Bruiser says, his voice even and calm. "But I've watched you over the course of the week—I've watched you get more competitive and cocky with every training session, and now I know why. Because your ego is getting in the way."

"My ego?" I sputter. "This has *nothing* to do with my ego. Don't give me that bullshit. I know what this is. I'm not an idiot. I saw your face that first morning when you saw my legs. I've seen that look enough times to know exactly what it means."

A shadow of remembrance passes over his face as he stares down at his hands clasped on the desk. "There's more to it than you think, kid."

"Oh yeah? Like what?" I cross my arms over my chest, nailing him with my gaze. "Enlighten me."

But he doesn't. He just sits there, avoiding eye contact, his resting grumpy face as hard as granite.

I scoff under my breath, shaking my head. "I thought you were different."

He looks up, meeting my eyes.

"That first day," I continue, "when you tested me and put me through all those hellish drills, I thought, 'This guy is actually going to give me a chance.' I wanted to work for you because you treated me like an equal. But then you changed. You started acting like I have special needs or something. So what the hell *was* that first day? Were you just trying to scare me off so you wouldn't have to deal with me?"

"Weston—"

"I don't want to work for someone who treats me like I'm broken." My voice shatters on the last word, angry tears stinging my eyes. I throw the envelope down on the desk. "Keep your money, sir. I don't want it."

With that, I turn and storm out of the boxing gym, letting the door slam behind me. My hands tremble with pent-up rage as

I walk down the street to my mom's car and collapse into the driver's seat.

There's a forest fire in my chest, and I can't hold it in any longer. I slam my hand into the steering wheel over and over again, every hit making the pain in my side flare up, but I don't care—I'm so burning mad, I could put a hole through this steering wheel.

SLAM, SLAM, SLAM.

I crumple forward with my face in my hands just as the tears spill down.

Weston:
Hey
Are you still awake?

> **Tessa:**
> Yeah
> What's up?

Weston:
Can I come over?
I know it's super late but
I want to see you

> **Tessa:**
> Of course.
> I'm staying over at my mom's apt tonight
> but she's already gone to bed
> Is everything ok?

I don't answer that last question because I don't need to. It's obvious when Tessa opens the door of her mother's apartment and sees me standing on the porch, holding my side.

"Oh my god, what happened? Are you hurt?"

I shrug one shoulder. "Not really. I got hit while sparring, but I'm okay."

Tessa knows me better than that. She knows I'm not okay.

Without a word, she takes my arm and escorts me into the tiny living room. It's dark but for the soft light of a few lamps. Tessa is wearing fuzzy slippers and one of my hoodies. She looks ready for bed. Is it really that late? I glance at the clock. 10:30. *I guess so.*

Tessa drags me over to the couch and makes me sit down. "When did you get out of the gym?"

"Hours ago."

"And you didn't go home?"

I shake my head. "I just drove around for a while. I wanted to be by myself. And then I wanted to see you."

Tessa looks up at me, worry swimming in her big blue eyes. I don't know if it's because I'm still gripping my side like a horse kicked me in the liver or because I just confessed that I wanted to be *alone*, which is about as weird for me as a snowstorm in Hawaii.

"What happened, Wes?"

When I don't reply, Tessa investigates for herself—pulling up the hem of my T-shirt to check out my injury.

"Oh, are we taking each other's clothes off while Mom's in bed?" I joke, falling back on my best coping mechanism: the dirty humor Tessa hates.

She clicks her tongue and grimaces—not at my innuendo, but at the nasty bruise darkening my ribs. "Weston, who did this?"

"Just some jerk I was sparring with. Come on, it's not that bad."

"It *is* bad. You're in pain—I can tell." She takes me by the shoulders and forces me to lie back on the sofa. "Just sit still and let me get you a cold compress."

I tip my head back against the pillows, shutting my eyes. *God, I'm so sore.* Tessa returns moments later with a bag of crushed ice wrapped in a dishcloth and places it on my side. It feels like a sharp blade sinking between my ribs.

I recoil in surprise, cussing like a truck driver. Tessa winces— at my pain or my language, I'm not sure which.

"Sorry, I know it hurts… but this will help the swelling."

I nod stiffly, holding the ice against my ribs. "It's okay. I've dealt with worse."

Tessa manages a sad smile, propping another pillow behind my head. "Are you comfortable? Here, take these off." She reaches for the ankle zipper on my track pants, sliding it up to access the prosthetic leg closest to her.

"Take what off, my pants?" I tease her between moans of pain. "Jeez, you really do get wild after your mom goes to bed."

Tessa rolls her eyes and blushes. "Shut up."

I feel her fingers brush over my knee, searching for the release on the socket. She's watched me take off my prostheses enough times to know how they work—but this is the first time she's ever done it *for* me. I never thought I'd say this, but it's strangely… arousing. I start to notice how incredibly sexy she looks, sitting there in my oversized hoodie, her messy hair like two curtains framing the sunny window that is her face.

With a *click*, my left leg releases, and Tessa gently places it on the floor before moving on to the right. I try not to think about the fact that her hands are *inside my pants right now, dear god*—

I press the bag of ice into my side to distract myself with a fresh jolt of pain. It's a surefire way to make any pleasant feelings go away. Once both my legs are on the floor, Tessa rolls up the bottoms of my track pants and peels off my prosthetic socks, which are soaked in sweat.

She winces when she sees my stumps. "Weston… you have blisters."

I close my eyes. "I know."

"You shouldn't be walking on them. Don't you know they'll just get worse?"

"Yeah. But I don't have time to dry my legs between classes. I can't help that I sweat a lot."

"You wouldn't be sweating so much if you wore shorts," Tessa argues.

"I can't wear shorts."

"Why not? You wear shorts all the time when you're training at school, doing track meets—"

"Track is different. School is different. Everyone knows me. They don't ask stupid questions."

Tessa falls silent, tracing her soft fingertips over my knee. "I know," she whispers. "I'll be right back." She stands and walks down the hallway to the bathroom, returning moments later with a damp cloth and a tube of ointment. "Scootch over," she says, sitting down and pulling my legs across her lap.

When she begins washing my stumps, I sit upright. "You don't have to do that, Tessa. It's gross."

She pushes me back against the cushions and leans in to kiss me softly on the lips. "No part of you is gross."

Maybe it's the way she says that—so sweet and honest—or

maybe it's the way she kisses me, or maybe it's the argument I had with Bruiser tonight, or maybe it's just a mix of the pain and the exhaustion and the effort of swallowing back everything I've wanted to say for the past seven days...

I don't know what it is, but at that moment, something inside me just *gives out*.

A knot tightens in my throat, and I press my eyes shut, covering my face with one hand because I'm too ashamed to let Tessa see me in tears.

See me in pieces.

Broken.

"Oh, Weston." She puts down the cloth and wraps me in a hug. "What happened? Please tell me."

My voice comes out thick as I fight back the tears I refuse to let fall. "Bruiser let me go."

"Why?"

"Because of who I am," I whisper. "*What* I am."

"Did he say that?"

I shake my head. "No, he tried to make some excuse about it not being the 'right time' to work for him. He said I needed to fix my attitude, that I was letting my ego get in the way. Maybe it's partially my fault. Maybe I pushed him over the edge tonight with Devon."

Tessa frowns. "Who's Devon?"

That's when I realize how little she knows about this whole mess.

So I start at the very beginning and tell her everything—from the first day when Bruiser dropped his coffee cup on the floor to all those little moments when he treated me with kid gloves, to Leia's game of mouse-and-mousetrap, to the sparring match with

Devon and the way Bruiser said, *There's more to it than you think, kid,* but wouldn't tell me what "more" there was.

Tessa listens to the whole long-winded story as she smooths ointment over my blisters. When she's finished, she leans back with my knees in her lap, her fingers threaded through mine.

"Well, maybe there *is* more to it than you think," she offers gently. "I mean… maybe Bruiser has a point."

"A point about what?"

Tessa tips her head to the side, like she isn't sure how to say what's on her mind. "Well, you can be a little…"

I narrow my eyes at her. "A little *what?*"

"Like that," she says with a smirk. "Defensive. Cocky. Protective of your ego."

"Pfft—what ego? I don't even *have* an ego."

Tessa laughs, tossing her head back. "Don't get offended, Wes."

"I'm not offended," I fire back, crossing my arms over my chest. "See, a guy with a big ego would be offended, but I'm *not.* You can say whatever you want to me. Anybody can—I don't care."

"Yet you care what Bruiser thinks of you," Tessa argues. "You've spent the past week throwing your back out to impress him. Why?"

I'm quiet for a moment. I've never really stopped to face that question head-on. Maybe she's right; maybe I have been too defensive to be honest with myself. But it's easier to let my guard down here, with Tessa's hand in mine and ice on my ribs and a quarter of my body parts sprawled on the floor.

"I guess I wanted to impress him because he's the kind of guy who *won't* be impressed by anyone. And I was… *cocky* enough to think that I could be the one to impress him."

Tessa nods slowly, tracing her soft fingertip over my rough knuckles. "So you wanted him to think you were special… different. But then, when he treated you like you were different, it made you angry."

I frown at her for a long moment, bending my brain to see it from this perspective. "Don't do that."

"Do what?"

"Reinterpret events in this really philosophical, mature way that makes me feel like a stupid little five-year-old."

Tessa snorts a surprised laugh. "That's not what I'm doing. I'm just *saying*… and I could be wrong, okay? This guy could be a total jerk. I don't know him. I just think sometimes we get used to being treated a certain way by other people, and we start to assume *everyone* is going to treat us like that, when really, it's just… well, to be honest, it's another kind of prejudice, isn't it? To assume you know what someone thinks of you just because lots of other people think that way about you?"

I shrug one shoulder, contemplating it. "Yeah, I guess you're right."

Tessa gives me a weak smile, reaching over to play with my hair. "I think maybe you should talk to him about how you feel. Just be honest. Be yourself. And I don't mean the *bulldozer* version of you who gets all angry and stubborn and huffs and puffs and refuses to look at anything from someone else's point of view."

I scoff. "Are you saying all this offensive shit about me because I literally can't get off this couch and walk away?"

Tessa smirks, raising her eyebrows. "Offensive? I thought you weren't offended by anything."

God, she pisses me off like nobody else.

She also turns me on like nobody else.

"Come here," I growl, pulling her down to my level and kissing her—slow, deep, like nothing else matters. Because right now, nothing does.

She's the opposite of everything at the boxing gym—all silky skin and soft lips and strawberry-scented hair and flowers on her pajama pants. As she cups my face in her hands and kisses me, I get lost in this feeling of us together. It's like stumbling upon the gates of heaven after an agonizing road trip through hell.

"Weston?" Tessa whispers, pulling back a few inches to look me in the eye. "That girl you said was… coming onto you…"

I try not to smirk at that halting, jealous undertone in her voice. Maybe it's my "ego," but there's something satisfying about seeing Tessa unnerved by the idea of another girl making a pass at me.

"Is she pretty?"

I shrug. "I don't know. Couldn't say. I only have eyes for you."

A smile melts over Tessa's lips, her gaze softening as she leans in and kisses me again. Her fingers curl through my hair, and my hands cradle her waist—accidentally slipping under her hoodie and skimming the smooth, bare skin of her lower back. I'm acutely aware of the fact that she's sinking closer and closer, but I don't realize just how close until her elbow jams into my side.

"Ow!" I blurt out, breaking our kiss—except I say more than just *ow*. I say things that probably make Tessa feel tainted from kissing my "potty mouth."

She doesn't call me out on it this time because I have a good excuse. She just struggles upright, all pink-faced and cute, gasping,

"Oh gosh, I'm sorry. We shouldn't do that tonight. You should sleep."

I groan, shifting onto my uninjured side. "I'd sleep better if I could cuddle you."

Tessa thinks about it, eyeing the space on the couch where her body would fit perfectly next to mine. I give her sad-puppy eyes to force the issue. Finally, she relents.

"Okay, but just for a few minutes."

"Yes, ma'am."

"And no dirty jokes."

"Yes, ma'am."

"And no—"

"Oh, just shut up and let me cuddle you."

She rolls her eyes, snuggling close to spoon with me. She rests her cheek on my bicep, and I sling one arm around her waist. Within seconds, I'm asleep.

———————

I spend all of Saturday with Tessa, doing absolutely nothing. We watch movies and eat food that's no good for us and occasionally get distracted kissing on the couch. Tessa keeps telling me I need to rest and let myself recover, and I guess she's right. I'm sore as hell—even more than last night—and my blisters need time to heal, which means spending as much time as possible with my prosthetic legs off.

Tessa usually has her days calendar-blocked from dawn to dusk with work (yes, even weekends) but she clears her schedule for me. She bakes chocolate chip cookies and insists we watch *The Princess Bride*, and she commentates it for me, like I did with *The*

Sound of Music back when she was blind. In the late afternoon, she takes me outside to the hammock in her backyard, and we cuddle together under the swaying sunlit trees, listening to the birds.

Tessa falls asleep like that, her head on my chest and her leg draped over my waist. *This is what life should be*, I think. Lazing around, having fun with my girlfriend, doing *nothing*. Who wants to spend their free time training their ass off at a boxing gym, pounding heavy bags and sweating bullets?

I do.

Despite how many times I try to convince myself I don't care about the job, I don't care what Bruiser thinks, I'm better off never speaking to him again…

I'm not buying it. Deep down, I know what Tessa said last night was true. I need to straighten things out between me and my ex-almost-boss. If I don't at least *try* to straighten things out, it will always bother me.

————————————

On Sunday morning, my opportunity arrives.

Tessa is at church with her family, which always leaves me feeling lonely for at least three hours per week. A good thing if you want to eliminate distractions and get shit done. Also a good thing if you're my mother, who has a running list of "chores for boys who have nothing to do." That's one thing about my mom: if you tell her you're bored, she'll make sure you're not bored for long.

On the top of her list today is dropping off a donation box at Goodwill—something Dad keeps forgetting because it's in the opposite direction of the *Chronicle*, and that's pretty much the only place he drives every day.

Mom knows how hard I've been working all week, and she can see how much I'm feeling it today, but she doesn't let me use that as an excuse to lie around feeling sorry for myself. So I toss the box into the backseat of her car and drive down to Goodwill to drop it off.

I drive by Bruiser's on the way, but the windows are dark, and I don't see his truck parked outside. The gym is closed for the weekend. Which would be the perfect excuse to avoid Bruiser altogether and put off this imaginary, uncomfortable conversation that's been stewing in the back of my mind for the past twenty-four hours.

He's not there. I can't talk to him. I don't even have his phone number. I don't even know where he lives.

Just when I think I'll be able to postpone the Talk for another day, I drive by the diner on Main Street and see a lifted Chevy pickup with US Marine stickers all over the back window. I know Bruiser must be inside.

And I know if I keep driving, I'll feel like a pansy-ass for the rest of my life.

So I swing the car into a space across the street and park.

It's now or never.

The door chime rings as I step into the diner and glance around. I spot him right away, drinking coffee alone at a booth, the back of his buzzed head looking less intimidating outside of the boxing gym. He doesn't see me until I drop into the booth seat across from him.

Our eyes lock, but the look on his face is not at all surprised. Has he been expecting me to hunt him down? Did he know this conversation was bound to happen sooner or later? He nods once in acknowledgment of my presence, but says nothing. And somehow, the silence isn't awkward or tense. It's weirdly, unexpectedly… comfortable.

Bruiser sips his coffee and waits for me to break the ice. There are two little empty shots of cream sitting on the table. I never would have guessed a guy like Bruiser would take cream in his coffee. He seems more like the type who would chew the actual coffee grounds because you can't let good caffeine go to waste.

That's when it suddenly occurs to me that I don't really know anything about this guy. Whether he's married or has kids or has a dog. Over the past week, I've only gotten to know Bruiser, the owner of the boxing gym. Bruiser the beast.

Not Bruiser, the man.

Now seems like a good time to start.

"Guess you're not much of a churchgoer, huh?" That's the first thing that comes out of my mouth.

Bruiser grunts into his mug. "Look who's talking."

I manage a half-grin. "My girlfriend is trying to convert me."

He sits back, studying me for a second, an unreadable look in his eyes. Maybe he's just now realizing that he doesn't know much about *me*, either. He's never asked me about my personal life—what I do besides boxing, if I have plans for my future, if I have siblings or a girlfriend or a dog.

Strangest of all, he's never asked me *the* question everyone asks: how I lost my legs.

I stare out between the slats in the window blinds, trying to figure out what to say next. Nothing seems right. A waitress saves me just in time, swooping over to ask if she can get me a coffee.

"That would be great, thank you."

She hurries off to the counter and returns a moment later with a mug of steaming dark roast. When she walks away, Bruiser finally speaks, his gaze fixed on the street outside, his voice low and defenseless.

"That picture you were asking me about... the one in my office. The one I told you was taken in Iraq?"

"Uh, yeah. The one of you with the rock-on guy?"

"His name was Rafe," Bruiser says, the look in his eyes miles away. Maybe countries away. "He was one of the best men I've ever had the privilege to work beside—to fight beside. Rafe was the kinda guy who would give you the shirt off his back. The kinda guy who wouldn't let you down. You needed help any time of day or night, he was there for you. We trained together way back, then wound up in the same platoon over there." Bruiser pauses, like there's a hell of a lot more to the story, but he either doesn't want to relive it or doesn't want to bore me with the details. "You got a best friend, Weston? Someone you know has your back come hell or high water?"

I think of Rudy. I think of Tessa, too.

"Yeah," I say.

Bruiser nods slowly, something in his eyes a thousand years old. "Well, I hope you'll never find out what it feels like to lose them."

My voice comes out hesitant. "Was your buddy Rafe... killed in combat?"

Bruiser shakes his head. "Not technically *combat*. We were on patrol. He stepped on an IED. It didn't kill him right away, but..." Bruiser looks down at his hands clasped on the table. Knuckles white. "He got his legs blown off."

That's when it clicks.

The way Bruiser dropped his coffee cup on the floor when he saw me that first morning.

The way he looked at me like he'd seen a ghost.

He had.

There's more to it than you think, kid.

And there I was, assuming my disability could be the only reason for his reaction.

"The other night, you told me to enlighten you," Bruiser continues, his voice low and grave, his eyes fixed on something out the window. "And I should have. But it's not easy to talk about it, kid. And it doesn't get any easier with time. I don't care how many years pass, how many therapy sessions the VA tries to put you through, how much medication they give you to help you sleep at night and not see that shit in your dreams… It never gets easy to talk about watching your best friend bleed to death in front of you and knowing it was your fault."

I shake my head, reeling inside. "Wait, how was it *your* fault?"

Bruiser doesn't answer right away. He stares into his half-empty coffee mug, letting a silence pass before speaking again.

"Rafe was a couple of years younger than me. I was kinda like the big brother he never had. And like a little brother, he was always trying to impress me. Always going out of his way to be the toughest, baddest guy in the room. That wasn't really who he *was*, you know? It was just who he wanted to be. How he wanted the other guys to see him."

I'm not sure why I feel attacked as Bruiser says all this. Maybe because I know he's not just talking about his buddy Rafe.

"No moment of glory is worth risking your life for. Remember that, kid. It's a lesson some people learn too late." Bruiser sighs, shaking his head. "So many things went wrong that day. We were at odds over some stupid shit, and Rafe thought I was underestimating him—undermining his authority. When we were out on patrol that day, he fought to swap places with me and take up the lead. He needed to feel like he was the top dog, you know? He needed to boost his ego. And then the world exploded." Bruiser's voice fades to a rough whisper. "We tried to rush him to the medics, but… it was too late."

I sink back in the booth seat, imagining what a hellish experience that must have been. Not just to live *through*, but to live *with*. I can tell by the gutted look in his eyes how much it haunts him.

I guess we all have scars. Some are just more visible than others.

Bruiser finishes by saying, "If Rafe hadn't been trying so damn hard to impress everyone—me most of all—he'd be alive right now. He would be here instead of me."

I lean forward with my elbows on the table. "You can't blame yourself. I mean, it could have happened to anyone. Right?"

Bruiser says nothing in reply. He just sits there with his arms crossed over his chest, eyes slitted, staring out the window.

"So that was the deal?" I ask after a moment. "Did you let me go because I just remind you too much of Rafe? And… what happened to him?"

Bruiser grunts a humorless laugh. "I guess that comes with being young, doesn't it?"

"What?"

"Thinking you're the center of the damn universe."

Okay, fine, that makes my ego bristle just a little. But I guess I've got to admit, he has a point. I *have* been looking at everything from my perspective. What Tessa said about me is true—when I go into bulldozer mode, it's like nothing else exists. I *am* the center of the damn universe.

Maybe self-pity is the highest form of arrogance.

"It was never about your legs, kid. As far as I can tell, it doesn't seem to stop you from doing much. And to be honest, I think that's pretty incredible." He says it with unvarnished honesty, looking me right in the eyes. "It was never about *you*, Weston. I wasn't going easy on you because I thought you were broken. I was trying to make sure I didn't make the same mistake with you that I made with Rafe. When you start looking up to someone, trying to make them proud, it's not..." He shakes his head, shoulders stiffening as he averts his gaze again. "I'm no good for you, kid. That's it. That's the truth. I'm no good."

I sit back, looking at this guy and finally *seeing* him for the first time. He's not a beast, not an ex-Marine with menacing tattoos and pecs of steel. He's just a man who blames himself for getting his brother-in-arms blown to pieces.

He's the center of his own damn universe, and he doesn't even see it.

"With all due respect, sir... that's a load of shit."

Bruiser's gaze snaps back to me, surprised.

I smile. Because that look tells me I've caught him off guard. And that's a satisfying feeling.

"If I've learned anything from losing my legs, it's that regretting past mistakes... is the slowest way to die." I shrug one shoulder. "Maybe, if you had a time machine, you could go back and do something differently on that patrol, and maybe Rafe would be alive right now. And maybe if I had a time machine, I wouldn't be sitting here as an amputee. But we can't change the past. We can only change the future."

A weak half-smile tugs at one side of Bruiser's tight-lipped frown.

"What?" I ask.

"You sound just like him."

I look down at our two cups of coffee on the table. "I'm sorry for getting angry the other night. I shouldn't have assumed those things about you. It's just when you walk around in my shoes for a while, you get used to people looking at you a certain way. Or not looking, in a way that's almost worse."

Bruiser listens, his expression stony and unreadable. I get the feeling he understands, even though he could never *really* understand.

"And I guess I was also pissed because you told Devon about my legs to make him feel bad and apologize for hitting me."

Bruiser frowns, confusion written all over his face. "I never told Devon that."

"But he said… I saw you talking to him after the sparring match, and he came over and said he was sorry—"

"Because I could see right through his competitive dickhead attitude and told him that my gym was no place to get even with someone over personal shit. I told him if he couldn't put his inflated ego in check and show some sportsmanship and respect, he could consider himself barred from training at my gym for the rest of his life." Bruiser grunts into his coffee mug. "The kid clearly has no father keeping him in line at home."

The last of my self-doubt melts away in that moment as I realize what this means.

I've been wrong.

About everything.

This whole time.

I've been an idiot. The center of my universe. A black hole of self-pity, self-destruction. I've been so caught up in what I thought was happening, it made me completely blind to what was *actually* happening.

Now, reflecting on the past week, it's like I can finally see clearly. And it's like the weight of the world has lifted off my shoulders.

As much as it pains me to admit it, Tessa is right. I'm too defensive for my own good. I *am* an arrogant moron.

But sometimes arrogance can be a virtue.

Like now.

"Sir, I know you think you're no good for me—and this job is no good for me. And maybe you're right. Maybe you bring out the worst in me. Maybe you bring out the worst in everyone. I don't know. Maybe I'm just a competitive jackass who wants to be the greatest of all time. But to be honest… I think *I'm* good for *you*."

Again, I take Bruiser by surprise. His eyebrows tick upward like, *Oh really, kid?*

"I realize how cocky that sounds," I'm quick to add, "which just goes to prove your point that I have too big an ego and need to adjust my attitude… but I'm willing to do that. It would be good for me to do that. I just think if I walk away from this job, I'll always regret it. And I think… maybe you'll regret it, too."

Bruiser watches me for a long moment, a thousand unspoken words flickering through his ice-cold eyes. It feels like an eternity passes before he breaks the silence.

"You think *you're* good for *me*?"

The way he poses the question would make anyone else shut their mouth and realize he's being rhetorical—sarcastic, even.

But I have the nerve to nod and say, "Yeah. I do. Because even though I don't know what it's like to go through a war… I do know what it's like to live every day with something that you can't escape—something that makes you miss the person you used to be. Something nobody else can ever *truly* understand. I know it's two completely different things, but… sometimes it helps just to know someone else who has…" I look down, my throat tightening around the last few words. "Stuff they can't talk about."

That's when the waitress comes by and refills our coffee mugs. A moment of silence comes and goes. Bruiser finally sighs through his nose and says, "You're right, kid."

Which prompts me to ask, "About… which thing?"

"You're an arrogant jackass."

My shoulders slump.

Bruiser hides his grin in his coffee cup, making me wait before adding, "You're right about me, too. I like having you around. You remind me of myself when I was your age."

"Really?"

"Why are you smiling? It wasn't a compliment."

I laugh.

"If you want to give it another shot… I'm willing to put up with your shit if you're willing to put up with mine."

I raise one eyebrow. "Wait, are you offering me the job?"

"If you have to ask, you weren't listening."

"No, I was listening."

"What'd I say?"

"You're hired."

Bruiser laughs. Yes, actually *laughs*. For the first time since I met him.

"Good answer, kid."

———————————

When I show up for work at Bruiser's Boxing Gym on Monday night, I'm wearing basketball shorts. It feels a little like that moment when you brace yourself before diving into a freezing lake. But once you take the plunge and your body gets used to it, you're like, *Hey, this water's not bad.*

That's how it is every time I let someone *see* that I'm an amputee.

I don't do it for Tessa. I don't do it for Bruiser.

I do it for myself.

Because if I can't be one hundred percent myself—damn the consequences—then there's no point to this job at all. I promised Bruiser I would adjust my attitude and put my ego in check. I vowed to be a better version of myself.

And tonight, as I was getting ready, I asked myself what the best version of Weston Ludovico would wear to the boxing gym.

Basketball shorts. Every time. Because the best version of Weston doesn't give a shit what people think, how much they look or don't look, or what stupid questions they ask.

That's the Weston I'm going to be from now on.

I know some days, I'll fail. But that's okay. Because I'll always get the chance to try again.

That's the thing about boxing—and life: everybody gets knocked down, but what makes you a fighter is getting back up and going another round.

When people start showing up for class, I don't look at them—but they look at me. As Bruiser calls the students to line up in front of us, they go through all the usual Reactions. Some people don't seem to care. Little Steve Rogers stares at me like I'm his new favorite Avenger. Princess Leia looks like she can't believe she kissed me. (And jeez, if I'd known my prosthetic legs would have warded off her creepy stalking, I would have revealed them a long time ago.) Devon looks the most shocked of them all—his mouth is hanging open in disbelief as he sees me in a whole new light.

Bruiser crosses his arms over his chest and leans closer to stage-whisper loud enough for everyone else to hear, "Do you see any flying *donuts* around here, Weston?"

I swallow a laugh. "No, sir. I don't."

"Then why the hell are all these mouths hanging open?"

I pretend to think about it, then answer, "I think they want to do knuckle pushups, sir."

Bruiser nods, grinning just enough for me to see. "I think you're right, kid." He slaps my shoulder. "Count 'em out."

PROM & PRINCIPLES
A Westess Story

"HOW MUCH FARTHER?"

"Tessa, you've asked me that five times in the past five minutes."

"And you've answered in the same unsatisfactory way every time," I say with an indignant huff. "'Not far.' You know, that's not the answer I was—"

Whoa.

I stop dead in my tracks when we emerge from the woods and find ourselves at the edge of a secluded little pond with a gazebo in the center and a boardwalk leading out to it. The gazebo's interior is decorated with twinkle lights and hanging flower baskets.

It's like something from a fairytale.

Weston holds his hand out to me, watching my reaction as if it's the best part of his day. "Shall we?"

Arm in arm, we stroll down the boardwalk to the gazebo.

"How did you find this place?" I breathe. "It's magical."

Weston shrugs. "Just came across it one day."

Once we're inside, I stop and turn in a slow circle, tipping my head back to take it all in. Sunset light kisses the pond's surface in a shimmer of rose gold, turning the water to pink champagne. Benches circle the gazebo's interior, making it the perfect place to soak in the view—or the perfect place to dance.

"You know what this reminds me of?" I say, turning to find Weston fidgeting with his phone. "The gazebo in *The Sound of—*"

"Shh, don't say it," Weston cuts in. "You'll ruin everything."

I frown, puzzled, until I hear the unmistakable first notes of a song I know by heart. Only this time, the voice accompanying the music is Weston's as he turns around theatrically and takes my hands in his.

"You wait, little girl, on an empty stage… for fate to turn the light on."

A surprised laugh jumps out of me, and my heart instantly melts at his honey-rich voice singing me one of my favorite songs from my favorite movie of all time.

"Your life, little girl, is an empty page you'll find something to write on."

"That's not—"

"To *wriiiiiite onnnnn…*" He gives me a pointed look, as if to say, *Don't correct my mistakes right now, Tessa.*

So I keep my lips sealed. Because it doesn't matter if he gets some words wrong. This is quite possibly the most romantic thing he's ever done for me.

As the music changes tempo, Weston begins leading me in slow circles around the gazebo, his eyes sparkling, his grin love-struck. "You are seventeen going on eighteen, baby, you're on the brink… of making me fall down dead at your feet—oh, what would my parents think?"

I burst out laughing, realizing now that he's deliberately changing the lyrics—and I like his version much better. I hop up on one of the benches, still holding his hand like the starry-eyed Liesl dancing with her secret lover in a moonlit garden. I'm glad I wore my twirliest dress for this date—it swirls around my legs as I skip from bench to bench, laughing the whole time.

"I need someone younger and wiser correcting my grammar for meeeee." Weston's voice carries the rewritten lyrics with cheery confidence. "You look like a dream, what I really mean is—" He grasps my waist and sweeps me off the bench as if I weigh no more than a feather. Suddenly, I'm standing right in front of him, and he's sinking down on one knee, making my heart flop backward in my chest. With an impossibly cute smile, he looks up into my face and sings the question, "Will you come to prom with me?"

I gasp, my hands flying to my mouth. "Oh my god, I thought you were going to ask me something else for a second."

Weston freezes, his eyes darting around as the karaoke song continues playing on his phone.

"Yes, of course. I will absolutely go to prom with you."

As understanding hits him, he springs to his feet. "You thought I was gonna ask you to marry me?"

I laugh, shaking my head because it sounds ridiculous when he says it out loud.

"We're seventeen, Tessa," he reminds me with a wink. "But someday, I absolutely will propose to you."

My heart squeezes as he catches my waist and pulls me close, resting his forehead gently against mine.

"For now, it's just a *promposal*."

I kiss him, lacing my fingers behind his neck and basking in the perfection of this moment and all its sweetness—the sparkling pink water all around us, the music drifting through the evening, the soft press of Weston's lips against mine.

"It was perfect," I whisper.

WESTON

"IT WAS KIND OF PERFECT." I SWERVE RUDY A GRIN AS we walk into the locker room after track practice the following day. "If anything, she was disappointed it wasn't a *real* proposal."

Rudy laughs, shrugging off his backpack. "Can't do a real proposal without a ring," he says. "And you can't get a ring when you're flat broke."

I punch him in the shoulder, but he's right; I have no money for diamond rings. We make our way through the chaotic locker room, which is a madhouse of sweaty guys shooting the shit, throwing dirty socks around, slamming lockers, and telling dumb jokes.

A crowded locker room has never been my favorite place to change out of my running blades and into my everyday prosthetic legs. But hell, over the past four years, I've had no choice but to get used to it. Everyone else has gotten used to it, too. They don't stare anymore.

I grab my stuff and claim a spot on a free bench—uncomfortably close to the captain of the football team, Neil Ferguson. Yep, *that* Neil Ferguson. The first one to welcome me back to school with scathing insults after my amputation all those years ago. He goes by "Ferg" these days because he thinks it sounds cooler. But a skunk is a skunk by any other name.

He's shirtless right now, a damp towel hanging around his neck as he shoots his mouth off about some girl he's taking to prom, bragging about how hot she is—in explicit detail—like his single most important goal in life is to make the whole damn world jealous of him.

I try to zone out of his obnoxious voice as I bend over to release the prosthesis from my left leg.

"You ask Clara yet?" I question Rudy over my shoulder.

He smirks, toeing off his running shoes. "She asked *me*, actually."

"Damn. Girl knows what she wants."

Rudy grunts. "She's threatening to wear sweatpants just to be rebellious. I don't think she's caught the drift that my family doesn't exactly like *rebellion* when it comes to tradition."

"You're getting them used to it, though," I say, grabbing a towel from my backpack. "Wouldn't they have preferred you asked some cute Jewish girl from synagogue?"

Rudy relents to a sheepish smile. "Yeah. They would've. But you can't help who you fall for."

"Ain't that the truth."

"You bet your ass we'll be up at Hickley Point before any of you losers get to second base." Ferg's sneering voice rises above the murmur of the crowded room. He leans back against the lockers, his arms crossed over his chest and a smug grin on his slappable face.

"What's Hickley Point?" asks Kent, a transfer student. He's been here long enough not to stare at my legs, but not long enough to know what Hickley Point is.

Ferg laughs at the question. "You serious, man? Well, I guess you have an excuse. You're fresh meat. Not yet *tenderized*." He smacks Kent on the shoulder, making him jump in surprise. "Hickley Point is where it happens."

"Where what happens?" Kent asks, apparently not as bright as he looks.

"Oh, man. Here it comes," Rudy mutters under his breath, rising from the bench to shove his running shoes back into his locker.

Ferg goes on to explain—in explicit detail—what exactly happens when you take your girl up to Hickley Point at night. The spot is so notorious that someone even blacked out the letter *L* on the sign and added some very imaginative doodles to emphasize the actual function of the place. Despite its reputation, Hickley Point is a perfectly G-rated public park—the main attraction being a lookout point where you can park your car and enjoy the view of Rockford sprawled in the valley below. I've driven Tessa up there a few times during the day (she either never noticed the defaced sign or was too sophisticated to say anything about it).

While Kent has his eyes opened about Hickley Point and all the luck to be found there, I towel-dry my stumps and slide my prosthetic socks back on.

The sooner I get out of Ferg's proximity, the better.

"Man, I wish I had a date to take to prom," Kent says with a sigh, shaking his head.

Ferg chuckles, yanking on his T-shirt. "Hey, I'll give you a tip."

Kent perks up, eager to learn.

"Pick a girl with glasses. Then, before you ask her, do this." He pulls Kent's glasses off his face in one quick motion, holding them out of reach. "You'll look a lot better—trust me!"

A couple of dumbass guys laugh at his joke, but something in me bristles. My muscles lock up as I watch Kent blindly grope for his glasses.

"Hey, Ferguson!" my voice booms out, killing the laughter. "Knock it off."

A flash of irritation sparks in his eyes as he swivels away from Kent and turns his bloodthirsty smile on me.

"Aw, what's the matter, Ludovico? Feeling left out?" He shoves Kent's glasses at his chest, stepping closer to look down his nose at me. "We all know *you* won't take your girl to Hickley Point on prom night."

His entourage of deadbeats makes a collective "ohhh" of understanding and starts laughing.

"The holy virgin would never let you go that far." Ferg grins down at me, his tongue in his cheek. "Would she, Ludovico?"

A coil of anger tightens in the pit of my stomach as I slide my gaze up to his. "I'd shut my mouth right about now if I were you, Ferg."

"Oh, I stand corrected—you're *both* holy virgins!"

I shouldn't let that bother me.

It doesn't bother me.

It *doesn't*.

But I can't deny that it gives me a strong, unstoppable urge to punch him in the face.

I shove the violent desire back down, focusing on the task at hand: putting my prosthetic legs on. I slide my right stump into the socket, but it doesn't fit. *Wrong leg. Idiot.* I switch to the left and push the pin into the lock until it clicks, ignoring Ferg's obnoxious voice the whole time.

"Tell us, Weston. We're all dying to know—has she inducted you into her cult yet? A life of celibacy and never keeping her up past her bedtime?"

I clench my teeth, fire building in my core as the urge to punch him grows even stronger. I cut Rudy a sideways glance, and he shakes his head slowly as if to say, *Don't fall for it.*

Normally, I wouldn't. I've had some practice letting offensive remarks roll off me, not rising to the bullshit that kids like Neil Ferguson throw around to make themselves feel more important. I've endured lots of locker room talk in the past four years. But this is different. It's not about me.

It's about Tessa.

With every cutting word that comes out of Ferg's mouth, something in me winds tighter and tighter… getting ready to snap.

He pushes me too far when he leans down and says in a stage whisper loud enough for everyone to hear, "I'll take her up to Hickley Point myself if you ain't got the balls."

I lurch to my feet, ready to knock his teeth out—

Correction: I lurch to my *foot.*

I stumble, falling face-first into the lockers but catching myself just in time. My backpack flies off the bench in the process, spilling my running blades onto the floor.

There's a burst of laughter as my ears blaze red-hot with embarrassment.

I sit back down, not looking at Rudy, even though I can sense him staring at me.

Ferg smiles and slaps me on the shoulder like I'm some football buddy of his. "Hey, I'm just kidding, Ludovico. Don't sweat it. After all, you've got the perfect excuse." He nudges my running blade on the floor with the toe of his shoe. "No girl's parents would be worried about *you* taking their daughter to prom."

My gaze snaps to his. "What the hell is that supposed to mean?"

But I know exactly what it's supposed to mean.

And I hate the way it makes me feel: like he just scored the final point of a boxing match, and I'm on the ropes with blood in my mouth and a sickening knot in my stomach.

Ferg grunts a laugh and walks off, exiting the locker room with his moronic disciples trailing after him.

Neil Ferguson's stupid accusations haunt me for the rest of the day, unpunched punches thrumming in my fists. Man, I should have decked him when I had the chance. So what if I only had one leg on? I could take that sleazebag on with no legs and one hand tied behind my back. I could have made him pay for talking shit about Tessa. I *should* have.

"Would you stop thinking about this? It's over," Rudy says with a sigh later that day when we're training on the heavy bag in my garage. "Why is it still bothering you?"

"It's not bothering me. It's just…" I shake my head, crossing my arms over my chest. "That's not the reason Tessa and I don't… you know. It's because she has boundaries. She believes in purity and stuff. And I'm fine with that."

Rudy wipes the sweat off his forehead with the back of his boxing glove. "Why are you telling me this, Wes? Who cares what Ferg says? He's a moron, always has been."

"I know. He is."

We switch places—Rudy moves on to shadowboxing while I blister the heavy bag, giving it a face. Neil Ferguson's face. I unleash all the violent energy boiling in my veins, pounding the piss out of the bag and hoping it will improve my mood.

But even after I'm dead tired and covered in sweat, those words still echo through my mind.

You've got the perfect excuse.

No girl's parents would be worried about you *taking their daughter to prom.*

Was he right? Is that why Tessa's grandparents have never had reservations about me being alone with her? About leaving us in the house together unsupervised? Did they trust me because they figured I couldn't try anything with their granddaughter?

They've liked me from the beginning, and I wore that approval like a badge of honor. I have nothing but respect for Mr. and Mrs. Dickinson, so it made me proud to think they had respect for me, too—that they trusted me.

But now I'm starting to wonder if *trust* is something I should be proud to have.

I decide to come right out and ask Tessa about it that night as we're driving to see a movie together. She's in the passenger seat, sneaking me smiles and telling me to keep my eyes on the road when I get distracted looking at her.

That's when I pop the question.

"Do your grandparents ever get worried about you going out alone with me?"

Tessa frowns, puzzled. "What do you mean, worried?"

I shrug. "I don't know, like… say we stayed out past your curfew. Say we stayed out… all night. Would they be worried?"

Tessa falls silent, considering it. "No. I don't think they'd worry—not like *that*, anyway. I'm sure they'd assume we had a reasonable explanation. They trust you."

They trust me.

I would have preferred it if she said her grandparents would call the cops on me.

I'm not the kind of guy who needs to break the law and have some "bad boy" reputation to feel cool. But God, is there anything more disappointing than being so trustworthy that you could keep a girl out all night long and her grandparents wouldn't worry even the slightest bit?

"And… why do they trust me?" I ask, pressing her to see if I can get the whole truth.

"Why are you asking me all these questions?" She narrows her eyes, looking suspicious but amused.

"I don't know," I say with an easy laugh. "I was just curious."

Tessa smiles and threads her fingers through mine. "They trust you because they know you're not like other guys."

She probably means it to be a compliment, but tonight, it feels more like an accidental elbow in the ribs, hitting a bruise still tender from this morning.

Not like other guys.

That's me, alright.

TESSA

———————

I'VE NEVER BEEN TO A DANCE BEFORE. JANE AUSTEN movies have set the bar unrealistically high for me when it comes to formal gatherings involving music, dancing, and socializing in beautiful ballgowns. But something tells me Weston's senior prom isn't going to fulfill my fantasies of stepping into Elizabeth Bennet's shoes and being swept off my feet by some dashing stranger with a British accent.

Weston is my Mr. Darcy, and I'm happy anywhere as long as he's by my side.

I still spend an unhealthy amount of time scrolling through Pinterest for dress ideas. It's a challenge to find something that meets my standards and isn't three hundred dollars.

Eventually, I wind up in a subcategory of gowns referred to as "fairytale prom dresses," and I can sense that I'm getting closer to *the one*. I know it when I see it: a tulle skirt made of the palest pink with matching balloon sleeves and a ruffly sweetheart neckline. Pastel embroidered flowers cover the whole bodice, like a spring garden blooming across the dress—blossoms floating between layers of impossibly light fabric.

The best part is that the dress is reasonably priced and available through an online thrift shop. It's one size too big for me, but Grandma says she'll have no trouble taking it in.

Weston badgers me to see a picture of the dress, but I tell him it's a surprise and he will just have to be patient. Truth be told, I can't wait to show him—hoping the flowers will remind him of the time we first met. How he brought me all those flowers when I was blind, how he helped me learn to love life again.

"This is what I'm wearing," Weston says whenever I deny him a peek at the dress. He'll gesture at himself just to drive me crazy—since he is usually wearing gym shorts and a hoodie.

"If you don't show up at my door looking like you're attending the Netherfield ball, I'm not getting in the car with you."

Weston only laughs at that and volleys back, "Who says you can't wear sweats to a ball?"

The anticipation builds with every passing day, and one afternoon, Mom and I have a hairstyling session—going through my entire Pinterest board of favorite updos and testing them out to see which ones are too complicated or painful to achieve on prom night.

Mom is a genius with hair, though I must admit all the braiding, twisting, and pin-stabbing is rather agonizing. Between yelps of pain, we discuss the dos and don'ts of senior prom. Being homeschooled my whole life, I'm not fully up-to-date on typical teenager etiquette—the behavior of high-schoolers is a baffling mystery to me. But if I stay close to Weston, I'll be alright. I know Rudy and Clara well enough to consider them friends, too. Everything will be fine.

At least, that's what I think until Mom throws a monkey wrench into the situation by adding, "I lost my virginity at my senior prom."

My gaze snaps to hers through the mirror. "That's not… a prerequisite to prom, right?"

Mom laughs, as though I just asked her to tell me what it *means* to lose one's virginity. "No, of course not. But… it happens. More often than you might think. Sometimes when you least expect it."

"Mom," I huff, watching my cheeks blaze pink in the vanity mirror, "I'm not like that. And neither is Weston."

"Sweetie, all boys are the same. Horny and hopeless."

"I dispute that. Weston isn't like other guys; you've said so yourself. He respects my boundaries—it's something we've talked about. Not in explicit detail, but… he knows I want to save my first time for my wedding night. And he's cool with that."

Mom tilts her head noncommittally as she slides a few more pins into my hair. "You say that now, but sometimes things get out of hand, and before you know it… Well, it's better to be safe than sorry. I can buy you what you need—"

"No, Mom. I don't need protection. This is going to be just like any other date Weston has ever taken me on. There's no reason to get all worked up about it. Let's face it: I'm about as wild as an elderly woman whose highlight of the week is perusing the romance section of the bookstore."

Mom has no clever comeback for that. She just lets out a dry chuckle and says, "Perusing," with an air of mockery.

I'm right, and she knows it. There's nothing to be worried about. Weston and I will dress up nice, go to prom, dance, and laugh, and have a good time together. It will be lighthearted and fun, and the trickiest bit will be enduring all that social interaction. The only thing I'll have to worry about is introducing myself to strangers and draining my introvert batteries. But even then, Weston assured me we can leave whenever I want—and we're under no obligation to attend After Prom, which is the next phase for extroverts who don't need things like sleep and sanity.

Mom may have a point—all guys might be the same.

But Weston is different.

WESTON

"SEVENTY BUCKS PLUS TAX TO RENT A TUX FOR ONE night? It's times like these when I wish I had an older brother to steal clothes from."

Rudy laughs from the passenger seat of my truck. Two plastic-sleeved clothing bags hang in the backseat, swishing noisily at every stop sign.

"Maybe you should've *bought* a tux and split it four ways with your brothers," Rudy suggests. "That way, they'd all get a turn wearing it when they get old enough to go to prom."

I snap my fingers. "Good idea. Except Henry's already taller than me, so I doubt he'd get much use out of it." I tap on my directional and swing into the parking lot of the florist shop. With our formal attire taken care of, Rudy and I are now in pursuit of corsages for our respective dates. It's totally antiquated and border-line ridiculous, but according to my mom, it's still the custom.

I pinch my nose to stop myself from sneezing the minute I walk in the door. Flowers are everywhere—stacked in vases on floor-to-ceiling shelves, crowded on table displays, and filling refrigerator cases.

"Can I help you guys?" asks a tall young woman with blonde hair. She's standing behind the counter, wrapping up a gift basket of flowers in cellophane.

Rudy steps forward to brief her on our mission. "We're going to prom; we need corsages." A very brief brief.

"Absolutely," the florist says with a sunny smile. "Right this way."

She leads us over to a refrigerator case filled with little bundles of flowers in every color imaginable. Some have ribbons, beads, and sparkly stuff—it's like an ice-cream bar with too many flavors to choose from.

"What colors are you guys looking for?"

I shrug. "I don't know." Turning to Rudy, I ask, "Does it have to be a specific color?"

Before he can answer, the florist says, "Usually, you try to match with the color your date is wearing."

I frown, trying to figure out how Tessa will match her corsage to the color "her date" is wearing when that date is me, and I'm wearing a black-and-white tux.

"But we're both going to be wearing tuxedos," I say, gesturing between me and Rudy.

The florist's eyebrows rise like she wasn't expecting to hear that, but she nods and smiles understandingly. "Oh! Okay, well, what color ties are you guys wearing?"

Rudy blinks, looking utterly confused. "Uh… blue."

"Red," I reply.

"So… you two want to match each other?"

I squint at her for a second before the realization hits me—

and I can't help but burst out laughing when it does. "He's not my date!"

"He's not *my* date," Rudy adds, shaking his head like the florist just accused him of taking an orangutan to prom. "We're not going *together*."

I'm cracking up too hard at this point to see the florist's face when she realizes her mistake. Rudy punches my shoulder to make me knock it off and says, "We're supposed to match the corsages to our dates' *dresses*. What color is Tessa wearing?"

"No idea. She refuses to tell me anything about it. But I'm guessing it will be pink. Light pink. It's her favorite."

The florist selects a corsage made up of tiny pink roses and a few sprigs of lavender. Good enough. Rudy texts Clara to find out what color her dress is; it turns out to be blue.

We pay for the corsages (which luckily don't break the bank like the tux rentals did), and the florist advises us to store them in the refrigerator until prom night.

Back in the parking lot, I stop Rudy before he can get into my truck.

"Hey, Rudy?"

"Yeah?"

I grin, extending the little plastic to-go box of pink flowers. "Will you go to prom with me?"

He responds by giving me an affectionate whack on the head. "You're such an idiot."

———————————

Tessa texts me hours ahead of time to let me know when I should pick her up. I've already given her the rundown for the night:

dinner out with me, her, Rudy, and Clara, and then onward to the dance, which is being held in the gymnasium at my high school.

Her grandparents gave her permission to bend her curfew tonight as long as I bring her back home before midnight. The idea of bent curfews and all-nighters immediately gives me flashbacks to Neil Fergeson's gibes from the locker room a few days ago.

No girl's parents would be worried about you *taking their daughter to prom.*

I remember what Tessa said when I asked her what her grandparents would think if I kept her out all night.

They trust you… because they know you're not like other guys.

Not like other guys.

Not

like

other

guys.

My knuckles tighten around the steering wheel as I try to shove that squirming, pansy-ass insecurity to the back of my mind. Rudy's right—Ferg is a moron, and so are all the guys who hang out with him.

I shouldn't care what they think of me.

I don't.

Not tonight.

I pull into Tessa's driveway at five thirty and snatch the corsage from my passenger seat before hopping out of the truck. After knocking three times on the front door, I take a deep breath and summon my most heart-melting smile, holding out the corsage.

When the door starts to swing open, I blurt out, "Hello, beauti… ful."

Mr. Dickinson stands in the doorway with a friendly pastorish grin on his lips. "Hello, Weston."

The corsage zips back to my side. I clear my throat awkwardly, heat blazing through my face. "Uh, hello, Mr. Dickinson. I thought you'd be Tessa."

"She's almost ready. Come on in."

I step into the foyer and turn at the sound of thunderous footsteps racing down the stairs. Tessa's mom, Heather, flies over to crush me in a hug and tell me how handsome I look.

"Tessa's on her way down." She whips out her phone, apparently having planned to film this moment. It feels like a rehearsal for our wedding. "Okay, sweetie, you can come down now!"

It's just a school dance—something I've always thought was overrated and overpriced—but I'd be lying if I said my heart doesn't lift into my throat with anticipation as Tessa walks down the stairs. First, all I see is a glimpse of swirling gauzy fabric through the spindles of the stair railing—flashes of her shoes beneath the hem of her skirt.

It's light pink, just as I thought it would be. And it's covered in flowers. And she's the most beautiful girl I've ever seen.

I'm paralyzed—speechless—as she stops at the bottom of the stairs and looks at me, a smile lighting up her eyes as she takes me in. Her hair is twisted into an updo, tiny sprigs of lily of the valley tucked in between her golden curls. Even from five feet away, she smells *incredible*.

Heather laughs behind her phone, which she's still using to film us. "Well, aren't you gonna say something, Weston?"

Tessa blushes and groans, "Mom," in a way that sounds

embarrassed—but she's smiling too much to be embarrassed.

I shake myself out of my stunned daze and step closer, taking her hand and looking down into her beautiful eyes.

"Wow," I rasp, my gaze sliding over the curve of her sparkly cheekbones, the gold chain around her throat, the ruffled edge of her neckline. "You look… breathtaking."

I don't know if this is the right moment to kiss her—with Heather filming and her grandfather watching a few feet away. But I can't help myself. This close, I can almost *taste* the scent of lily of the valley, which reminds me of the summer I first fell in love with her.

I lean down and capture her lips in a kiss G-rated enough to be immortalized on her mother's photo roll. When I straighten back up, she's looking at me like she wants me to kiss her again. A hundred times. The feeling is mutual, but there's a time and place. For now, I give her the little plastic container with the corsage inside.

Tessa gasps when she sees it. "Did Mom tell you what color my dress was?"

I shake my head, giving her a wink. "Nope. Just a lucky guess."

TESSA

HIGH SCHOOL PROM COULDN'T BE MORE DIFFERENT from a Regency ball. But I would feel like a princess on Weston's arm no matter where he takes me.

He is my safe place—my lifeline in a sea of strangers as we weave through the vast, low-lit gymnasium strobing with purple lights and pulsing with dance music. Apparently, we showed up late and missed the popularity contest that kicked off the night— the whole "Prom King and Prom Queen" ceremony. I laugh into Weston's ear that the royal couple looks utterly ridiculous in their bejeweled crowns and sashes, and he agrees. Secretly, I'm glad he's not popular enough to win such a trivial competition.

We hang out with Rudy and Clara, though a few other students occasionally rope Weston into conversations. Some such students are girls in shimmery dresses who tell him they voted for him to be Prom King, which leads to Weston introducing them to *me*, which leads to insincere smiles and quick departures on their part.

Clara leans into my ear at one point and says, "You have no idea how jealous they are of you."

I laugh, something like warm sunshine lighting up in my chest as I stare at Weston, who looks so devastatingly handsome in his tux, the disco ball overhead casting a hundred moving shards of light over him. He's talking to Rudy now, making all sorts of cute faces and wild gestures to emphasize what he's saying.

I link arms with Clara and say, "Maybe we should make the *boys* jealous."

She nods approvingly, her dark eyes glinting at the idea. "Good thinking, Tessa. Let me introduce you to a few guys I know."

And with that, she leads me to a different corner of the room, weaving through the chaotic crowd. I envy her easy-breezy confidence and her ability to tap shoulders and strike up conversations. Small talk comes as naturally to her as breathing. Not so for me. But luckily, the music is too loud to carry on a substantial conversation with anyone.

I smile and nod when it seems like the right thing to do, and I laugh when Clara laughs even if I don't hear the joke someone made. Eventually, I wind up with a glass of fruit punch in my hand that I most certainly didn't ask for. Is it spiked? No—of course not. We're at a school event being monitored by school faculty. I sip the punch with caution and feel more and more like a socially awkward homeschool girl as I drift to the margins of the group.

Clara has been siphoned into a gossipy conversation with one of her girlfriends, which leaves me alone and friendless. I glance around for Weston—but he's nowhere to be found in the sea of strangers. It's dizzying, all of it: the sheer number of people in this room, the bright strobing lights, the pounding beat of bass in the floor.

Where did he go?

I'm about to reach into my dress's hidden pocket and pull out my phone when two strong hands slide around my waist, warm and sure and familiar.

"There you are," Weston murmurs into my ear, pulling me backward and away from the circle of Clara's friends. "Come on. Let's dance."

I spin to face him, a twinge of anxiety flickering in my chest. "But… I've never danced like *this* before." I nod towards the others flailing wildly under the strobe lights to the high-energy music. "And I'm… holding this drink someone gave me."

Weston smirks, taking the cup out of my hand and abandoning it on a nearby table. "There's no science to it, Tessa. You don't need to know how to dance in order to dance."

"That seems scientifically impossible!" I laugh into his ear.

It's a bit intimidating to plunge into a crowd of glamorous strangers. But with Weston's hands in mine, I'm not scared of anything. He leads me onto the dance floor, and we throw ourselves into the rhythm of the song with reckless abandon—Weston occasionally twirling me around.

I laugh every time I trip over the hem of my dress, and he laughs every time he trips over his feet. We are graceless, breathless, and spectacularly bad at this, but that makes it more fun. The only thing that could make it better is… fewer people. The room is so crowded that I keep bumping into bodies, and once, I narrowly miss getting my skirt splashed by someone's drink.

It's a relief when the song changes to something smooth and

romantic—all the energy mellowing as couples melt into each other's arms for a slow dance.

Weston's hands encircle my waist as I slide my fingers up to the lapel of his jacket. The room liquefies in shades of rose gold as we sway in leisurely circles around the dance floor, star confetti sparkling under our shoes.

At one point, I step on Weston's toes and say, "Oh—sorry," out of instinct.

He only smiles and shrugs. "You can step on my feet all you like."

I laugh and rest my face against his chest, breathing in his spicy scent as I spread my hands over his back. I don't know this song, but it feels like warm honey melting over my skin, making me forget anyone else exists. There is nothing but the perfect harmony of us together, slow-dancing in gentle circles, Weston's hands heavy on my hips.

"You're so beautiful," he whispers into my ear, his warm breath leaving chills on my neck. "The most beautiful girl here. The most beautiful girl in the *world*."

A little laugh catches in my throat as I tilt my head back to look at him. "Flattery."

"Truth." He dips down to kiss the tip of my nose. "Scientific fact."

WESTON

"Multiplication?" I say, casting Rudy a dubious look as I shadow him down the hallway toward the bathrooms. "That's the secret weapon?"

He nods. "Works every time."

"You're telling me you were mentally going through your frickin' *times tables* back there while you were slow-dancing with Clara?"

Rudy casts a smirk over his shoulder. "Takes your mind off other things."

By "other things," of course, he means the cause-and-effect results of being in close proximity to your dancing partner, who happens to be a girl you're crazy about and who smells so good you can practically taste her with every breath you take.

"Well, shit, man." I sigh, shaking my head. "You've been keeping this a secret all this time? Too bad I can't remember my multiplication tables."

He laughs, dodging a couple making out awkwardly close to the bathrooms. As he pushes through the swinging door, I follow him into the crowded, noisy men's room. One booming voice rises above the rest, and the second I recognize it, my defenses go up.

Ferguson.

I glimpse him in my peripheral vision. As usual, a pack of dimwits crowd around him, acting like animals. I see cash changing hands and can't help the dry laugh that escapes me as I walk past.

"Thought your drug-dealing days were over, Ferg."

He glances up at the sound of my voice and says, "I'm in a different business now… selling insurance policies. Five bucks a pop." He brandishes a box of condoms, and all I can do is roll my eyes.

Of course, only Neil Ferguson would be lame enough to spend prom night in the bathroom, scalping condoms at inflated prices to horny guys who didn't come prepared. It's pathetic. I would almost feel bad for him if he weren't such an asshole.

"You sure you don't need one?" he yells at the back of my head. "Oh, wait—that's right. You're not getting laid tonight. Or ever."

A coil of anger tightens in my stomach, but I force myself to walk away. To not even spare him a glance over my shoulder.

"Ignore him," Rudy mutters under his breath, stopping at the urinal next to mine. "You and Tessa getting out of here soon, or what?"

I nod, staring straight ahead at the ugly tiled wall. "Probably. She said she's tired of all the people. It's still early, though. We might drive somewhere."

"Oh yeah? Where? Hickley Point?"

I grin, shrugging one shoulder. "Maybe. Not for *that*, obviously. Just to hang out. Talk. It's a good place to look at the stars. And make out."

Rudy doesn't have a chance to reply before another voice pipes up from the urinal on the other side of me. Kent, the kid I took fire for in the locker room—I recognize his glasses out of the corner of my eye.

"What's a good place to make out?" he asks, turning to look me in the eyes—a universal no-no for communication at urinals.

"Uh, Hickley Point," I say, zipping up my fly and stepping away from the wall.

"Hickley Point?" Kent echoes, loud enough for the entire freaking bathroom to hear it. "Man, you're so lucky!"

Actually, I'm not—not the way he *imagines*. But it's too late to correct him or tell him to keep it to himself. The cat is out of the bag. And, of course, Ferg is the first to grab that cat by the tail.

"What's this?" He speaks up, abandoning his post by the door to come over to the sinks, where I'm now washing my hands. "Ludovico's taking the holy virgin up to the point? Well, color me impressed."

If I had to guess, I wouldn't say he's so much *impressed* as he is *jealous*.

"What's the matter, Ferg?" I don't bother looking at him as I tear a paper towel from the dispenser and dry my hands. "Did your hot date fall through the cracks or something? Thought *you* were supposed to be up at Hickley Point before the rest of us."

Ferg stares at me, a single muscle ticking in his jaw. I can't help but notice—the bathroom has fallen silent. Everyone watches the two of us, like they think a fistfight is about to break out any second now. A long, tense pause stretches between us, filled by the sound of muffled hip-hop through the walls.

Then Ferg breaks into an icy smile. "It's only ten o'clock. I've got plenty of time to make a *few* trips up to the point. Whereas *you* gotta hurry up before you need to get your girl back home for her curfew."

Anger clenches in my gut as I stare at him, balling up the paper towel in my fist. The other guys watch us, silently waiting for someone to throw a punch. But that's exactly what Ferguson is expecting—hoping for. That I'll lose my shit because he's poked this bear one too many times.

I don't give him the satisfaction. I just stand my ground, holding his eye contact. He doesn't back off. Instead, he takes one of his "insurance policies" out of the box and holds it out to me.

"Guess you're gonna need one of these," he says with a wicked smile, flicking the foil wrapper between his fingers. "Go on, take it. It's on the house."

I know what he expects me to do: walk away. Let him score the final shot, leave me on the ropes, and have the last laugh. But I'm sick of letting him have the last laugh. I'm sick of letting his insults roll off me like water.

I'm sick of being an easy target.

Different.

Disabled.

Like somehow, just because I'm an amputee, I'm less of a man.

Not like other guys.

I don't want to prove him right—prove all of them right. I'm done cowering away from Ferg's attacks and letting him think he's won.

This time, *I'm* going to score the last shot.

So I take the little foil package from his hand, shove it into the pocket of my tux, and say, "Thanks, *Neil*." I drop his real name in his face like a final stinger and walk away, not looking back—not once.

A few other guys make a collective "ohhh" of animalistic respect for me as a red-blooded man as I stride past them all to get out of the bathroom. But the momentary blip of victory is short-lived.

"Why did you do that?" Rudy asks me as soon as we're back in the hallway. I can tell he thinks I'm an idiot for caving to Ferg's bullshit.

Honestly, it probably *was* an idiotic thing to do. But my knee-jerk reaction is to justify it. So I say, "To prove a point."

"Why do you need to prove a point to those guys? They're a bunch of losers."

"Because I'm sick of them making me feel like I'm not… not one of them."

"You're *not* one of them. You're better. At least, I thought you were."

I turn to give him a sharp look. "Look, I'm not gonna *use* it, Rudy. I'm gonna throw it away right now."

"Do that. Before Tessa sees it."

"She wouldn't even know what it is."

Rudy raises his eyebrows. "I wouldn't be too sure of that."

I can see the disappointment in his eyes as he walks off to rejoin Clara. It makes me feel even more slimy for what I did back there in the bathroom.

Rudy's right. I shouldn't have needed to prove a damn thing

to those guys. Why do I care so much about what they think? They aren't my friends; they never have been.

Part of me wishes I could go back and do it differently. But I can't.

So, instead, I shake the whole thing off and head straight for the nearest trash can, insurance policy in hand.

But before I make it there, Tessa appears—latching onto my arm. "Wes, there you are."

Shit.

I shove my hand back into my pocket before she sees what I'm holding. "Hey," I greet her with an easy smile, kissing her cheek. "What's up?"

"Nothing," Tessa replies, twisting the fabric of her skirt between her fingers. She looks flushed and disoriented.

"You okay?"

"Yeah, it's just… really crowded in here. Can we pop outside and get some air?"

"Absolutely."

With Tessa's arm looped through mine, we make our way out of the noisy, hot gymnasium and through an exit door. The cool evening air feels good after the suffocating combination of cologne and body odor.

Tessa lets out a deep, long sigh. Just looking at her, I can tell she's not eager to go back inside anytime soon.

"You want to get out of here, don't you?"

She tips her head against my shoulder, even more beautiful in the dim wash of the parking lot lights.

"Well, I won't make us leave if *you'd* like to stay longer," she confesses. "But… I'd rather go somewhere else, just the two of us. I'm not… ready to go home yet." She lifts onto her tiptoes and catches my lips in a slow, lingering kiss. My hands fall to her waistline, holding her for a moment as we taste each other in the darkness.

It's a teaser trailer for something more, something that sparkles in her eyes as she draws back to look up at me expectantly—her pupils dilated and her cheeks rosy.

"Uh, we could go up to Hickley Point," I suggest. "Look at the stars."

She smiles, fingering the edge of my necktie. "That sounds perfect."

TESSA

____

IRRESISTIBLE. THAT'S THE ONLY ACCURATE WORD FOR the way Weston looks tonight. I've seen him twice before in formal attire, but never in a tux with a boutonniere pinned to his lapel— his blond hair so perfectly tousled, it begs me to run my fingers through it.

As I stressed to my mother a few days ago, I am *not* a girl who gets carried away by her emotions. There are some things I can resist. But kissing Weston in the front seat of his truck at the top of Hickley Point is not one of them.

Our favorite love songs play softly on the radio as we melt into each other's arms, reality slipping away with every kiss, every touch, every heartbeat.

This is my desire—the simple pleasure of being held by him, loved by him. It's more dazzling than a hundred disco balls and a hundred proms to go with them. My ears are still ringing from the loud music and merry chaos of the dance, but there's a kind of heavenly peace here with nobody but Weston.

He's taken me up to this lookout point before. It's spectacular at sunset and breathtaking on a starry night like this. But I'm not much interested in stargazing right now. Weston has my full attention, his fingers in my hair as we kiss by the dashboard lights. When one of the braided coils falls away from the rest of my updo, Weston draws back.

"Oops, sorry," he whispers, holding up a pearl-tipped hairpin. "Wrecked your hair."

I bite back a smile. "It's okay. Nobody else is going to see me tonight. You can take it all down if you want."

Weston looks stunned—as though I've given him permission to undress me. "Really?"

I shrug. "As long as you don't pull my hair and make me scream."

He murmurs a laugh under his breath, leaning in to kiss me as he releases another pin from my elaborate updo. One by one, the braids tumble down, little sprigs of lily of the valley falling into my lap as my hair comes undone. Weston takes one blossom between his fingers and lifts it to his nose.

"I love that you remember this," he says.

"Of course. I'll never forget." I lace my hands behind his neck and lean in for another kiss, crushing my lips to his and losing myself in the perfection of this moment.

Weston gently works the tiny elastics off the ends of my braids and runs his fingers through my hair, letting it all flow loose and free around my shoulders. Something is different about the way he looks at me—a thousand unspoken emotions smoldering in his eyes like a wildfire.

"You're *so*... beautiful."

It's the hundredth time he's told me that tonight, but now

his words hit differently. As though we're both trapped in a spell—in a dream. The lucid kind that's too good to be true... but I don't want to wake up.

I want to keep dreaming forever.

My heartbeat quickens as Weston lowers his mouth to the hollow beneath my earlobe and presses a torturously soft kiss there. Everything in me melts, and my fingers curl around his tie, drawing him closer. For a moment, I am swept away by a force beyond my control.

When I find my footing again, I lower my forehead to his shoulder, a breathless laugh shivering out of me. "Wes... if we don't stop now... I'm not sure we'll be able to stop at all."

He exhales against the curve of my neck, his heart pounding under my fingertips. "Would that be such a bad thing?"

"It would be a wonderful thing," I admit, easing back to give him a soft smile. "But not here. Not now."

He nods understandingly, his fingers tucking a strand of hair behind my ear. "I know." And there's no mistaking the crestfallen look in his eyes.

"Are you... disappointed?"

"What? No." He shakes his head. "That's not... no. I know how you feel about it. I respect your boundaries, Tessa. I admire them. I admire your... self-control." A smirk plays at his lips as he closes his hand over mine. "I admire you in so many ways. You put me to shame."

"Shame?" I volley the word back, arching one eyebrow playfully. "Why? Because you're sitting here having all kinds of dirty thoughts about me?"

A pained little laugh escapes him. "No. I'm not. It's not... that."

He doesn't say what it is, but I can tell *something* is getting under his skin. I don't like any miscommunication between us, so I decide to clear the air.

"We can talk about it if you want."

"Talk about what?"

I shrug. "Sex."

Weston's eyes clash with mine, as if I just uttered some shocking form of profanity.

"What? It's not like you're the only one dealing with certain… urges."

Now he laughs, one of his easy laughs—tipping his head back against the driver's seat. "I know. And we don't need to talk about it. I just…" He swallows, looking down at our fingers interlaced in my lap. "I wonder if sometimes we do things because we want to look a certain way to other people, you know? We might say things we don't really mean just to keep up a reputation. To feel like we belong."

"Some people might feel that way," I say softly, "but for me, it's not about what other people think of me. I don't care about that. They can think whatever they want. What's important is what *I* think of me. And if I let myself… *go there* with you…" I look down, a blush warming my cheeks. "I'd feel like I let myself down. And I'd always regret not waiting. Not being true to myself. You know?"

Weston nods slowly, taking in my speech with such a solemn sweetness in his eyes. He looks hypnotized for a moment before he finally speaks, his voice a thready whisper.

"What did I ever do to deserve you?"

I smile, dipping my head self-consciously.

"No, I mean it," Weston says, lifting my knuckles to his lips and kissing them. "You're so perfect. So beautiful and strong and confident and comfortable in your own skin…" His voice wavers on that last compliment, and I see a ghost of a sour memory pass through his eyes. He looks down. "You've made me a better person just by knowing you."

"The feeling is mutual, I assure you." I lean in to press a featherlight kiss to his lips. "You know, I'm pretty sure most guys would be disappointed to find themselves with a girl like me tonight."

"Oh yeah? Why?"

"Because." I tip my head to the side. "According to my mom, most guys have certain *expectations* after prom."

A fleeting, indecipherable expression crosses Weston's face, then gives way to a soft smile. "Well, I'm not like other guys," he says, that steady self-assurance returning to his voice.

I rest my head against his shoulder, and he circles one arm around my back. For a while, we sit gazing out over the lights of Rockford and the scattering of stars in the velvety black sky.

I turn up the volume on our playlist and thread my fingers through Weston's, happy to be held by him. We don't kiss much after that. Instead, we talk about prom, laughing over silly moments we witnessed, while I marvel at the bizarre customs of public schoolers. In conclusion, I give the entire experience three out of five stars.

"Wow," Weston says. "Generous."

"I would've liked it better if it was just you and me," I admit. "What fun that would be, right? Like that scene in *Pride and Prejudice*, where Lizzy and Darcy are dancing together at the ball, and suddenly everyone is gone, and it's just the two of them? That would be so perfect. Prom for two."

Weston chuckles. "For me and you?"

I nod, grinning up at him. "Mm-hmm. And we wouldn't play any of that mainstream pop music. We'd play romantic oldies like this."

I reach over to crank up the volume on "Bridge Over Troubled Water" by Simon and Garfunkel, and in that moment, it feels like *our* song. We both fall silent, listening to the music—my head on his chest and his hand cradling my waist.

When the song finishes, there's a beat of silence. And in that breathless quiet, Weston whispers, "I love you, Tessa."

I swallow back the lump in my throat and squeeze his hand. "I love you too."

WESTON

AS I SIT IN THE FRONT SEAT OF MY TRUCK WITH TESSA in my arms, I'm overwhelmed by every stroke of luck that brought us together. It's nothing short of a miracle. *She's* nothing short of a miracle, a lifeline pulling me back from the edge of self-doubt and stupid fears.

Her goodness makes me ashamed of the way I acted in the school bathroom when Ferguson confronted me. How dumb could I have been to cave in to his taunts? To let that squirming voice of insecurity get the better of me? I envy Tessa's ability to not give a crap about what people think of her.

She makes me realize I don't care either, deep down. All I care about is what *she* thinks of me. All I want to be is worthy of her love, worthy of her kisses, worthy of unraveling her beautiful hair in the moonlight.

Sure, every other couple parked at Hickley Point might be getting hot and heavy in their cars right now, but Tessa and I aren't like every other couple. She's different. I'm different. We're different together, and it's not a bad thing.

As we drive back towards town, I notice that my truck is running low on gas. Tessa says she doesn't mind if I swing into the gas station to fill up. I park at a vacant pump and hop out, but before I shut the door, Tessa says, "Oh, could you also grab me a bottle of water? I'm so thirsty."

I wink at her. "Thirsty for me? Water won't fix that."

She lets out a righteous little scoff, rolling her eyes. But she's grinning.

I feel ten feet tall as I pump the gas, then stride across the parking lot into the convenience store to buy Tessa a bottle of water. The guy at the checkout is unfazed by my tux, which makes me think I must not be the first senior prom attendee who's stopped here tonight. I take out my wallet to pay for the water, and that's when I realize… my wallet is the only thing in my pocket.

The insurance policy is gone.

My stomach plummets to my shoes.

Did it fall out in the truck?

I whip out a ten-dollar bill and slap it on the counter with a hurried, "Keep the change!" In a flash, I grab the bottle of water and race back out to my truck—heart pounding, armpits sweating—and swing open the driver's door.

I don't even glance at Tessa. I just shove the water bottle in her direction and start frantically searching the driver's seat and floor mat for the little foil-wrapped package.

Damn it, damn it, I should've thrown it away when I had the chance.

"Did you lose something, Weston?" Tessa asks, her voice low and uninterested.

I brush off the question with a nervous laugh. "Yeah, uh, no—it's nothing, really. Just, uh…"

It's gone. It's gone.

"A condom?"

I look up so fast I bash my head against the steering wheel. But I can't even process how much it hurts because Tessa is holding the foil wrapper between her fingers, betrayal written all over her face.

For an excruciatingly long moment, I can't speak. I'm dumbstruck, staring at her, wanting so much to say the right thing. But brilliantly, all I can manage is: "You… weren't supposed to see that."

It's not the right thing to say.

Tessa narrows her eyes at me, holy hellfire sizzling behind the blue. "When were you planning to *use this*, Weston?"

God help me.

I don't know how to explain. How to make her see that I didn't even want to take the stupid condom; it was *forced* on me. I had no choice, right?

But I did.

And I've never been more ashamed of myself.

"Look," I begin, my voice wavering. "It's not what you think. It's not even *mine*."

Tessa frowns, suspicion and disbelief twisting her brow.

"Okay, it *is* mine. But it's not like I have more of them at home or something. I just… happened to have that one tonight because—"

"Tonight?!" Tessa bursts out, cutting me off. "Because, what? It's senior prom, and that's what all the guys do?"

Damn it, what can I say? I'm afraid if I open my mouth again, I'll just keep digging myself deeper and deeper into this hole.

"So *that's* why you were trying to talk me into having sex with you," Tessa says, throwing the insurance policy down in disgust.

"I wasn't trying to talk you into having sex—"

"Oh, so you just thought I'd *want* to?" she fires back. "You figured I'd go along if I knew it was *safe*?"

"No—no, Tessa, that's not how it was at all. I wasn't planning to use it, okay? I was gonna throw it away—"

"Of course you were. After I drew the line."

"No, I was gonna throw it away before that. Hours ago, right after I got it."

Tessa squints at me, because this makes no logical sense when I say it out loud. "Then why would you get it in the first place?"

"Because…" The explanation dies in my throat.

I should tell her the truth. But the truth is an ugly, complicated, twisted thing—something I don't want to admit because Tessa will see how spineless I am. How much of a pansy-ass I've been. Trying to protect my manly ego. Trying to fit in with the locker room guys. To not be the "holy virgin" on top of being the guy without legs.

I can't tell her all that. I'm too mortified.

So instead, I just stand here, like an idiot, and say nothing.

Tessa finally scoffs and sits back hard in her seat, crossing her arms over her chest. "I guess my mom was right," she murmurs, voice thick with tears. "I guess all guys *are* the same."

It cuts when Tessa says that. It cuts to know *this* is how she sees me. Like every other stupid, horny guy who has no self-control. Like Ferg and the locker room losers. All this time, it's been bothering me to not be "one of them"—bothering me because I didn't fit in, didn't belong. But now, hearing Tessa lump me in with that group… it's horrible.

All this time, I didn't want to be seen as different. An outlier. An out*cast*.

But *God*. Right now, I would give anything to make Tessa see me as different. *Her* kind of different.

"Take me home, Weston."

Just like that, the discussion is over. There's nothing else I can say. I have no good excuse for what I did.

It was wrong.

I slide into the driver's seat and start my truck—my knuckles white around the steering wheel. We drive back to Tessa's house in silence. I feel sick to my stomach the whole way there, angry enough to kick myself.

When I pull into Tessa's driveway, she doesn't kiss me or even say goodnight. She just gets out of the truck and runs to her front door in her fancy ballgown—looking like a princess with a broken heart.

MOM IS THE ONLY ONE STILL AWAKE WHEN I WALK through the front door. She turns away from the reality TV show she's watching to cast me a smile. But the smile dies as soon as she sees my expression.

"Tessa, is something wrong?"

I shake my head firmly, quiet rage boiling in my chest. "No. I'm fine. Just tired. I'm going to bed." Before she can ask any more questions, I pivot and go upstairs—heading straight for my room.

I shut the door quietly so as not to disturb Grandma and Grandpa, who are asleep down the hallway. Nervous energy buzzes in my veins as I turn on the lamp beside my bed, pull my nightshirt out of a drawer, and feel around for the zipper on my dress. I need a mirror to see what I'm doing, but when I catch sight of my reflection…

I lose it.

A silent sob wrenches out of me as I take in my beautiful gown covered in flowers. My undone hair, messy from Weston's fingers unraveling my braids in the darkness. My corsage, still tied to my wrist, pink petals matching the fabric of my dress.

It all breaks my heart because it's so perfect.

This whole night was perfect—before I found that *thing* in Weston's truck.

Now my face crumples with furious tears, and all I want is to forget all of it. I reach behind my back to grab the zipper, jerking it down. It's stuck. Mom helped me put this dress on, and I didn't consider the difficulty of taking it off on my own.

I struggle in silence for a moment, mascara beginning to run down my cheeks as I fight with the zipper, then—

A soft knock echoes through my bedroom door.

"Can I come in?" Mom asks.

I sniff, swiping tears off my face, but only succeed in smearing my makeup. Instead of replying, I cross the room and swing open the door.

Mom's eyes widen in dismay when she sees what a wreck I am. "Sweetie, what happened?"

I swallow a sob, not ready to spill the awful truth. "I can't get this stupid dress off."

Mom wordlessly turns me around, gently brushes my hair aside, and unzips the back of the gown, letting it pool around my ankles. I step out of the gauzy pile of fabric and reach for my oversized nightshirt. It's one I stole from Weston, but I don't have the energy to look for anything else to wear.

"Why don't you tell me what happened," Mom suggests gently, picking up my dress from the floor and smoothing it out on the bed. "Is it something Weston did?"

"Yes," I croak through my tears, snatching a makeup wipe from my vanity and cleaning the mascara off my cheeks. "Well, not so much something he *did* as something he was *hoping* to do—planning to do…" My voice chokes around the words.

"And what is it he was hoping to do?" Mom asks, zipping up the dress and sliding it onto a hanger. "Rob a bank?"

I grunt. "No."

"Ask you to marry him?"

"No, of course not."

"Have sex with you?"

I can't reply to that one. I just shut my eyes and let the tears fall, nodding quickly.

Mom places her hand on my shoulder. "Come on. Tell me what happened."

So I do. I stretch out on my bed and go through half a box of tissues as I tell Mom about the whole condom conundrum. How everything was so wonderful up until the moment I found it and confronted Weston.

By the end of the story, Mom looks surprised that's all that happened—as if my reaction is unreasonably dramatic for something this serious.

"It's not *that* big a deal," she says, blunt and unfeeling as ever. "I mean, you can't blame the guy for trying his luck."

I drop my hands from my red face, appalled by how she makes the whole thing sound like a carnival game. "But Weston already knows how I feel about sex before marriage. We've talked about it before, and then in the truck tonight, it came up again, and he seemed okay with it. I *thought* he was okay with it. He was so sweet and understanding—even though I could tell there was something he wasn't telling me. But we had a good talk about principles and the reasons behind them and everything." I sniff, drying my cheeks with a balled-up tissue. "He said all these nice things about how he doesn't deserve me, how I'm so beautiful and confident in my own skin. He said he *respected* my boundaries. But the whole time, he had that… *thing* in his pocket."

Mom falls silent for a long moment, turning it over in her mind as she gently strokes her fingers over my knee.

"And then," I add, "to make it even *worse*, he acted like he never intended to use the thing. When I found it and confronted him about it, he said he planned to throw it away—hours before we even went up to Hickley Point. Which doesn't make any sense."

Mom frowns and tilts her head, as if this new piece of information changes the whole story. "Where do you think he got it?"

"I don't know. I didn't ask. Does it matter? It's not like it fell out of the sky into his pocket, it was a conscious decision, and there can only be one reason a guy would make that decision."

"Not necessarily."

"Mom, if you're going to take his side—"

"I'm not taking sides, Tessa. I'm just saying you don't know what high school is like. Peer pressure alone can make you do stupid things for stupid reasons."

I shrug. "I guess so. But I thought Weston was different."

"He *is* different," Mom says. "And it must not be easy to be different when you're him."

I feel a stitch of guilt at the idea of it. Navigating the cruel, unpredictable world of high school is bad enough for kids with acne or a big nose. Though I've never experienced bullying first-hand, I know how mean-spirited people can turn even the most minor flaw into ammunition to hurt you with.

"You think he's being bullied?" I ask, looking up at Mom.

"He's never mentioned that to me."

"No, he doesn't seem like the type who would talk about it. Especially not to you."

Somehow, that makes it all the more heartbreaking: the possibility that someone at school is being cruel to Weston because of his disability—and he can't talk to anyone about it, not even me.

"Still," I say with a righteous sniff, "it doesn't justify what he did. It doesn't make it okay."

"No," Mom agrees. "But you said yourself he didn't push you when you told him how you felt. He *did* respect your boundaries. Right? Even if he thought there was a slim possibility for something more—"

"If he thought there was a slim possibility, then he doesn't know me at all." I cross my arms over my stomach and stare at the ceiling stubbornly.

After a moment, Mom starts laughing.

"What's so funny?"

She taps my nose with one finger. "You. And all your strict moral principles."

"I don't see what's funny about that."

"You were making out with the guy," Mom says, arching her eyebrows. "Don't deny it; I can see the rash coming."

My hand instinctively flies to the edge of my jaw and neck, where Weston's face brushed against mine as we kissed.

Mom smirks; her suspicions are confirmed when my cheeks flush pink. "You let him take down your hair, and you were probably playing love songs in the car while you made out with him."

"Well... yeah. But we didn't do anything improper."

Mom grunts. "You didn't have to. That was enough. Can you even imagine how turned on he must've been?"

"Ugh, Mom, *please*." I drag my hands over my reddening face.

"I'm just saying. Guys don't have much self-control. And when I say 'not much,' I mean 'none at all.'"

A miserable laugh catches in my throat. I remember Weston saying tonight that he admires my self-control.

I admire you in so many ways.

My heart melted when he said that. But now the memory is like a thorn on a beautiful rose. Pricking me with a stab of bittersweet pain.

I sigh, closing my tired eyes. "I don't know, Mom. I don't know what to think. When we were up at the lookout together, I felt like he knew me better than anyone in the world. And then, after we fought… he seemed like a stranger."

Mom nods slowly, brushing a strand of hair off my forehead. "I think you should tell him that. Talk to him. Be honest with each other. And listen to his side of the story, too."

That's the last thing I want to do. Weston had his chance to tell me his side of the story on the drive home tonight—and he didn't. He just sat there *silent* in the driver's seat because he couldn't bring himself to tell me the truth.

And if the truth is that terrible, I'm not sure I want to hear it.

WESTON

———————

I'M AWAKE ALL NIGHT. KICKING MYSELF. OVER AND over and over again.

I can't stop replaying everything that happened—not just at prom with Ferguson and his moronic friends, but before that. The countless times he nagged me in the locker room, trying to get under my skin. Trying to drag me down to his level.

Tonight, I fell for it.

What an idiot I was. Weak, insecure, struggling to keep my pride intact. Everything I hate—that's what I've been. In a lame attempt to impress a few guys who don't even care about me, I lost the only thing that truly matters: Tessa's trust.

Will she ever look at me the same way again?

Will she ever forgive me?

I wouldn't blame her if she didn't. I don't deserve her forgiveness, her trust… her love.

I don't deserve *her*.

At school the next day, I barely speak to anyone—but my bad mood and the dark circles under my eyes don't go unnoticed by Neil Ferguson. In the locker room after gym, he smacks my shoulder with his sweat-soaked T-shirt and says, "Correct me if I'm off base, Ludovico, but you do *not* look like you got laid last night."

I slam my locker shut, jaw clenched. "It's none of your damn business, Ferg."

"Oh, you *definitely* didn't!" He throws his head back and laughs. "Should've known you'd be all talk and no action. Let me guess—you got close, but then she broke the news that she's becoming a nun."

He doubles over at his own stupid joke, and a few of his dimwitted disciples laugh with him. I don't react. I just sling my backpack over one shoulder and make myself scarce.

I couldn't care less what Ferguson says anymore. He can taunt me all he likes, call me a virgin, try to get under my skin. It doesn't matter to me what any of them think.

The only thing I'm concerned about is how to make things right with Tessa.

I've been texting her all day, asking if I can come over after school and talk to her. I've called her, left her voice messages, but never got a word back. I've apologized, admitted what I did was wrong, asked her if she'll forgive me.

So far, no response.

Finally, I decide to ask Rudy for advice. He always knows the right thing to do. The worst part is having to tell him the whole ugly truth of what happened last night after Tessa and I left prom.

No, actually—the worst part is admitting that I was wrong, and he was right, and I should never have put that stupid "insurance policy" in my pocket.

"So she *did* know what it was," he says, with a smug, smart-ass smirk on his face.

"Don't say I told you so, Rudy… Just don't say it."

"Wasn't going to. You know I told you so. No need to remind you that I told you so."

I sigh, thumping my head back against the row of lockers. We're loitering in the main hallway as school empties out for the day.

"I was an idiot, it's true," I admit. "I acted like… a pansy-ass. And I regret it. And now Tessa's not speaking to me, and I have no idea how to make it right."

"Why don't you just try telling her the truth?"

"I did tell her the truth."

"Really?" Rudy looks unconvinced. "The *whole* truth? About what happened between you and Ferguson in the bathroom?"

I shake my head, looking down at the scuffed tile floor. "Not that part."

"Well, that's the part she needs to know."

He's right. Still, I cringe inwardly, just imagining making a confession like that—how would I even begin? *See, there's this sleazeball named Ferguson who's been trying to make me feel small and weird and broken ever since I lost my legs…*

"It's no excuse," I mutter, more to myself than Rudy. "It doesn't make what I did okay."

"No, but it's the truth." Rudy shuts his locker, hooking his backpack over his shoulder. "And Tessa deserves to know the truth. Don't you think?"

"Yeah." I nod, forking my hand through my hair. "But I can't just… show up at her door, spill my guts, and beg her forgiveness. Hopefully, she *will* forgive me, but… I want to make it up to her somehow. Give her something that shows her how much I really care about her."

"Well," Rudy says as I shadow him down the hallway, "how big a makeup gift are we talking? Flowers? Chocolates? A Tesla?"

I grunt, knowing my wallet won't stretch far—especially after the prom tickets and tux rental. "It would have to be something only I could give her," I say, thinking aloud as I catch the door and follow Rudy outside. "A wish she would never expect to actually come true, like…"

That's when an idea hits me.

A crazy one, probably. But if I could pull it off… it would be perfect.

Rudy notices the scheming look on my face and braces himself. "I sense a bad idea incoming."

"No, it's a good idea. A really good idea. But I'll need your help."

He frowns, suspicious. "With what?"

"Bribing the prom committee. And your mom."

"My mom?"

"Yep." I smile as the possibilities come together in my mind. "She's still the events coordinator at the country club, right?"

THAT EVENING, AS I'M STRESS-BAKING THREE FLAVORS of babka bread (chocolate, cinnamon, and raspberry) while miserably pondering the future of my and Weston's relationship, I hear him knock on the front door.

I know it's him before Grandma even goes to answer it. He's been trying to call me and text me all day, offering many flavors of apologies (I'm sorry, please forgive me, I was wrong) with no response from me.

Maybe it was savage and petty to leave him on read. To not ring him back. To not feel ready to forgive him. But after all, I'm not the one who betrayed his trust—*he* betrayed *mine*.

Moments later, Grandma walks into the kitchen and says, "Weston is here to see you."

I haven't told her about last night—but I suspect Mom has, and no doubt they have both been wise enough to keep it from Grandpa. I stiffen, rinsing my sugary hands at the sink and snatching a dishtowel.

"Well? Where is he?"

"On the porch," Grandma replies softly. "He wants to speak with you alone."

I dry my hands fiercely on the towel before slapping it down on the counter and storming to the front door. When I step out into the cool twilight, I immediately lock eyes with Weston, who stands under the porch light, looking equal parts hopeful and sick to his stomach.

I don't say hello. I don't say a word. I just stand frozen in place with my chin tipped up—determined *not* to notice how cute he looks in his bomber jacket, his blond hair a soft, rumpled mess.

"Tessa," he begins, clearing his throat. "First… I must tell you that I've been an unmitigated and comprehensive ass."

Something in me falters at the reference. But I refuse to be charmed by his humor this time.

"Don't think you can redeem yourself by quoting *Pride and Prejudice*," I bite out.

Weston is not put off by my icy response. If anything, he looks more determined to continue.

"I don't know if I can redeem myself at all," he confesses. "But… I want to tell you something you don't know."

"And what is that?"

He takes a deep breath and shakes his head, like he's not sure where to begin. "I've been an idiot."

"I thought you were going to tell me something I *don't* know."

A twitch of a smile teases the side of his mouth. When he speaks again, his voice is low and serious—his eyes burning with resolve. "I never even *contemplated* the idea of having sex with you last night."

A sharp laugh hitches in my throat. "Really? Well, I found evidence to the contrary."

"That had nothing to do with you," Weston says, moving closer and holding my eye contact firmly. "It was stupid and wrong, but it wasn't because of you. It was this guy in my class—he's been a jerk to me ever since eighth grade."

Eighth grade. I remember the significance of that year for Weston.

"Since the amputation?" I ask softly.

He swallows. Nods. Looks down at his shoes. "I shouldn't let him get to me. I usually don't. But last night, he was really on my case, and one thing led to another, and… long story short, he's the reason I had the…"

"Evidence," I supply, too sophisticated to call it what it is.

Weston nods. "He was scalping them in the bathroom during prom. I didn't even want to talk to him, but we wound up in this stupid argument, and… I guess I just had a moment of weakness. I couldn't back down and let him win. I wanted to prove a point. So I took the thing. And I regretted it as soon as I walked out of there. I realized how dumb it was, and I was going to throw it away. But then you showed up."

I press my lips together, looking at the story in a new light. It's not a redeemable light—but it's less incriminating than my suspicions were.

"So you're saying that you made this decision purely out of cowardice and male ego." I sum up the situation with frigid clarity.

Weston nods.

"Well, that's still despicable."

"I know. And I'm sorry." His eyes are full of remorse as he studies my face in the soft light of the porch. "Please forgive me,

Tessa. I'll never do something that stupid again."

I look away, my gaze trailing over the lampposts lining the street, illuminating the navy-blue twilight.

Forgive him.

He makes it sound so easy. But he doesn't know how much I cried last night. How my heart ached to think of us separated by something as important as the principles we live by.

"It wasn't just the condom, Wes. It was that you couldn't tell me the truth even when you saw how much it hurt me."

"I couldn't tell you the truth because—" His voice breaks off in a miserable sigh, and he looks away, shaking his head. "Because I was ashamed."

I fall silent, watching him in the amber glow of the porch light.

Mom was right—no one is immune to peer pressure. Not even Weston, with all his confidence and fortitude. He still fails sometimes. And maybe, if I were in his shoes, I would fail sometimes too. I'm not so self-assured to claim I know what it's like to be him. To be so obviously, painfully *different* that every day becomes a merciless trial by a jury of your peers.

"I forgive your reasons," I relent finally, "even though they were wrong. But Wes... I can't help feeling like you *were* disappointed last night. Because of... my beliefs."

"On sex?"

I glance around instinctively, not that anyone is within earshot—but still, it's a rather intimate subject to be discussing on the front porch.

"Let me tell you what *I* think about sex," Weston says, stepping closer until we are barely a foot apart. His eyes dart between mine, full of something urgent and honest. "I think if a man loves a woman enough to have sex with her, he should love her enough to marry her. He should love her enough to *wait*… a hundred years. A thousand years. However long it takes. I think if he really loves her, he'll be happy to wait. Happy just to be with her—just to make her smile, make her laugh… even if he never got to kiss her. That's how I feel about *you*, Tessa." His voice softens to a threadbare whisper. "That's how I love *you*."

For a moment, I can't speak. There's a knot in my throat, and tears threaten to blur my vision as I stare up into Weston's face. Part of me wants to throw my arms around his neck and let him hold me. To tell him that's how I love him, too.

But there's still an unresolved conflict weighing on my mind.

"What about the fact that all these guys at your school now think I'm… promiscuous?"

Weston frowns, puzzled. "Wait, what does that mean?"

I lower my voice to a discreet whisper and give him a simpler synonym. "A slut."

His eyebrows jump in surprise. "What? They don't think that."

"Well, they thought you were going to sleep with me last night—"

"They know it didn't happen. I was so pissed off at school today, they could tell I didn't… They think you're a nun! Okay? That's what one of them said." Weston shakes his head, a teasing spark in his eyes. "Knowing you and your love for *The Sound of Music*, you'd probably like that rumor."

I press my lips together, refusing to find this joke amusing. "You're not going to make me laugh right now, Weston. You might never make me laugh again."

Weston smirks in that sinfully adorable way of his. "I highly doubt that."

I'd be lying if I said my heart doesn't flop when he gives me that look. Those eyes. I'd be lying if I said I don't have the urge to kiss him right now despite everything.

"Give me one shot—*one* chance to make it up to you."

I cross my arms over my chest. "And how do you plan to do that?"

Weston reaches into his back pocket and produces a fancy invitation card with gold edging and swirly handwriting across the front.

You are formally invited to the Glasswater Lake Country Club on May 22nd at 8:00 p.m. Formal dress required. RSVP in person immediately upon request.

"This is your mom's handwriting, isn't it?"

Weston only grins and nods.

"Did you tell her the despicable reason you needed to write such an invitation?"

"She knew it was for a good cause." He taps the card. "And when I say formal dress, what you wore last night would be perfect."

"I'm going to wear a T-shirt and sweatpants," I growl bitterly. "How's that?"

Weston twitches his eyebrows. "As long as it's one of *my* T-shirts."

I narrow my eyes at him with suspicion. "Why are you smiling?"

"Because. You just RSVPed."

"No, I didn't. I never said I was coming."

"Yes, you did. Can't go back on your word now." Weston descends the porch steps and walks across the driveway to his truck. "I'll see you tomorrow night," he calls over his shoulder.

"Dinner at a fancy country club isn't going to fix this, Weston!"

He stops, turns, and nods contemplatively. "No, you're right. Dinner won't fix this."

His parting words are bizarre but hopeful, as is that reckless glint in his eyes. I watch from the porch as he hops into his truck and drives off into the night.

I'm still mad at him.

But I'm more curious than anything.

———————————

The following day, Weston makes himself scarce. I receive only a few optimistic text messages reminding me about tonight's invitation to the country club. As I'm getting ready, trying to decide what to wear (sweatpants are too unsophisticated, even though it would prove a point), I overhear Mom talking on the phone with Weston. She's already agreed to give me a ride tonight, but that's not the subject on her lips when she comes into my room to help me choose my "formal attire."

"You should wear your prom dress," she advises, reaching into my closet to slip the flowery gown off its hanger. "Trust me, you'll wish you had if you don't."

I narrow my eyes at her suspiciously. "Do you know what Weston has up his sleeve?"

Mom purses her lips and shakes her head, but she's not just

the worst liar in the world—she's the worst liar in the *history* of the world.

"Come on, Mom. I heard you on the phone with him. What's he scheming? Some sort of ridiculously elaborate dinner? Don't you think I'll look absurd sitting there in this sparkly gown?" I hold it up to my body like she hasn't seen me in it already.

"I think…" She pauses, biting her lip. "When you pay that much for a dress, you should wear it more than once."

I give in, knowing Mom is clued in on Weston's plan, even though she won't divulge the smallest hint of that plan to me. So she helps me put on the fairytale dress and zip up the back. I tell her I don't want to fuss with my hair this time, but she insists on sitting me down at my desk to weave together a quick princess braid that crowns my head, allowing my golden waves to flow freely like a waterfall behind me.

"You look beautiful," she says, kissing my cheek.

"Thank you." I give myself a once-over in the mirror before admitting, "I *do* look pretty. Prettier than Weston deserves."

Mom chuckles at my icy comment. "Oh, I'm sure Weston is well aware of how lucky he is."

We make our way downstairs, outside, and into Mom's Subaru. I remain silent the whole drive to the Glasswater Lake Country Club—a tangle of emotions warring in my heart. I keep glancing at the dash clock as though my obsessive time-checking will convince the minutes to move faster.

At eight o'clock sharp, we pull into the parking lot of the sprawling, white-columned country club.

"Well, this is the end of the line for me," Mom says. "Just

walk over to the big steps. You'll find your way." With a wink, she shoos me out of the car.

I assume Weston is going to be the one to drive me home as I watch Mom's taillights roll down the road and vanish into the night. The warm glow of the country club guides me onward, down the path towards the cascading staircase that leads up to a magnificent wraparound porch.

I see someone waiting at the base of the steps for me, but as I draw closer, I realize it's not Weston.

"Rudy?" I frown in puzzlement as I look him up and down. "What are you doing here?"

He grins mischievously and offers his arm with a flourish, like he's an usher at a royal wedding. "I've been instructed to escort you."

"Instructed by Weston?"

He nods. "He's waiting for you inside."

Truthfully, I'm surprised he's not out here to "escort me" himself. But I assume it all ties into the mysterious plan as I loop my arm through Rudy's and walk up the stairs with him. Once inside, I pivot towards the restaurant entrance, but Rudy tugs me back and says, "This way."

I frown. "But I thought…"

Rudy brings one finger to his lips in a gesture that tells me all will be revealed in a matter of minutes. He leads me down a posh hallway lined with oil paintings, finally stopping at a pair of double doors marked *Kensington Ballroom*.

The name alone is fancy enough to make me glad I decided to wear my prom dress.

Rudy knocks on the door in a rhythmic pattern—a secret

code. He steps back, hands folded, like a very official security guard.

I raise an eyebrow at him. "What are we waiting for?"

"Music."

But not just any music. The *Pride and Prejudice* soundtrack. I instantly recognize the familiar piano melody oozing from the other side. And now the suspense is *killing* me.

Rudy steps forward on cue and throws the double doors open, revealing the ballroom beyond. I gasp, my hands flying to my lips as I take in the sight before me.

The first thing I notice is an archway decorated with silk flowers and ribbons—like a gateway to a magical realm. A hand-painted sign curves above the arch, declaring in glittery letters:

PROM FOR TWO

My heart melts as I step through the archway and into the ballroom, which is decked out just like the Rockford High gymnasium was the other night. But unlike the dance floor at the school, this place is gloriously, spectacularly *empty.*

Strobe lights caramelize the room in shades of pink and gold, reflecting off the disco ball spinning from the ceiling and scattering stardust over everything in sight.

Including Weston.

He stands in the middle of it all, wearing a white button-down shirt and a black vest, looking unfairly handsome—a hopeful smile on his face as he watches me absorb this dazzling sight.

He made my wish come true.

Happy tears spring to my eyes as I lift the hem of my skirt and run to him. The music crescendos just as we crash into each other—and it makes my heart swell with love for him.

"You look breathtaking," he rasps, holding me tight for a moment before stepping back to take me in.

"So do you," I say, gazing up at him in the syrupy rose-gold light.

"I would've worn a tux, but my rental expired."

I laugh just as a tear escapes down my cheek. "How did you pull this off?"

Weston shrugs, a smile toying with his lips. "I may or may not have bribed the prom committee to let me borrow their decorations. Everything was already packed up from the other night."

"And this ballroom? It must've cost an arm and a leg to rent it."

Weston nods. "It cost *two* legs, actually. Did you not notice I'm missing limbs?"

I fall against his chest in a flurry of laughter. He laughs, too, and before I know it, I'm crying, and there's a sweet ache in my heart from all the hurt melting away.

"Oh, Wes… I'm sorry."

"I'm sorry, too." He kisses the top of my head. "I kept wishing we could go back and do prom over again. So that's what I thought we could do right now. Prom for two—me and you. If you don't count Rudy. He promised to stay out of sight and be our DJ. It's all thanks to his mom that we got the ballroom for tonight. There was a last-minute cancellation, so I guess it was meant to be."

I smile, blinking away my tears. "I can't believe you did all this… just for me."

"Tessa, I would move heaven and earth for you."

A ball of emotion rises into my throat, and it's impossible to speak—all I can do is mouth the words *I love you.*

He catches my hand and gives it an affectionate squeeze, his lips forming the same words. *I love you, too.*

The distance between us is suddenly unbearable. I slide my fingers around his neck and pull him down to my level, kissing him deep and slow. His hands encircle my waist as his lips move over mine with tenderness and passion, saying more than his words ever could.

That's when the music changes, as if by magic. Another familiar piano tune starts playing, and when I recognize it, I nearly start crying again.

Bridge Over Troubled Water.

It really does feel like *our* song now, especially when Weston threads his fingers through mine and smoothly leads me into a slow dance. The disco ball shimmers overhead as we fall into rhythm with each other, moving in graceful circles around the ballroom floor. He gazes down at me with love in his eyes, and I smile up at him with happy tears in mine.

And it's even better than that scene in *Pride and Prejudice.*

A thousand times better.

THE WRITING CLASS

A Tessa Story

———

MY HEART LODGES IN MY THROAT, BEATING DOUBLE time as Weston turns the page. He's on the final scene now. I can see the blank space at the bottom of the paper from across the sunroom coffee table. It takes all my self-control not to dive onto the wicker couch with him and read over his shoulder.

Instead, I purse my lips and draw in a deep breath, trying to steady my nerves. I shouldn't be nervous. It's only Weston—my second self. He's read everything I've ever written, including some extremely private love poems for his eyes only.

But I've never written anything quite like this before.

Wringing my hands in tortured silence, I take my attention off Weston and gaze out the sunroom windows to the swirling autumn leaves outside. The backyard is an impressionist painting of wild colors—burnt orange and satiny gold and bright red. My mind turns to the task of finding a new word to describe *red*. Not bright; bright is too common an adjective…

The red maples flare like pockets of fire among the cool dark greens of the pines. I like that—*pockets of fire.*

The page flips again. My gaze snaps up to Weston, who stares at the back of the final page in disbelief, as if expecting some secret message to be written there.

"That's *it*?"

An unexpected laugh stumbles out of me. "You wanted it to be longer?"

"Yeah. Come on, it was just getting started!"

I grin, hope taking flight in my chest. "So you liked it? You thought it was good?"

Weston nods, shuffling the pages back into some clumsy semblance of order. "Yeah, it was great. And I'm *not* a person who likes reading. In fact, I hate reading."

"I know. It's preposterous." I spring to my feet and sit beside him on the couch. "So what did you like about it?"

Weston shuffles his hand through his messy blond hair, letting out a contemplative sigh. "Uh, well… I liked the girl a lot."

"Mabel."

He nods. "She's you, isn't she?"

"Well, she's not *me* exactly."

"Oh, come on. She's blind, she's sweet and cute and funny and has a great sense of humor—she's totally you." He winks. "And the good-looking war hero is me."

"He's not *you*."

"Oh, come on," Weston says again, grinning even more now. "He got his leg blown off. Who else could he be?"

"Only one leg, though."

"Okay, so he's fifty percent less badass than me," Weston decides. "And he lost his limb saving his friend in the war, whereas I lost my limbs by doing something dumb to look cool in front of my friends."

I tip my head. "Exactly."

"But the roles are kind of reversed," Weston muses, flipping through the pages in his lap. "I mean, it's Mabel who has the good attitude all the time and makes the grumpy guy—Lieutenant Barnes—see that he needs to learn how to punch life in the face. So really, she's me, and you're him."

"Okay, fine. It's inspired by how we met," I admit, leaning closer to rest my chin on his shoulder. "Do you think it's too… unoriginal?"

"Are you kidding? You're supposed to get inspiration from real life, I thought."

"Yeah. You are, that's true."

"Except you might have to give me a cut of the profits for using my line," Weston adds with a cheeky smirk, pointing out some dialogue at the bottom of a page. "When Mabel says, 'There's nothing you can't do.'"

"You don't own the rights to that phrase." I laugh, shoving him playfully. "Besides, it's not good enough to publish. Not like this, anyway. It's just a short story—a rough idea."

"Doesn't seem 'rough' to me," Weston says. "It's awesome. It felt like watching a movie."

"Really?" I light up at the compliment. "Which parts?"

"I don't know—all of it."

"Do you have any critiques?"

Weston shakes his head and shrugs. "I don't know. I'm not a writer."

"Yeah, but you don't need to be a writer to see problems with a story. Was there anything you had to read twice to understand?"

He frowns thoughtfully, flipping back through the pages.

"Uh, let's see… This word here. 'Multifarious.' I have no idea what that means."

"It means like… varied. Diverse. Lots of different things."

Weston grunts. "Must've been one of those SAT words I threw in my mental trash bin as soon as I passed the test."

I laugh. "I can change it."

"No, no, I'm sure your readers will be more literate than me." Weston turns to press a featherlight kiss to my forehead. "You're like a walking dictionary. I learn a new word every time I hang out with you. And then I immediately forget it."

I press my lips to his because I can't resist when he's this close and wearing his soft gray UFC hoodie and smells like crisp autumn air and that musky, spicy aftershave I love so much. He's started shaving all the time, for my sake. I can't stand the rash he leaves on my face after kissing me with even the *slightest* hint of stubble on his jaw. He says it makes him feel more "manly" to keep his face clean for "his woman." I always object to being called *his* woman, but secretly, it gives me the urge to crawl inside his hoodie and smother him with kisses.

"I want to know what happens next," Weston whispers against my lips, tucking a strand of hair behind my ear. "Does the lieutenant learn to live again? Does he tell Mabel about his leg? Do they fall in love?" He nuzzles my neck, fingers cradling my waist. "Do they make out? Hop in the sack together?"

"Weston—!" I laugh, holding him back—although the urge to climb into his lap and kiss him harder is becoming increasingly difficult to resist. "I can't tell you what happens next. I don't know."

"But you've thought about it."

"I *have*…" I lower my gaze, threading my fingers through his.

"I've had some ideas for turning it into something longer, like…
a novel."

His eyebrows rise. "A novel?"

"Crazy, I know."

"It's not crazy. That's a great idea."

"You think so?"

He nods without hesitation.

"But I don't know the first thing about writing a novel," I
confess softly, tracing the rough and calloused spots on Weston's
hand. They're strong and much bigger than mine. A fighter's
hands. The knuckles of his index and middle fingers are more
pronounced than the others, from years of punching heavy bags.
I've been obsessed with these hands since the day he first guided
me, back when I was blind.

"Seems to me like you already know a lot about writing,"
Weston says, lifting one shoulder. "You've got a talent for it, Tes.
You always have."

"Well, thank you. I appreciate you saying that, and I know I
have some talent, but… that's not enough to be a *master* at something. I feel like I need to learn more about it all. There's so much
I don't know."

Weston tips his head back against the couch, narrowing his
eyes speculatively at me. "Why do I get the feeling this is building
up to some kind of announcement?"

I groan, tipping my head back. "Because you can read my
mind before I even tell you what I want to tell you!"

"Tell me," he says, his eyes full of mischief. "Or I'll tickle it
out of you."

"Don't—don't you dare."

He's the most brutal of ticklers and likes nothing more than pushing me to the laughing brink of violence, at which point I will start aggressively grappling with him to make him stop. The last time we descended into such a wrestling match, I ended up leaving a visible scratch on his neck. He relished the chance to display my "love mark" for the rest of the week.

To avoid a repeat of *that* embarrassment, I come right out and tell him my news. "I signed up for a creative writing class."

"Seriously?"

"Seriously."

"Like a real-life, in-person *class*. In a classroom. With other people."

My shoulders sag. "I'm not as sheltered as you think."

He laughs, unconvinced. "I'm just surprised you didn't go for, like, an online class or something."

"Well, it was partly my mom who convinced me to do a class in person. She thinks it would be good for me to meet other writers and stuff." I shrug. There's a nervous flutter in my stomach when I think about braving a classroom of strangers. "It's three nights per week, and the classes are held at the college. I was wondering if you'd mind driving me, since you'll be in town anyway for work. The schedule lines up perfectly with your shifts at the gym."

"Sure, I'd be happy to drive you," Weston says with a nod. "Think you can handle socializing that much every week?"

"I'll survive. And we'll make up for it by cuddling and watching movies together when we get home."

"Sounds perfect." Weston sets my short story aside and scoops me into his lap, as if eager to get a head start on the cuddling. "There's nothing like coming home after a brutal training session to fall asleep on the couch with you."

"Yeah, you only make it, like, ten minutes into a movie before you pass out."

Weston laughs. "What can I say? Bruiser works me like a dog. And you always smell so good, like fresh laundry and coconuts…" He buries his face in my neck and breathes me in, his mouth dangerously close to my skin. I wrench his head back.

"Don't you go doing anything nasty to me before my first appearance in class," I warn him, pressing one finger to his lips.

"What, you're afraid I'll give you a love mark?"

"I wouldn't put it past you."

But Weston only laughs and tips his head back, toying with the ends of my hair. "When's your first class?"

"This Monday, at six. I'm kind of anxious about it, honestly. I wish you were doing it with me."

Weston grunts, like he can more easily see himself taking a class on pig farming or asteroid mining. "I'd be about as far outside my element with a bunch of literary nerds as *you'd* be in the boxing gym."

"Hey, I could learn how to fight if I really wanted to."

"You could. Absolutely. You would look like a total badass in boxing gloves." Weston's eyes twinkle at the mere idea of that, a smile twitching at his lips. "But it's not you."

I grunt. "No. It's not."

"And creative writing is not me," he says, with a quiet huff of a laugh. "So you can write stories for me. And I'll beat people up for you."

I grin. "Sounds like a plan."

———

White button-down, dark flare jeans, brown cardigan, boots. It's the perfect outfit for my first-ever appearance in a classroom. Not too overly academic, but also not so casual that it appears I haven't *tried* to look put together.

"You're beautiful," Weston says when he drops me off at the college entrance on Friday evening. He's wearing his usual boxing gym clothes: T-shirt, hoodie, and track pants. Definitely out of place among the historical brick buildings scattered across the campus.

"Hopefully I won't be too awkward," I murmur, looping my book bag over my shoulder.

"You'll be great," Weston assures me, leaning down to kiss my cheek. "If you need anything, just call me."

"Thanks, Wes. Love you."

"I love you, too."

And with that, we part ways—him back to his idling truck, me down the long, winding pathways through the college campus. For a diehard homeschooler, I've always been unreasonably obsessed with this place, especially in the autumn. There's something romantic about the red-brick lecture halls, oozing their Oxford charm among the old-growth trees and blankets of crisp orange leaves. When I was a kid, in the summer, Grandma and I would have picnics under the big oaks with piles of books from the library. I remember graham crackers and lemonade and falling asleep in feather-soft patches of sunlit grass.

Tonight, the lampposts are shining in the twilight, guiding me down the walkway towards Avery Hall, where the writing class is held. Mom and I scoped it out ahead of time so I wouldn't get lost in the mazelike campus. It looked more imposing in the light of day. Now, with the warm tungsten glow of the gridded windows, it looks like a cozy refuge for creative minds to escape the cold, dark unkindness of the real world.

As I approach, I see a group of people filing into the building ahead of me. Voices lift on the night wind as the door swings open and shut. The person at the back of the group hears my footsteps and pauses, holding the door for me.

"Thank you!" I say gratefully, rushing up the rest of the stairs to meet the boy who waited for me.

Perhaps *young man* is a better way to describe him. He looks a few years older than Weston, but that might be due to his studious square glasses, which frame a set of intensely dark eyes. His hair is chestnut brown and combed back in a way that echoes forgotten '60s fashion, which pairs well with his blazer, plaid scarf, and Oxford shoes.

"After you," he says with a bashful smile, gesturing towards the warmly lit foyer.

"Thank you," comes my automatic reply, and as I step inside, I realize I already thanked him when he first caught the door for me.

So much for not being socially awkward.

I follow the sound of voices to classroom B, where a placard outside displays the class schedule and the professor's name: Dr. Travis Middleton, PhD. I haven't met him yet, but I'm hoping he'll be less intimidating than his name and title suggest.

The classroom is bustling with students chatting and settling themselves behind desks. A whiteboard on one wall looms over an enormous mahogany desk, where an elegantly dressed woman with auburn hair sorts out some papers.

My gaze doesn't linger on her as I pass, but when she glances up at me and says, "Good evening," with a cheery smile, I can't help but stop.

"Hello," I say tentatively. "How are you?"

"I'm fantastic," she replies, her voice buoyant and bright, as she circles the desk and extends a handshake. "Travis Middleton. And your name is…?"

My eyebrows jump in surprise. "Oh. I'm sorry, I thought Travis was—"

"A man?" she guesses with an easy laugh. "You wouldn't be the first. You should've seen how confusing it was when *I* was in school. So many mix-ups with clubs and sports teams." She sighs, rolling her eyes in a good-natured way. "I guarantee, whatever your name is, I will envy it."

I grin. "It's Tessa. Tessa Dickinson."

"Oh! It even *starts* with a *T*. Why, Mom? Why couldn't you have named me Tessa instead?" She clasps her hands together and moans the question dramatically at the ceiling, making me dissolve into laughter. "You share a surname with a great writer, too."

I blush self-consciously. "Emily Dickinson is my favorite poet."

She winks. "Mine too. I'm glad you could join us tonight, Tessa. Please have a seat. Anywhere you'd like." Her beaded bracelets clink together as she swings her arm in a wide gesture, raising her voice for all the students to hear. "In fact, everyone, feel free to move your desks around! Just make sure you're not blocking anyone's view of the whiteboard, okay? We don't want chaos, but we don't want constriction—we want that fun gray area in between the two!"

This is not the way I expected a traditional classroom to be run—especially by a professor whose name sounds sanctimonious enough to be a Charles Dickens character. But apparently, Dr. Travis is a free spirit who marches to the beat of her own drum. I like her already.

Being an "obsessive perfectionist" (Weston's words, not mine), I decide not to rearrange my desk and instead keep it aligned with the back wall. As we all settle down and pull out our notebooks and laptops, I scan the classroom. I can tell that a lot of the attendees are college students cramming in extra studies in their downtime, which immediately makes me feel like both an amateur *and* an outsider.

"Looking for someone?" a girl stage-whispers next to me, dragging her desk closer to mine and tilting it at a slight angle. She's tall and lithe, with warm brown skin and a gorgeous afro, thick gold hoops swinging from her ears. She plops a glittery MacBook on the desk in front of her and swings it open, fingernails flying over the keyboard as she types in her password.

"Who, me? No." I laugh, my cheeks pinking as I fish my laptop out of my bag. "No, I'm not looking for anyone. I'm just…"

"Silently judging your fellow scholars?" she finishes with a covert wink.

"No, no, of course not."

"It's okay. I do it all the time. Makes for good story inspiration." Her smile is dazzlingly white as she extends a handshake. "I'm Shoshanna, by the way."

"Tessa." I shake her hand. "Good to meet you."

"Yeah, same. So now that we're on first-name terms and everything, you can divulge who you were looking at." Shoshanna swerves me a knowing side-eye. "Let me guess. Grayson Rhodes?"

"Who's that?"

She tips her chin towards a student sitting a few desks in front of us. I don't recognize the back of his head, but I glimpse a brown plaid scarf draped over his chair. The young man who held the door for me.

"Oh, him? No. No, I wasn't looking at *him*."

"I wouldn't blame you, girl; he's a total hottie."

I bite back a surprised laugh. As if anyone could qualify as a "hottie" in my world other than Weston. I'm a one-man woman through and through—however, I will admit that Grayson *does* have aesthetic appeal. But just because a guy is nice to look at doesn't mean I'm going to look. Not like *that*, anyway.

"So, what do you write?" Shoshanna asks me, pivoting the topic with the effortless grace of someone who is an expert at social interactions. "You seem like a rom-com kinda girl."

"Close," I admit. "I mostly write poetry, but I'm working on a historical romance. Sort of. What about you?"

"Fantasy series," comes her reply. "High fantasy, Tolkien level. Like elves, faeries, dragons… and I have multiple languages and storyworld maps all over my dorm. It's intense."

"Sounds… intense."

I can't imagine having so many ideas I'd need *maps* to draw them out. It's tricky enough to make the English language do what I want—but inventing *other* languages for the world of my characters? That's mind-bending to think about.

"I have a feeling you all are much more serious writers than I am," I confess meekly, opening up a Word document and fooling around with fonts just to give my fingers something to do.

"That's crap," Shoshanna returns with a swat of one hand. "You're sitting here, aren't you? You're serious. I'm sure your story is awesome. Most of these people are probably here for the extra credit or job benefits for being a student. You're here because you love writing. I can tell."

Dr. Travis claps her hands together and calls the class to attention. All heads turn to where she stands at the front of the room. She's written four words out on the whiteboard in tall, slanted letters.

YOUR STORY MATTERS. WHY?

"Welcome, everyone," she greets the class with a sunny grin. "I'm so glad to see all your smiling faces tonight, and I'm honored to be able to be a guide to you in your creative writing endeavors."

I feel a pair of eyes on me and try very hard not to let anything distract me—but after a moment, I can't help letting my gaze drift to the one head that's turned in my direction.

Grayson's dark eyes lock on mine. A little smile twitches at one side of his mouth. I return the smile because that's the friendly thing to do, right? Then I tug my gaze back to the professor, determined to stay focused.

"To begin our first lesson, I'd like to talk about why your story *matters*…"

———————————

The class finishes at seven forty-five, but I wind up staying later to let Shoshanna introduce me to a few of her friends—whom she refers to as the "Inklings." Shamelessly stolen from C. S. Lewis and Tolkien, she's quick to confess, but I assure her that her literary heroes would approve of such theft.

As it turns out, Grayson Rhodes is part of this Inklings group. Shoshanna looks enthused to introduce us to each other, and even more enthused to let us walk out of the lecture hall together at the back of the group, side by side.

"I'm surprised I haven't seen you around campus before," Grayson says, scrutinizing me through his square-framed glasses. "You don't go to school here, do you?"

"No. I'm not going to college. Probably ever."

Grayson lets out a surprised laugh at my blunt response. "Good for you. I wish I had that attitude sometimes. But I'm afraid my parents would self-combust if I spoke against the hallowed institution of higher education." He says it in a droning, pompous way that's meant to sound mocking, but I have a feeling it's not far from the truth. "They think it's bad enough that I'm pursuing writing as a profession. They think it's a safety net. But honestly? It's my parachute. If I can't get it to work, I'm screwed because I won't be able to tolerate doing anything else for a living. Climbing the corporate ladder sounds like… a slow death. Not that it's a bad thing; I just think it's too ordinary and intellectually sterile for people with more creative, complex personalities."

"That's probably true," I admit, snuggling my cardigan up around my neck to block out the October wind. Shoshanna and her friends are light-years ahead of us now, two of them splitting off from the group and heading for the parking lot with hollers of "goodnight" and "see you Monday!"

I glance around for Weston's truck, but I don't see any sign of him. My watch reads 8:05. He should be here any minute.

"I'm sorry," Grayson says. "I rambled so much, I didn't get to hear anything about you." He stops under a lamppost along the path, and I'm not sure *why* he's stopping here, but I can't very well continue walking when he's just asked me a question, so I stop too.

"Uh, I'm not… very interesting." I shrug. "No grand ambitions for my life yet; I'm just… I'm writing a novel."

"What's it about?"

I make a little noise of hesitation, shrugging and rubbing my arms for warmth.

"I know, I know—the three most terrifying words to utter in the presence of a writer." Grayson flashes me a grin, and I catch a glimpse of something a tad conceited in his dark eyes. "Should I go first?"

"Please," I urge him, nodding.

"Well, it doesn't have a name yet or a definite genre."

"Okay…"

"It could be considered a psychological thriller or possibly literary fiction. Let's go with literary fiction. In a nutshell, it's about a psychiatrist and his patient who is suicidal, very depressed, just… in a dark place after the loss of his wife. The whole novel basically takes place within the walls of the psychiatrist's office, and the character arcs are juxtaposed with each other—negative and positive. So while the patient becomes mentally healthier and more stable, the psychiatrist slowly becomes more and more depressed and, eventually, suicidal. And it's going to end with him killing himself."

"Oh. My." The right response to his story idea has vaporized somewhere in the mist of *juxtaposed character arcs*. All I can think to say is, "Not a happy ending, then?"

"Well, it depends on your perspective," Grayson says, adjusting his glasses. "The psychiatrist starts out happy, then gradually experiences a mental downfall. The patient starts out at his lowest moment, but ends the story quite happy and fulfilled with a promising future. I'm trying to explore the idea of our lives conforming to preconceived notions of success and how the great endeavor of intellectual ascension can eventually cause the mind to turn inward and destroy itself."

Again, I'm lost for what to say. I just stare at him for a long moment, my lips parted, like a beached fish.

"Oh God, that sounds really pretentious, doesn't it?" Grayson rubs his forehead and chuckles.

"No, no, it doesn't sound pretentious at all," I assure him. "It sounds very… thought-provoking. I certainly couldn't write something like that."

It's true—it would torture me to write such dark subject matter. I expect Grayson Rhodes is the sort who will end up retired in a library, surrounded by first-edition collectibles, with a skull on his writing desk, and probably smoke a pipe like an academic from a bygone era. He already has the wardrobe for that kind of retirement.

"Anyway, your turn," he says, shoving his hands into the pockets of his blazer. "Tell me what your story is about."

"Well," I begin, a bit more confident now that he's shared his project so willingly, "it's a love story. In England. During World War One. It's about a young woman who's blind and how she falls in love with a soldier who lost his leg in the war—but she doesn't know he's lost his leg because he doesn't tell her and she can't see him."

Grayson smiles. "That's brilliant."

My heart tumbles unexpectedly. "You think so?"

He nods without hesitation. "Yes. What a great hook—I can see the emotional conflict right away, all the little nuances their relationship would create with that secret between them. How many words have you written?"

"Uh, well, not many yet. It's really just a short story right now. But I want to make it into a novel, somehow. That's why I'm here. To learn."

"Well, you already know how to come up with genius ideas," Grayson says, the light from the lamppost twinkling in his eyes. "Where'd you get your inspiration?"

"Just from life," I answer without ceremony. "Actually, it's sort of inspired by how I met my boyfriend."

His smile dwindles for a split second, then quickly rights itself. "Oh yeah? Is he in the military?"

A little laugh catches in my throat. "The military? No."

Headlights sweep across the darkened parking lot, and I glance up just in time to see Weston's pickup truck come rolling to a stop. Perfect excuse to break away from Grayson without appearing rude.

"Oh, there he is now. I'd better go; I don't want to keep him waiting." I back-step toward the parking lot, pulling my cardigan close around me. "It was really nice to meet you, Grayson. I'll see you on Wednesday?"

He nods, his smile like a struggling flame as he eyes Weston's truck cautiously. "Yes, absolutely. Wednesday. It was enchanting to meet you, Tessa Dickinson."

Enchanting? That's a word you don't hear every day.

I give him an awkward little wave and make my exit—dashing across the parking lot, flinging open the passenger door. Once I'm in the truck, I lean over the center console to give Weston a quick kiss. But before I can sink back into my seat, he pulls me into a second kiss—this one so long, the ceiling light dies before it's over. His lips are deliciously warm compared to mine, and he smells like sweat, the good kind, earned from hard work.

"You must've missed me," I say breathlessly, falling back into my seat and buckling up.

Weston narrows his eyes, looking out the window to where Grayson is walking down the path toward the dormitories.

"Who's that guy you were talking to?"

"Oh, he's just a writer in my class. Grayson. He's a student here at the college."

"Yeah? Looked like he was enjoying talking to you. Alone." Weston thrusts the truck into reverse and backs up to pull out onto the main road. For a moment, I can't account for his irked attitude. Then it clicks.

"Oh my god, are you *jealous*?" I needle him, a flattered smile curving onto my lips. "Jealousy doesn't look good on you, Wes."

"Me? Jealous?" Weston scoffs, shaking his head. "I'm not jealous of that college guy. What does he have that I don't, besides warm toes? I am *not* jealous, Tessa. I'm possibly the slightest, smallest, *tiniest* bit murderous."

"Oooh, you mean *possessive*."

He brakes at a stop sign, looking over at me with hard, un-amused eyes. I can't help but laugh and lean closer over the center console to cup his face in my hands, brushing his nose with mine.

I sink my mouth into his, capturing his lips in another long, deep kiss—easing off after a moment to whisper, "Possessive looks good on you."

WESTON

____

WHEN MY BROTHERS AND I WERE YOUNGER, WE raised monarch butterflies as a science experiment. The glass terrarium lived on our front porch, and Mom was constantly inventing new ways to stop Aidan from opening the lid and letting the caterpillars roam free. It was fun watching them until they wrapped themselves in their chrysalises and did absolutely nothing for about two weeks. Henry was the only one who didn't give up on the monarchs. He documented every update in his science notebook like an entomologist, checking on them each morning and night.

He woke me up early one Saturday and dragged me out to the front porch to see the first butterfly emerging from its chrysalis. It wasn't much to look at—just some crumpled orange wings struggling against the sticky film of the chrysalis. He wanted to open the lid and help it along, but Mom told him that he could hurt the butterfly if he tried to do that.

"Leave it alone," she said. "This is something it has to do on its own."

So we waited and watched and, slowly, the butterfly made it out of the chrysalis on its own. They all did. When the terrarium was filled with papery orange wings, we took the lid off in the backyard and set them free to fly away.

That's how it feels to watch Tessa over the first week of her writing class. She emerges from the chrysalis, one wing at a time. That first night I dropped her off, she was anxious about being awkward around other people, but on Wednesday, she seems more sure of herself as she walks off toward the lecture hall. By Friday, she's got a confident swing in her hips as she strides onto the college campus.

Sometimes I see that guy Grayson meet her on the path—the college guy with the glasses. He dresses like he's from another century, and I can't help noticing how he smiles and waves every time he sees Tessa or parts ways with her when I come to pick her up after class.

I'd be lying if I said my defenses don't lock up whenever I catch sight of him. Tessa called it *possessiveness*, but that's not the right word for it—because I don't want to possess Tessa. I don't want to keep her inside a chrysalis. I want to see those wings unfold and take flight. I want her to see what she can do on her own, without the shelter of a terrarium around her.

It's good for her to get out of her shell and do something all on her own, without me or her family there as a safety net to fall back on.

So each time I drop her off at the college, I immediately head to Bruiser's, taking out any leftover aggression on the heavy bags. Every night as I drive Tessa back home, she tells me how her class went—and though most of the writer lingo flies right over my head, it's nice to hear her talk about it. I can't help but notice how much more enthused she is about her writing—like she no longer sees it as a side hobby, but something serious.

On Friday night, we make good on our promise to cuddle and watch TV together. Tessa has a Jane Austen movie she wants me to see, and sure enough, I get through about fifteen minutes of it before dozing off with her in my arms. I can't help it. Between the combination of British accents, slow violin music, the sweet scent of Tessa's hair, and the warmth of her body curled into mine… damn. It's impossible to stay awake.

When I open my eyes again, she's no longer lying beside me but sitting on the floor with her back against the couch, laptop on the coffee table in front of her. The movie is still playing on the TV, but I can tell I've missed a lot. The main girl character was all happy and in love when I fell asleep, and now she's crying her eyes out. Apparently, some stuff happened. But I'm more interested in knowing what Tessa's up to.

Her hair is within my reach, so I catch a strand between my fingers and whisper, "What are you writing?"

She gasps, turning to me with surprise. "I thought you were asleep."

"I was," I groan, rubbing a hand over my face. "This crying chick woke me up."

Tessa murmurs a laugh and reaches for the remote, lowering the volume. "I just had some ideas I wanted to write down."

"For the book?"

She nods.

"Can you tell me about them?" I roll onto my back, tucking one hand behind my head. "Or is it top secret? Or is it a sexy, spicy love scene that you're too embarrassed to share with me?"

Tessa grunts, tipping her head back dramatically. "Oh, yeah, that. Definitely." She types a few more words into her document before swiveling to face me, folding her arms on the edge of the couch—new ideas sparkling in her eyes. "I had a crazy thought. What if I made the story dual point of view?"

"What does that mean?"

"Like switching back and forth between Mabel and Lieutenant Barnes. So, right now it's third person omniscient, but if I did this dual-point-of-view thing, it would be first person close."

She might as well be speaking another language. When it becomes obvious that I have no idea what terms like "third person omniscient" and "first person close" mean, she explains.

"Dr. Travis was talking about tenses and perspectives tonight—the differences between them and how they can change the way you engage with a story. And as she was talking, I realized that my favorite perspective to read is first person—where the pronouns are *I, me, my,* etcetera. So it feels like the character is the one telling you the story." Tessa waits to make sure I'm tracking. When I nod, she continues, "So that got me thinking… it would be kind of fun to write both sides of this story, first person. But I might need your help."

"My help?" I quirk one eyebrow. "I'm no writer, Tes. I don't even understand half the stuff you said about perspectives—"

"I don't mean the writing part," she says with a grin, taking my hand in hers and gently stroking her silky-soft thumb over my rough knuckles. "I mean… writing from Lieutenant Barnes's perspective. I want it to be realistic. The stuff about him losing his leg."

"Well, I'm sure you can find an amputee who would be willing to answer your questions." I give her a sleepy wink. "What is it you want to know?"

She glances down, pressing her lips together. I know that look—the color in her cheeks, the shy smile she uses to cover up awkward feelings.

"Seriously, you can ask me anything, Tessa. I don't mind talking about it."

"You sure? Because I don't want to make you... relive it."

"It's not like I actually went through a war."

"No, but it was still traumatic." Her gaze falls on my prosthetic legs, which are lying on the floor. I always take them off when we snuggle on the couch together. It's incredibly satisfying after a long, sweaty workout and shower to just lie here and let my stumps breathe. Bonus points when I get to make out with Tessa at the same time.

"What did it feel like?" she asks softly, lifting her gaze to mine. "I don't mean the operation; I know you were under anesthesia for that... but after. When you woke up."

If I close my eyes, I'm back there—lying in that hospital bed with machines beeping and IV poles looming over my head and Mom's hand clutching mine. I never told Tessa all the horrible details, and she's never asked me to talk about it.

"I couldn't really feel anything," I murmur. "I was pretty loaded with painkillers. But they didn't have any of that stuff back in the day when your story takes place. They had morphine, I think. Man, that shit must've hurt." I shudder inwardly at the thought. Having your legs amputated while you're dead to the world is one thing. But I don't know if I would've gotten through it if I'd actually had to see my blood on the surgeon's tools.

Luckily, I don't think Tessa is getting *that* graphic with her story, so I tell her the things that might be useful. I explain how phantom pain feels—how sometimes it's just a sensation like the missing limb is still there, and other times it's as if your legs are melting under a pile of burning hot coals. She asks me about recovery time, rehabilitation, adapting to ordinary life when you're missing something you used to depend on every single day.

I tell Tessa what I know from experience, and she takes notes on her laptop, hands flying over the keys as she writes down all my answers. Finally, she moves back onto the couch with me, sliding my knees into her lap and stroking her fingers gently over my stumps—the faint white line where the surgeon sewed me up five years ago.

"What is the biggest thing people don't understand about it?" she asks me, her voice so sweet and honest. So willing to listen, to know me better. It's moments like these that make me think even if she hadn't met me when she was blind and couldn't see my missing pieces, we still would have ended up together—she still would have wanted me. She still would have fallen in love with me.

And I still would have fallen in love with her.

"I think the answer to that question would be different for everyone," I say, my voice low as Tessa's beautiful hands caress my scars. "For me, the thing I feel like most people don't understand is... how your sense of self gets lost in it."

Tessa tilts her head, silently asking me to elaborate.

"It's like, you go from being... whoever you were before to being known as 'the guy with the missing leg.' Or legs, plural, in my case." I let out a dry, mirthless laugh. "People start identifying you with it. Like that's where you begin and end. And they think anything you do is incredible, even if it's just pumping gas or going for a run—all because you're missing a limb. That shit gets old really fast."

"Because you feel like that's all they're thinking about? The fact you're an amputee?"

I nod slowly, meeting her eyes. "It's like your guy—Lieutenant Barnes. He's still the same person he was before the war. But he's different. But he's the same. You know? There's more to him than… surviving something awful."

Tessa turns my words over in her mind and smiles a little, her gaze softening as she lowers herself to my level and presses a soft, paralyzing kiss to my lips. I reach up to cradle her waist, my fingertips accidentally sliding under her T-shirt and brushing against smooth, bare skin. It's enough to shake up a bottle of intense desires within me.

"You're right," she whispers, her warm breath on my cheek as she breaks away to look into my eyes. "There's *so much* more to him than that."

ON MONDAY NIGHT, DR. TRAVIS TEACHES ABOUT THE importance of feedback and critiques—how to take constructive criticism, learn from it, and implement ideas into our stories. It all leads up to a moment halfway through the lecture when she drops an unexpected bombshell on the class.

"Now that we've all gotten to know each other a bit better, I'd like for each of you to pair up with another writer who will be your critique partner." Dr. Travis smiles, taking in our surprised expressions. Some students were expecting this. Others were not. I belong to the latter category. "Don't worry about your partner's reading preferences. Even if you write in very different genres, you'll still be able to help each other and provide valuable feedback. I find this one-on-one approach to be much more effective than a group workshop setting, although we *will* be doing some workshopping next month. For now, I just want you all to work with one other writer and swap pages—however much you're comfortable sharing with each other. *Don't* choose the person sitting next to you."

This last caveat comes just as Shoshanna turns to me and I turn to her, our fingers poised to choose each other as partners. *Busted.* We both freeze, then dissolve into laughter. Shoshanna thumps her forehead on her laptop and reluctantly stands to go seek out a different partner. Is that what *I'm* supposed to do now? My heart lurches into my throat at the prospect of roaming around this classroom asking some random stranger to be my critique partner. What if everyone I ask says no? My confidence wilts like a flower in the sun as I stare down at my sweaty palms.

"Tessa?"

My gaze jolts upward at the sound of Grayson's smooth voice. He's standing right in front of my desk, with a crooked but hopeful smile on his face.

"Would you want to be my critique partner?"

Relief washes over me, and I nod—perhaps *too* quickly. "That… would be great."

His eyes light up, and he pulls over a vacant chair, straddling it backwards and leaning on his elbows. "I know my work in progress isn't really your thing, but I can tell you have a real talent for coming up with original ideas—and I could use some of that talent."

A self-conscious blush pinks my cheeks. "Well, I don't think my work in progress is *your* cup of tea, so I guess we're even."

He straightens up, surprised at my allegation. "What makes you think I don't like romance?"

"Well, given your obsession with mortality and the darker parts of human nature, you probably aren't a fan of happily-ever-afters." I raise my eyebrows, dipping my chin to study him. "Am I right?"

Grayson smiles, slow and soft like a summer rain—his dark

eyes scanning my face as though he's taking in details he wants to write about. "I think anything that came out of your head would be brilliant."

The compliment makes my stomach dip. But I tell myself, *It's something he would've said to anyone. He's just being friendly.*

"You might change your mind once you actually *read* my story," I warn him, returning my gaze to my laptop.

I send him my first chapter that night, and he emails me the prologue of his story, whose document is titled simply: the-suicidal-psychiatrist.docx

I fire back a quick response to let him know I received it.

Got it. Can't wait to jump in. Critique #1: think of a better title.
-Tessa

He responds to my email within minutes.

Got yours too. Thank you for trusting me with it. I'm open to title suggestions anytime. ;)
-Gray

I stare at the computer for a full three minutes, overthinking that semicolon and parenthesis. A winking smiley face. Is it meant to be friendly? Or flirtatious?

I decide to file it under *friendly* and move on—because if I even consider the possibility of Grayson flirting with me, I'll start psychoanalyzing every interaction we've had thus far and wind up feeling extremely weird about reading his book at all.

It's nothing, I tell myself. He's probably just trying to make me more comfortable about sharing my story with him. But a squirmy little voice in the back of my mind keeps haunting me with unfounded fears, like *what if he steals my ideas?* But those suspicions are baseless and ridiculous. Grayson writes in a completely different genre—and if he wants to be friends, he won't do something as sly and underhanded as plagiarizing me.

In truth, I'm hesitant to open up Grayson's document and start reading his story—not because the subject matter is darker than my usual literary fare, but because I'm afraid I might hate it. What if he's a terrible writer? What if I can't find anything to praise? What if he puts me on the spot and tells me to be honest with him, and I end up hurting his feelings?

Worst-case scenarios crowd my mind until I decide it won't hurt to put off reading his first chapter. I'm sure he's not going to read *mine* straight away.

Clicking back to my inbox, I find a new email from Shoshanna titled **Inklings meeting!!!!** When I open it up, I discover she has copied all the members of her writing group, including Grayson. Including *me*.

Apparently, we are all invited to the Trolley Station Café for a brainstorm session on Wednesday afternoon. Her requirements are to "bring your book and your brain and some capacity to buy yourself a coffee because I will NOT be buying a round for everyone."

A mixture of excitement and dread twists in my chest. I fight the urge to reply to Shoshanna privately and ask her if she's sure she wants *me* to join this brainstorming session. I don't know if

I'm at the level of group meetings with writers at cafés, swapping ideas over coffee and being… well… *brilliant.*

Sitting in class and receiving information is one thing. Being part of Shoshanna's effervescent tribe of creative geniuses is quite another.

But when I tell Weston of my dilemma the following morning, he puts to death all my doubts.

"What do these other writers have that you don't?" he asks, looking impossibly cute as he leans on the porch railing, wind tousling his hair as the fiery maple tree sheds its red leaves behind him.

I shrug from where I'm sitting on the swing. "I don't know. They're just more… academic than I am."

"So that means they have more boring ideas," Weston fires back. "Whereas *you* were homeschooled, so you still have your genius creativity intact. It hasn't been beaten out of you by dumb shit like trigonometry."

I smile and blush, looking down at the paper-clipped pages in my lap: Grayson's prologue. I haven't begun reading yet, but I can already tell by the opening line it's going to take all my concentration to focus on this story.

"Is that the next chapter of your book?" Weston asks, jerking his chin toward the pages.

"This? No, this is Grayson's book, actually."

"Grayson?" His raised eyebrow says it all. "Why are you reading *his* story?"

"We're critique partners. Dr. Travis had everyone in the class pair up with someone else. I was going to choose Shoshanna, but we couldn't pick the person sitting next to us, so… Grayson asked me if I'd be his partner. And I said that I would."

A muscle in Weston's jaw twitches, but he only nods.

"Don't look at me like that. Grayson's a nice guy—he's just trying to be friendly."

This makes Weston choke back a laugh. "Friendly, huh?"

I tip my chin up defiantly. "I told him I'd read his prologue and give him feedback. He's going to read my first chapter and give me feedback. That's how this writing class works. We're just trying to help each other."

Weston takes a long, deep breath, like he has a thousand protests but can't bring himself to verbalize any of them. Instead, he crosses the porch and sits down on the swing beside me, reading over my shoulder.

I let him, because it's no skin off my nose—and I enjoy having him close by whenever I can, even if we're just sitting in companionable silence together.

I dip my gaze to the page and begin reading.

You can learn a lot about a man by watching the way he attempts to kill himself. For some, the cool press of the pistol against the temple is a rattle of redemption's gates. For others, the silent choke of poison brings more ease and comfort through the dark cavern into death. For others still, a rope and a high place will beckon like the cursed song of Persephone, calling a new miserable soul to the underworld.

For Peter Hunsecker, it was a bridge.

"Well, this is depressing." Weston speaks up beside me.

I drop the pages into my lap. "I know. It's not... my cup of tea, but it's what he writes. The story is about a suicidal guy going to a psychiatrist."

"Sounds boring as all hell," Weston says, yawning for emphasis. "Plus, his writing is horrible. I mean, 'the cursed song of Persephone, calling a new miserable soul to the underworld'?" He underscores the line with his finger as he reads it. "Who the hell talks like that?"

"It's literary fiction. It's supposed to be…"

"Depressing?"

I give him a no-nonsense side-eye. "Intellectual."

"I don't see how it's intellectual to use a bunch of fluffy words nobody actually uses in real life."

"Well, you don't read. You're not a reader. You've only read my stuff, so you can't really judge someone else's stuff with an objective mind."

Weston grunts, standing and putting his hands up defensively. "Well, I guess I'll just take my nonobjective, unintellectual mind elsewhere."

"Don't be like that."

"Like what?"

"Don't be offended and upset just because Grayson chose me as his critique partner—"

"I'm not offended or upset," Weston argues, crossing his arms over his chest. "I just want you to be careful."

"Careful of what?"

"Of this guy *Grayson*. You could write circles around him. I hope you realize that. Don't let his highfalutin mumbo-jumbo make you think that's the only way to be 'intellectual' or whatever."

I sputter a disgusted noise. "We have completely different writing styles, Wes. All I'm doing is reading his first chapter and giving him feedback, and if you don't mind, I'd like to get it done before I meet them all at the café tomorrow."

I don't mean for it to sound like an invitation to leave, but that's how Weston takes it. I can tell by the flinch of his eyes, the way he spears a hand through his hair and heads for the porch steps.

"Guess I'll see you later, then."

"Wes."

He pauses on the second step, and I walk over to meet him—to press a soft kiss to his lips.

"I'm sorry. I don't want to fight about this… I just promised Grayson I'd read it."

"I understand," he says, his voice soft and his eyes full of earnest sweetness. "I just want you to be… cautious. *Suspicious.* See, you're teaching me how to find the right word."

I frown. "Suspicious of what?"

Weston's gaze roams over my face, and he smiles sadly, like he could explain it a hundred different ways and I still wouldn't understand. "You're beautiful, Tessa. You're brilliant and funny and interesting and sweet… You haven't been around a lot of guys. You don't know how they… look at you."

"Wes, Grayson's not like that."

"*All* men are like that," he corrects, pretty sure of himself for someone who's never properly met Grayson. "Trust me, I know. He chose you as his critique partner for a reason."

"He knows I have a boyfriend."

"Doesn't matter. If you'd had a boyfriend when I met you, that wouldn't have stopped me from wanting you. Wouldn't have stopped me from trying to get you. I would've moved heaven and earth to be your man." He catches my hand in his and gives it a quick squeeze, leaning in to press another kiss to my lips. "Just be on your guard, okay?"

I'm still flustered after Weston's truck backs out of the driveway and heads down the street. His warning lingers in my mind like a pebble in my shoe—just sharp enough to be a bother. It's not that he mistrusts Grayson's intentions towards me. It's that Weston mistrusts *me*, alone with Grayson.

"Jane Austen."

"Stephen King."

"J. K. Rowling."

"Tolkien… duh."

Grayson points at me, and all heads swivel in my direction.

"Uh, Emily Dickinson," I say quietly.

There are a few hums and nods of agreement around our table, which is tucked away in the back corner of the coffee shop and crowded with laptops, notebooks, and cappuccinos. It's unexpectedly delightful to be a part of this sacred gathering of writers. On my way here, I was afraid I might feel like an outsider—stuck on the fringe, unable to contribute to the conversation. But Grayson met me at the door with a bright smile and pulled out a chair right beside his near the center of the table.

I made sure to put an appropriate amount of space between us.

Though laptops were flung open and drinks were ordered, the brainstorming has yet to begin—and Shoshanna treats the proceedings with the utmost respect, proving that this part of the meeting is perhaps more important than the actual agenda.

We've been going around the table, naming the authors who first inspired us to become writers. I'm the only one who's chosen a poet, which makes me feel like the odd woman out, until Grayson chimes in, "Mine is John Keats."

Shoshanna groans and thuds back in her chair. "Oh, come on—"

"What's wrong with Keats?"

She makes a show of looking at her wrist, which has no watch on it. "We don't have time to go over *all* the reasons."

Her objection makes the whole table erupt in opinions—some in favor of Keats, others against him. Grayson laughs and puts his hands up, but the twinkle in his eye tells me he intended to start a conflict with this controversial opinion.

"I want to hear what Tessa thinks," he says, silencing the gabble like a judge in a noisy courtroom. My cheeks heat up as he turns to put the spotlight on me again. "Since it sounds like you're the only one who reads poetry around here."

Shoshanna objects to that, but Grayson puts up one finger to halt the traffic for my opinion.

"I, uh… haven't read a ton of Keats. I like his letters more than his poems, honestly."

Grayson frowns, tilting his head to the side. "His letters?"

I nod. "When he was in a relationship with Fanny Brawne, he wrote her love letters when they couldn't be together. Actually, the poem 'Bright Star' was written about her. And there's a line from one of his letters—I can't remember the exact words, but it goes something like…" I close my eyes because I know I'll fumble if I can see everyone watching me. "'I wish we were butterflies and lived but three summer days. Three days with you I could fill with more joy than fifty common years could contain.'"

When I open my eyes, Grayson is looking at me with a soft, mesmerized expression, like I just melted him with that line of Keats. Weston's warning from yesterday comes rearing up in my mind.

You don't know how guys look at you.

Is this the look he was talking about? The one that singles me out, like I'm the only girl sitting at this table?

I break eye contact with Grayson, drying my damp palms on my jeans. "So, yeah, I almost wonder if Keats was more poetic when he wasn't *trying* to be poetic."

This idea sparks a new debate about the use of metaphors and similes in writing—when it should be done, when it is overdone, etc. The artistic rhetoric soon becomes too dizzying for me to keep up with, but I enjoy listening. Surrounding myself with this sort of conversation makes me feel like a real writer. And yet, that twinge of self-doubt resurrects itself every time I ask someone to explain a literary term or introduce me to a famous author I've never heard of.

I feel like I belong here, but at the same time... I don't belong.

Eventually, all of us Inklings descend into our private worlds of brainstorming—speaking only to our designated critique partners for ideas, and occasionally putting the whole group to a vote on the more complex decision-making.

I tell Grayson what I thought of his first chapter, and watch over his shoulder as he reworks sentences based on my opinions. I compiled a list of constructive feedback last night, with an 80:20 ratio of positive to critical thoughts.

"You didn't like the opening line?" he asks, quirking one eyebrow over the rim of his square glasses.

"Well, it's not that I didn't *like* it—I mean, it was good. You just got a bit wordy with all the things it *wasn't* before finally leading up to the scene with Peter on the bridge. What if you cut out that whole first paragraph and began with, 'You can learn a lot about a man by watching the way he attempts to kill himself… For Peter Hunsecker, it was a bridge.'"

Grayson nods slowly, looking at the opening line in a new light. He highlights all the wordy parts and, with one click, deletes them.

"Genius." He casts me a grin. "I think you might be my muse, Tessa."

I sputter an appalled scoff and roll my eyes. "I doubt that very much. Your writing is really good—I like it. And that's saying a lot because I would normally *never* read this type of book."

Grayson laughs and pops open a different Word document minimized on his screen. *My* first chapter. When I see it, my heart flops. He hasn't given me any feedback so far; he just sent an email late last night that simply read, *I finished yours. Wow.*

But I couldn't tell if that was a good wow or a "wow, your writing is atrocious" kind of wow.

Now his critiques are inescapable as he sits beside me and highlights the first few paragraphs of my chapter.

"This," he says, nodding to the screen, "was absolutely brilliant."

I smile, my heart swelling. "Really?"

"Yeah. I was hooked right away. Couldn't put it down."

"Oh my gosh, seriously?"

Grayson laughs. "Don't sound so surprised. You're a very talented writer, Tessa."

A self-conscious blush warms my cheeks, and I shrug

modestly. "I'm… glad you liked it. At first, I was going to start with Mabel's point of view, but I decided to change it to begin with Lieutenant Barnes's."

"You wrote it so well, too," Grayson says. "I was especially impressed by the medical stuff. I can tell you really did your research."

That makes me smile to myself. I don't know if talking to my boyfriend while cuddling on the couch counts as research, but if it does, I'm pretty sure "research" is my favorite part of the writing process.

"I did have an idea, though."

I glance up at him, my confidence flickering. "Yeah?"

"Well, this *is* a brainstorm session, after all. And feel free to tell me to go pound sand—but I was thinking as I read it… what if Mabel and the lieutenant already knew each other? What if they were in love before the war even started, and she thinks they can just pick up where they left off, but Barnes feels like he's not enough for her now?"

The idea sparks new possibilities in my mind. "That's… an interesting thought."

"And what if—I know you're not going to like this one." Grayson smirks, folding his hands over his laptop in a scholarly fashion. "What if Barnes is actually dying from his wounds, and Mabel doesn't find out the reason why until it's too late—"

"No, no. Nobody's dying. This is a *romance*. It's going to have a happy ending."

Grayson chuckles at my adamancy.

"And speaking of happy endings," I add, "I think I figured out a way for your book to have one—"

"Oh God, no." He tips his head back defiantly. "Don't say

you want the psychiatrist to live. He *needs* to die. It's part of the overarching symbolism."

"Yes, I know, but *what if…* the patient is the one who ends up saving his life? Peter. And you could still have that juxtaposition of the negative and positive arc, but it would be even *juicier* because if Peter had jumped off the bridge at the beginning of the story, he wouldn't have been alive to save the psychiatrist."

"But the psychiatrist wouldn't have become suicidal if it weren't for Peter."

I shrug. "Even more reason for Peter to save his life."

Grayson thinks about it for a long moment, stroking his chin thoughtfully as he stares at his laptop, once again a judge in a courtroom—only this time, he's deciding the fate of his characters.

"I also had another thought, but you won't like it." I turn back to my own laptop with a cryptic smile, opening up my first chapter and pretending to make minor edits.

"What is it?"

"Nope, not saying. You'll laugh."

"I won't laugh, I promise. Tell me. I need your creative genius to summon my soul from the depths of literary despair."

I roll my eyes. "You *have* read too much Keats."

"What. Is. The idea?"

I turn to face him, propping my chin on my fist. "Make it a love story."

He lets out a sigh, which gives way to a laugh as he sinks his face into his hands.

"What if instead of Peter you had… Patricia?"

"Patricia?"

"Yeah. What if the patient was a woman? Who lost her husband? And the whole story could unfold the same way, except the psychiatrist falls in love with Patricia, but he can't have her—and maybe he's already married so he feels like a terrible person for even *wanting* her… but he can't help himself."

Grayson's expression of doubt melts into something more serious and dreamy. He falls into a reflective trance as his gaze roams over my face, stalling on my lips for a second.

"He can't help himself," he whispers.

I turn back to my keyboard, a prickle of unease breathing down my neck. "Just a thought."

"It's a good thought," he assures me with a half-smile. "It's a thought worth thinking about."

WESTON

OVER THE COURSE OF THE NEXT TWO WEEKS, I WATCH the monarch butterfly slowly lose her strength to fly. It's not that she *can't* fly—her wings are just as capable as they were before. But something is weighing her down.

I first notice it on the drives home from Tessa's writing class. When this thing first started, she'd be all bubbly and talkative when she'd hop in my truck—telling me everything her professor lectured about, then starting to think up new ways to apply it to her story—and I would just listen because I couldn't get excited about creative writing any more than she could get excited about MMA knockouts.

Still, I loved listening to her talk—even if most of the lingo went over my head. I loved seeing her light up over something that was all her own. I loved watching her fly.

Now, she doesn't say much on the drives home. When I ask her what she's thinking about, she replies, "The book." If I urge her to tell me, "What about the book?" she shakes her head and says, "It's too hard to explain."

On the nights that I hang out at her place to watch movies and snuggle on the couch with her, I always wake up at some point to find her sitting on the floor with her laptop, typing away. Sometimes she's working on her own book. Other times she's working on *his*.

Grayson Rhodes. The smart-ass college student with the glasses and the fifty-cent words. I'd be lying if I said I don't bristle inside every time I catch Tessa reading his work.

"Stop taking it so personally," she says one night when we're supposed to be hanging out together, but she's got a pile of his stupid writing in her lap and a red pen to mark up errors.

I *do* take it personally. I want to snatch that red pen of hers and slash it through every line on the page. I don't like Tessa reading that crap about suicide and psychiatrists and death. It's not her. She hates it; I know she does. But she's reading it anyway, willingly—happily. *Why?*

What the hell is so special about this guy?

"Well, I hope he doesn't have that many edits for *your* writing," I say in response, nodding toward the papers in her lap. "Because if he does, I'm going to have to wring his neck."

"Pfft. Stop. Grayson *does* have suggestions for me and some edits, yeah. He can see things in my writing that you can't."

"Because he's smarter? More intellectual? Has a bigger vocabulary?"

Tessa rolls her eyes. "I never said that, Wes. He's just… a writer, okay? You're not. So he can see errors in my writing that you can't see."

"Is that why you've been sad?"

"Sad?"

"Yeah, gloomy. Glum. Whatever the hell the right word is."

"I haven't been gloomy or glum," Tessa objects, but the way she turns back to her laptop and lets a curtain of hair fall into her face is proof she wants to hide from my words—because they're true. "I just... I want to improve my writing, that's all. I want my book to be perfect."

That's not unusual for Tessa. She always wants *everything* to be perfect. But I've watched the way her perfectionism makes her spiral into a hole of self-doubt and anxiety.

"You're a really good writer, Tessa," I assure her, sitting upright on the couch and gently running my fingers through her long hair. "I know I'm biased when it comes to you, and my word might not count for much because I'm not some literary scholar... but I suspect you're more of a writer than any of those other students are."

Tessa caps her red pen and sets the pile of papers aside. "Your word *does* count, Weston. I value your opinion. And besides..." She smiles, crawling over the couch cushions and sinking into my lap, her soft hands latching behind my head—pulling me close to her lips. "A big vocabulary is *not* what I look for in a man."

I can't help the smile that breaks onto my face. "That... sounds kinda dirty."

She rolls her eyes. "It wasn't meant to sound *dirty*."

"Even better." I kiss her, winding one arm around her back and scooping the other under her knees, drawing her in closer, closer, never close enough. She kisses me hard, hungrily—like she didn't realize how much she was craving this until now.

The feeling is mutual.

Her skin smells so good, and it tastes even better as I kiss my way down the curve of her jaw, to the hollow beneath her ear. For some reason, this spot always drives her crazy—her fingers turn into claws and her body curls tighter around me like a boa constrictor going in for the kill.

Aaaaand that's when her cell phone starts ringing.

I loosen my hold, letting her crawl back over the couch to snatch her vibrating phone from the coffee table.

"Who's rudely interrupting our makeout session?" I ask, still too high on the rush of dopamine and other good feelings to be pissed off at this interruption.

"I don't know. Probably spam." She swipes to answer the call, holding it to her ear. "Hello?"

A tinny guy's voice comes through the speaker, making Tessa jolt upright.

"Oh. Grayson, hi."

Good feelings gone.

Tessa turns to give me a face, but I can't tell what kind of face it is—sorry she picked up? Or just sorry that *I* happened to be here, making out with her, when she picked up?

I sit here for a minute listening to the muffled sound of his voice through the phone. Tessa nods and "mm-hmms," but she keeps looking at me and parting her lips like she wants to tell Grayson she has to go. Her attempts are useless.

I'm tempted to grab the phone from her ear and tell him to screw off—but something tells me that wouldn't put Tessa in the mood to continue kissing me.

After a few minutes of sitting here feeling like a spare part, I decide to make it easier for her. I mouth the words *It's okay* and reach for my prostheses, which are lying on the floor by the couch. Tessa dives before I can, wrestling my left leg away from me.

Stay, she mouths.

And to ensure I do, she climbs back into my lap—still on the phone with Grayson, whose voice I can hear more clearly now that she's closer.

"Anyway," he says, "I was really calling to ask if you want to meet up tomorrow at the Trolley Station, go over a few of these ideas you sent me."

Tessa glances up at me, hesitation in her eyes. "Oh, um… I didn't see an email from Shoshanna."

"No, the next Inklings meeting is on Thursday. I thought you and I could have some one-on-one time. We'd get more done that way."

Every muscle in my body locks up at his choice of words. *One-on-one time?* My reaction doesn't escape Tessa. She feels it in the squeeze of my hands around her hips before she even looks up into my face.

Say no.

It's not something I tell her or even secretly mouth to her. It's just a whisper in the back of my mind. A want. A fear. A twist in my gut that I hope she'll feel too.

"Are you busy tomorrow afternoon?" Grayson presses her, making me want to reach through the phone and pop him one.

"Uh, no, I'm not… I can make time." Tessa bites her lip, scanning my face and then sliding her hand down to cover mine. "Would it be okay if my boyfriend came along?"

Well, that's a wild card I wasn't expecting her to play.

Silence from Grayson while he thinks about it. "Uh, yeah, sure. That'd be fine. I'd like to meet him, actually. Sounds great. Three o'clock?"

Tessa's gaze slides back to me, a slow smile pushing over her lips. God, that look is enough to burn me down like a forest fire. "Three o'clock."

She hangs up, dropping the phone on the coffee table.

"He doesn't want to meet me," I say in a low growl, brushing a strand of hair off her cheek. "He doesn't even *know* how much he doesn't want to meet me."

Tessa murmurs a laugh, fingers clawing at my neck. I guess animal aggression turns her on?

"Well, *I* want you to meet *him*," she says. "I want you to see that he's absolutely no threat to us. He's just a friend."

I almost laugh—I *would* if it weren't so damn frustrating. This is what I love about Tessa. She gives everyone the benefit of the doubt. Trusts them, thinks the best of them, too sweet to see past the masks people wear.

Grayson may not be a threat to us, but I'm sure as hell a threat to Grayson. And there's no way he's looking forward to this meeting tomorrow—not now that Tessa invited *me* to join them.

"Be nice to him, okay?" Tessa traces her fingertip along my jawline, her beautiful eyes glittering in the lamplight. "Don't get all… proprietorial."

"If I knew what the hell that meant, I might know how not to be it," I whisper, catching her lips for a kiss, then another, and another. She hums contentedly, burying her fingers in my hair as I nuzzle her neck. "I could give you a *proprietorial* love mark here. That'd do the job, wouldn't it?"

Tessa squeaks a little laugh and wriggles her neck away from my mouth. "Maybe I'll give *you* one instead. That would also 'do the job.'"

"Even better." I kiss the tip of her nose. "Let Grayson see what he's missing out on."

The next day, we walk into the Trolley Station hand in hand. I make *sure* we're hand in hand because I want Grayson to understand the stakes of this "one-on-one" time with Tessa. I'm the only one who can set those stakes.

And no, I don't think that's *proprietorial* of me. (I looked that word up, so I know what it means. And I'm not it.)

Tessa waves with her free hand as soon as she spots Grayson hunched over his laptop at a corner table, two cups of coffee beside him.

One for him, one for Tessa.

He knows her drink order.

For some reason, this knowledge makes me want to hook-punch him in the liver. And we haven't even been introduced yet.

I'm wearing jeans and Jordans, so we get to skip the Reaction. I have no idea if Tessa told him I'm an amputee, but I assume not since he seems to have no awkward reservations about treating me like your average Joe Blow.

He smiles and gets to his feet, sauntering over to meet us halfway across the café. Yes, *sauntering*—that's the right word. A form of walking exclusive to college guys with big vocabularies and even bigger egos.

"Wes, right?"

"Weston," I correct him, reaching for a handshake. He accepts it, and I deliberately crush his finger bones with a friendly smile on my face. There it is—the flinch in his eyes. Warning taken. I ease off, letting my hand return to Tessa's. "Good to meet you, Grayson."

"Yeah, good to meet you too," he says with some effort, flexing his hand at his side. *Pansy-ass.* "Uh, Tessa, I got you a cap with oat milk. I didn't know what Weston likes."

"I'll get my own."

Tessa smiles appreciatively at Grayson. "That was nice of you, Gray. Thanks."

Gray?

She has a nickname for him, and he knows she likes oat milk in her cappuccino? If this was one of Tessa's period dramas, I'd be throwing a glove at this guy and calling for a duel.

I decide to walk away before I say something *unfriendly*, but not before I lean in and kiss Tessa's cheek—right in front of Grayson. Call it upping the ante. Call it proprietorial. I don't even care.

I'd want her to do the same to me if there was some girl I had to meet for a study session. That's how I decide to look at it as I stand in line for a black coffee, watching Tessa and Grayson at the corner table. If this were the other way around, and I brought her to meet a girl I worked with who had the hots for me, it would be to make a point.

I'm taken. I'm hers. She's mine. Get the picture?

Tessa told me to be "nice" to this guy, but I wonder if that's just her soft, people-pleaser side trying to be a diplomat. Deep down, she wants Grayson to know she's off-limits. Why else would she have invited me to join this meeting when I have absolutely nothing to add to the conversation?

She's laughing at something he said as I take a seat in the chair beside her. "What's funny?"

Tessa shakes her head. "Oh—nothing."

Apparently, the joke was too intellectual for my ears. Grayson clears his throat and sips his drink, which looks suspiciously like a latte.

Again, I think, *Pansy-ass.*

"So, Tessa was telling me that this book she's writing is

actually inspired by the way you two met." Grayson points back and forth between us. "You never finished explaining why that is, Tessa."

"Oh," she says, glancing at me. "Um, well… I met Weston a few years ago, right after I was in a car accident and lost my eyesight."

"Oh wow." Grayson's eyebrows arch with surprise. "Seriously?"

"Yeah, it was just temporary. For about three months, I was completely blind. Weston came to help me run my blog and transcribe my poetry for me." Tessa grins at the memory, threading her fingers through mine under the table. "I wound up falling for him before I ever saw him."

"Ohhh, okay." Grayson nods. "So that's where the idea for Mabel's blindness came from." He turns to me with a stupid smirk to add, "And it looks like you have two legs, so I guess the similarities end there."

Tessa chokes on her cappuccino, but I just shrug and say, "I guess they must."

He doesn't need to know. It wouldn't change anything about this situation, after all. The stakes are the same.

For the next hour, I sit beside Tessa and try not to look bored. It's a challenge once she and Grayson start going back and forth over the tops of their computers, playing a volleyball match with words like *inciting incident* and *fatal flaws* and *alliteration* and *prose*. Hanging out on the sidelines of this discussion would be a lot easier if I were still in school and had some homework to busy myself with. But my work these days is all hands-on—instructing at the boxing gym and filling part-time day shifts as an apprentice at the *Chronicle*. There's no take-home work to keep myself busy when I've got nothing better to do. Which is great. Except for times like this, when I have nothing better to do.

So I write out a few training schedule ideas on my phone for a kids' boxing class I've been trying to convince Bruiser to start doing at the gym. I come up with a week's worth of drills easy enough for kids to handle without dying. After that, I watch UFC compilation videos on mute, analyzing the best knockouts—simultaneously listening to Tessa and Grayson debate over some aspect of his stupid book.

Between fighting matches, I steal glances upward. I watch the way Grayson looks at Tessa. To her, it might seem platonic and harmless. But as someone who has a similar weakness, I know exactly what that look means.

And let's just say the violence on my phone screen perfectly illustrates how I feel about it.

Over an hour later, the topic pivots to *Tessa's* book, and she starts debating a timeline issue. I'm zoned out for most of it, watching two Brazilian guys grapple each other bloody, until Tessa turns to *me* with a question out of the blue.

"Wes, would three weeks be too soon for Barnes's sutures to heal?"

"Uh, it depends on how many stitches he had. Was it AK or BK?"

"BK."

"So, not as big an incision," I conclude. "Yeah, he'd be healed up in three weeks, but he wouldn't be able to put much pressure on it for a few months."

When I glance up from my phone, I find Grayson staring with a bewildered expression, clueless as to why I'm a font of amputee wisdom.

It would be the easiest thing in the world to explain. But it's more fun to skirt around the truth and say, "I've got a friend who lost his legs."

Tessa grunts, going back to her laptop.

Grayson's eyebrows jump. "Really. Wait, is he… the runner?"

"The runner?"

"Yeah, I've seen this guy running sometimes—he has these prosthetic legs; they're like the ones you see in the Paralympics."

"Running blades," I supply, draining what's left of my now-cold coffee. "Yep, that's him."

Tessa cuts me a thorny look, like *Why are you lying to him?* But I just shrug and give her a smirk, pretending I don't know what she's so annoyed about.

The last thing in the world I want Grayson Rhodes to feel for me is *pity*. Blood-curdling fear and intimidation, maybe. But not pity.

So I let him think I'm buddies with the Paralympic runner whose face he apparently never looked at closely enough to recognize that he's sitting across from said runner right now.

Hey, it's not my fault the guy has bad facial recognition.

He and Tessa go back to talking about the highfalutin literary aspects of the story, excluding me from the conversation for a while. I eventually get up and clear the empty cups from the table, asking Tessa if she wants anything else to drink or eat. She shakes her head no and encourages *me* to get something if I want—or, she says, if I'd rather go somewhere else, I can feel free to do so.

Is she encouraging me to leave? Or just trying to be nice because she can tell I'm bored out of my mind? I insist that I'm fine and sit back down, checking the time on my phone. Four forty-five. I don't have to be at Bruiser's until six. Will there be any hope of dragging Tessa out of here before then?

I sigh under my breath, rocking my chair onto its back legs. Tessa stops typing, stands, and touches my shoulder. "Wes."

I glance up, and she jerks her head in the direction of the door. I ignore the burn of Grayson's gaze tracking me as I follow Tessa over to the entrance.

"Weston, I know you're bored," she says in a low voice. "Why don't you go? You have better things to do with your time."

"You're the one who invited me to come."

"I know, and I shouldn't have. I didn't think about how dull it would be for you—I'm sorry."

I shrug. "I don't mind. I like being with you, no matter what."

She crosses her arms over her chest. "Well, don't you have to get ready for work?"

"Not for another hour."

She looks disappointed to hear that. Her gaze pivots out the windows to the street.

"What's that face?" I take a step closer and put a hand on her shoulder. "You *want* me to leave, Tes, is that it?"

"I think that might be best."

Something tightens in the pit of my stomach when she says that. My hand lowers, retreating to my side. "You saying you'd rather be... *alone* with him?"

"That's not what I'm saying. Don't twist my words. We just have a lot of work to do, and I don't want you to—"

"Send me away now, and you know what that says to him." My voice drops to a gravelly rasp. "You know what he'll think, right?"

She doesn't know. She's clueless. But her blue eyes are smoldering with intensity as she looks up into my face.

"Why are you so jealous?"

I let out a grunt that's more like a scoff. "I'm not jealous. I don't have anything to be jealous of, Tessa. Do I?"

That question mark is the tip of a blade, and I know she feels the sharp edge of it.

"I can't believe you would say such a thing," she whispers. "You're being so… so—"

"Proprietorial?" I offer.

Her eyebrows lower into an icy frown. "Yes. And I wouldn't be like that about you with your friends."

"This is different. This is 'one-on-one time' with a guy who wants to—" I back up, finishing that sentence a different way. "A guy who likes you as *more* than a friend."

"So? Even if he does, that doesn't mean I like him back that way. I *don't*. You of all people should know that. I shouldn't have to *prove* it twenty-four seven."

I gently take her arm. "Tessa, I never said—"

"You don't own me, Wes." She jerks her arm out of my grasp, and that one little gesture hits me like a kick in the gut. "I really think you should go."

With that final word, she spins on her heel and marches back to the table to sit across from Grayson. My blood boils, pressure building in my veins until I can't take it anymore.

I want to punch someone. *Him.*

But instead, I thrust open the door of the coffee shop and charge down Main Street, passing my pickup truck—don't care. The boxing gym is only two blocks away, and I could use the cold bite of fresh air after that suffocating coffee shop.

It kills me to walk away, to leave Tessa there with *that guy.* All alone. Laughing at his stupid literary jokes.

Part of me wants to turn around, go back.

But she asked me to leave. She *told* me to leave.

She wanted me to leave.

Bruiser won't be at the gym yet, but I've earned the responsibility of carrying a spare key. It burns in my hand all the way there, and when I reach the entrance door, I let myself in. Lock it behind me. Turn on the lights, then the radio, volume full blast on some '90s rock station.

I don't care that I'm wearing jeans and street shoes. I set myself up in front of a heavy bag and start punching, punching, punching.

I punch until my hands bleed.

WHENEVER I SHOW UP AT MY MOM'S APARTMENT with grocery bags of ingredients and start making a mess of her kitchen, she always knows something has happened to set me off. She says the magnitude of the mess is a good indicator of how stressed I am. When baking calmly, I tidy as I go—sweeping up flour spills and washing dishes between uses. But tonight, I'm chaotic. Mixing bowls, wooden spoons, and measuring spoons crowd every inch of counter space, surrounding me in disorder.

I guess that means I'm pretty high on the "stressed" end of the baking spectrum. But it's not my fault. It's Weston's. He's the one who started this whole miserable muddle.

"Don't you think he was overreacting?" I ask Mom when she appears in the kitchen to show me an outfit option for her date with a work "friend" tonight—a gray turtleneck sweater and jeans with black boots. "I mean, he acted like I was doing something wrong with Grayson—something… inappropriate. I don't even know *what* he thought. He was so weird about it."

Mom sighs, gesturing towards her outfit. "Help?"

"Uh, do you have a black sweater? I think that would go better with the boots. Oh, and a houndstooth blazer on top would look cute."

Mom grunts. "I don't have fancy stuff like that, Tessa."

I shrug, turning back to my chocolate chip cookie dough as Mom disappears to search for a black sweater.

"Did you hear what I said about Weston?" I holler after her.

"Yeah," comes her muffled reply from the bedroom.

"And do you think I'm right?"

"I don't know."

I huff, swiping a handful of chocolate chips and tossing them into my mouth. Stress baking also includes stress binging on sugar, which is possibly not the healthiest way to expel negative emotions, but oh well.

"I just don't understand why Weston is so possessive of me all the time," I grumble, irritably stirring the cookie dough. "I didn't invite him to the coffee shop today because I wanted him to be all grumpy and alpha male towards Grayson."

"Alpha male?" Mom echoes, appearing in the kitchen doorway with a scrunched-up expression. "Is that some literary term?"

"No, it's just… like when a guy is all competitive towards another guy, trying to be the dominant one. You know? It smacks of patriarchal pontification." I swipe a bite of cookie dough from the bowl. *Mmm, perfection.*

"Pontification?" Mom chuckles, shaking her head at me. "I think it's kind of sweet that Weston wants to protect you all the time. Be your number one."

"He *is* my number one, but I don't need protection from

Grayson. He's harmless." I look her up and down. "I like that sweater. Looks much better with the boots."

"You think so? Doesn't make me look fat?"

"Oh my god, Mom. Stop." I pop another bite of cookie dough into my mouth. "*I'm* the one who's going to be fat if Weston keeps stressing me into baking cookies all the time."

Mom kisses my cheek, tugging at the waistband of my sweats. "I can lend you some stretchy pants."

I grunt a wry laugh, kissing her back. "I'm gonna need them. Have fun on your date."

"Thanks. I shouldn't be gone too long, but feel free to stay the night. And feel free to have Wes come over and keep you company." She winks at me in a way that makes me think "keep you company" is a euphemism for something else. "He can stay the night too, if he wants."

"Mom!"

"I'm just joking, sweetie." She whacks my arm playfully, grabbing her purse on her way to the door. "But seriously, you should invite him. Talk it out, make things right. You'll feel better."

"He's still working," I say, pointing at the clock, which reads five minutes to seven. "And I'm sure he'll be exhausted and hungry after his class finishes up."

"Even more of a reason to feed him cookies and give him kisses and a sensual massage." She bites back a grin. "I'm telling you, that is the best way to a man's heart."

"And I suppose that's not at all patriarchal."

Mom shakes her head, grabbing her car keys. "It's what alpha women do."

I laugh and blow her one last kiss goodbye. Once she leaves

and I'm alone in the silent apartment, I have time to ruminate on everything in a new light.

Maybe Mom is right. Maybe *I'm* the one who overreacted in the café earlier. I did, after all, drag Weston there with me—I didn't want him to feel left out, like I was prioritizing Grayson over him. I also wanted him to see proof with his own eyes that my relationship with Grayson is purely platonic. Perhaps it was unfair of me to invite Weston to come and then ask him to leave— perhaps I handled the whole thing badly.

The silence wears away at my conscience until finally, when the cookies are done and I've eaten way too many of them, I pick up my phone and send Weston a text.

TESSA:

Hey

I'm alone at my mom's place if you want to come over

I'd like to see you

It's only a few minutes after eight, which means his last class is just wrapping up. I wait on tenterhooks for his reply, the possibility that he might say *no, I'm too tired* making me anxious enough to devour another cookie.

Moments later, my phone buzzes with a new message.

WESTON:

I want to see you too

I'm going to shower first then I'll come over

That good?

I write back, *Sounds good.* A little while later, he's walking through the front door with messy damp hair and a bunch of pink carnations in his hands.

"Oh, Wes!" I fall on him with kisses, breathing in the sinfully good scent of him freshly showered; all lean muscle under the softness of his hoodie. "I'm sorry about earlier," I whisper against his chest, holding him tight.

He kisses the top of my head. "I'm sorry too."

"I baked you cookies."

"I brought you flowers."

I laugh, easing back to look up into his face. "I guess we both have different ways of relieving our stress."

Weston's grin is a crooked but adorable thing. "Well, buying flowers isn't much stress relief. I had to go punch things for three hours first." He holds up his bruised, blistered knuckles.

I click my tongue, breath catching when I see his poor, abused hands. The irony of it all strikes me as funny. "So you go split your knuckles open training like a beast… and meanwhile I gain ten pounds eating cookies."

Weston murmurs a husky laugh, sliding his free hand around my waist. "Ten extra pounds of you to cuddle with? Sounds good to me."

"Oh, stop." I blush, taking the flowers over to the kitchen to fetch a jar of water. Weston shadows me, snatching a cookie off the cooling tray on his way over.

"Bruiser *was* surprised to see me already sweating like a pig when he showed up for our first class."

I unwrap the carnations from their plastic sleeve and begin snipping them to the proper height. "I'm… sorry I made you angry. About Grayson."

"You didn't make me angry, Tessa. You never make me angry."

"Well, you seemed so…" I shrug, searching for the right word. "Annoyed. When you left."

Weston remains silent for a moment, leaning back against the counter as he watches me trim the carnations and arrange them in the mason jar.

"I wasn't annoyed with *you*," he says at last. "I was just… I was *annoyed* because I saw something I was afraid I'd see."

I cast him a questioning frown over my shoulder. "And what was that?"

"Grayson," he bites out the name, "looking at you like he wanted to…" He pauses, starting a different way. "Like if I wasn't there, if I didn't exist, he'd be taking the next step by this point."

"The next step?" I repeat, on the edge of a laugh. "And what is that next step?" The question is borderline rhetorical, but Weston answers it honestly, straight-faced.

"Kissing you. Making out with you. Getting his hands on you—alone, preferably in his dorm room."

"Oh my god, stop. That's not how he thinks about me."

"He's a guy. Okay? He's got XY chromosomes." Weston shoves off the counter, stepping closer to me. "Despite his coffee preference, he is full of testosterone, and you're a beautiful girl who discusses poetry and 'allegories' with him. No straight single guy is going to prefer to be *platonic friends* with you."

I plunk the last carnation into the jar and whirl to face him. "I could say the same about you."

Weston's eyebrows rise. "You think all the guys are after me?"

"No, I mean—" I sigh, shutting my eyes. "I could be suspicious and jealous every time I caught another girl checking *you* out. But I wouldn't be ready to attack her because I'd know that you're mine and she doesn't have a chance."

"Wait a minute, wait a minute." Weston points to himself. "*I'm* yours. But you're not mine. How does that work?"

"I didn't say I wasn't yours."

"Today in the café, you said, 'You don't own me.'"

"Well, you *don't* own me."

Weston groans, tipping his head back. "I don't *want* to own you—I just don't want some other guy thinking he can—"

"Can what? Spend time with me? Discuss books and ideas with me?"

"If only that was all he wanted."

I cross my arms over my chest. "I think that *is* all he wants. I think you're *inventing* everything else because you're secretly afraid I'll be unfaithful to you or something. And I have no idea why you would think that when I've never looked twice at anyone but you—"

"I don't think you're unfaithful, Tessa," he cuts in, softening his voice and gently resting his hands on my shoulders. "I just… I think you like this guy more than you want to admit. Even to yourself. And I know it's all platonic on your side, but on his… it's not. And I think you should just be hyperaware of that. Because some of the things you do…" He shrugs stiffly, like he's bracing himself for what comes next. "He could take it as encouragement."

My eyebrows arch. "Encouragement? You think… you think I've been flirting with him?"

"Not intentionally—"

"What have I done that's flirty?"

"Oh, I don't know," he returns with a hint of mockery.

"Being his critique partner, throwing your own book by the wayside so that you can work on *his* stupid book night and day, giving him all this feedback and ways to improve his story—"

"I've been helping him as a friend. I'd do the same for Shoshanna if *she* were my critique partner." I pivot back to the counter, sweeping the flower-stem clippings into the trash bin. "And I have *not* thrown my own book by the wayside to work on Grayson's. I've spent a lot of time working on my own writing."

"Yeah, well, you spend a lot of time working on *his*, too. And I just think you're selling yourself short."

"I'm not selling myself, period. I'm helping him out as a critique partner. That's all." My voice hardens as I turn to look at him through narrowed eyes. "It's one thing to be possessive of me, Wes. It's another thing entirely to forbid me from having any friends."

Weston lets out a sharp exhale that sounds more like a scoff. "I'm not forbidding you from having friends—I have friends. From school, from the boxing gym… But how would you feel if I hung out with this *one girl* from the gym all the time, went to coffee shops with her to 'talk about training' or stayed up late writing her emails, trying to help her do better? How would that make you feel, Tessa?"

I stiffen; the mere image is enough to turn my stomach. "It's not the same thing—"

"It *is* the same thing," Weston insists, lowering his voice and taking a step closer. "And if you would have a problem with *me* doing that, you should understand why I have a problem with *you* doing this thing with Grayson."

Righteous anger bubbles up in me, curling my fingers into fists. I feel my cheeks blazing hot, unformed words boiling on my tongue as I stare at him.

"You'd be jealous, too," Weston rasps, his eyes unraveling me with a single glance. "It's the same rule both ways, Tessa."

"No, it's *not* the same." My jaw clenches, voice wobbling as angry tears blur my vision. "It's different. Because if it were the other way around, I wouldn't doubt you for a minute. I wouldn't come over trying to educate you about how 'women look at you,' I wouldn't tell you to stop working with this girl because everything you did was some kind of coded flirtation—"

"I never said that, Tessa—"

"You don't trust me!" I burst out, pulling back when he reaches for me. "That's the truth, Weston—just say it. You're afraid that I'll fall for some other guy just because he's a writer, and he's more book-smart than you and quotes poetry—"

"I don't give a shit about any of that. It's not that I don't trust you—I don't trust *him*!"

"Well, I do."

My words hit Weston like a slap. He freezes, face going slack as understanding sinks in.

"I'm my own person, Wes. I won't be instructed by you—or anyone else—on whom I can and cannot be friends with." I cross my arms firmly over my chest, my voice pitching higher, thick with coming tears. "If you have a problem with that, then maybe I'm not the right girl for you."

A muscle in his jaw twitches, and he nods slowly, something icing over in his blue eyes. "And maybe I'm not the right *guy* for *you.*"

It sends a knife through my heart.

All I can do is watch as he strides back over to the front door and lets himself out. As soon as he's gone, I collapse against the counter with my face in my hands. Sobbing.

____

I LIFT MY BRUISED KNUCKLES TO DAD'S OFFICE DOOR and knock twice.

"Come," he says from the other side.

I let myself in, greeted by the familiar sight of my father sitting behind the big mahogany desk. Fingers hammering at the keyboard. Motivational quotes on the wall.

"What's up?" he asks without looking away from the computer screen.

"I just wanted to let you know that I checked with Marcus, and he said there's no additional comment from the board of trustees on the librarian dismissal story."

Dad glances up at me, his glasses slipping to the edge of his nose. "I'm surprised Marcus didn't tell me himself."

"I think he wants to make sure I get the full experience as an apprentice. He had me make him a Keurig, too. Apparently, that falls under the umbrella of 'administrative tasks.'"

Dad grunts. "Well, you can tell him I said that one day you'll be *his* boss—if you want to take my place here, that is. Probably not exciting enough for you." With a wry laugh, he leans back in his desk chair, studying me. "You got something you want to get off your chest?"

I'm not sure how he guessed—maybe because I barely slept last night and have the dark circles under my eyes to prove it. Or maybe because when I showed up at the *Chronicle* for work and he asked me how I was, I said, "Fine." Not "Never been better," like I always do.

The truth is, I have been better. A *lot* better. Even just two days ago, when I held Tessa in my arms and kissed her on the couch and she told me that she valued my opinion.

Apparently, none of that was true.

Her parting words to me last night eclipse every other thing she said. *Maybe I'm not the right girl for you.*

I sigh, shutting my eyes and rubbing the ache in my forehead. "Have you ever said something that pissed Mom off so much she… basically told you to go jump in a lake?"

Dad hums a tired laugh. "Once a week, at least."

I relent to a weak smile and slump defeatedly into the chair across from Dad's desk. "What do you do when she won't see something from your perspective?"

"Well." He steeples his hands, thinking about it. "First, after I cool off, I try to analyze the situation. See if there's something I missed. Try to see it from *her* perspective."

Her perspective. Just like that, I'm back in the café, watching Tessa and Grayson bouncing ideas off each other, her eyes full of excitement and new possibilities.

She trusts him. That's her perspective—she told me last

night. She thinks I'm inventing all this stuff because I'm secretly afraid of losing her.

Maybe some part of me *is* afraid of that. I mean, isn't that the primal fear behind jealousy? Losing what you've got to someone else? But this is so much more complicated than simple *jealousy*.

When I say nothing, Dad continues, "Marriage is an education, Wes. I've been married to your mom for nearly two decades now, and I swear I learn something new about her every day."

"I'm not married to Tessa," I mutter.

"No, but you've been with her for a few years. The two of you seem happy together. Any long-term relationship is a test of love. And if I've learned anything over the past two decades, it's that love is a choice. Sometimes not the easiest choice, but... a choice nonetheless."

"And what does that choice look like? If she doesn't agree with you, and you don't agree with her, and this *thing* is getting between you, pushing you apart?"

Dad slides his glasses off and folds them carefully in his hands. "Well, it's hard to say when I don't really know what this 'thing' is that's getting between you two—"

"Another guy."

Dad's gaze snaps up to mine. I can tell he wasn't expecting that.

"She doesn't like him like that," I quickly explain. "But he... likes her. I can tell. She thinks I'm overreacting. That's about the size of it."

"Well, in that case, I wouldn't let the grass grow under your feet."

"How do you mean?"

"There's a time to leave a woman alone, and a time to be

there for her. I'd say this case falls into the latter category." Dad levels a serious look at me. "If this other guy is trying to get close to Tessa, you don't want him to be there for her when you're not. You want to prove to her that you're constant—that you're always there, no matter what."

He's right. Even though I don't have a clue how I'm going to smooth things over on the whole Grayson issue, I know there's truth in what my dad is saying. I need to prove to Tessa that my love is constant—that it won't waver just because some literary latte-drinker in a blazer caught her attention.

I take a deep breath, leaning forward to rest my elbows on my knees. "What about the other guy? How do I get rid of him?"

Dad gives me a stern look. "Well, I wouldn't recommend violence."

"What makes you think I'd be violent?" I manage a wry smirk as I hold up my split knuckles.

"Don't worry about the other guy," Dad says. "Once he realizes he doesn't have a shot with Tessa, he'll drift out of her life without you having to do anything about it. If I were you, I'd trust Tessa to handle that side of things."

"And what if…" My voice dies in my throat, and I look down, squeezing my hand into a fist and then releasing it. I'm ashamed to finish the question—ashamed that there's still a twinge of self-doubt cowering in the pit of my stomach. "What if he *does* have a shot with her? What if she likes him way more than she'll admit, even to me? Even to herself?"

Dad contemplates for a minute before answering, "Then she was never the right girl for you."

It's like an uppercut to the chest, hearing Dad echo the same words Tessa threw in my face last night. I don't want to believe there's any truth in them, but it's impossible to ignore the way my stomach twists with dread at the thought of Tessa loving someone else.

It sparks a fear in me I've never experienced before. I hate how helpless I feel, facing an opponent I can't fight back against— not with words, not with fists, not with anything.

I rise to my feet, walking over to the window and looking out at the streets of Rockford. The sun is sinking low in the sky. Quarter past five, according to the wall clock. Tessa will be heading to her writing class soon. She'll get a ride from someone else tonight. Her mom, maybe.

Or Grayson.

The possibility is enough to make my hands coil into fists at my sides. The thought of her walking into class with him, laughing at private jokes with him, letting him open doors for her, flirt with her, be there for her when I'm not… it's enough to light a fuse inside me.

No. I will be there for her. Always.

"Hey, Dad?" I turn to look at him. "Would it be okay if I left now? I want to see if I can catch Tessa before her class starts."

He nods with an approving smile. "I think that's a good idea."

TESSA

MY HEART IS RACING AS I SHUT MOM'S PASSENGER door behind me and wave goodbye through the window. To prove that I'm *not* nervous about this, I turn and start walking purposefully down the campus path. But as soon as Mom's car is out of sight, I stop dead in my tracks.

I hate confrontation.

I tap my foot nervously on the leaf-scattered sidewalk as I stand frozen under the enormous oaks, mentally preparing myself for the conversation I'm about to have with Grayson.

I need to clear the air between us. I need to prove to Weston—and to myself—that his fears are unfounded.

Ever since our argument last night, I haven't been able to stop thinking about this conflict between us. I didn't mean it when I told Weston that maybe I wasn't the right girl for him—I *know* I'm the right girl for him, and he'll always be the right guy for me.

But can't he see I need to be free to make my own choices? I'm not as naïve and foolish as he thinks I am. And I'm about to prove it.

I've already planned a speech—of sorts. I'm going to tell Grayson the truth about Weston's suspicions, without beating around the bush. And as much as the mere idea of confrontation sends my heart flying into a panic, I know I have to do this. I have to be strong, independent. I don't need Weston to protect me.

Steeling myself with a deep breath of resolve, I march down the snaking walkway toward Avery Hall. The lampposts are shining, though twilight hasn't quite blanketed the sky in purple-blue. It's still bright enough to see a familiar, long-legged boy in glasses and a blazer come striding down the intersecting path towards me.

"Tessa!" He waves, his smile a flash of white in the indigo dusk. "Wait up!"

My heart flops. *No time like the present, I guess.*

"Hey, Grayson," I greet him with a wary smile. "I'm glad I caught you. I was hoping we'd... get a chance to talk alone before class."

Grayson's eyes light up with interest. "Oh? I've got time after class too, if you want to discuss our books more. You can come back to my dorm afterwards."

Perhaps that invitation would have struck me as benign and platonic before last night—but now all I can hear is Weston's voice echoing in my memory: *If I didn't exist, he'd be taking the next step... Getting his hands on you—alone, preferably in his dorm room.*

I shake my head, dispelling those ridiculous thoughts from my mind. "Uh, actually, this isn't about our books."

Grayson's steps slow over the pavement as we near the corner of an old brick building. We're a stone's throw from the lecture hall, where the windows are already seeping golden light, and I can see students filing through the front door. But if I don't get this conversation over with, it will be impossible to focus on anything else.

So I stop, turning to face Grayson. "Look, I… don't know how to say this. So I'm just going to say it. Okay?"

A little smirk twitches at his mouth as he slides his hands into his pockets. "Please do."

I reel in another slow, deep breath, glancing around to make sure we are truly, absolutely *alone* before I speak.

"You've been a really good friend to me, Gray. You've been so nice about my writing and such a helpful critique partner. I really value your feedback, and I've enjoyed our discussions about literature…"

That sounded smooth, I encourage myself. *Now for the hard part.*

"This is going to sound ridiculous, but… over the past week, my boyfriend, Weston, seems to think there's some sort of… romantic attraction between us. I know that probably sounds crazy, but—"

"You're asking if I'm falling for you?"

My gaze snaps up to his, breath catching in my throat. "Well… yeah, I guess I am."

Grayson's eyes roam over my face, his expression softening. After a moment of hesitation, he nods. "Yeah. I think I am."

The confirmation knocks the wind out of me. I stare at him, speechless.

"Don't look so surprised," he says. "Who wouldn't fall for you, Tessa? You're beautiful and intellectual and funny… You're the first girl I've ever met who truly *understands* me."

"Grayson—"

"I know there's… your boyfriend. But honestly, what do you

have in common with him? You and I are so similar. We read the same books; we like the same things. I could talk to you for hours and never get bored. Most girls think I'm freaky, they think my writing is weird and depressing, but you don't—you *get* me."

His confession rushes out so quickly and without warning, I can't make my voice work to reply. I'm dizzy, overwhelmed, frozen where I stand—unable to move even when Grayson steps closer and envelops my cold hands in his warm ones.

"Don't pretend you haven't felt it, too," he murmurs, his breath clouding in the chilly air. "There's some kind of… chemistry between us, Tessa. You light me up every time you walk in the room, every time I see a new email from you—"

"Grayson, please."

"I know—you feel bad because of Weston. Maybe he's the one who made you feel you shouldn't get close to me—"

"That's not… You don't understand—"

"I *do* understand," he insists, his voice a rough whisper as he reaches up to brush a strand of hair behind my ear, his hand lingering on my neck. "I understand you better than *he* ever could. And you understand me in a way no one ever has."

Before I can take my next breath to reply—

He's kissing me.

It happens in a heartbeat, so fast I don't have time to back away. His lips move over mine in a soft, lingering kiss before I lurch backwards.

"Grayson," I gasp, rattled to my core. The shock of someone else's mouth on mine is both startling and invasive. "I don't like you like that. There's… *nothing* between us except friendship. I thought that's what you were—my friend."

I try to take a step back, but his hands catch me by the waist, holding me where I am.

"Don't say that," Grayson rasps, something wounded in his eyes. "I know I'm more than just a friend to you. I knew what it meant yesterday when you sent your boyfriend away so you and I could be alone."

My stomach sinks, the choke of regret tightening around my throat. "No, Grayson—that wasn't what you thought it was. I don't… I don't want to hurt you. But you're deluding yourself. I love Weston. I *like* you, as a friend, but… that's it."

Grayson stares at me for a long moment, his hands still encircling my waist. The tiniest smile curves at the edges of his mouth, determination setting fire to the rejection in his eyes. "I don't believe you," he whispers. "I think you're just telling yourself that because you feel bad for your boyfriend—but you shouldn't."

He moves in to kiss me again, his fingers tightening around my waist as he pulls me closer. A surge of panic rises in my chest, and I reel backward, breaking away from his lips.

"Grayson, stop." My voice cracks, thick with tears, as my eyes well up. "You need to stop, okay? You need to leave."

"Leave?" That single word knocks the air out of his lungs. "You can't mean that, Tessa." He steps closer, putting his hands on my shoulders.

"I *do* mean it," I say firmly, squirming out of his grip. "Let go of me."

That's when I hear footsteps pounding over the pavement. A hand claps down on Grayson's shoulder, wrenching him away from me. I stumble backward in confusion.

And there stands Weston—murder in his eyes.

WESTON

I'M GOING TO KILL HIM.

That's the first thought that crosses my mind when I spot Grayson Rhodes kissing Tessa like he's got the right to.

It's getting dark, but not too dark to see her shove him back—breaking the kiss and trying to put space between them. Grayson, apparently, isn't the kind of guy who takes no for an answer. He moves in closer, putting his hands on her shoulders.

I break into a run, which is not the easiest thing to do in everyday prosthetic legs, but I don't care—I would crawl over broken glass with no legs at all to get to her.

Red-hot rage boils up inside me as I close the distance. I hear Tessa saying, "Let go of me," but Grayson doesn't move an inch—that is, until I grab him by the shoulders and jerk him backwards. Tessa's eyes widen; her cheeks are wet with tears. The sight of her crying is enough to make me go batshit.

Grayson puts his hands up in some pansy-ass plea of innocence. But I know what I just saw. And I'm not letting him off the hook that easily.

I punch him in the jaw, sending his glasses flying off his face. Good—I hope he can't see a damn thing without them. Anger courses through my veins as I catch his arm, twisting his wrist at an impossible angle and dropping him to his knees with a guttural cry of pain.

I've got his fingers—his whole career—in my hands. I want to break every one of them. I want him to be sorry for this for the rest of his pathetic life.

He flinches as he kneels there, his eyes wild with fear, as I push his tendons to the brink of snapping.

"Wes."

Tessa's voice pulls me out of my rage. I glance at her for a second, but she only shakes her head, something quiet and fierce in her eyes.

"Let him go."

I've made the point. Anything more would make her see me as a monster.

I wouldn't mind being a monster if I happened to be alone in a dark alley with Grayson Rhodes. But here, now, in front of Tessa—I can't lower myself to *his* level.

So I let him keep his fingers and his stupid writing career.

"Get out of my sight," I seethe through gritted teeth. "And stay the hell away from Tessa—got it?"

Grayson doesn't so much nod as *tremble*, scrambling backwards on his ass to put space between us. He crawls to his feet, grabs his glasses, and limps back down the path—possibly to go call the cops on me. I don't care.

All I care about is Tessa. As soon as that scumbag is out of sight, I rush to her.

"God, are you alright?"

She falls on me in tears, wrapping her arms around my neck and gasping into my chest. I hold her close, my knuckles still throbbing from decking Grayson in the jaw. He'll have a bruise for weeks. But he deserved worse.

"Shh, I'm here. You're safe." I whisper those words over and over again into her soft hair. And when she calms down enough to breathe and speak normally, I ease back to look her in the eyes. "Did he hurt you?"

She shakes her head. "No… I'm fine."

"Are you sure?"

"Yes… I'm just—so… so ashamed. I was so stupid. You were right—I was wrong. I'm sorry I didn't trust your judgment. I should've known you were warning me because you loved me…"

"You weren't stupid," I assure her softly, brushing the tears off her cheeks. "You just think the best of people. That's not a bad thing. Until you come across an asshole like that guy."

She sniffs, wiping her nose and looking up at me with her huge blue eyes filled with tears. "Thank you for being here for me, Wes."

I gently rest my forehead against hers. "I will *always* be here for you," I promise in a whisper. "But… I still think it might be a good idea to teach you how to throw a punch."

TESSA

Lieutenant William Barnes was the most beautiful man Mabel had ever seen. And she had seen many beautiful things before her sight deserted her, leaving her in a world of darkness. Perhaps, one day, she would see him again—if the optimistic doctors were right and her vision healed with time.

Until then, Mabel was determined to love him more than ever. The war had left them both with scars. They had both been broken, one way or another.

But her love for William would never break. Never fail.

"I can't believe you kept your wound a secret from me for so long," she said to him one evening as they sat in the garden together, side by side, soaking in the last rays of warmth the setting sun had to offer.

William's hand slipped effortlessly into hers. "Wounds heal, Mabel. Mine never shall... I'll never be quite the same as I was before."

Mabel laced her fingers through his and squeezed his hand. "The war has changed everyone. But you are the same man, inside. And that's the only thing that matters. We'll both learn how to laugh again—together." She reached up and found the smooth edge of his jaw, tipping his face towards hers.

Their kiss began featherlight and grew more passionate as he wound his fingers into her hair and she gripped his jacket's lapel. Across the garden, a robin sang her sunset song. And in that moment of perfection, it was like all the suffering that came before had never happened at all.

They still had each other. And they would never let go.

I'm not sure if the story is finished until I sit back and stare at that final line for a long moment—feeling a slow smile take over my face. It's the perfect scene to end on. And even though my imagination wants to explore what might happen next to these two characters I've slowly fallen in love with… this is all for now.

I type "the end" at the bottom of the document and hit save. It's bittersweet, seeing those final words. I don't want the story to be over, but there's a kindling fire of anticipation in my heart for all the *other* stories I'm bound to write.

"Hey." Weston's voice comes from behind the chair where I've parked myself with my laptop. I'm at his house today, dog-sitting Thor while the boys are at school and Weston's mom is running errands. It's been a quiet afternoon of writing with the sweet golden retriever snoozing at my feet. Weston has been infinitely patient, making an effort to not disturb me until this moment. Now he sneaks up to whisper into my hair, "Can I interrupt the creative genius?"

"Mm-hmm," I hum, shutting my laptop and tipping my head back to look up at him. "I just finished."

"Finished? The whole thing?"

"The whole thing."

Weston cheers and applauds, coming around the other side of my chair to whisk me to my feet and twirl me triumphantly. I burst out laughing at his huge reaction, and Thor thwacks his tail, spinning in circles as if joining in on the excitement.

"I can't wait to read it," Weston says. "I'm sure it's awesome."

"I'm looking forward to hearing what you think of it." I grin up at him. "There's a sappy kiss at the end."

He laughs, tipping his head back. "You've brainwashed me with all the Jane Austen movies. I can handle a little sappiness at this point."

I smack him on the arm. "Okay, why did you want to interrupt me, anyway? You look like you're… up to something."

"It's time for our lesson." Weston gives me a meaningful wink and takes my hand, leading me to the garage—Thor trailing after us like an eager spectator.

Weston stops beside the heavy bag swaying from the ceiling and turns down the volume on the radio, which is playing an '80s rock station.

"You were serious about this?"

Weston snatches a pair of boxing gloves from his gym bag and turns to give me a frown. "Of course I was serious. Everyone should know how to defend themselves. Plus, I've always wanted to see you in boxing gloves."

"Well, I guess it's not the most scandalous thing a guy could want to see me in."

Weston laughs and helps me into the gloves, fastening the Velcro straps around my wrists. "Now," he says, taking a step backwards and tapping his chest. "Hit me like you don't like me."

"What? I can't."

"You've gotta. Come on. Hit me."

I throw a feeble punch at Weston's chest. He doesn't flinch or even blink.

"Seriously?"

I strike him again, putting a little more force into it.

"I said hit me like *you don't like me*," Weston reminds me, impatience flaring in his eyes. "Or maybe I should say: hit me like I'm Grayson Rhodes."

That uncorks a bottle of leftover anger in me. The force of my punch makes Weston jolt backwards a little. A satisfied smile curves onto his face. "*That's* what I'm talking about. Again." He taps his chest.

"I don't want to just keep hitting *you*."

"Oh, I think I can take it. You hit like a girl."

I punch him again, so hard it forces him back a whole step.

"Ow!" He exaggerates a glare, rubbing his chest where I landed my jab. "What the hell…"

"I'm sorry—"

"Shh. Never be sorry for punching a guy who's asking for it." Weston steps in close, gently tucking a piece of hair behind my ear.

He kisses me softly, and I kiss him back, my hands moving up to his neck—but my bulky gloves only thump gracelessly against his head, making him laugh.

"I was right, by the way," he whispers against my forehead. "You look really badass in boxing gloves."

ADVENTURES IN CHAPERONING

A Westess Story

WESTON

____

MY BROTHER HENRY HAS ALWAYS BEEN THERE FOR ME. Even at times when I didn't *want* him to be there. That's just how it is with little brothers. Once you've got them, there's no getting rid of them—for better or for worse. Growing up together, we had a healthy mixture of both. Good times and bad times. All three of my brothers had an incredible knack for being a pain in the ass when they wanted to be, but still—I would have killed anyone who tried to hurt them.

We're all three years apart, but Henry was the one who showed up first and made me a big brother, so naturally, we wound up closer to each other than anyone else. There was a time when I felt like the center of Henry's solar system—wherever I went, he followed. It was like his entire world circled around what I did. And there was no better feeling than that: to be your little brother's hero.

It stayed that way even after I lost my legs. He was there when I pulled an idiotic skateboard trick to impress my friends and ended up hurting myself. He was there after the amputation, looking at me like he'd just watched Superman get run over by a bus. He was there when I almost fell down the stairs on my new prosthetic legs, and suddenly our roles were reversed—he was the one holding *me* up.

Maybe it was trauma bonding. Or maybe it was just plain old brotherhood. Either way, Henry has always been the better version of me. But I've never been jealous of him for getting better grades, winning Mom's favoritism, being unofficially crowned the "golden child" of the family. Honestly, I'm glad he's the favorite. Takes the pressure off me to be good all the time.

But being the golden child comes at a cost—the cost of Mom's Concern. I say "Concern" with a capital *C* because it's not the average concern you'd feel for an injured dog or an old lady who looks like she can't cross the street on her own. No, Mom's special brand of Concern for Henry goes beyond the borders of parenting and into the deadly quicksand of mollycoddling. He didn't used to mind it back when he was younger and mollycoddling had its benefits. The slightest runny nose and she'd let him stay home from school. The smallest scrape or bruise and she'd bandage him up. The first hint that he wanted something and she'd try to fulfill it—just to make him happy, because Henry rarely asked for anything.

There are some undeniable benefits to having a mom always there for you. Someone to wash your underwear. Cook your favorite foods. Give you birthday gifts and hugs and make you feel special.

There are also some undeniable downsides to having a mom always there for you. Like when she tells embarrassing stories about you in front of your friends. Or randomly knocks on the bathroom door to ask if you're okay in there. Or tries to stop you from doing anything potentially dangerous but absolutely necessary to maintain your reputation as a cool guy.

In some ways, I feel like I skipped the awkward transition from being Momma's little boy to being my own man. Maybe it was because I lost my legs right around that age and had no choice but to rely on my mother until I got back on my feet—literally. She held my hand in the hospital, read books to me in rehab, helped me take showers until I learned how to do that by myself.

I guess that's one bonus of going through something super traumatic—less traumatic things are suddenly not traumatic at all in comparison. The amputation forced me to grow up fast. Henry, on the other hand, still hasn't shaken his status as Momma's little boy.

And now that he's fifteen, I think the downfalls are starting to outweigh the benefits.

This becomes obvious to me one morning at the breakfast table when Henry asks me if I'd mind giving him a ride somewhere tomorrow night. He says it because he thinks Mom is out of earshot, flipping pancakes in the kitchen, but apparently, he hasn't learned one crucial thing about our mother: she has the hearing of an elephant—with hearing aids.

"Where do you need to go tomorrow night?" she calls from the kitchen.

Henry slumps in his chair, tipping his head back. "Just… to the movies. With a friend."

"What friend?"

He looks to me, an unmistakable plea from one red-blooded man to another. But I don't know who this friend is or why it has to be a secret from Mom. So I just shrug and mouth the word, "Lie."

Deception is always a surefire way to weasel your way out of an awkward conversation with the woman who raised you.

But Henry only scrunches his eyebrows and turns up his hands like his brain stalls at the mere idea of telling a lie. I step in to help him by answering his question.

"Yeah, sure. I'll give you a ride. No problem."

"What. Friend." Mom steps into the dining room, frying pan in one hand, spatula in the other. She's giving Henry the stare—the one that makes you feel like you're being held by the back of your shirt over a pool of quicksand.

The quicksand of mollycoddling.

Henry takes the honest way out, as usual. "Vivi Reynolds."

Across the table, Aiden bursts out laughing and jeers, "Oooh, Henry has a girlfriend!"

"Shut up," he snaps, throwing a balled-up napkin at Aiden as his face turns red.

Aiden volleys the napkin straight back and starts crunching up another one to use as ammunition. Mom usually shuts down any use of projectiles at the table, but right now she's hung up on the last thing Henry said.

"Vivi Reynolds? And who else is going with you two?"

Henry sighs, looking down at his plate. "Nobody. Just us."

"Better sit in the back of the theater," Aiden says with a laugh, "so nobody will have to watch you sucking each other's faces!"

I kick him under the table with my prosthetic foot.

"Ow!"

Mom flops pancakes onto our plates, passive-aggressive and silent. Henry watches her out of the corner of his eye, his face still flaming red from Aiden's jokes. No one says a word for a minute.

Then, finally, Mom speaks. "I don't know if it's proper for you to go out all alone with Vivi. How old is she?"

"Sixteen."

"Well, how did you two become so close? You've never mentioned her before."

Of course he didn't. A potentially romantic relationship with an older woman isn't exactly the kind of subject you chat about with your mother. Especially not at the breakfast table.

Henry shrugs and plays it cool. "You never asked."

"Well, why don't you tell me a little bit about her?"

I come to the rescue. "Mom, he's old enough to go on a date with a girl. It's just the movies. Who cares? Henry, pass the maple syrup."

Mom stands there for a moment with her frying pan, watching her baby boy transform into a mysterious stranger right before her eyes. Henry passes me the syrup and continues eating his pancakes, not looking at Mom.

I wonder if she can see how much he's dying inside, or if moms are immune to secondhand embarrassment.

"Alright," she relents with a sigh. "But I want you back home by eleven, alright?"

"Yes, Mom," Henry grumbles.

The conversation seems to be over. Case closed. But I can tell by the way Mom slides her gaze from Henry to me that she's not going to forget about it *that* easily.

———————————

Mom ambushes me in the garage that night as I'm doing rounds on the heavy bag. I'm covered in sweat, locked in the zone, '80s rock blasting so loud from the radio, I don't even hear her come in. I flurry the bag hard and fast as the song comes to an end—out of breath.

That's when Mom clears her throat. "Sorry to interrupt."

I spin to face her as I pull off my gloves. "Here to train with me?"

She laughs and rolls her eyes. "No."

"Come on, it's fun. I'll show you how to knock someone on their ass."

"Listen. I want to talk to you about something serious."

I wipe my sweaty forehead with the crook of my elbow. "Something serious? Sounds more like Henry's kinda thing."

"It's Henry I want to talk to you about," Mom says, instinctively tidying the workbench where Dad has left tools scattered around. "And I have a favor to ask of you."

Oh boy.

"Does this have to do with his date tomorrow night?"

Mom puts up one finger. "Don't—don't give me that face. I'm not being overprotective."

"Yeah, you are."

"I'm just concerned about him."

Concerned. With a capital *C*.

"How come he's never talked about this girl before?" Mom frowns, crossing her arms over her chest. "For all I know, she could be…"

I wait for the punchline, eyebrows raised. "What? A prostitute?"

Mom clicks her tongue. "Weston—"

"A drug addict? A stabber? What do you think is gonna

happen, Mom? They're going to the movies together. Big deal."

"It *is* a big deal. This is *Henry*. He's never shown an interest in girls before."

I smirk, throwing light punches at the heavy bag. "Not that he's talked about, anyway."

Just like that, Mom's Concern doubles in size.

"Look, he's fifteen years old, Mom. Give him some room to breathe. You never worried about *me* going out with girls."

"Yes, well, Henry's not like you."

"Because he has all his limbs intact?"

Mom sighs, giving me a look like *that's not what I meant and you know it.* "Because he keeps everything to himself. Unlike you, I don't know what's going on in that head of his. And don't you think he was acting a little strange about this Vivi girl when I asked him about her this morning?"

"I think he was dying of embarrassment and didn't want to talk about any girl he has a crush on." I shrug, rolling the ache out of my shoulders. "It doesn't mean she's a seductress or something. There are just certain things a guy doesn't want to talk about with his mom."

I watch this painful realization slowly sink in, darkening my mother's eyes. It's times like these when I know exactly what she's wishing: that she had four daughters instead of four sons. It seems like the older girls get, the more they spill their guts to their mothers—if Tessa is any indicator of female behavior. Men, on the other hand, need their space. The social distancing begins at birth and just gains momentum as the years go on.

Henry is slipping out of bounds, and Mom isn't ready to let go. But there's nothing I can do about it, so I just shrug and put my boxing gloves back on.

"In that case, I need to ask a favor of you."

Apparently, I spoke too soon. There *is* something I can do about it. And that something looks like a bad idea glinting in Mom's eyes.

"What kind of favor?" I ask, bracing myself for the answer.

"Well, you said you'd give Henry a ride tomorrow night," she begins slowly, crossing her arms over her chest. "I was wondering if maybe you could just… keep an eye on him."

"You mean… *chaperone* him?"

"No, obviously not. He wouldn't need to know you're there. I thought you could take Tessa out, and just… happen to go to the same places Henry takes this new girl of his."

"You mean… *stalk* him."

Mom sighs, tipping her head back. "No. It wouldn't be stalking for you to wind up in the same restaurant or movie theater, close enough that you can see what he's doing."

"That is the literal definition of stalking, Mom."

"Oh, stop it. He's your brother. Aren't you concerned about him?"

"Concerned?" I almost laugh at the second appearance of that word. "No, I think if I were him, I wouldn't want my big brother stalking me or chaperoning me or 'keeping an eye on me' on my first real date with a girl I liked. Can you even imagine how humiliating that would be?"

"He wouldn't be humiliated if he didn't know you were there."

I shake my head, throwing combos at the heavy bag. "I can't do it, Mom."

"Then I will."

I whirl to face her. "No. No, no, no, you can't—"

"I'm not going to stand by and let him go off alone with some older girl I've never even met before. Who knows what they might get up to. Who knows if they're really going to go to the movies or if that's just an excuse."

I'm not even the one being chaperoned/stalked, and it makes me cringe to imagine it: Mom hovering just out of sight, spying on Henry's every move—sitting at the back of the theater or in the margins of a restaurant. It's not just embarrassing. It's… emasculating.

But there's no way to explain that to Mom, who still sees Henry as her little baby. So instead, I do the only thing I can think of to save my brother's manliness.

I lie.

"On second thought, I think I should… do it."

Mom tilts her head to the side, suspicious of my tone. She has a nose for bullshit—especially mine. "Are you sure? You're not just saying that to make me feel better?"

"No, I will. I'll do it. I'll take Tessa out on a date, and we'll just… *happen* to go to the same places Henry goes. And we'll stay out of sight, and I'll make sure he doesn't get into any trouble with this girl, okay? You don't have to worry about any of it." I tag a convincing smile onto the end of my pledge to soften her up.

Sure enough, it works. Her shoulders relax, and her eyes brighten. "Thank you, Weston. I know I might seem overprotective, but… I regret not being more protective of my boys in the past."

I know exactly what she's thinking when she says that.

"Past is in the past, Mom. You couldn't have stopped me from doing dumb shit when I was younger. In fact, I probably would've wanted to do it more if you'd told me not to."

She laughs a little, but there's a glint of tears in her eyes as she walks over and hugs me.

"I love you," she whispers, her voice all watery—which makes me feel bad for lying about stalking Henry on his date. But I make it up to her by kissing the top of her head and patting her back with one boxing glove.

"Henry will be fine, Mom. I promise."

———————

The following morning, I give Henry a ride to school. I can tell something is eating him by the sheer number of times he sighs and messes his hands through his hair. With anyone else, I'd wait for them to speak first. But my brother is the type who will keep everything bottled up if nobody comes out and formally invites him to get it off his chest.

So about halfway to school, I break out the trusty bottle opener.

"Go on, spill it."

Henry turns to squint at me. "Spill what?"

"Whatever's been making you sigh and fidget for the past half hour."

"We've only been driving for ten minutes."

"Is it about Vivi?"

Henry slumps in his seat defeatedly. "It's about Mom. Don't you think she's kind of... overreacting?"

If only he knew about the deluxe version of her Overreaction that I listened to in the garage last night.

"Yeah, well, you know Mom. She's always worried about everything."

"But she's not like that with you," Henry volleys back. "You and Tessa get to go out wherever you want, whenever you want, and she never tries to stop you."

I shrug. "That's just because I'm the oldest. And she knows I'm a lost cause. You're her favorite."

"I don't *want* to be her favorite. Not if she's gonna treat me like a baby."

Ah, the universal struggle of boys on the cusp of manhood and mothers on the cusp of losing their boys to manhood. The last thing I want is to be caught in the middle. In fact, I think I'd rather be caught in the middle of a dodgeball court. Without my prosthetic legs on.

"Look, Henry, Mom will always be Mom. You just gotta tell her what she wants to hear, make her happy, and then go do whatever you want. Within reason, obviously. Don't go jumping off a bridge after Vivi or something."

Henry rolls his eyes. "You'd do something dumb like that before I would."

He's right—I thought as much myself last night in the garage. Out of all four of us, Henry is the boy most likely to succeed and make his mother proud. I don't know where all this suspicion and Concern is coming from all of a sudden. Some of us are born to get in trouble; others are not. Clearly, I belong to the former category. But Henry is about as squeaky clean as a bottle of hand sanitizer dipped in bleach. He wouldn't get into trouble if it held a gun to his head and demanded he surrender himself to it. He'd sooner be shot.

And that's why, tonight, Tessa and I will not be stalking my little brother on his first date with Vivi. We'll go somewhere totally different, stay out just as late, and I'll come back home with

Henry at eleven o'clock, and Mom will rest easy thinking that her favorite son's innocence hasn't been lost.

"So," I say, rapping my fingers on the steering wheel, "where are you taking Vivi?"

"To the movies," he replies. "Maybe we'll go out for pizza first. I don't know."

"What movie are you going to see?"

"The new *Star Wars* one."

I nod, slowing for a stop sign and noticing how Henry is *still* fidgeting relentlessly even after spilling his guts about Mom. Something else is eating him. The bottle isn't empty yet.

This time, I wait. And after a minute, he can't keep it in any longer.

"Wes?"

"Yeah?"

He messes up his hair again. "Well, I was just wondering… how do you…" The rest of the sentence gets stuck in his throat, and he sighs. "Never mind."

"Come on, what is it? You can ask me anything, man."

Apparently, it's the kind of question that makes your face turn red just thinking about it. Henry struggles to put it into words.

"How do you… kiss a girl?"

I bite back a laugh as I turn to look at him. "You've never kissed her?"

Henry shrugs. "I mean, we've *kissed*, but we haven't… you know."

"Made out," I supply.

"It's not that I want to *make out* with her," Henry says defensively. "It's just, I want to… y'know…"

"Make out with her."

My brother heaves a sigh, crossing his arms over his chest. "Well, it's just that I know she's dated older guys, and I want to be able to… do it right. Like, how do you know if a girl wants to make out with you?"

"Uh…" I laugh, caught off guard by the bluntness of his question. "I don't know. You just kind of… read the terrain."

"What's the terrain? Her body?"

I shrug one shoulder. "Yeah, I guess. Sort of. If she starts leaning into you, putting her hands on you… it's a sign that you can keep going."

Henry nods eagerly, looking about ready to start taking notes. "And after that? Like, how do you know you're kissing good? What do you do with your tongue? Do you breathe through your nose or your mouth?"

I grin. "Believe me, once you're kissing her, you're not going to be thinking about whether you should breathe through your nose or your mouth."

I immediately think of Tessa—and how good it feels every time she melts into my arms, her lips moving under mine and her fingers curling through my hair. I usually let her take the lead, and sometimes she surprises me with a love scratch on the neck or a gentle bite on my lower lip. God, I wish I could drive to her house and make out with her right now.

"And what happens after that?" Henry asks, pulling me out of my thoughts.

"After what?"

"Kissing. I mean, that's just first base, right?"

"Well, when I was *your* age, first base was holding hands."

Henry scoffs, crossing his arms over his chest. "If you don't know, then forget it."

"Of course I know." I flex my fingers around the steering wheel, playing it cool. "After *that*, you… start touching her. Not in a creepy way, but like… playing with her hair. Holding her waist. Pulling her closer and seeing how she reacts. If she doesn't push you away, you're good. If she crawls into your lap, then you're *really* good."

"Uh-huh. And after that?"

There is no "after that"—at least, not for me and Tessa.

There's a line in the sand we just don't cross, because she has strict boundaries, and I have nothing but respect for those boundaries, even though I'd have zero complaints if they disappeared tomorrow.

But what do you tell your little brother when he's looking to you as the fount of all carnal knowledge and it's becoming obvious that he's way more of a red-blooded ladies' man than you are?

"Uh, well." I clear my throat, turning into the school parking lot. "What comes after that probably isn't a card you wanna play on the first date. You've gotta give a girl something to look forward to, you know?"

Henry smirks. "Yeah. Yeah, I know what you mean. Leave them hungry for more."

"Exactly." I nod smoothly. "You just have to follow her lead." But in the back of my mind, I'm thinking, *Hungry for more? Jeez.* Maybe Mom has good reason to be concerned about her precious baby boy. Maybe he's not as innocent as we all think he is.

I pull up to the entrance of the high school and drop Henry off, giving him finger guns as we part ways.

It's not until I pull out of the parking lot that it hits me:

Did I just seal my brother's fate? Did I just give him terrible advice and let him loose on Vivi Reynolds? Now, if he *does* get into some kind of trouble, and I'm not there to watch out for him, Mom will hold *me* responsible for giving him bad advice.

Damn it.

There's only one way to save my skin. I'll have to stick to the promise I made Mom last night. As much as it pains me to stalk my brother and possibly mortify him for the rest of his life, it'll be easier than facing the consequences of being the big brother who corrupted him.

I slide my phone out of my pocket and punch in Tessa's number. She answers on the second ring, her sweet voice filling my ear.

"Hey, sunshine."

"Hey, beautiful. Want to go out tonight?"

TESSA

IT DOESN'T TAKE MUCH TO MAKE ME SAY YES TO a surprise date with Weston Ludovico. Any time of day, any day of the year, I'm his. It doesn't matter if the date consists of a romantic dinner out or playing ultimate Frisbee with his brothers or cuddling and watching a movie at home, which usually ends in the two of us falling asleep on the couch together.

Over the past year, I've learned a lot about love. How it doesn't need to be packaged in fancy paper and a bow. Real love is perennial—it blooms in any kind of weather. That's how I feel about Weston. He is the sunlight of my life. So when he calls me randomly to ask me out and tells me where we're going is a surprise, I don't press him for answers. I just ask him how I should dress (since his interests range wildly in variety, from rock-climbing to shark-diving). He says, "Like you usually dress." Which isn't exactly helpful. In the end, I decide that a pair of jeans and a cashmere sweater are appropriate for almost any setting.

When Weston picks me up at seven, I'm relieved to see him wearing jeans too.

"So, where are we going?" I ask, too curious to hold back any longer. "Hopefully somewhere to eat, because I'm starving."

Weston nods, lacing his fingers through mine over the center console. "I thought we'd go out for pizza first."

"Pizza?" I volley back the word with raised eyebrows. Not that I have anything *against* pizza; it's just that we haven't followed our typical protocol for deciding where to eat. Usually, Weston asks me where I want to eat, I tell him I don't know, then he says *he* already has reservations somewhere (though he never actually does) and tells me I have three guesses as to which restaurant that may be. One of those three options always ends up being the place we go to eat.

It's safe to say Weston has cracked a code I didn't even know I had.

But tonight, he puts me through no such inquisition. He simply declares he wants pizza, and the topic is closed.

"Okay," I say with an easy shrug. "Pizza's fine with me."

"Good."

I tilt my head, studying his profile with a quizzical smirk. "Is everything alright?"

"Yeah." He nods quickly, squeezing my hand. "Yeah, everything's great. How was your day?"

We make pleasant small talk about our respective days for the rest of the drive, until at last Weston parks the truck outside the pizza place, and we head inside, hand in hand. Weston stops short as soon as we walk in the door, scanning the restaurant as if he's looking for someone.

It's the sort of place where you seat yourself. Usually, at moments like these, Weston's standard operating procedure is to turn to me and ask where I prefer to sit. But tonight, he simply takes my hand and leads me over to a booth at the far corner of the restaurant.

"This okay?"

I nod and slide onto the bench seat across from him. He immediately snatches a menu from the table and holds it up in front of his face. I glance over my shoulder, scanning the pizza place, but nothing looks amiss.

Leaning across the table, I hook one finger over the top of Weston's menu and pull it down to look him in the eyes. "You're acting increasingly suspicious, Wes."

He forks one hand through his tousled blond hair. "What do you mean?"

"I mean all of this. You choosing where we eat, choosing where we sit, looking around like someone's going to catch you doing something wrong—"

"Look, if you didn't want pizza, you should've said something—"

"It's not that I don't want pizza. I'm fine with pizza. I just—"

"Heyyyyy, my name's Charlene. I'll be your server tonight." A waitress in a checkered apron stops beside our table, chewing gum impatiently. "Can I get you guys started with something to drink?"

I order an unsweetened iced tea. Weston orders a Coke. As soon as the waitress walks away, I tell him that he shouldn't drink Coke—it's full of sugar.

"You only live once," comes his usual answer. Then up goes the menu once more, hiding his face from public view.

"Okay, what is going on?" I demand, crossing my arms over my chest.

"I'm... reading the menu."

"You've been here hundreds of times. You know everything on that menu, and it doesn't even matter what's on the menu because you know we're going to order one large cheese pizza, half with spinach and feta for me, half with bacon and pineapple for you." I snatch the menu out of his hand, stealing his security blanket and making his blue eyes flare in a way that is both frustrating and incredibly cute.

"Tessa—"

"What. Is going. On. Who are you hiding from?" I turn to glance over my shoulder again, scanning the occupants of the restaurant.

"Don't look," Weston hisses, nudging my foot under the table.

But it's too late. I've already seen the person in question.

"Henry?" I turn back to Weston with a puzzled frown. "It's your brother, Wes."

"I know it's my brother. Don't let him see you."

"Why?"

Weston sighs, slumping forward on the table and shielding the side of his face with one hand. "I don't want him to know I'm here."

"You mean…" I narrow my eyes, piecing it together. "This isn't a coincidence."

Weston shuts his eyes defeatedly. Busted.

Despite his warnings, I look again. Henry is sitting across from a pretty girl with long brown hair wearing a magenta miniskirt, fishnet tights, and combat boots. I can't tell if it's just the edgy outfit, but she looks a bit older than Henry—though I suppose his string-bean height makes up for any age gap between them.

They appear to be halfway through a pizza and struggling with awkward first-date chat. Henry keeps drying his hands on the napkin in his lap, and the girl keeps fidgeting with her fishnets under the table.

"Okay, that's enough," Weston grumbles, reaching over to tip my chin back towards him. "They're gonna see you watching them."

I shake my head, fighting back a grin. "I don't get it. Why did you decide to come here if you don't want Henry to see you?"

Weston takes a deep breath, about to give me the answer, when—

"Here's the Coke, and here's the iced tea." Charlene the waitress slides two frosty glasses onto the table. "Have we made up our minds?"

I order for us—the usual pizza we always order. When Charlene walks away, I rap my fingers on the table and stare Weston down, waiting for an explanation. He chugs his Coke to avoid talking until I finally reach across the table and take it away from him.

"Tell me what's going on, or I'm not giving this back."

Faced with these dire consequences, Weston finally comes clean. "Alright, fine. My mom asked me if I'd keep an eye on Henry. This is the first time he's ever really taken a girl out on his own, and she's… I don't know. Worried he'll get into trouble."

"So you're stalking him."

"I'm not *stalking* him. Just… keeping an eye on him. And I don't want him to *know* I'm keeping an eye on him."

"That's literally the definition of stalking, Wes."

He lets out a dry laugh, dropping his face into his hands. "I know."

I frown, taking a cautious sip of the Coke and shuddering as I set it back down. "That's... kind of invasive, don't you think? Poor Henry. He's such a sweetheart—he won't get into any trouble with this girl."

"Yeah, well, that's what I thought," Weston agrees. "But Mom was going to stalk him *herself* if I didn't do it, so I told her I would. It was kind of a lie at the time because I was planning on just dropping Henry off and going somewhere else with you. But then he started asking me all these questions this morning, on the ride to school."

I narrow my eyes. "What kind of questions?"

Weston stifles a grin, sitting back smugly in his seat. "Y'know, just... guy stuff."

"Okay, in that case, I don't *want* to know."

"It wasn't anything that bad," Weston clarifies. "But I may or may not have... given him more advice than I should've."

My eyebrows jump. "Weston!"

"What? I'm his brother, not his dad. Why shouldn't he live a little? Mom's always breathing down his neck, treating him like a baby. He's tired of it. A man needs some space, okay?"

"A man?" I toss the word back at him. "He's fifteen, Wes."

Weston rolls his eyes, about to retort, but I cut him off.

"And why are you stalking him if you're not worried about him too?"

"Because," Weston lowers his voice, leaning closer, "if he *does* get into some kind of trouble with Vivi, I'll be the one who gets blamed."

"For corrupting him?"

"Corruption is... a strong word." Weston tips his head noncommittally. "I'd say more like... giving him ideas."

"Somehow, that sounds worse."

"Look. All we have to do is follow him around and stay out of sight. Supposedly he's going to the movies with her afterwards, to see the new *Star Wars*. So we'll follow them there and keep an eye out. Mom wants him back home by eleven, so it's not like much can happen before then, right?"

I arch one eyebrow pointedly. "Depends on how many *ideas* you gave him."

Weston sighs wearily, about done debating this topic with me. After a moment of contemplation, I decide to go easy on him. Whatever his reasons, it's sweet of him to be concerned about his little brother. Even if the primary motivation is to avoid a tongue-lashing from his mother.

Perhaps it *is* invasive to stalk poor Henry on his very first date with a girl he likes. But Weston's mother has a point—it can't hurt to be too careful.

"Alright, fine," I relent at last. "I'll help you keep an eye on him. Are you sure he said he was going to see *Star Wars*?"

Weston nods.

I groan, tipping my head back. "I hate *Star Wars*."

"I know." He smirks, fidgeting with his straw wrapper. "But we don't have to *watch* it the whole time... We could do other things."

I roll my eyes, about to shut down his naughty insinuations, when—

"Hey, Wes."

We both freeze and turn to look at Henry, who is suddenly right beside our table with his arms crossed over his chest and a suspicious look on his face.

Oh dear.

"Henry… Hey." Weston laughs easily, leaning back in the booth seat. "What are the chances of this?"

Henry doesn't buy his brother's casual smile. "Are you following me?"

"What? No."

"No, of course not," I add with a shake of my head. "In fact, Weston didn't even want to come here because he didn't want you to feel awkward if you saw us. But I was really craving pizza, so he finally gave in."

Weston nods in agreement, nudging my foot gently under the table in a way that says *thank you*.

"Oh." Henry lowers his defenses, hands retreating to his pockets. "So what are you guys doing after this?"

"Uh, we were thinking of going to the—"

"Skating rink," Weston cuts in before the words *movie theater* can slip off my tongue.

Henry's eyebrows scrunch with confusion. "Skating? Since when do you skate?"

Weston shrugs. "Since… today. Tessa likes it, and I've never tried it, so…"

"You're gonna fall on your ass so many times, man." Henry shakes his head, looking amused by the prospect.

"Falling on my ass is one of my specialties," Weston returns smugly, toasting Henry with his glass of Coke.

I just roll my eyes and smile indulgently. The charade seems to work, because moments later Henry says, "Well, you guys have fun. See you later, Wes."

"See ya."

With that, Henry returns to his table and his waiting girlfriend. Weston lets out a sigh as soon as he's out of earshot.

"Told you not to look over at them."

My mouth drops open. "Are you blaming me for getting us caught?"

"Well, you could've been a little more covert about it—"

"And you could've chosen to sit somewhere that wasn't so visible."

"Where else could we have sat?" Weston volleys back. "This place is tiny. There's no way we could've stayed completely out of sight. Unless we ate in the parking lot."

I sip my iced tea with righteous indignation. "You're welcome, by the way. For covering up your reasons for coming here."

"Thank you," Weston says, a bit too late. "And *you're* welcome for making up the story about going ice skating. Were you seriously going to tell him we were going to the movies?"

"I wasn't going to say *Star Wars*."

"Doesn't matter." Weston shakes his head. "He would've known. He still thinks I'm up to something; I can tell."

I lift my eyebrows. "Oh? I guess you need to be more *covert*, then."

WESTON

TESSA IS ALWAYS MORE BEAUTIFUL WHEN SHE'S PISSED off at me. As a matter of fact, I think that's how I fell in love with her in the first place. There's nothing like the righteous fury of a pretty girl to knock you off your (proverbial) feet and make you forget you ever had any other goals in life except to make her smile.

Tessa has that glint of holy hellfire in her eyes right now as she sits across from me in the pizza place. We've dropped the subject of Henry, but she keeps stealing glances over at him and Vivi, and I keep kicking her foot under the table to make her stop.

By the time *our* pizza arrives, Henry is already paying his tab, and Vivi is sneaking off for a pre-departure restroom break.

"Damn it, they're gonna leave," I mutter, tearing off a slice and devouring half of it in a single bite. "Hurry—we have to eat this fast so we can keep following them."

Tessa rolls her eyes. "Don't you think that'll look a little suspicious? Us inhaling this pizza and chasing after them?"

I shrug. She has a point, I guess. Not that I would have a

problem winning a pizza-eating contest against Tessa. But judging by the speed at which she takes her first bite, I can tell she wouldn't be much competition. She's too sophisticated for stuff like that.

"Besides," she adds, sipping her iced tea, "you already said Henry's taking Vivi to the movies. So we know exactly where they'll be."

I grunt. "*Supposedly*. But maybe Mom's right—maybe that was just an excuse. Maybe they're going to do something else."

"Like what?"

"I don't know, like…" So many different ways to finish that sentence, all of which would make Tessa cringe. My suspicions are confirmed when I risk a glance at Henry and catch him checking Vivi out as she strides back to their table, all long legs and combat boots. Those fishnet tights don't leave much to the imagination— and by the way my little brother is looking at her, I can tell his imagination is running wild.

Not that I can blame him—my own imagination runs wild sometimes, with Tessa. It can't be helped. Especially in the summer when she's wearing a swimsuit and slathering sunscreen over her smooth, bare legs. Or when she stretches and her shirt rides up her waist, flashing a pair of freckles just above her bellybutton. Once I tried to kiss those freckles and got a savage whack in the head.

"Look it up on your phone."

I turn back to Tessa. "Look what up?"

"The time the movie starts. Duh."

"Oh." I pull my phone out of my pocket and pull up the showtimes at the Rockford Cinema. "*Star Wars* starts at eight o'clock."

"And right now it's seven thirty," Tessa adds. "No doubt

they're heading to the theater next, and we'll catch up with them. I don't care if we miss half the movie, do you?"

I sigh, reaching for another slice of pizza. "That's not the point. As soon as he walks out that door, I won't know *where* he's going."

"Oh, stop it." Tessa drops her unwanted crust onto my plate. "Henry's a good boy. He won't get into any trouble with Vivi. He probably won't even work up the courage to kiss her."

I grunt. "You wanna bet?"

"Sure. How much?"

My eyebrows jump. I wasn't expecting her to take the offer seriously, but hell—why not? A wager always makes babysitting more fun. "How about… winner gets to choose the next place we go on a date. And it can be something the other person hates."

Tessa takes a passive-aggressive bite of her pizza. "That's not fair."

"Why not?"

"Because I hate more things than you do."

I laugh, shaking my head. "Well, maybe you just need to broaden your horizons."

She narrows her eyes in a glare. "I won't need to. Because I'm sure Henry will have a perfectly G-rated date and I'll win this bet."

I cut another glance across the pizza place and see Henry take Vivi's hand as they walk out together.

"My money's on PG-14."

———————

By the time we finish eating and pay the tab, it's eight o'clock. Time is running out. We get back into my truck and drive to the cinema, and the whole way there, Tessa keeps telling me, "Slow down. We won't get there any faster if you get pulled over for speeding."

It takes a few laps around the parking lot to find an empty space, but we finally manage to grab one and ditch the truck. Tessa laughs as we dash across the parking lot, her breath clouding in the cold.

Once inside, we walk up to the ticket kiosk and ask for two tickets to *Star Wars*. The lady behind the plexiglass looks puzzled.

"That showing started twenty minutes ago," she tells us. "There's another one starting at nine—"

"That's okay. We like walking in halfway through a movie," I tell her with an irresistible smile. "Besides, my girlfriend hates *Star Wars*."

Tessa elbows me in the side, but she's grinning. The lady takes my money and slips me two tickets. I hand one to Tessa and say, "Candy?"

"We just ate."

"How come you always say that? It's not like candy is a *meal*."

She rolls her beautiful eyes and goes along, following me to the concessions and criticizing all my choices. It's one of the many ways I know to hack her brain. If I pick out some type of candy she hates, she'll always step in and override my decision, choosing some type of candy *she* likes. It's science.

After I've emptied my wallet on concessions, we go hunt down the screen playing *Star Wars*. Even outside the door, I can feel the rumbling sound effects of exploding spaceships. I stop Tessa before she can enter the theater.

"Remember, we don't want them to see us. So keep your

head down when you walk in and don't look at anyone until we get to the back row. Okay?"

Tessa tilts her head. "And what if Henry and Vivi are sitting in the back row?"

"Then we're screwed."

She laughs, shoulders open the door, and we walk down the long, dark hallway into the theater. I keep my head down and my arm hooked through Tessa's as I climb the low-lit stairs. Luckily, I don't trip and fall on my face.

When we reach the back row, I dare to look up—and thankfully, Henry isn't among the wallflowers hiding up here in the nosebleeds. I let out a relieved sigh and sink into a seat beside Tessa.

There's an intergalactic battle unfolding onscreen, explosions thundering through the surround sound, but I'm not paying attention to the movie. I'm busy scanning the audience in front of us, looking for two silhouettes that look like my brother and his girlfriend.

"Do you see them?" I ask, leaning close to Tessa's ear and getting a whiff of her incredible-smelling shampoo.

She shakes her head, blue eyes sparkling as they scan the theater. I do my own search and immediately freeze when my gaze lands on a couple towards the front. The guy is about the right height to be Henry, and though I can't see the girl very well, she seems to have a lot of hair, just like Vivi.

More to the point: they're making out.

I lean over to tell Tessa, "I think I see them," at the exact same moment she leans over to tell me, "I think I see them."

We both laugh; then Tessa points discreetly at a couple seated five rows ahead of us on the end. Not the same slobbery couple *I* was spying on a few seconds ago. These two are just sitting stoically side by side, watching the movie like they're genuinely interested in seeing which spaceship is left standing by the end of this scene.

"That's not them," I argue, gesturing toward the kissing couple—who have sunk even lower in their seats now, still lip-locked as CGI gunfire flashes over their heads. "*That's* them."

Tessa wrinkles her nose in disbelief. "That guy is too big to be Henry. Look at his shoulders."

"You think I don't know my own brother when I see him?"

"No, you obviously don't." Tessa reaches into the paper bag in my lap and pulls out a package of KitKats, tearing it open. "Besides, they wouldn't be making out *this* soon into the movie."

"Why not? They don't have a second to waste."

"Henry's better than that, and you know it." She jerks her head in the direction of *her* prospects and says with finality, "They're right there. I'd stake my life on it."

"Oh, come on. Those two aren't even touching each other. Henry would at *least* have his arm around her shoulders at this point."

"Well, you're more flirtatious than he is, and *you* don't have your arm around *my* shoulders," Tessa says matter-of-factly.

I take it as my cue to put one arm around her—better late than never.

Tessa laughs and shoves half the KitKat into my mouth. "I guess we'll just have to wait until the lights go up to see who's right."

It's a bet within a bet. And I'm game for any wager that involves holding Tessa Dickinson in the dark and being fed candy while listening to her savage, one-star commentary on a movie she's never seen before. I've never been much of a film critic, but

Tessa (being a writer) has made it her responsibility to educate me on what a good story looks like, and I (being madly in love with her) have to agree with all her criticisms, even if I still enjoy a "plot-driven CGI pew-pew-fest" once in a while. (Her words, not mine.)

All throughout the movie, I keep my eye on the two couples in front of us, trying to figure out which one is Henry and Vivi. The kissers, who have a pattern of falling on each other's lips during every battle sequence? Or the stoics, who don't take their eyes off the screen the whole time, but occasionally lean into each other's ears to whisper something?

I guess it doesn't matter which couple is Henry and Vivi. It's enough to know that they're in the same room as me, safe and sound. Now, I can just relax and pretend this is a *real* date, not a stealthy stalker-fest. Though I hate to admit it, Tessa was right: Henry *did* stick to his word. Whether he's the lucky guy making out with his girl near the front or the less-lucky guy whispering sweet nothings in his girl's ear, the important part is this: he didn't lie about going to the movies.

Tessa: 1. Me: 0.

So far, the odds aren't in my favor. It's possible Tessa could win this wager. I start imagining the possibilities of a date I would hate. Jane Austen movie marathon? Ballroom dancing lessons? Pottery class? Is it crazy to admit that I wouldn't even mind doing any of those things as long as I could do them with her?

Unfortunately, I don't think Tessa would feel the same way about activities like rock-climbing or hand-to-hand combat.

Two hours later, the movie comes to a dramatic end, and Tessa whimpers, "Thank God," against my neck, which makes me laugh and pat her on the back.

"You made it, Tes."

"I was fighting to stay awake," she admits, kissing my cheek. "Sugar and loud noises were the only things keeping me from dozing off."

As the credits roll, the lights go up, and I'm on the edge of my seat because *this* is the moment I've been waiting for: to see who guessed the right couple based on their silhouettes.

The kissers stand up and gather their stuff. My heart sinks when I realize they're not Henry and Vivi. Tessa was right, damn it. That guy *does* have boulder shoulders—definitely not my little brother.

I'm about to admit defeat and let Tessa enjoy her win, but when I swivel to look at the stoics she pointed out earlier, I do a double take.

That couple isn't Henry and Vivi, either.

Tessa's face goes white as a ghost. We both frantically scan the audience as everyone starts filing out of the theater, but Henry and Vivi are nowhere to be found.

They were never here at all.

"*I TOLD YOU THAT GUY WASN'T HENRY,*" *WESTON SAYS* as we hurry down the stairs and toward the exit, dodging and weaving around moviegoers.

"Well, *your* guy wasn't Henry, either," I volley back, shadowing him out the door and into the main hallway of the cinema. "You were *so* sure of yourself—"

"Look, I don't want to talk about what's past." Weston stops short, scanning the crowd of people making their way toward the lobby. "I can't believe this…"

"He might still be here," I offer. "Maybe he went to the nine o'clock showing. Or maybe they went to see a different movie altogether. Vivi probably hates *Star Wars* like I do, and Henry let *her* choose the movie instead."

Weston turns to me, a spark of hope in his eyes. "Good thinking." He grabs my hand and starts leading me back down the hallway in the direction we came.

"Wait, where are we going?"

Weston stops at the door to a different auditorium and shoots me a look over his shoulder. "We're going to check them all."

"Wes, we can't just—"

Too late. He's already shoved open the door, completely disregarding the rules. I'm no authority on multiplex cinema laws, but you can't just sneak into every auditorium without buying a ticket to that showing. Not that we'll be hanging around to watch the movie being screened inside, but it still feels somehow… criminal.

I scan the movie poster and overhead screen displaying the film's title, rating, and showtime. *The Silent Assassin*. Rated R. It hardly sounds like romantic first-date fare, but if Weston is serious about checking each theater for his missing brother, I can't leave him to do this search alone.

Pushing through the door, I creep down the low-lit hallway, bracing myself for grisly assassin vibes as soon as I round the corner. But I don't make it far before I crash straight into Weston.

"They're not in here. Come on, next one." He grabs my elbow and drags me out of the auditorium, then straight into the one beside it.

This movie is called *Forbidden Desires* and is also rated R— though not for violence. As soon as we step through the door, I am accosted by the sound of gasping and moaning, but Weston mercifully shields my eyes before I can glimpse what's happening on the screen.

We scan the half-filled audience of scandalized moviegoers— some of whom are fulfilling their own "forbidden desires" by kissing and necking in the dark. I try not to look *too* long as I search for Henry and Vivi amid the lip-locked couples. But thankfully, our truants aren't in this auditorium, either.

I retreat as quickly as possible, and Weston meets me in the hallway.

"That was assaulting," I say with a shudder. "Three down, four to go."

Weston is about to plow through the next door when I stop him.

"*Pony Pal Adventures?*" I point to the sign above the door. "When I said Henry would have a G-rated date, I didn't mean he'd go see a movie that's literally made for five-year-olds."

Weston gives the sign a double take and laughs, shaking his head. "You're probably right."

The next auditorium is between showings—nobody inside except the staff, cleaning up spilled popcorn and forgotten trash. Racing against the clock, Weston and I zigzag between the last two screens: one is playing the nine o'clock showing of *Star Wars*, the other a romantic comedy that I wish we had watched instead of *Star Wars*—since our presence here was totally pointless anyway.

I can't decide what is more disappointing: the fact that Weston has not only led his little brother astray but also lost sight of him, or the two hours of my life I spent watching space battles.

Back in the main hallway, Weston sighs and forks his hands through his hair. "Shit, shit, *shit.*"

"Do you have to swear?"

He fists a hand in his hair. "Shit's not a swear word."

"Well, it's not a nice word, either. Now just… think for a minute. Where else could Henry possibly have gone? Did he have a plan B? In case Vivi didn't want to go to the movies?"

Weston shrugs. "Not that he told me. I should've grilled him more about it. But at the time, I didn't think I was actually going to stalk him."

I cross my arms over my chest, pondering for a moment. "Does he have any friends from school? Someone else they might have made plans to hang out with?"

No sooner have the words crossed my lips than—

"Ludovico!"

The voice is booming, nasally, and eerily reminiscent of fingernails on a chalkboard. Weston's whole countenance falls when he hears his name and secretly shoots me a miserable glance before slowly turning around.

"Ferguson."

I've only had the displeasure of meeting Weston's nemesis, Neil Ferguson, once before, an interaction that mainly consisted of him giving me backhanded compliments and objectifying once-overs while Weston quietly resisted the urge to punch him in the teeth.

There's no escaping Neil Ferguson's notice at this point—not when he walks up to us, trailing some unlucky girl behind him.

Weston is the first to speak. "How did you like *Pony Pal Adventures*, Ferg? On a scale of one to ten?"

Ferguson grins hatefully. "Very funny, Ludovico. Enjoying a nice little chick flick with your girlfriend?" He nods toward the rom-com poster on the wall. "Man, you two are just the *perfect* PG couple."

Weston lets the insult roll off him like water. "Well, I guess some people need to watch movies about stuff they don't get to experience in real life." He loops one arm around my shoulders. "Isn't that right, Tessa?"

I nod, biting back a smirk as I lace my fingers through his. "That's right."

The joke goes right over Ferguson's head. He pulls his girl-friend against his side possessively, but she's too busy texting to even glance up at him.

"Guess you're not going to Nicky Savage's party tonight." Ferguson says it like a dare, his gaze darting between me and Weston. "Heard it's gonna be a real rager. You should come."

I raise my eyebrows at the mere idea of attending *any* party, never mind one considered to be a "rager."

Weston shakes his head with an easy laugh. "Ragers are for people who don't know how to have a good time at home."

Ferguson narrows his eyes, fighting back a smirk. "Oh yeah? Well, I heard your little brother Henry was gonna be there."

Weston's arm stiffens around my shoulders. "What? Who told you that?"

"Nicky did. Apparently, her sister is best friends with Vivi Reynolds. Isn't your brother going out with her?"

I gulp, looking up at Weston, who has gone white as a sheet.

"That's right," Weston says.

Ferguson grins and rocks back on his heels. "Man, the kid's gonna have his eyes opened tonight. Might even beat you to losing his V-card, Ludovico."

Weston doesn't dignify that comment with a response; he just steers me away from Ferguson, not sparing him a goodbye or a backward glance. "Come on, let's get out of here."

I don't say a word until we've exited the cinema. "You think he's serious about Henry going to this party? Or was he just trying to get your goat?"

"Not sure," Weston says, keys jangling in his hand as we dash back across the parking lot toward his truck. "But there's only one way to find out."

And that's how we find ourselves driving to a late-night "rager" held by a mysterious girl named Nicky Savage, whom I have never seen in my life. Weston gives me the Spark Notes summary of the situation on the ride across town. Apparently, Nicky is a senior socialite with a reputation for throwing lively, boozy parties and inviting anyone and everyone between the ages of thirteen and twenty.

"Does that mean we can just walk into this party uninvited?" I ask as Weston slows down for the multitude of parallel-parked cars lining the street. I have a feeling we're getting close to Nicky's house.

"I don't care if we weren't invited," Weston says, swerving the truck to a stop along the side of the road. "If Henry's at this party, having his 'eyes opened,' Mom's gonna take it out of my hide."

We hop out of the truck and hurry down the street, hand in hand. Weston leads me up the driveway of an unassuming split-level house with the name Savage printed on the mailbox. I can hear the muffled thumping of bass-boosted music, but there doesn't seem to be much "raging" going on.

Weston climbs the steps to the front door and knocks three times. It swings open seconds later on a grumpy-faced middle-aged woman wearing a cat sweater.

"Back door, for the *hundredth* time!" she snaps before promptly swinging the door shut in Weston's face.

He turns to me with a shrug. "Back door, I guess. They should have signs."

"How can this girl host a lively, boozy party when her parents are home?" I ask, shadowing Weston around the back of the house.

He only says, "That's Nicky Savage for you. Her parents put up with anything."

The pounding bass grows louder as we round the back corner of the house. There's a frosted glass door leading to the walkout basement, and inside, I see a thick crowd of teenagers swaying to the dance music, red plastic cups in hand. Some of them are already making out.

I catch Weston's hand before he can open the door. "We're not going to have to, like, hang out with these people, right?"

He laughs. "Of course not. We're just here to look for Henry."

He's right. This mission is purely virtuous, and the ends justify the means—but stepping through those sliding glass doors into a bona fide high school party feels strangely like stepping into the outer circle of Dante's *Inferno*. The music instantly swallows me up, bass thumping through my whole body as I hold on to Weston's hand for dear life. He parts the crowd for me, scanning the basement for any sign of Henry and Vivi as we weave around dancers and wallflowers.

"Weston!" A high-pitched female voice erupts from behind us. We both spin around as a curvy blonde girl with sparkles on her face prances over with a dazzling smile. I'm a little affronted when she grabs Weston by the neck, bold as brass, and plants a kiss on each of his cheeks. "I didn't know you were gonna be here tonight! And you brought your girlfriend! Tessa, right?"

"Uh, yeah, this is Tessa. Tessa, this is Nicky."

She swoops in and kisses *me* on both cheeks. I suppose Nicky *doesn't* have a crush on my boyfriend—she's just a girl who appreciates flamboyant French mannerisms.

"Sweet! I'm so glad you both came. Drinks are on the wet

bar! Help yourselves. We've got vodka and alllll the mixers. But don't tell my parents." She puts a finger to her lips and winks at me, then vanishes into the crowd.

"Wait—Nicky!" Weston's voice is drowned out by the deafening music. He growls and tips his head back. "I was gonna ask her if she'd seen Henry."

"Do *you* see him?" I ask, lifting up on my tiptoes and squinting to identify faces in the dim purple light. "I'm too short to see—and there are too many people here."

No sooner are the words out of my mouth than some random guy steps on my heels and sends me stumbling into Weston's arms. My cheeks flush furious red as I look up at him.

"Maybe we should check over here," he suggests, whisking me away from the bustling dance floor. (If thirty square feet of space can be called a *dance floor*.) As Weston heads for the margins of the room, I know exactly what he's thinking: that if Henry and Vivi have been at this party for the past two hours (while we were obliviously watching *Star Wars*), they will have moved beyond the dancing and drinking phase by this point.

Moving with the caution of spies in enemy territory, Weston and I prowl the perimeter of the basement—twice—dodging kissing couples.

Henry and Vivi are not among them.

Finally, I pull Weston into the darkest, quietest corner of the basement and blurt out, "How could you have let this happen?"

"How could *I* have let this happen?" Weston points to himself in disbelief. "You're the one who said beyond the shadow of a doubt that Henry would be at the movies watching *Star Wars*—"

"Well, if it weren't for you trying so hard not to be seen in the theater, maybe we wouldn't have had to sit there for two hours before realizing that they weren't even there in the first place!"

"Shh! Calm down, okay?" Weston puts his hands on my shoulders, his eyes glinting in the candy-colored light. "I'm not blaming you, Tessa. It was my responsibility to keep an eye on Henry—"

"Yes, it was. And now God only knows where he is, and we're stuck at this crazy, inappropriate party with underage teens drinking *vodka.*"

Weston chuckles. "Are you mad at me?"

"Yes!"

"Why?"

"Because! You've dragged me all over the place tonight, doing things I didn't want to do, and for what? You're an irresponsible brother and a disappointing boyfriend. One-star review for *you,* Weston Ludovico."

He narrows his eyes at me, jaw twitching. In a flash, he catches my hips and spins me around, pinning me against the wall and lowering his forehead to mine. "Have I ever told you how beautiful you are when you're mad at me?"

"Have I ever told you how insufferable you are when you refuse to admit you're in the wrong?"

He stifles a reckless little smirk. "Insufferable, huh?"

"Yes."

"Show me how insufferable you think I am."

For a breathless moment, all I can do is look up into his dazzling eyes, my heart pumping faster as the bass-boosted music transitions to something slow with reverb. Weston stares down at me, his closeness like a force of gravity, his spicy scent filling my lungs, his hands still circling my waist.

Irritated as I am, I can't resist him a second longer.

Despite my frustration (or perhaps because of it), I grab his face and crush my lips to his. It's the first time I've truly kissed him tonight, and somehow, it feels like every little tiff has built up to this moment of unleashed passion. Weston lights up as he kisses me back hungrily. I melt at his touch, my lips softening, my heart thumping against my ribcage harder than the bass line of the music rumbling through the sound system.

Somehow, I know this is a bad idea. But now that I'm kissing him, I can't stop. His hands tighten around my hips, fingers hooking through my belt loops, and I blindly follow his lead, cradling his face the whole time, saying everything I want to say with my lips on his.

He runs his fingers through my hair, his breath skimming across my left cheek, then lingering at the hollow beneath my ear. I shiver at the mere sensation of his skin on mine, but when a sting of pain comes instead of a kiss, I jolt back.

"Ow! What are you doing?"

Weston laughs, looking rumpled and far too pleased with himself. "I'm giving you a hickey to prove you went to a 'crazy, inappropriate party.'"

"That was *not* a hickey," I argue, reaching up to touch my neck. "You straight-up *bit* me."

"Sorry." He grins sheepishly, tucking a strand of hair behind my ear. "Want me to try again?"

"No. This is ridiculous; we're supposed to be looking for Henry—"

"Well, you're the one who started making out with me."

"I *kissed* you," I correct. "*You're* the one who started making out with *me*."

"You enjoyed it." Weston winks at me. "Admit it."

I open my mouth to say something witty and scathing, but that's when Nicky appears in our corner of the basement, shouting, "Did you guys get drinks yet?"

"Better question." Weston raises his voice to be heard over the music. "Have you seen my brother Henry tonight?"

Nicky nods. "Yeah, he showed up with Vivi Reynolds—a while ago. They went upstairs, I think."

Weston shoots me a look over his shoulder, eyes wide with panic. "Upstairs?"

WESTON

———————

MOM'S GOING TO KILL ME.

That's all I can think as I grab Tessa's hand and drag her up the stairs of Nicky Savage's basement, leaving the party behind.

Henry and Vivi *did* come here. Hours ago. And apparently, they graduated beyond drinking and dancing and making out… to *sneaking upstairs.*

My hands are slick with cold sweat as I shove through the basement door and race up another flight of stairs, Tessa on my heels. At last, we reach the second floor—and that's when Tessa stops me.

"What are you thinking, Wes?" she whispers fiercely. "We can't just snoop around someone else's house!"

I put a finger to my lips. "Shhh. Listen."

Tessa falls silent, and we both stand frozen for a moment, ears open. Moving as quietly as possible, I creep down the hallway, pausing outside each closed bedroom door, dreading what I might hear on the other side. Hoping my suspicions are wrong. Maybe he didn't take Vivi upstairs. Maybe he took her home. Maybe—

A girlish laugh sends a wrecking ball through my train of thought. Vivi's muffled voice comes from behind one of the closed doors. "Henry, stop—that's cheating."

My brother's unmistakable laugh echoes after hers, and it's enough to make my stomach plummet to my shoes.

Neil Ferguson's sneering jokes from earlier come back to haunt me. *The kid's gonna have his eyes opened tonight. Might even beat you to losing his V-card.*

Tessa's eyes flare with anxiety as I approach the door, dread coiling in my gut. My hand reaches out and closes around the knob. I don't want to turn it. I don't want to throw open this door and catch my little brother red-handed. But I have no choice.

This is just about the most mortifying position I've ever found myself in. And yet, my gut tells me it'll be worse if I turn a blind eye.

So I take a deep breath and throw open the bedroom door. "Henry—"

The rest of my sentence freezes in my throat.

Henry and Vivi sit cross-legged on the floor beside a fluffy pink bed, along with another girl—Nicky's little sister, Florence. All three of them turn to gape at Tessa and me as we stand in the doorway. There's a Monopoly board on the floor between them.

"Weston?" Henry blurts out, stunned embarrassment all over his face. "What the hell are you doing here?"

Vivi and Florence burst out giggling into their hands, and Henry's face goes bright pink. He springs to his feet and steps over the Monopoly board, marching across the room to look me in the eyes.

"What are you doing here? Are you following me again?"

"Uh—no," I stammer, shaking my head. "No, we're not. We just…"

"How did you find me, then?"

"Nicky said you were up here."

Henry's eyebrows arch as he looks between me and Tessa. "You guys came to Nicky's party?" His suspicions are confirmed as he studies the two of us—clothes rumpled, hair a mess. I'm pretty sure I have lipstick on my jaw from Tessa's kisses, and there's a visible red bite mark taking shape on her neck.

Henry makes an expression between a smirk and a grimace when he sees it. "So *that's* why you made up the whole story about going to the skating rink. I *knew* you were bullshitting me."

Tessa's cheeks blaze with color, and her hand flies up to cover her neck.

"We weren't *planning* on coming to Nicky's party," I defend myself quickly. "We went to the movies and bumped into Ferguson, and he said you were coming here tonight. What was I supposed to do? Stand by and let you…"

Henry narrows his eyes, waiting for the end of that sentence, but it never comes. "You went to the movies? Why, because I told you I was going there with Vivi?"

I suck in a deep breath, then let it all out in a defeated sigh. "Yeah," I admit. "I lied, okay? I didn't want to… but I promised Mom I'd keep an eye on you."

"Unbelievable." Henry shakes his head. "I can't believe this—"

"Well, hey, you lied too."

"I didn't lie. I thought we *were* going to go to the movies, but then I found out that Vivi has epilepsy and can't watch movies like that in a theater."

I glance over his shoulder at Vivi, who is sitting on the floor beside her best friend, the two of them giggling over something on her phone.

Henry continues in a low voice, "She knew Florence would be on her own tonight because she doesn't do her sister's crazy parties, and… Vivi thought it would be nice to keep her company. So we decided to come over here and play Monopoly instead."

I am an idiot. The biggest idiot of all time.

"That's so sweet of you," Tessa says, with an indulgent smile for my brother and a critical look for me. "Weston didn't want to embarrass you, Henry. He was just worried, that's all."

Henry scoffs. "Worried? What the hell, man?" He shakes his head, looking at me like I just ran over his dog. "I never would've expected *you* to be worried."

"I wasn't worried," I argue. "Mom was worried, and you know how she gets. I was just… trying to make her happy. I'm sorry, okay? It was out of line. I should've given you your space."

"No shit you should've—"

"And I said I was sorry!" I toss up my hands. "What else can I do, man?"

Henry takes his sweet time thinking about it before cocking his head to the side and saying, "You could do all my chores for a week."

"A whole week?" I sigh, tipping my head back defeatedly. "Okay. Deal."

That manages to resurrect Henry's grin, the leftover anger melting from his eyes. "I'm looking forward to telling Mom all about what happened tonight," he says. "Next time, I'll be the one she's asking to keep an eye on *you*."

Henry returns to his board game, and Tessa pulls me back

into the hallway, shutting the door before she bursts out laughing, covering her mouth with her hands. I shake my head, giving up and laughing with her. It *is* pretty funny, in retrospect, to think about all the stupid, crazy stuff we did tonight in the name of protecting my little brother—and, meanwhile, he was staying out of trouble just fine on his own.

"You were right," I admit. "Henry's too good for his own good."

"I'm always right," Tessa declares with a righteous little smirk. "And you know what that means: I win the wager."

I nod in dismay. "You win the wager. But mark my words; you're going to have a hard time finding something I hate to torture me with on our next date."

"Maybe so," Tessa murmurs, clasping my hand as we head back down the stairs. "But I'm sure I'll think of something."

FIRE ON FORSYTHIA LANE

A Westess Mystery

WESTON

ROCKFORD, NEW YORK, IS ONE OF THOSE SMALL country towns where nothing ever happens—which makes my father's newspaper, *The Rockford Chronicle*, pretty desperate for interesting stories to report about.

While papers in Albany and Schenectady are running stories about burglaries and political scandals, the most sensational news our town has to offer is the outcome of local sports games or the annual fishing derby. I guess it's kind of nice to live in a place where crime is basically nonexistent and the worst thing you have to worry about after dark is getting sprayed by a skunk.

Luckily, my job at the *Chronicle* doesn't involve sitting in front of a computer trying to write a one-thousand-word article about the world's most boring local events. I'm what Dad calls an "administrative supervisor"—which includes running background checks (aka Google searches), fact-checks (aka more Google searches), and occasionally calling people to see if they have additional comments to add to a story. My apprenticeship also includes leaving sticky-note jokes on everyone's desks (with the punchlines written on the backs), making Keurigs for people who are too important to do it themselves (aka Marcus, the Manhattanite who thinks he still works at the *New York Times*), and occasionally taking out the trash. (In the words of my dad, nothing is too lowly for a true leader to take care of.)

All that to say: nothing exciting ever happens in Rockford. That is, until one cold night in mid-April, when I jolt awake at one o'clock to the sound of fire engines bellowing through town, one after another. Usually, the fire department is called out for false alarms or because someone's overzealous bonfire scared the old folks next door. But it's not the season for bonfires. And it sounds like some of those fire engines are coming from neighboring towns.

When I see the hallway light turn on and hear the murmured voices of my parents outside my bedroom door, I know something is wrong. Moving as quickly and quietly as possible, I fit on my prosthetic legs and climb out of bed, stumbling into a pair of pants and grabbing a hoodie on my way to the door.

Mom and Dad are downstairs now, talking in low voices so as not to wake my brothers.

"I don't like this any more than you do," Dad says, his words diced by the jangle of his car keys. "But I know how Marcus likes to be in at the kill. He's probably down there already, and I don't want him sticking his nose where it doesn't belong. He represents the *Chronicle*, which means he represents *me*."

I frown, slinking down the stairs but staying out of sight when I reach the bottom. Part of me is dying to step out and ask what the heck is going on, what's on fire, and what Marcus has to do with it—but I know Mom will dismiss the whole thing and send me back to bed, like I'm no bigger than Noah.

Instead, I sneak down the hallway and let myself out the back door, into the pitch-dark night. As I circle around the back of the house, I hear the crunch of Dad's footsteps on the gravel driveway, approaching his pickup truck.

"Dad," I whisper hoarsely, rushing over, "where are you going? What's happening?"

He grumbles a sigh as he swings open the driver's door. "Wes, you shouldn't be out here. Go back to bed."

"But I want to come with you," I protest, walking around the truck to the passenger side. "Please, Dad. I won't get in the way—I swear. Let me come."

"Fine," he mutters. "Get in. Hurry up. We don't have much time."

I don't need to be told twice. Hopping into the passenger seat, I buckle up. "What's going on? Something on fire?"

Dad nods, pulling out onto the street and driving south. "Montgomery's place."

"Which one? Doesn't that guy have, like, three different houses?"

Dad grunts. "The one that was being renovated on Forsythia Lane. Old Victorian house, remember?"

"Yeah, I remember. Must be a pretty bad fire if they've been calling out of town for help. What's Marcus doing there?"

Dad lets out an irritated sigh. "What Marcus does best. Getting into trouble."

We drive in silence, the empty dark streets seeming more eerie with sirens wailing in the distance. I have a hundred questions, but I keep my mouth shut and let Dad concentrate on driving.

Forsythia Lane stretches over a hill, on the outskirts of town—which means we can see the fire before we even get close enough to smell it. The whole crest of the hill is glowing beyond the skeletons of leafless trees, sending billows of smoke into the night sky.

We pull over to let another fire truck zoom past, then cautiously make our way to Forsythia Lane. Dad pulls the truck onto the side of the road, out of the way of any emergency vehicles that need to pass. The Montgomery house is farther up the hill—all we can see from this distance is a haunting red glow against the inky sky.

Marcus's little white Prius is parked on the opposite side of the road.

No Marcus in sight.

Dad curses again and shoves open his door. I get out of the truck and immediately breathe in a lungful of smoky air. I've never been this close to a structure fire before—and somehow, it's even creepier when you can't actually *see* what's burning. Just a massive plume of smoke flickering orange, flakes of ash floating down like snow and disintegrating when they hit the ground. I can hear a chaos of noise farther up the road: voices shouting over the rumble of vehicles and equipment, the roar of the fire boiling under it all.

Dad yells Marcus's name and looks in the windows of his car, but he's nowhere to be found.

"He's probably up there, taking pictures of the fire," I say, pointing to the ominous glow.

Dad starts walking up the hill, yelling over his shoulder, "Stay close to me—understand? Don't get in anyone's way. This is a dangerous situation."

As we near the crest of the hill, the air grows warmer and thicker with smoke and ash. Fire engines line the street, crushed together as close as possible and blocking the view of the burning house. Dad and I stay clear of the firefighters as they rush between vehicles, barking orders to each other.

I've driven by the Montgomery place a hundred times—but it's never looked as big as it does now, engulfed in flames. The firefighters have already put out the worst of the blaze, but I don't need to be an expert to know that the whole house is lost. It used to be three stories high, with a turret on one corner. Now all that's left is the first floor and the skeletal structure of the second floor. Flames still feast on the remaining wood, and firefighters blast water everywhere, but it won't be enough to save any part of the house.

"Marcus!" Dad shouts when he sees the prodigal reporter crouched behind one of the fire trucks, snapping pictures with his phone. Not only did the guy have the nerve to strut onto the scene of a disaster in the middle of the night, but he apparently had the time to put on a suit jacket.

No joke.

"What the hell are you doing?" Dad demands, sounding more like a father than a boss as he grabs Marcus by the arm and drags him away from the fire truck. Maybe it's easy for him to use his Dad Voice because Marcus is barely four years older than me—still a kid, despite the custom-printed business cards he carries in his suit pocket.

"Mr. Ludovico, I was just—"

"I know what you were doing," Dad cuts him off gruffly.

"That's not what I meant when I said 'what the hell are you doing.'"

Marcus blinks, looking like a flustered rookie for a second. Then his gaze flicks to me, and he seems to rediscover his professional pride.

"I knew we'd want to cover this story in the *Chronicle*," he explains calmly. "So I came to gather photographic evidence and document any witness statements."

"Well, I don't want you or *anyone* getting hurt for the sake of news reporting. Understood? Stay back, out of the way. Let the firemen do their jobs. You can take pictures from here, and you can question witnesses once the danger has been mitigated."

Marcus looks like a kid who's been grounded for a week. But he nods reluctantly and obeys my father's orders—if only to keep his job.

"When did the fire start?" I ask, coughing into my sleeve as more smoke billows up from the rubble.

"I heard one of the firemen say they got the call at twelve forty-five," Marcus answers, looking down at his fancy wristwatch. "So about half an hour ago."

"Do you sleep with your watch on?" I joke, just to throw him off. Marcus Verne is a guy who isn't easily *thrown off*—or easily amused.

He ignores my comment and turns to Dad instead. "The house burned faster than normal, wouldn't you say? It doesn't seem like an accident."

"It could've had a number of accidental causes," Dad adds before Marcus can start jumping to criminal conclusions. "Who called the fire department?"

"The lady who lives over there," Marcus explains, turning to point at the farmhouse about two hundred feet away. Even from

this distance, I can see a white-haired woman in a bathrobe standing in the middle of her driveway, hugging herself as she watches
her neighbor's house burn to the ground. "I'm going to question
her some more about what exactly she saw, but I wanted to get
photos while it still looked good."

I guess, in Marcus's strange little world of reporting, a house
engulfed in flames in the middle of the night looks "good." Makes
me wonder if he's secretly a pyromaniac. Maybe he set the house
on fire himself just to have something interesting to write about
for the *Chronicle*.

"You're free to question witnesses," Dad says sternly. "But
don't press the woman for information. I'm sure she's been
through enough stress tonight."

"Absolutely," Marcus agrees with a nod. "I fully respect the
boundaries of ethics in the investigative process."

I can't help rolling my eyes at his choice of words. "Where's
the owner? Montgomery?"

"Not here, obviously," Marcus replies. "I'm sure they're trying to get in touch with him. But he's probably out of town."

"At least nobody was living in that house," Dad murmurs,
taking in the disaster sight across the street. "Shame it burned
before it even went up for sale."

Marcus snaps a few more pictures with his phone, then pivots
on his heel and starts for the neighboring house, where the robed
woman can still be seen standing in her driveway.

"Follow him," Dad murmurs to me. "Make sure he doesn't
put his foot in his mouth."

I shadow Marcus down the side of the road, staying far
enough back that he doesn't even notice I'm stalking him.

"Excuse me!" he yells to the robed woman in the driveway.
"Excuse me, ma'am, can I ask you a few questions? My name is

Marcus Verne. I'm with *The Rockford Chronicle*, and I'd like to ask—"

"No questions," the woman's shrill voice comes back trembling, almost scared. "No—just… leave me alone." She turns and charges back to her porch, hugging herself the whole time until she vanishes behind a slamming door.

Marcus stops short at the end of her driveway, cussing on the end of a sigh.

"Lost your touch?"

He whirls around to find me standing a few feet away. The flash of surprise in his eyes is quickly replaced by icy irritation. "What the hell are *you* doing here, anyway? This is no place for *kids*."

I wonder, did he consider himself a "kid" when *he* was eighteen years old? Not to mention, he has to look *up* to address me because I'm at least two inches taller than him.

I let the insult roll off me with a shrug. "Just thought I'd come see what all the hype was about. Now I'm starting to wish I'd stayed in bed."

Marcus narrows his eyes as he studies me in the pale moonlight. "Well, if you're getting cold feet… maybe you should go back home. Leave the dirty work to those of us who can handle it."

A half-smile twitches at my lips as I take a step closer. "Oh, I *never* get cold feet. It's one of the few benefits of being a double amputee."

As usual, Marcus is not amused. He's about to parry back when I hear a rustling in the bushes to my left. At first, I think it's an animal—a skunk, hopefully—and I'm about to take off and leave Marcus to confront the encounter on his own…

But that's when a man comes stumbling out of the woods—

a ratty baseball cap on his head and a cigarette glowing between his fingers. I stiffen, defenses up, as I watch the man stagger out onto the dirt road, his jolty gait proof that he's either injured or drunk.

I can tell it's the latter when he gets close enough to where Marcus and I are standing. Even over the stench of smoke hanging in the air, I can smell whiskey. It's almost as recognizable as skunk.

The guy stops short when he sees us, bristling like someone just pulled a gun on him.

Marcus puts his hands up in some pansy-ass gesture, as if to say, *I come in peace.* I keep my fists behind my back, letting this guy wonder if I'm hiding something he should be worried about.

As he tips his head back to look at us, a slice of moonlight spreads across his features—and recognition hits me like an uppercut.

Jonathan Boone. I only know his face because I used to see him on this road years ago. Out in his front yard, mowing the grass or working on his car. But that was before he went to prison.

Marcus isn't a local, so he doesn't know any of the history I do about this guy—how the story of his arrest wound up in the *Chronicle*. How Montgomery was the one to take Boone's name off the mailbox at the end of the driveway. How, when you're out in the sticks of upstate New York, you don't introduce yourself to local drunks who come stumbling out of the woods at one o'clock in the morning.

"Hello, sir. My name is Marcus Verne—"

"Why the hell you telling me your name, kid?" Boone slurs in response—and I almost laugh at the use of *kid.*

Boone, on the other hand, seems very amused at the sight of the burning house, which is now just a skeleton. He points with his withered cigarette and collapses into rough, wheezing laughter—the lights of the first-responder trucks blinking across his craggy face.

"What a sight, huh?" He chuckles, lifting the cigarette to his lips. "The bastard finally got what was coming to him."

And with that, Jonathan Boone continues staggering down the road, veering off towards the woods to avoid the cluster of firefighters. Or maybe to avoid being *seen* by anyone.

"Who the hell was *that*?" Marcus rasps, staring after Boone as he disappears into the night. "Did you hear what he said?"

"Yep." I sigh, shoving my hands into my pockets and heading back in the direction of the fire trucks. "And I don't think he's the only one who feels that way about Montgomery."

"What do you mean?" Marcus says, catching up to me. "Does he have a lot of enemies?"

I shrug. "I don't know. He's made a lot of money buying foreclosed houses and reselling them at a profit. Some of those previous owners aren't the biggest fans of him, for obvious reasons."

"You know who that guy was, don't you?" Marcus pries eagerly, trotting along beside me. "What's his name?"

"Jonathan Boone. He used to live in that house."

"What house?"

For an investigative reporter with business cards and the ability to put on a suit jacket in the middle of the night, Marcus Verne isn't very sharp. The penny doesn't drop for him until I stop in my tracks and point at the smoking structure of the Montgomery place.

"*That* house."

TESSA

____

"OH, MY GOODNESS… THAT'S TERRIBLE." I BREATHE the words through my fingers as I stare at the video playing on my laptop screen—a blazing inferno swallowing up that beautiful old Victorian house Mr. Montgomery put so much work into remodeling.

I woke up sometime after midnight to the distant wailing of fire engines—but Forsythia Lane was too far away for us to see anything from our house on the east side of Rockford. Estimating from the number of emergency vehicles I heard, I assumed the blaze was unusually chaotic. But I didn't know just how disastrous it was until Weston sent me the story featured on the homepage of *The Rockford Chronicle*'s website, complete with video clips of the fire.

The article doesn't provide much insight about how it happened, saying only that the fire department was summoned at twelve forty-five by a concerned neighbor. According to the fire chief, the cause of the fire is still unknown and under investigation.

I don't get the full scoop until Weston comes over to see me later that morning. I'm in the midst of spring cleaning, and today that project involves emptying my bedroom closet, sorting donations, and organizing the rest of my things into labeled bins and baskets. Weston's blue eyes widen adorably as he leans against the doorjamb, taking in the apocalyptic mess surrounding me.

"You're becoming predictable, you know that?" He grins, and it's the first ray of sunshine I've seen today. "Whenever I show up at your house uninvited, I'm guaranteed to find you either baking, cleaning, or writing."

I laugh, tiptoeing my way through the chaos to get to him. "Well, you're rather predictable, too. I usually find you either punching something, working out, or eating."

"Hey, I still play the ukulele," he argues. "I'm a very complex and multilayered guy."

I smirk, grabbing the drawstrings of his hoodie to tug him down to my lips. "You are," I whisper, and kiss him softly. The smell of smoke lingers on his clothes, making me draw back with surprise.

"Have you been *smoking*?"

A laugh startles out of him. "What? No—"

"You smell like smoke."

"Oh, it's probably just my hoodie," he explains, lifting his sleeve to his nose and taking a sniff. "I wore this last night when me and Dad went up to see the fire."

"You were *there*?"

He nods. "We wouldn't have been if it weren't for Marcus. He's the one who got the video and wrote that article I sent you. Dad was worried he'd get a little overzealous. This is the first exciting thing that's happened since Main Street flooded last fall."

"I don't know if I'd call a house burning down *exciting*," I say with a shudder. "At least nobody was hurt or killed. Do they know anything else about how it started?"

Weston shrugs, shaking his head. "According to my dad, the fire marshal was called to investigate, which means there's enough evidence for them to suspect arson."

My eyes widen. "Do you think someone burned it down on purpose? Why? I mean, what would be the point of burning down a house nobody's living in?"

Weston leans back against the doorframe as I return to my task of sorting and organizing a pile of giveaway clothes.

At last, he answers my question with one word. "Revenge."

I frown. "Who would want to get revenge on Mr. Montgomery?"

Weston goes on to tell me about another person he saw last night—Jonathan Boone, the former owner of the house that burned. As he tells the story, I vaguely remember seeing news of Boone's arrest in the papers a few years ago. He was arrested for his second DWI and sentenced to prison for three years.

"Rumor has it, by the time he got out, he was so deep in debt he couldn't pay the mortgage on his house," Weston explains, sitting on my bed now and fiddling with a Rubik's Cube he found in my "miscellaneous" basket. "The house went into foreclosure, and Montgomery bought it at auction for a real good price. Then, of course, he renovated it so he could resell it for twice as much, like he usually does."

"So you think this Boone guy is still holding a grudge against Montgomery for buying his house?"

Weston shrugs, spinning the cube. "I don't know. Sounded like it from what he said last night. I mean, he *laughed* as he watched the house burn. And he said something like, 'That bastard finally got what was coming to him.'"

"Did you notice anything else strange about him?"

"Other than the fact that he was drunk?" Weston ponders it for a moment. "He was smoking a cigarette."

I bite my lip, sliding a stack of clothes into a box for donations and folding the flap shut. "That sounds… suspicious. And you said he came out of the woods?"

"Yeah, but would you really do that? I mean, if you burned someone's house down, would you hang around the scene of the crime just to watch it burn? I guess if you were a psycho, maybe… but you'd think an ex-con would be a little more careful to not get arrested again."

"Well, you said he was drunk. People do stupid things when they're drunk." I look down at the floor, unpleasant memories of my own springing to mind—the drunk driver who caused the car accident that rendered me blind two summers ago. "Were you the only one who saw this Boone guy?"

"No." Weston sighs. "Marcus was there, too. He heard everything and probably wrote it down. He's all gung-ho about making sure the *Chronicle* is the first outlet to break this story. Which really means making sure *he's* the first one to break the story."

I study him for a moment, reading between the lines. "I take it you and Marcus don't see eye-to-eye on a lot of things."

Weston lets out a sarcastic laugh. "The guy's on a major ego trip. Thinks he's still working for the *New York Times* and I'm just his water boy. Or… Keurig boy, I guess."

"Why did he leave the *Times*?"

"He didn't leave; he was laid off. He only worked there for a few months, fact-checking obituaries or something." Weston leans forward on his knees, scrabbling the Rubik's Cube faster now. "I think this is the first job he's ever had with a little bit of authority, and it's already gone to his head. But Dad's pretty desperate for writers, so I've been choking down my pride." He shoots me an impossibly cute smirk. "You looking for a job? You could fill his place."

I hum a laugh, tipping my head back. "That's not the sort of writing I do, Wes."

"Benefits are pretty good," he assures me with a wink. "I'll bring you coffee every hour—or tea, if you prefer. I'll give you neck massages, foot massages... We can make out in your cubicle when nobody's looking."

I roll my eyes, grinning at the highly improbable fantasy. "If you start a fiction or poetry column, maybe I'll consider it."

Weston slumps defeatedly, tilting the Rubik's Cube at different angles. He's managed to solve two sides of it—red and yellow—but the rest is a jumble. "This thing is impossible to solve."

"Not true," I needle him, snatching the cube out of his hands. "I solved it once, when I was younger."

"Of course you did, you frickin' genius." He flops backward on the bed with a sigh, watching me fiddle with the cube. "Let me guess: you were four years old."

"No, not *that* little. The trick is to break the problem down into smaller steps... Sometimes the move that looks the most wrong is actually the right one."

I fidget with the cube for a moment while Weston watches me, uncharacteristically silent. At first, I think he's just *that* entranced by watching me try to solve the Rubik's Cube, but when I glance up at him, he's lost in thought, his eyes dazed.

"What's that scheming face for?" I ask. "You're still thinking about the fire, aren't you?"

He confirms my suspicions by diving right back into the topic. "The neighbor who called the fire department… she lives across the street from the Montgomery place. Marcus tried to question her, but she ran back inside her house like she was scared to talk about it."

"You think she knows something?"

"I think if *anyone* knows something, it would be her." Weston gets to his feet and leans down to kiss the top of my head. "I have to go to work. Marcus will be thirsty for his midmorning coffee right about now."

I laugh, squeezing his hand before he walks away.

"Good luck solving that cube."

WESTON

SURE ENOUGH, AS SOON AS I SHOW UP AT THE
Chronicle, Marcus's first words to me are, "Weston, sleeping in
again? Well, I guess you *were* up past your bedtime last night.
Coffee would be nice. Just when you get the chance." He cuts me
a withering smile, then swivels back around to face his computer.

He's wearing a different suit jacket this morning. Navy blue,
with a matching tie. He has all the style of a New York stockbroker
and all the charm of a colonoscopy.

"Coming right up," I answer with an unbothered smile,
dropping the act as soon as my back is turned.

I find Rachel at the Keurig machine, whipping up her usual
hazelnut decaf with a packet of stevia. She's still a goddess, still has
the longest eyelashes I've ever seen, and I'm pretty sure she's still
secretly in love with me (despite the giant engagement ring on her
left hand).

"Good morning, Weston. You look like you didn't sleep
much last night."

That gets us talking about the fire on Forsythia Lane and all the mysterious rumors surrounding it. Apparently, Marcus has already been blabbing about the run-in we had last night with Boone, because Rachel seems pretty convinced he is the prime suspect in a case of revenge arson.

"It *does* seem pretty coincidental that the former owner of the house is an ex-con who just happened to be nearby at the time of the fire," she says, stirring stevia into her coffee while I start making a cup for Marcus. Just to get under his skin, I decide to make him a hazelnut decaf too—because I know he hates it.

"I think they're still investigating the cause," I point out. "There's no proof it was intentional."

"Oh, there's proof, alright." Rachel blinks her gigantic eyelashes over the rim of her coffee mug. "My fiancé has a cousin on the fire squad, and he said—off the record—that they found evidence of accelerant that must've been used to start the fire. That's why it spread so fast. But, y'know, this is all hush-hush. Apparently, if there's any possibility of arson, it's usually kept quiet until the investigation is complete. So you didn't hear that from me."

"My lips are sealed," I assure her.

I wish I could say the same for my highbrow coworker.

Rachel sighs. "Well, I'd better get back to writing this week's obits. Not that they're going anywhere."

I grunt a laugh at her morbid joke and pull Marcus's coffee out as soon as the Keurig stops grumbling. Seconds later, I'm plunking the mug down on his desk.

"What've you been telling people about Boone?"

Marcus frowns, eyeballing me the way a celebrity might look at a pleb who broke past a velvet rope to ask him an unsolicited question. "I've only told the truth about what I saw last night. What I heard."

He picks up the mug of coffee and takes a long swig, not realizing what flavor it is until he swallows. I get the satisfaction of watching him grimace and clear his throat.

"In the world of investigative reporting, you need to consider even the smallest indicators that point to something being not quite *right*. You were there, Weston. You probably shouldn't have been, but you were. You saw what I saw."

"I'm not sure what I saw. A drunk dude coming out of the woods saying Montgomery finally got what was coming to him." I place my fists on the desk, leaning closer and lowering my voice. "You don't know that he's guilty of anything except laughing at someone else's loss."

"Did you know Jonathan Boone has a prison record?"

"Yeah, for driving while intoxicated. Not for arson."

"That doesn't mean he's not capable of arson."

"Anyone is capable of arson," I volley back. "You, me, Rachel. Just because someone is capable of committing a crime doesn't mean they're guilty of it. For example, I'm within poisoning proximity of your hazelnut decaf. Not that I would actually poison you. But I *am* capable of it. See the difference?"

Marcus stares at me for a long moment—looking a bit unnerved—before he finally chuckles, shaking his head. "You should be a lawyer when you grow up, Weston."

When you grow up. Inwardly, I bristle at the veiled insult. Outwardly, I grin.

"I think I'd rather be an MMA fighter. I've heard it's considered rude to punch people in the courtroom."

Marcus shakes his head, swerving back to his computer to

click open a minimized window. "I've done some digging," he says. "Jonathan Boone's criminal records, traffic violations, previous addresses, and his current residence."

With another click, he brings up a map of Rockford. I can't help noticing that he's already routed the distance between the Montgomery house and the backwoods trailer park on the end of Wolf Spider Hollow, where Boone must be living now.

"Look at that," Marcus says, pointing to the sidebar displaying the route. "Two point seven miles from the Montgomery house. He couldn't have walked from there to the fire unless he was nearby *before* the fire started."

"First of all, he didn't come down the road; he came out of the woods. And who says he walked from his house? He was probably out drinking in town. The local bar stays open till midnight."

"Which would still have given him enough time to leave the bar and go set the Montgomery house on fire."

I frown, narrowing my eyes at him. "You don't know that's what happened."

"And you don't know that's *not* what happened," Marcus insists. "I'm not casting blame on anyone; I'm merely deducing and conjecturing. That's my job."

"Really? Thought you were a reporter, not a detective."

Marcus sighs. "Look. As long as this investigation is kept under wraps, nobody has proof of anything. Montgomery has made no public comments thus far—he's refusing to talk to anyone but his lawyers."

"Was he really out of town when it happened?"

Marcus tips his head in a half-nod. "He was staying at a hotel near the Albany airport when he got the call from the fire department."

"Why a hotel?"

"Apparently, he had plans to catch an early flight to LA this morning. But I'm sure canceling his business trip is the least of his worries at this point." Marcus leans back, shaking his head. "This whole thing is a tricky situation, but I intend to find my own answers."

I frown, crossing my arms over my chest. "How?"

"Questioning witnesses, starting with Mr. Boone."

"What are you gonna do, just show up at his house? In your little white Prius?"

A muscle tics in Marcus's jaw as he copies the Wolf Spider Hollow address into his phone. "I'm not afraid of mud or ex-convicts who may or may not have something to hide." His reply is cocky and fearless, matching his ridiculous Brooks Brothers blazer. "And if you're about to tell me there are actual wolf spiders on Wolf Spider Hollow, I'm not afraid of those either."

"Never seen wolf spiders up there, no," I return coolly, shoving my hands into the pockets of my Carhartt jacket. "But I *have* seen cars like yours stuck on the side of the road. You're gonna need four-wheel drive."

And that's how I wind up driving Marcus Verne into the backwoods outskirts of Rockford, him riding shotgun in my pickup truck, obsessively checking his phone for the route directions. I know exactly where I'm going, but he calls out every turn for me anyway. Finally, I tune out the sound of his voice and turn up the volume on the radio, forcing him to listen to country rock hits. Somehow, he strikes me as more of a Taylor Swift kind of guy.

Eventually we turn down the bumpy dirt road called Wolf Spider Hollow. It's one of those places that rich Manhattan tourists like to pretend *don't* exist. One of those sketchy, overgrown trailer parks where the residents have more dogs than teeth.

And speaking of dogs, Boone has one chained to the side of his discolored trailer—a snarling Doberman with a spiked collar and an obvious appetite for flesh. As soon as I pull my truck up and park, the dog lunges to the end of his chain, making Marcus bristle in the passenger seat.

"This the right one?" I ask, nodding towards the crooked numbers above the door.

Marcus swallows hard and checks his phone. "Uh, yes. It is."

"Well," I say, leaning back in my seat with a grin, "enjoy your interview."

Marcus pales, glancing from me to the Doberman that's blocking the path to Boone's place with bared teeth and pricked ears.

"Maybe you should come too," he offers, smoothing a hand over his hair. "It doesn't seem like a safe place to just sit in your car."

I grunt, scanning the sagging trailers surrounding us. "Yeah, well… it *does* seem like a place where everyone carries."

"Carries what?"

I block a laugh with my fist. And as usual, Marcus Verne is one hundred percent serious. My gaze slides out the window to the pissed-off Doberman jerking his chain.

"Dog treats," I answer at last.

Marcus's eyebrows jump halfway up his forehead. "Dog treats?"

"Yep." I flip open my center console and pull out a Milk-Bone. "My brother has a dog, so we're in luck. But this is the only treat I have, so be ready to run."

Together, we get out of the truck, and I break the Milk-Bone in two, putting half in my pocket for an emergency escape tactic. Marcus looks ready to get back in the truck, and I have to bite my tongue to stop myself from laughing.

If a wolf spider jumped out right now, I'm pretty sure it would be the last straw. He'd run screaming.

"Hey, big guy," I greet the Doberman with a friendly smile, waving half of the treat in the air. "I'll give you a cookie if you don't bite my leg off. Seriously, if you bite my leg, you're going to regret it."

The dog's ears flatten submissively when he spots the treat. He licks his black lips, whining and pawing the ground.

"You hungry?"

"Yeah, I think he's hungry for more than half a cookie," Marcus grumbles behind me. "He looks hungry for human flesh."

"Well, the guy behind me has more of that than I do," I tell the dog in a stage whisper loud enough for Marcus to hear.

As soon as I'm close enough, I toss the treat on the ground, far enough away to get the dog out of our path. While he dives for it, Marcus rushes up to the door and knocks hard three times. He waits, eyeing the dog with visible terror.

Seconds later, the door swings open, and there stands Jonathan Boone with a baseball bat in his hand.

Marcus reels back a few steps, putting his hands up. "I-I'm not looking for any trouble, sir. My name is Marcus Verne. I'm with *The Rockford Chronicle*."

"I seen you last night," Boone growls, his craggy face twisted in a scowl as he turns his gaze on me. "And *you.*"

I don't tell him my name. I'm pretty sure it's the last thing he's interested in knowing.

The Doberman wanders back over to me and sniffs at my pockets, looking for more food. I break off another piece of the Milk-Bone and toss it onto the ground.

"If you boys are sniffing around for answers about the Montgomery fire, you can just get back in your truck and get the hell out of here."

"You were a witness to the fire," Marcus begins, like he's conducting an interview for TV. "Can you tell us more about where you were last night around twelve o'clock?"

"I was at the bar in town," Boone says in a low voice—a voice that doesn't invite a counter question.

But Marcus can't help himself. "Is that where you were when you first saw the fire? What brought you all the way up to Forsythia Lane?"

Boone stands frozen in the doorway, thumping his baseball bat against his thigh. The dog trots over and starts licking my hand, so I scratch him behind the ears.

"I don't have to answer none of your questions," Boone snarls. "You're not the police. You're not the fire department. You want answers? Talk to them. And get the hell off my property."

"Marcus," I say under my breath, tipping my head towards my truck.

But he won't be told what to do. Especially by me.

"All I want to know is when *you* saw the fire, Mr. Boone. Your answers, if printed, will be credited anonymously."

"I ain't giving you any answers," Boone says. "Now get off my property and don't make me say it again."

He slams the door shut, making the whole place rattle from the impact. Marcus back-steps away from the door as the dog nuzzles my pockets, searching for the rest of the treat. I give it to him, wondering if it's the only food he's had today, and calmly walk back to my truck. Marcus takes his time following me, whipping out his phone and snapping a photo of Boone's place. I don't know why he does it until we're back in the truck and he points out the window at something plastic and red hidden in the weeds.

Gas cans.

"He refused to give any answers." Marcus recaps the situation as if I weren't standing right there, a victorious spark in his eyes. "He refused to give an alibi. And he has cans of accelerant on his property. Still think he's not guilty, Weston?"

————————————

A few gas cans might be enough for a guy like Marcus to sentence someone to prison (again), but it's not enough evidence for me. So after I drop him back off at the *Chronicle*, I decide to make some inquiries of my own. I park my truck on the street outside The Howling Coydog—which is the only bar Boone could've been referring to when he said "the bar in town." (The other candidate is a pub that serves alcohol but closes at eight o'clock. Not the kind of place a guy like Jonathan Boone would go to drown his sorrows.)

The Howling Coydog doesn't open until five o'clock, but the lights are on inside, and I can see the bartender moving crates around when I tent my hands to peer through the glass door. It takes a few minutes of waving before I catch his attention.

The door swings open on a tall, bearded man in a flannel shirt.

"We don't open till five," he informs me, "and I don't think you'll be old enough to drink by then. Sorry, kid."

"No, I'm not… here for that. I wanted to ask you a few questions, if you don't mind. My name's Weston. I'm from *The Rockford Chronicle*. Covering the story of the Montgomery fire."

The bartender's eyebrows rise. "Are you, now? Well, can't tell you much about it. I was here till late, then went home and crashed for the night. I heard the sirens like everyone else around one o'clock in the morning."

"Do you know Jonathan Boone?"

The bartender nods. "Yep. He was here last night. Last one here, actually. I had to kick him out to lock up."

"At midnight?"

"That's right."

"And did you happen to notice if he got into a vehicle?"

The bartender shakes his head. "He walked. Told me he wasn't going to make the same mistakes he did before, so he left his truck home. I don't know where he went, but he wasn't too steady on his feet at that point—he might not have made it home at all."

"Did he talk to you about anything else?" I ask. "Did he seem angry about anything? Any*one*?"

The bartender shrugs. "No more than usual. Boone isn't exactly a ray of sunshine."

With that, I thank the guy for talking to me and let him get back to work. On the sidewalk outside The Howling Coydog, I pivot to face the direction of the Montgomery house. It's at least two miles away from where I'm standing.

He left on foot.

At midnight.

If the neighbor lady called the fire department at twelve forty-five, the fire would've had to break out at least ten minutes before she realized there was a problem.

That means Boone would've had to walk from this spot to Forsythia Lane in thirty minutes or less.

Is that even possible?

Only one way to find out.

A MAP OF ROCKFORD LIES SPREAD OPEN ON THE coffee table in the Ludovicos' living room, Weston leaning over it with a red marker in one hand. His brothers are all seated around the table to the left and right of me, watching as Weston draws landmarks on the map.

"The Montgomery house is here." He makes an X halfway down Forsythia Lane. "And Boone's place is two point seven miles away… here." He leaves a single red dot on Wolf Spider Hollow. "But he wasn't home on the night of the fire. He was drinking in town, at The Howling Coydog." He makes another red dot on the bar on Main Street. "I talked to the bartender yesterday. He said Boone stayed till midnight and walked from there."

"That's a long walk," Henry concludes, leaning his elbows on his knees as he studies the map. "You think he could've walked to the Montgomery house with enough time to light the fire?"

Weston shakes his head. "No. I walked it myself to check— cutting through the woods, so it was the shortest possible route.

The bartender said Boone was unsteady on his feet, so I figure he walked at the pace *I* can walk through the woods with prosthetic legs. And it took me a little over an hour to get to the Montgomery house."

I pinch my lip between my forefinger and thumb. "So it's not possible for Boone to have gotten there in time."

Weston nods, looking across the map at me. "Boone has a solid alibi, which means motive isn't enough to make him a prime suspect."

"Why do you want to prove this guy innocent, anyway?" Aidan says, squinting incredulously at his brother. I still haven't gotten used to his voice, which is huskier and deeper now that he's crossed the threshold of thirteen. "I mean, he's a criminal—right?"

"He went to prison, yeah," Weston says, spinning the marker between his fingers. "But just because he messed up once doesn't make him a criminal now. Everybody's innocent until proven guilty. And I just think some people are too quick to want to prove guilt instead of innocence."

When he says "some people," I know exactly whom he's referring to: Marcus, the reporter who is determined to get to the bottom of this case before anyone else does. As I sit across from Weston, watching his eyes dart over the map, I can't help but wonder if solving this mystery is personal to him, too. If it has less to do with proving Jonathan Boone innocent and more to do with proving Marcus Verne wrong.

"I just think there are more possibilities to consider," Weston says, spinning the marker over the map. "I mean, it's like solving a Rubik's Cube. Right, Tessa? Sometimes the least obvious move is the one you have to make. Sometimes the least obvious suspect is the one who's guilty."

"So who's the least obvious suspect?" I pose the question to all the Ludovico boys, leaning back against the base of the couch.

Noah is the first to answer. "Dad!"

Weston rolls his eyes, cracking a smile and giving his littlest brother a playful shove. "You can't incriminate your own family, Noah."

"The old lady across the street?" Henry offers. "You said she's the one who called the fire department."

"Why would an arsonist call the fire department to come put out a fire they started?" Aidan volleys back, slumping into an armchair. "That's just stupid. My money's on Boone."

"You don't have any money," Henry says with a smirk.

"What about Montgomery?" I interject, trying to think outside the box. "How solid was *his* alibi?"

Weston tilts his head noncommittally. "According to Marcus, he was staying at a hotel in Albany so he could catch an early flight the next morning. That's where he was when the fire broke out."

"Why would Montgomery burn down his own house?" Noah asks, his face twisted with the confusion of a child who is too innocent to understand adult corruption. Sometimes, I don't understand it either.

"Insurance fraud is a pretty common reason," Henry answers smartly, but this only makes his little brother more confused.

"What does *that* mean?"

"It means the insurance company will give you money if you lose your house in a fire," Weston says. "If the whole house is destroyed, they'll pay you whatever it was worth."

Aiden scrunches his nose. "Why wouldn't he just sell the

house instead of burning it down to collect the insurance? Someone would've bought it, eventually."

Weston frowns, nodding slowly. "Yeah, I agree, it seems unlikely. He did a ton of renovations on that place. Seemed pretty close to putting it on the market. And from what I've heard through the grapevine, Montgomery is really pissed about the whole thing."

"Sounds more like revenge to me," Aidan says with a smug little grin on his face. "I bet Boone wanted to get back at Montgomery for buying his house, so he went around with those gas cans in the middle of the night, soaked the place, and threw his cigarette in and—kaboom!" He makes an explosive gesture in Noah's face and laughs when his little brother shrinks away.

"We don't know that's what happened," Weston reminds him. "Dad says investigators look at two main things with arson cases: did the suspect have a motive to burn the house... and did the suspect know that the house was going to burn?"

"How can you prove that someone *knew* it was going to burn?" Aidan asks, squinting dubiously at his brother.

"There are clues," I answer. "You can look at what was destroyed in the house... If anything valuable was removed *before* the fire, that usually indicates the owner knew it was going to happen."

"If I knew our house was going to burn," Noah muses philosophically, "I would grab... Weston."

This makes Weston laugh and ruffle his little brother's hair. "Thanks, bro. I'm honored."

"If I knew our house was going to burn," Aidan chimes in, "I'd grab my Nerf guns."

"I'd grab Thor," Henry adds, reaching down to pat the sleepy golden retriever on the head.

"I'd grab my running blades," Weston says decidedly. "After getting Noah out, obviously. The rest of you would have to fend for yourselves."

Henry rolls his eyes in a good-natured way, but Aidan takes this as an opportunity to wage a wrestling match with Weston, tackling his brother to the floor. The two of them start grappling with each other, and I sigh, knowing this display of brotherly affection could take a while. I pull the map closer to examine it.

"Mr. Montgomery wouldn't have had to save anything from the fire because the house didn't have any personal belongings in it," I observe aloud, though I'm pretty sure Henry is the only one paying attention at this point. "So we'd need to find some other kind of proof that he knew the fire was going to happen and that he had a sufficient *motive* to burn the house for the insurance rather than just selling it."

"Maybe there was something wrong with the house," Henry offers, resting his chin on his fist. "Maybe he knew he wouldn't be able to sell it."

The gears in my mind start spinning at his suggestion. "Wes."

He's still grappling with Aidan on the floor, the two of them rolling around and coming dangerously close to toppling a table lamp.

"Agh! I'll pin you!" Aidan howls, arms flailing.

"You don't gotta hope in hell, little brother—"

"WES."

His head of messy blond hair pops up at the sound of my voice. "Yeah?"

"Can we please focus?"

Aidan takes the opportunity to get on top of Weston and nail him to the floor. "Pinned you!"

"Okay, you win," Weston relents, crawling back over to the coffee table and fixing his rumpled shirt. "Where were we?"

"Well, I was just thinking... isn't Rudy's dad a real estate attorney?"

Weston nods. "Yeah. Why?"

"How likely is it he'd do us a favor?"

"What kind of favor?"

"A title search on the Montgomery house. To see if there's anything irregular with the history of the property—something that was possibly overlooked during the sale. Something that would motivate him to burn the house down to collect the insurance."

Weston nods slowly, gears spinning behind his eyes now. "I can definitely bribe Rudy into asking his dad... Whether Rudy can bribe his dad is another story."

"Meanwhile," I add, "we should try to talk to the lady who lives across the street. What's her name? Does anyone know?"

"Mrs. Atwood," Henry supplies. "She's a recluse. Hasn't come out of her house since her husband died a few years back."

I frown, turning to look at him. "How do you know that?"

Henry messes a hand through his chestnut-brown hair. "There's a guy in my class who delivers groceries for her every week. He says he's gotta leave them on the porch 'cause she won't even open her door. She leaves the money out there for him, too."

"That must be why Marcus hasn't had any luck getting her to talk," Weston muses, rubbing his forehead. "Maybe Tessa can get her to open up. As one recluse to another?" He smirks at me, waggling his eyebrows.

I narrow my eyes into a teasing glare. "We're going to have to do better than that." My finger traces over the curve of Forsythia Lane, pausing on the red X. "And I think I know exactly where to start."

WESTON

I LOVE THIS SCHEMING, SNEAKY DETECTIVE VERSION of Tessa Dickinson. She's a girl of many talents—I've known that since the day I first met her. But I don't think she's ever looked more beautiful than she does when she's thinking like a criminal.

Together, we puzzle out the best way to get a recluse like Mrs. Atwood to open up her door and be willing to be interrogated by two teenagers about a crime she probably had nothing to do with.

Our first step is to talk to Rachel at the *Chronicle* and get her to dig up the archived obituary of Mr. Charles Atwood. She does this without question, of course, because she secretly loves me.

While she pecks away at her keyboard in search of the long-lost obit, Tessa anxiously taps her fingers on her chin beside me.

"So… let me get this straight," I say under my breath. "We're going to read this obituary inside out and upside down until we find something we can use as leverage to force Mrs. Atwood to open her door."

Tessa rolls her eyes lovingly at me. "You make it sound so… aggressive."

"I'm an aggressive guy."

"Well, I think a *gentle* approach is best in this case. Mrs. Atwood is probably still grieving over the loss of her husband. We need to show sympathy and compassion. And we need to know a little more than nothing about Mr. Atwood to prove we're not just trying to get her to talk about the fire."

I nod slowly, noticing how pretty she looks right now, in her soft pink sweater and matching headband. I can't help leaning in close to kiss her temple and whispering, "You'd make a good detective."

She blushes, looping her arm around my waist and grinning up at me. "So would you."

The hum of a printer jolts me out of my moonstruck daze.

"Okay, you two lovebirds," Rachel says, rolling back in her swivel chair to tug a paper out of the printing tray. "Here's the obituary. Anything else?"

"That'll do it." I take the page and give her a grateful smile. "Thanks, Rachel."

With Tessa's hand in mine, we walk to the coffee break room, where a bunch of office chairs surround a long pine table strewn with abandoned mugs and pens from the last time someone was here. Happily, I haven't seen Marcus since I walked in the door. And with any luck, I won't see him at all.

"Coffee?" I offer Tessa, pointing to the Keurig.

She smirks, pulling out one of the chairs and sitting down. "That's right, you're the resident barista around here."

I grunt, flipping over a clean mug. "You can call me anything, Tessa. But *don't* call me a barista."

She laughs. "You're a cute barista."

"Don't."

I know what she likes, so I don't have to ask. Decaf dark roast with two sugars, one cream. I set it beside her on the table and go back to the Keurig machine to make myself a full-caf dark roast, black. That's when a new voice slides into the room like a slithering, silver-tongued snake.

"Well, I didn't know it was bring-your-girlfriend-to-work day."

My muscles stiffen as I turn to look at him. New charcoal-gray suit, fancy wristwatch flashing in the light, hair slicked back like he's about to appear on a national news broadcast.

How the hell does a washed-up hack like him afford expensive new suits every time I turn around? Maybe he has rich parents and a trust fund, and the whole reporter thing is just an excuse to get out more and annoy people.

"You didn't know?" I say, rolling with his punches. "I guess it doesn't matter to you—I mean, it only applies if you have a girlfriend."

Tessa glances back and forth between the two of us, cautiously sipping her coffee like she's expecting someone to throw a punch any minute now.

Marcus lets my comeback roll off him with an easy laugh, his gaze landing on the paper in front of Tessa.

"Don't tell me you've roped your girlfriend into investigating the Montgomery fire," he says with a disgusted little laugh, strutting up to the coffee bar and snatching a cup for himself. I take my mug of coffee out of the Keurig before he can get any ideas about stealing it.

"Actually, we're just doing some background checking," I answer smoothly, shooting Tessa a look that I hope she translates as *Don't tell him anything.*

Marcus grunts, stabbing buttons on the Keurig. "Well, I'm afraid it's going to be 'case closed' pretty soon. I just got back from delivering my evidence to the police."

I set my coffee on the table with a *thud*, whirling back around to face him. "What? What evidence?"

Marcus crosses his arms over his chest, a shit-eating grin curving the corners of his lips. "The conversations I had with Jonathan Boone. The proof of accelerant found on his property. The way he refused to provide an alibi. I felt it was my civic duty to inform the police of what I know."

Civic duty, my ass.

"Boone *did* provide an alibi," I argue. "He told us he was at the bar in town the night of the fire."

"Oh, please. Any drunk would've said that to cover his tracks. Are you telling me you took his word for it?" A pitying laugh. "You really need to learn the rules of this game before you play it, little boss."

That shouldn't piss me off. That shouldn't make every muscle in my body lock up with the urgent and unquenchable desire to punch him in the face.

But it does.

I want to tell him that I confirmed Boone's alibi. That I questioned the bartender at The Howling Coydog and I hiked the whole two miles from Main Street to the Montgomery house just to figure out how long it would really take a stumbling drunk man to make that trek in the middle of the night. I want to tell him that he doesn't know what he's talking about. Hell, I want to go straight to my dad's office right now and tell him to fire Marcus Verne.

But that would be immature. That would prove him right—that I'm just a kid who can't take the heat.

So I draw in a slow, deep breath. Let it out. Sip my coffee. Look at Tessa, so quiet and beautiful and in control.

Then I turn back to Marcus. "Boone isn't the only suspect in this case, Verne. As a matter of fact, I'm starting to wonder how solid Montgomery's alibi is."

At this, Marcus bursts out laughing, like my suggestion is the most outrageous thing he's heard all day. "Montgomery? You've got to be kidding me."

"No. It's not unheard of for the owner of a property to commit arson. Or insurance fraud."

"Montgomery *knows* Boone's been after him, looking for revenge. He's been *threatened* by that drunk before this happened—did you know that?"

"Threatened? How."

"Emails. Unsigned and always from a different address."

"If they were unsigned, how does he know they were from Boone?"

Marcus sighs, shaking his head like he's been debating "why is the sky blue" with a toddler for too long and he's just now realizing what a waste of time it's been. "I need to get back to work. Have fun with your girlfriend. But not *too* much fun, please—this is a professional workplace." And with one final scathing smile, he takes his coffee and strides out of the room, back to his cubicle.

My blood is boiling as I sit down at the table beside Tessa. I don't notice that my hands are curled into fists until her smooth, warm fingers melt over my knuckles.

"I know you want to punch him," she murmurs, "but he's not worth it."

I shut my eyes, taking a deep breath and letting it all out again. "I guess I'm just not the kind of guy who can work in an office. I need a fighting ring to settle my differences with someone."

Tessa hums a little laugh, leaning over the corner of the table to brush her lips softly against mine. "Cool your jets, tough guy."

She kisses me slowly, pushing me back in my chair and melting my anger just like that. One minute I'm a weapon, locked and loaded; the next, I'm defenseless. Down for the count. All because of her lips on mine. They taste like sweet coffee, and I can't get enough of them. But apparently this isn't a makeout session; it's just a tactic to make me relax and forget about punching Marcus in the face. Tessa eases back after a moment with a triumphant smile and whispers, "Now. Let's get to work."

Side by side, Tessa and I study Charles Atwood's obituary like it contains a coded message that will solve this whole mystery.

Charles Atwood, a longtime resident of Rockford, NY, passed away on Thursday, January 22, due to heart failure. He was known and loved by many for his generous spirit and vibrant personality. Charles had a profound love of nature and enjoyed spending his time hiking and bird-watching. He was an avid reader, always with a new book at his side. His fascination with history and culture was infectious, inspiring many around him to embrace learning.

Throughout his life, Charles made significant contributions to various charities, including Limitless Life, reflecting his belief in the potential of every individual. He was a beacon of kindness and generosity in his community, always eager to lend a helping hand.

Charles is survived by his beloved wife, Marjorie, who stood by his side in every walk of life. He will be greatly missed by all who knew him. His legacy of love, generosity, and curiosity will continue to live on in the hearts of many.

"Limitless Life," I murmur, those two words standing out to me more than anything else in the obituary. "Why does that name sound familiar?"

"It's a charity," Tessa says, making a rapid-fire internet search on her phone. "Looks like... they help kids with disabilities."

I snap my fingers, remembering. "That's right. My mom applied to them back when we were trying to get my running blades. They help families who can't afford to buy higher-end equipment like running blades, power wheelchairs, stuff like that."

Tessa frowns. "Doesn't health insurance pay for that?"

"For the most basic stuff, yeah. But not for 'luxury' devices. They're not considered necessary. And they're really expensive."

Tessa slides her hand over mine, sad determination in her eyes. "Running isn't a luxury. It's a human right."

A smirk pulls at my mouth. "You sound like an activist, Tessa."

She laughs dismissively and turns her attention back to the webpage on her phone. "So, this charity... they helped you get your blades?"

"Mm-hmm. Thanks to my mom's persistence."

"And thanks to Charles Atwood's generous donations." She quirks her eyebrows at me, a sly smile on her lips. "I think we just found our leverage to open the door."

It takes a few seconds to click. "What, me? *I'm* the leverage?"

She nods.

"I don't know, Tessa." I sigh, rubbing my forehead. "You know how much I hate it when people pity me."

"I know… but don't the ends justify the means this time?"

Maybe she's right. But it still makes me cringe to imagine it: showing up at Mrs. Atwood's door with the intention of making her *look* at me and go through the Reaction and feel sorry for me and invite me inside.

"I'll go with you," Tessa offers eagerly, threading her fingers through mine again. "We'll do it together."

She makes it sound like something dangerous, something I'm afraid of. Maybe because she knows me so damn well, she can read my mind. She sees me inside out. Sees the stuff I don't want anyone to see.

I squeeze her hand back and say, "Okay."

TESSA

WESTON WEARS SHORTS, FOR OBVIOUS REASONS.

I stand beside him on Mrs. Atwood's front porch, proud to hold his hand as I ring the doorbell. When there's no answer in the first two minutes, I ring the bell again, and we wait.

And we wait.

And… we wait.

The door has a gridded window in the upper half, the inside covered in bubble wrap except for a tiny triangular hole in the middle that Mrs. Atwood must use as a peephole to see who's darkening her doorstep.

When a single blue eye appears in that triangle, I nearly jump out of my skin. Mrs. Atwood's voice hammers through the glass, bitter and shrill.

"Go away!"

"Wait—Mrs. Atwood," I begin desperately. "Please, can we talk to you? It's about your husband!"

That makes her freeze, blue eye blinking through the hole in the bubble wrap. I'm not sure the hole is big enough for her to see all of Weston, including his prosthetic legs. She'll need to open her door if this plan is going to work.

"What about my husband?" she asks, voice muffled through the window.

"He did something to help me once." Weston speaks up, his voice so sweet and warm, I don't know how anyone could turn him away. "Something that changed my life. And I'd like to thank you for it, since I can't thank him."

Mrs. Atwood frowns suspiciously behind the bubble wrap for a moment before I hear the telltale jangle of multiple locks being unbolted. Next thing I know, the door swings open, and Mrs. Atwood's petite, bathrobed frame comes into full view. She's about my height, so she has to look *up* into Weston's face as she braces herself in the doorway.

"Now, young man, what are you talking—" Her gaze lowers to his legs. And just like that, her guarded frown melts into a look of stupefied shock.

Weston doesn't crack a joke or say anything to soften the blow; he just lets her react. I give his hand a little squeeze. I know he knows what it means. He squeezes back.

Mrs. Atwood holds onto the door frame with one hand, her other hand clutching her robe around her chest. She seems lost for words, looking Weston up and down. That's when he takes the floor.

"Your husband donated to a charity called Limitless Life— and as it turns out, that charity helped my parents afford a certain kind of prosthesis that allows me to run. There was a time when I was afraid I might never be able to do that again. And I just wanted you to know how grateful I am for people like Mr. Atwood... who cared enough about kids like me who lost something we all take for granted." Weston lowers his gaze to the floor of the porch, giving an easy shrug. "I know you're not a big fan of visitors, and I don't want to bother you—"

"No, no," Mrs. Atwood says, stepping aside and holding the door open. "Come in. Both of you. It's cold out there."

Weston and I trade a quick smile, and I know we're both thinking the same thing.

Success.

Hand in hand, we step into the farmhouse, which is dimly lit by antique lamps and smells faintly of Bengay. Mrs. Atwood ushers us into the living room and encourages us to sit down. Almost every chair is covered in a hand-knitted afghan, and I count at least three cats snoozing on the furniture. Weston cautiously sits on the couch beside a napping tabby, and I take the seat beside him.

Mrs. Atwood mutters apologies for the mess, saying she's not used to having visitors. As she shuffles around the living room, clearing up old mugs and crumpled tissues, I want to tell her she doesn't have to tidy for us—but I completely understand the impulse to create order.

We don't touch the topic of the fire for at least fifteen minutes. Mrs. Atwood makes us tea and tells us about her late husband—how generous and hardworking he was, how he used to make birdhouses from scratch and watch the little winged creatures for hours, sketching them and learning their habits.

I start to relax when I realize Mrs. Atwood isn't going to put Weston through any kind of awkward inquisition about his legs. I was worried about putting him in the spotlight like this just to get Mrs. Atwood to open her door to us, but now that we're in her living room drinking tea and petting her cats, it seems to be the last thing on her mind.

At last, Weston finds a way to smoothly transition to the topic of the fire: Mrs. Atwood remarks on how quiet it usually is up here on Forsythia Lane.

"The night the Montgomery house burned down must've been the most excitement you've had up here in a long time," Weston says casually, scratching the tabby cat under her chin.

Mrs. Atwood shudders at the mere memory of the fire. "I just kept praying those firemen would be alright, and that they'd put it out before it spread down the street."

"You were the one who called the fire department, right?" Weston waits for her to nod before adding, "Good thing you happened to be awake."

Mrs. Atwood sips her tea and strokes a black cat that's snuggled in her lap. "It was strange, because I couldn't sleep at all that night. I'm usually in bed before ten o'clock, but that night I just lay awake for hours. Then, at about eleven thirty, I heard a car pull up to the Montgomery house."

My interest piques at this new piece of information. "A car?"

"I didn't get up to see whose car it was," Mrs. Atwood continues. "I figured it must've been Mr. Montgomery, since no one else was living there."

"Did you happen to hear when the car drove away?" Weston asks, letting the tabby climb into his lap and curl up in a purring ball of orange fluff. A longhaired gray one comes slinking over to join the snuggle fest, and I almost laugh because Weston looks impossibly cute engulfed in cats. He's like an animal magnet wherever he goes. And honestly, I can't blame any living creature for wanting to cuddle with him.

"I must've been asleep when the car left," Mrs. Atwood says, frowning as she recalls the night. "But I keep my windows open a crack at night this time of year. I love the cool mountain air when I'm sleeping… Only, that night, I could've sworn I smelled lighter fluid. It woke me up again around midnight, and *that's* when I got up to have a look around."

"Was that when you saw the fire?" Weston asks.

Mrs. Atwood shakes her head. "No… everything was dark over at the Montgomery place. No cars in the driveway. I thought maybe I imagined all of it. I tried to go back to sleep, but I couldn't. I kept feeling like something wasn't right… When I got up about a half hour later, I saw the whole top floor of the Montgomery house was on fire."

"Just the top floor?"

She nods. "The windows were either open or they'd been blown out—the fire was getting to the roof, and I knew that house was going to come down like a ton of bricks. I called the fire department as quickly as I could."

Weston thinks about this for a moment, stroking both cats simultaneously behind their velvety ears. I can tell the gears in his mind are turning a hundred miles an hour, but he doesn't share his deductions with Mrs. Atwood. Instead, he just gives her a sympathetic smile and says, "I'm sorry you had to go through that. It must've been scary."

"It was," she admits, caressing the black cat. "But my babies and I are safe—that's all that matters."

———————————

By the time we part ways with Mrs. Atwood, her cats have become inseparably attached to Weston. She invites us to stop by again, any time we want, and we both thank her profusely for her kindness.

Back in the front seat of Weston's truck, we sit parked in the driveway for a few minutes, discussing and deducing.

"So whoever set the house on fire showed up in a car," Weston concludes. "And they made sure the attic burned first so the whole house would become a sort of self-ventilating furnace and be totally destroyed. But somehow… the fire didn't start until at least thirty minutes after the arsonist left."

I tilt my head, turning over the possibilities in my mind. "We know they used lighter fluid because Mrs. Atwood smelled it."

"And the fire department found traces of accelerant."

"But if the arsonist lit a match, it would've started burning immediately," I add, pinching my lower lip between my fingers. "So maybe they lit something else… like a candle."

"A candle?"

"Yeah… That would've taken longer to burn out. And by the time it *did* burn to the end and ignited the accelerant, the arsonist would've been long gone. He would've had time to establish an alibi somewhere else."

Weston taps his fingers on the steering wheel. "Want to look around the crime scene before we head back?" he asks, quirking his eyebrows at me in a way that's impossible to refuse.

"Is that legal?"

"I'm pretty sure we can't do any more damage at this point," Weston says with a grunt, shifting the truck into reverse and pulling out onto the road. We stop in the driveway of the Montgomery house—which is just a pile of rubble and ash. Nothing but a blackened skeleton remains of the beautiful Victorian house that once stood here.

I hop out of the truck with Weston, and we cautiously approach the disaster zone, which is roped off with crime scene tape to keep intruders out.

"Don't get too close, Wes," I warn him, my head on a swivel as I check to make sure we're truly all alone. "I don't think we're supposed to be nosing around here."

"I'm not going to go in there," he says, gesturing towards the rubble. "I'm just looking for anything… out of the ordinary. Keep your eyes peeled."

I stay in the driveway, too nervous to go anywhere near the yellow tape. Instead, I keep my eyes trained on the gravel beneath my feet, searching for any left-behind clue the fire marshal may have missed. I don't know what I'm looking for until I see a glint of something shiny in the light.

Strange.

I reach down to brush aside a clump of dirt, picking up the shiny brass object. At first, I think it's a ring, then I realize something is hooked around the ring.

A key.

"Weston," I call to him, catching his attention. He squints when he sees what I'm holding up. "I found this at the edge of the driveway."

We meet each other at the crime scene tape. He's standing on the opposite side despite the bold message printed in black letters: **DO NOT CROSS.**

"A key?" he rasps under his breath, turning it over to get a closer look. "What do you think it unlocks? The house, maybe?"

I shrug. "I guess there's no way to find out."

Weston thinks about it for a moment before glancing over his shoulder at the charred remains of the Montgomery house. I know exactly what he's looking for: the front door. Surprisingly, it's one of the only parts of the house still intact—though it's blackened by smoke and lying facedown in the rubble of the front porch.

Weston takes the key and heads straight for the crime scene.

"Be careful, Wes. We're not supposed to be here—"

"Shh, it'll just take a sec. Don't you want to know if the key fits?"

I groan at his stubbornness, ducking under the yellow tape and following him—because if he gets hurt or disturbs something that *shouldn't* be disturbed, I'm not letting him face the consequences alone. We carefully pick our way through charred boards and broken glass until we reach the fallen front door.

Weston crouches down and slides the key into the antique knob.

"It fits," he announces, turning the handle and causing the metal bolt to slide out of the lock. "And who else would have a key to this house… besides Montgomery?"

I swallow, a chill racing down my arms as I watch Weston slide the key in and out of the lock. "Well, I don't think Jonathan Boone would've had a key."

"No. He wouldn't."

"But why would Montgomery have left it behind?"

"He probably dropped it by accident," Weston muses, pocketing the key and glancing around for any other clues lost in the rubble. "It was dark. If *you* only had thirty minutes to get to your alibi before your house burst into flames, would you waste any time looking around for a key to a door you're never going to unlock again?"

I shake my head, about to respond when—

"Hey!"

Weston and I both whirl at the sound of a gruff man's voice. My heart sinks into my stomach as soon as I see the unmistakable green sheriff's cruiser parked beside Weston's truck in the driveway.

A mustached man stands beside the cruiser, his arms crossed over his chest as he levels a frigid look at us. "I think you kids had better come with me."

Weston curses under his breath.

WESTON

I'VE ALWAYS WONDERED IF I'D WIND UP IN THE BACK of a sheriff's cruiser someday. The odds seemed likely, given how many times people have told me to stay out of trouble. But never did I ever imagine Tessa would be sitting beside me in the back of that sheriff's cruiser.

She's shooting daggers at me the whole ride back into town, her face as red as a tomato—righteous anger blazing in her eyes.

Honestly, I'm more worried about *her* punishment for me than the sheriff's. He and my dad go way back—one of the perks of living in a small town. Tessa, on the other hand, has never been caught doing something illegal before.

"I should be taking you two down to the station right now," Sheriff Walker warns us from the driver's seat. "Disturbing a crime scene could be considered tampering. And as I'm sure you both know, tampering is against the law."

I swallow stiffly, the Montgomery key burning a hole in my pocket. "But we weren't tampering with anything, sir. We were just looking. We were curious."

Sheriff Walker meets my eyes in the rearview mirror. "Curiosity can be a crime."

"Are you arresting us?" Tessa blurts beside me, anxiety swimming in her eyes.

Sheriff Walker grunts a dry laugh. "I'm giving you both an escort back to where you belong. But if I catch you kids snooping around the Montgomery place again, I'll have no choice but to charge you with disturbing a crime scene."

"It won't happen again," I assure him with a quick nod. "Promise."

I want to ask why he didn't let me drive my own truck back home, if this is nothing but an escort to "where I belong"—but I know better than to debate with an officer of the law who is choosing *not* to charge me with a mischief crime I am in fact guilty of.

He drops Tessa off at her house, then drives to Main Street and parks his cruiser right in front of the *Chronicle*, in full view of my dad's office window. I suppress a groan, tipping my head back against the seat.

"I'll walk you inside," the sheriff says with a sadistic grin. "Haven't seen your dad in a while."

Just my luck.

He doesn't frog-march me or anything. He just holds the door open, and we walk into the *Chronicle* together. It's humiliating enough. And of course, Marcus Verne is right there to witness my Walk of Shame. He leans against the wall with a flashy new tie around his neck and a shit-eating grin on his face.

My jaw twitches as our eyes connect, and in that instant, I know: he was the one to sic the sheriff on me. He had to be.

"Look who I found out by the Montgomery place," Sheriff

Walker announces to my dad as soon as we step into his office.

I can't look him in the eyes. I can't explain myself until we're alone, so I just stand there silently fingering the key in my pocket while Sheriff Walker catches up with my dad. After about fifteen minutes of jawboning, he makes his exit, and I watch from the window as the cruiser pulls back out onto Main Street and drives off.

Dad sinks back into his desk chair and lets out a long sigh. "What the hell got into you, Weston?"

My fist tightens around the key as I turn around to face him. "I wasn't doing anything wrong. I was just investigating."

"It's not your job to investigate," Dad shouts, anger sparking in his eyes. "That's up to the police and the state investigators, not *you*. And yes, you *did* do something wrong when you crossed that crime scene tape that said 'do not cross'!"

"Okay," I hiss. "Do you have to let the whole office know? I'm sorry. I told Sheriff Walker it won't happen again, and it *won't*." I look down, a knot of frustration tightening in my chest. My fingers still have ash on them from fooling around with the front-door lock of the burned house.

"Weston," Dad begins, then sighs again, rubbing his forehead wearily. "In the world of reporting, it's easy to get caught up in the excitement of breaking a story—especially a sensational one like this. But you have to remember, there are ethical rules we operate by. All that matters is getting the truth out to the public once we know for sure *what* the truth is. It doesn't matter who gets the glory."

An indignant laugh catches in my throat. "Maybe you should talk to Marcus about that. He's been snooping around in this case long before I was, trying to dig up all this evidence against

Jonathan Boone—he's going around telling the police stuff he doesn't even *know* for sure. He's the one who's been trying to get the glory, being a know-it-all jerk—"

"Stop letting Marcus bother you," Dad cuts in, leveling a stern look at me. "It doesn't matter what he thinks or says or does in his free time. I'm not going to tell him how to behave because he's not my son—you are."

I grit my teeth, every other accusation I was about to make sinking back down my throat.

"He's a decent writer," Dad continues, his tone clipped. "That's why I hired him. Now, I know there's a personality clash between you and Marcus, but I want you to be the better man, alright? Rise above it. Have a professional attitude and don't let your ego get involved. That's a lesson you're going to have to learn sooner or later if you stay in this line of work."

I want to tell him he doesn't really *know* Marcus—doesn't know what a slippery, scheming bottom-feeder he really is when "the boss" isn't looking. But somehow, I know anything I say will come out sounding petty and unprofessional.

And after seeing the look on my dad's face when Sheriff Walker escorted me into his office, all I want is to make him proud of me again.

So I say, "Yes, sir." And I leave his office.

When I pull out my phone, I find a new text from Tessa on the screen.

TESSA:
Did you get off okay?

A wry smirk tugs at one side of my mouth as I type back a reply.

She replies immediately.

I send her a row of kissing emojis in response to the death threat and pocket my phone, striding across the office to Marcus's cubicle. He's talking on the phone as I approach, his back to me, his perfectly groomed head nodding to the voice on the other end of the phone.

"Yes, sir. Absolutely. I understand… I can print those off here and deliver them by the end of the day."

I slow my steps, creeping silently closer as I eavesdrop on the call. But there's not much else to eavesdrop on because that's when Marcus says a curt goodbye and hangs up, turning back to his computer. It looks like he has an email up on the screen, but the window around the email doesn't look like an ordinary inbox. Before I can get a closer look, Marcus notices me approaching and minimizes the window, lightning-fast.

"Well, if it isn't the little boss himself. Just in time to get me a fresh coffee. Hey—how did it feel to get a police escort into work today? Must've been quite the honor."

I press a humorless smile onto my lips as I sling one arm over the edge of his cubicle. "An honor I have *you* to thank for, right?"

Marcus chuckles, straightening his tie. "You think I have nothing better to do than follow you around as you play your little detective games with your girlfriend?"

I study him, trying to peel apart the layers of that response. He seems uncharacteristically… twitchy. Almost *nervous*.

"What are you working on?" I ask, casually jerking my head towards the screen.

Marcus stiffens. "Fact-checking."

"Who were you on the phone with just now?"

His eyes narrow. "None of your business, little boss."

"I think it would be my *dad's* business, since you're on his payroll and you're technically supposed to be working right now."

"I am working," Marcus replies briskly, picking up his empty coffee mug and thrusting it into my free hand. "Dark roast. No cream or sugar."

TESSA

———————

OUT OF THE GOODNESS OF MY HEART, I DECIDE NOT to strangle Weston for almost getting me arrested. At least we got off with nothing more than the proverbial slap on the wrist. It might have been a different story if we wound up in a cell together, but thankfully the sheriff is good friends with Mr. Ludovico and didn't let his son—or me—get in any real trouble.

We've been strictly forbidden from snooping around the Montgomery property or "investigating" the fire, according to Weston. But that doesn't stop us from secretly meeting with Rudy later that week at the Trolley Station Café to go over the findings of the title search.

"Apparently, these records are all public—otherwise, I never would have been able to convince my dad to dig into this." Rudy pulls a folder out of his backpack and flips it open on the table, looking like a professional attorney himself. He's started wearing glasses for reading, and it only enhances the academic look of him. He slides a few pages across the table to me and Weston. "Here's what he found."

We lean over the page, scanning the records as Rudy explains them to us in a low voice.

"This shows the sale history of the property. Three years ago, when it went up for auction, Montgomery bought it for one hundred and twenty-five thousand dollars. According to my dad, auction sales always come with a 'buyer beware' scenario."

I frown, looking up at him. "Meaning what?"

"The house is sold on an 'as-is, where-is' basis," Rudy explains. "The buyer takes on every problem that comes with it. And as it turns out, Montgomery got more than he bargained for."

Weston flips to the next page, his eyes scanning eagerly for answers to his unspoken questions. Rudy points to a line of data halfway down the page.

"See that number?"

"Two hundred and twelve thousand," Weston murmurs. "That's not what he paid for the house, right?"

Rudy shakes his head. "No. That's the estimated cost of a remediation order the city hit him with after an inspection. Full asbestos and mold removal, plus lead paint abatement. They even issued a stop-work order. Until that's done, he can't sell or even rent it."

"So even if he finished the flip," I say, puzzle pieces fitting together in my mind, "he'd have to sink two hundred grand into making it legal. And after the price he paid for it, plus the reno-vations…"

"He would've sunk three hundred thousand dollars into the house," Weston concludes, his gaze locking on mine.

"But if the house burned," Rudy interjects, "he could claim the insurance for what it was worth. The house was valued at two hundred and fifty thousand."

I swallow hard, a knot tightening in my throat. "But wouldn't the insurance company run their own investigation?"

Rudy rests his chin thoughtfully on his fist. "Yeah, they ran their own investigation. But they found no evidence that Montgomery was involved."

"He'd already set himself up with the perfect alibi," Weston says. "He booked a hotel in Albany and stayed there on the night of the fire, to prove he was out of town and planning to fly out to LA the next morning."

"So you think that was just a setup?" I ask.

Weston shrugs. "It could've been. He would've booked the hotel for real, and the plane tickets. That's proof of an alibi."

Rudy eyes Weston cautiously. "You said you didn't like how Marcus was trying to implicate Boone without enough evidence. Careful you don't do the same thing to Montgomery."

"I'm not," Weston argues, crossing his arms as he sits back in his chair. "I just think this is a pretty strong motive. Before this, we couldn't find a motive for Montgomery. Now we know he couldn't have sold that house without forking over two hundred grand to bring it up to code."

"But he didn't make it look like an accident," I add, thinking out loud. "He could've if he wanted to... Most fires are started accidentally. But he used accelerant."

"Because he wanted the house to burn as fast as possible," Rudy puts in, rapping his fingers on the table. "And it didn't matter if he made it look like arson..."

"Because he was planning to pin this whole thing on Boone from the beginning," Weston says decidedly. "Think about it— the ex-convict with a shady past loses his house to the white-collar businessman... and in a fit of drunken rage one night, he goes around and burns down the house Montgomery took from him. It's the perfect story."

I frown, turning over all the possibilities in my mind. "And according to Marcus, there were threatening emails from Boone to Montgomery. He has records of malicious intentions, which would be the smoking gun the police need to prove Boone had a motive."

Weston nods slowly, a doubtful look creeping into his eyes as he thinks about it. "How the hell did Marcus know about those emails, anyway? He told me that Montgomery wasn't talking to anyone but his lawyers."

"Maybe Marcus camped out on Montgomery's front lawn until he agreed to answer his questions," Rudy offers with a wry smirk.

"I wouldn't put it past him," Weston grumbles. "He was acting weird the other day at the office. And I overheard him on the phone with someone he called 'sir,' saying he'd print something off and deliver it. Later, I saw him walking out with a yellow envelope."

"Do you know where he was going?" I ask.

Weston shakes his head. "I didn't have my truck, so I couldn't follow him. But now I think he was probably going to the police station."

"To take them evidence?" Rudy raises an eyebrow. "Why would he have any evidence to give them?"

Weston's gaze slides from me to Rudy, gears spinning behind his eyes. "Good question."

———————

After our meeting at the café, we go our separate ways, and I don't hear from Weston again until later that night, after my shower. I'm towel-drying my hair, wrapped in a bathrobe and ready to dive into a cozy mystery book before bed—and that's when my phone starts ringing.

"Hey, you still awake?"

"Weston, it's nine o'clock. I'm not *that* much of an old lady." I leave out the part about me planning to snuggle up with a blanket for the next hour reading a book.

"Feel like being my lookout?"

"What?"

"I'm going to go down to the *Chronicle*."

I frown, crossing my bedroom to draw my curtains closed. That's when I see Weston's truck idling in my driveway, the headlights misty in the rain that's beginning to fall.

"You're literally calling me from my driveway."

He laughs. "I was wondering when you'd notice. See? You'd make a great sleuth."

"And you'd make a terrible criminal."

"That's why I need you to come with me to the *Chronicle*."

"Why?" I put one hand on my hip, frowning out the window at his truck. "What are you doing that you have to sneak around at night?"

Weston sighs through the phone. "I need to figure out what Marcus was hiding."

"You're going to break into his computer?"

"It's a work computer, not *his*. It technically belongs to my dad, which means it kinda sorta belongs to me. So no, it's not illegal. And I won't even have to break into the office—I have a key."

"Did you steal it from your dad?"

"No, he gave it to me. He trusts me."

"Well, that makes one of us."

Weston groans. "Come on, Tessa. Please? I need your computer skills. If Marcus was doing something wrong, he would've covered his tracks well. And you know I'm not the most tech-savvy person in the world."

I think about it for a few moments, resting my forehead against the cool glass window as I consider my options. If I say no, Weston will go to the *Chronicle* anyway—and possibly get himself in more hot water than he can handle.

He's the most stubborn person I've ever met.

"You're not just doing this to get back at Marcus, are you? I know he's been getting on your nerves lately—"

"That's not what this is about," Weston insists, his voice firm with resolve. "I just want to get to the bottom of this. I want to know the truth. I want to solve the damn Rubik's Cube."

A little smile teases my lips as my gaze drifts to the unsolved cube sitting on my nightstand. I've made a little progress with it each night. Now only three sides remain scrambled.

I understand how Weston feels—I know this whole mystery has been getting under his skin like a splinter. It's done the same to me. Now, we may be on the cusp of finding answers. So, despite the little voice of hesitation in the back of my mind, I give in.

"If you get me arrested again, I *am* going to kill you this time."

"I know," Weston says, a smile in his voice.

"Slowly," I add.

"Yes."

"Painfully."

"I'd expect nothing less," he answers cheerily. "But we're not going to get arrested."

I step away from the window, shedding my bathrobe and reaching for a pair of jeans. "I'll be down in two minutes."

I CAN'T BELIEVE I CONVINCED TESSA TO SNEAK INTO the *Chronicle* with me after hours. But here she is, right by my side, her hair still wet from the shower. She looks extra beautiful when she's doing something she might get in trouble for.

The rain is falling hard by the time I park my truck outside the *Chronicle*; low rumbles of thunder are rolling through the sky, drawing closer.

We unlock the door, and I snap on the lights.

"Shouldn't we keep them off?" Tessa asks, wide eyes scanning the empty office like monsters might be lurking between the cubicles. "What if someone sees?"

"Rule number one when you're somewhere you shouldn't be," I say, striding down the row of cubicles. "Act like you *are* exactly where you should be."

Tessa sighs, rubbing her arms. "So you have a cover story, I assume?"

"Mm-hmm. Forgot my phone in the office. Can't remember where I left it."

"And you needed *me* to come help you find it?"

I tilt my head back and forth. "I needed someone to call the phone so I know where it is."

Tessa has no comeback for that, and I feel a blip of victory. My cover story is bulletproof enough that even *she* can't poke holes in it. We make our way across the office, stopping when we reach Marcus's cubicle. I drop into his desk chair, which stinks like his cologne, and reach over to power on his computer.

It takes only a few moments to boot up, and Tessa's head is on a swivel the whole time as she dutifully plays the lookout. When the desktop finally loads, I dive straight for the "recent items" menu in the upper left corner of the screen.

My eyes scan the list: internet browsers, word documents, printer, PDF reader, file converter... Photoshop.

"Why would Marcus be using Photoshop?" I murmur under my breath, double-clicking to open the program.

"Maybe he was working on some graphic design project?" Tessa suggests with her usual heart of gold.

I shake my head. "He doesn't do graphic design for us."

Once Photoshop loads, I scan the recent projects list—the one at the top has a filename of HM_DRAFT4.

HM as in Harrison Montgomery?

I try to open it up, but an error message pops onto the screen.

"Source files not found," I read quietly, turning to Tessa. "Do you know what that means?"

"It means whatever files he was working with are no longer located where they were before. He probably deleted them." She leans over my shoulder, taking the mouse and opening up the trash bin in the bottom right corner.

Sure enough, it's full of Photoshop files. Tessa's wet hair

brushes against my face as she leans closer to work her magic—selecting all the deleted files and recovering them in a few keystrokes.

"There. Try opening the project again."

I reclaim the mouse and reopen Photoshop, bringing up the document labeled HM_DRAFT4. I wait with bated breath for it to load, and when the project fills the screen, *holy shit*.

The air rushes out of my lungs.

It's a screenshot of an email—to Harrison Montgomery, from a gibberish email address. The subject line reads: **You'll be sorry.**

Chills crawl over the backs of my arms as I read the body of the email out loud.

"You'll be sorry for what you did to me, Montgomery. If you think you can take my home, then turn around and make bank off it… you've got another think coming. Watch your back."

"Why does Marcus have a screenshot of this email?" Tessa whispers close to my ear.

I shake my head, pointing to the sidebar menu on the screen. "It's not a screenshot. Look at all these text layers. He *created* this email. It's forged. And there are at least three others like it."

Tessa's breathing quickens as the truth hits us both, the final side of the Rubik's Cube coming together.

"Marcus has been working for Montgomery in secret," I murmur. "That's who he was on the phone with the other day. He was talking about printing these emails off here and delivering them… so Montgomery wouldn't have the files in *his* computer and it couldn't be traced back to him." A dry laugh rattles in my chest as it all pieces together. "No wonder Marcus was able to afford all those expensive suits. He's known it was Montgomery this whole time, and he's been getting hush money in exchange for helping the guy cover it up—and framing Boone for arson."

Tessa's eyes dart back and forth over the computer screen. "How do we get this to the police?"

"I'll take screenshots of the project files and send them to the printer. There are probably more emails like this in his recents. I'll check. You go to the printer room and get the papers as soon as they come out." I gesture behind me to the little room down the hallway where our printers and scanners are kept.

"Done," Tessa says, and takes off towards the printer room. I watch as she disappears through the door, then roll my chair back to the computer and start capturing screenshots—immediately sending them to print.

My heart pounds in my chest as I navigate back to the main menu and open the list of recent projects, finding another one called HM_DRAFT3.

Same deal as before. A threatening email from an encrypted address, the body of the message dripping with vengeance and warnings that Montgomery will "get what's coming to him."

I shake my head in disbelief, capturing another screenshot of the open project files. As I hit *print* on the third file, I hear the telltale creak of a door opening. I figure it's Tessa coming out of the printer room and say over my shoulder, "Hey, I've got a few more coming. Stand by."

That's when the lights go out.

I freeze, the glow of the computer screen suddenly blinding in the dark. For a second, I think the power went out because of the thunderstorm. But if it had, the computer would've died too.

Someone shut the lights off.

Someone is here.

My blood runs cold as a knot of dread tightens in the pit of my stomach. Slow footsteps echo over the floor, coming from my left or right, I can't tell—until they come to a stop right behind me.

"Still haven't learned the rules of the game, have you, little boss?"

WESTON

EVERY MUSCLE IN MY BODY LOCKS UP AT THE SOUND of Marcus's slithering voice. I'm about to whirl around and punch him so hard he'll see stars when—

Click.

My heart vaults into my throat.

"Put your hands over your head."

I obey his command, slowly bringing my hands up and regretting every decision I've ever made, especially bringing Tessa here with me tonight.

"Now back away from the computer," Marcus instructs, his voice a low growl. "And tell your little girlfriend to shred those papers you just printed."

"Or what?" I bite back. "You'll shoot me? Don't you think that'll land you in prison for more time than forgery?"

Okay, that was probably way too cocky a thing to say when you're being held at gunpoint. But this situation doesn't feel real to me. Marcus might be a con artist and a forger and a scummy hack, but he's not a cold-blooded killer. He's not even holding his pistol properly, I realize, when I turn around slowly and stand up, keeping the swivel chair between us. As I study him in the pale glow of the computer light, I wonder if this is the first time he's ever held a gun.

"I won't shoot you," he seethes with a bloodless smile. "I'll leave a few holes in the wall and call the police and have *you* arrested for attempted murder. These documents could easily be your handiwork." He jerks his head towards the Photoshop file on the computer screen. "This isn't *my* computer. It's your father's. And technically, everything that belongs to your father also belongs… to you."

My eyebrows rise. "You'd pin all this on me? Why? What the hell do you have to gain by seeing me punished for something you did? Are you literally *that* jealous of me?"

Marcus's grin looks evil in the ghostly blue light. His laugh comes out even more deranged. "Jealous? Why would I be jealous of an *amputee*?"

That's the last straw.

I may be an amputee, but I can still use my knees pretty well. And right now, I'm willing to bet my life on it.

Driving one knee up, I kick the swivel chair and send it flying straight into Marcus, knocking him flat on his back. The gun goes off, firing into the ceiling and making my ears ring. I don't waste a second. I dive on top of him, slamming my fist into his stomach, then hooking him hard in the face.

I can barely see, but I can feel well enough to ground and pound him—furious adrenaline rocketing through my veins. A guttural cry of pain erupts from Marcus as I drive my fist into his stomach again, struggling to blindly wrestle the gun out of his hands.

Tessa must hear all the ruckus, because suddenly the door to the printer room swings open, letting out a shaft of bright light.

"Stay back, Tessa!" I yell to her. "Call the police!"

She vanishes back through the door just as I manage to yank the pistol away from Marcus. I toss it into the darkness before he can use it against me—then we're back to grappling each other like animals. Without a weapon in the mix, I have the advantage over him. I may be just a "kid" in his eyes—and a disabled one at that—but I don't need legs to feed him a knuckle sandwich.

He gives me one, too—hooking me hard on the jaw by dumb luck. It's enough to throw me off guard for a second. Enough for him to trap my arms behind my back. I writhe on the floor, rolling over and thrusting a knee where I think his groin is. When he lets go with an animalistic moan of pain, I know I hit my target.

I clamber to my feet, trying to get away from him while I have the chance—but his hand reaches out and yanks my metal ankle joint, making me trip and fall on my face. Panic fires through me as I try to drag myself away.

Downside of having no feeling below my knees: I don't know how tight a grip my attacker has around my fake leg.

Upside: my fake leg is removable.

Thinking fast, I reach down and press the release on my left prosthesis, disconnecting the socket from my stump. I leave Marcus holding my leg while I crawl away like a madman to the safety of the printer room.

I slam the door shut as soon as I'm inside, reaching up to twist the lock.

"Weston! Oh my god." Tessa crashes to her knees beside me. "The police are on their way. Are you hurt? You're bleeding. Where's your leg?"

Despite everything, I almost laugh as I slump back against the door. "Marcus has it."

Tessa is breathing hard as she cups my face in her hands. "You stupid, stupid idiot—you could've gotten killed!" She brushes away the trail of blood on my lip with her finger. "You're lucky I was here to save your neck."

The distant wail of sirens grows louder until I see police lights blinking under the crack in the door. Moments later, chaos erupts outside—voices barking orders, footsteps pounding into the office.

"I *am* lucky to have you," I rasp, squeezing Tessa's hand and smiling through my split lip. "Partner in crime."

———————————

We're stuck at the *Chronicle* for what feels like the rest of the night—and this time, Sheriff Walker doesn't give me a tongue-lashing for being found in the middle of a crime scene.

I watch as the police lead Marcus away in handcuffs. I don't know what's more satisfying: to know that he'll pay for what he did, or to know that I'll never have to make his pitiful ass a Keurig ever again.

Tessa and I take turns explaining to the sheriff what happened and the files we found on Marcus's computer. We hand over the printed email forgeries, but the police end up seizing the whole computer hard drive for further investigation.

Meanwhile, first responders put me through the Spanish Inquisition of medical questions, and it takes a while to convince them that I ripped my leg off *on purpose*—and that, despite the blood on my lip and the hole in the ceiling, nobody was shot.

(Unless you count the nutshot I delivered to Marcus's groin when we were grappling on the floor. It makes me smile to know that he'll have sore balls while he sits in jail, awaiting trial.)

When Dad shows up at the *Chronicle*, he rushes over and hugs me so tight I think my ribs might break—and I hug him back just as hard. We don't get time to talk about everything until after the commotion has died down and Tessa has gotten a ride back home. The police are still poking around, taking photos and gathering evidence, but they've stopped asking us questions.

That's when Dad shakes his head in dismay and says, "I'm sorry, Wes. I should've taken your suspicions about Marcus more seriously... I should've paid closer attention to him. I should've noticed..."

"You have a lot on your plate, Dad," I assure him with a shrug. "And you weren't wrong—I *did* let Marcus piss me off. But it was more than a personality clash. More than rivalry."

Dad nods. "I know. And I'm sorry I misread the situation."

I give him a weak half-smile. "I'm sorry I didn't tell you where I was going tonight. I know I shouldn't have been... investigating. I know it's not my job here. And I understand if you want to fire me."

Dad laughs unexpectedly, his hand on my shoulder. "I think I'll let you off with a warning this time."

TESSA

ARSON VERDICT: LOCAL BUSINESSMAN GUILTY OF INSURANCE FRAUD; ACCOMPLICE CONVICTED FOR FORGERY

ROCKFORD – Rockford found itself at the center of a riveting courtroom drama on Thursday as Harrison Montgomery, 57, the owner of a once-stately residence, was pronounced guilty of insurance fraud after deliberately setting his own house ablaze.

The incident unfolded on April 17 when Montgomery, facing a city-issued stop-work order and an estimated $200,000 in mandated hazardous material remediation, opted for a reckless solution: burning his house to the ground. The motivation was a dubious attempt to claim insurance rather than address the costly repairs that stood in the way of selling the property.

Montgomery orchestrated the arson by dousing the attic in accelerant and igniting a candle, subsequently leaving town under the pretense of an early-morning flight to Los Angeles.

However, Montgomery's plan took an unexpected turn as he attempted to shift blame onto the previous property owner, Jonathan Boone. Montgomery alleged that Boone had sent him malicious emails, which he claimed revealed the motive behind the crime. Investigations, however, revealed these emails to be cunning forgeries, the handiwork of an accomplice in the crime, Marcus Verne, a 22-year-old implicated in the scheme.

Rockford's chief of police, Sheriff Walker, expressed his disdain for the ruse, stating, "Montgomery's actions not only endangered lives but also attempted to destroy the reputation of an innocent man."

In the verdict delivered yesterday, Montgomery was found guilty of insurance fraud and arson. He now faces a significant prison sentence and has been ordered to make restitution for the damages caused by the deliberately set fire.

Marcus Verne, the accomplice responsible for the forgery of evidence, will stand trial for multiple charges, including fabricating the emails to frame Jonathan Boone. Verne faces legal consequences for his complicity in this case.

I lower the newspaper when I finish the article and look at Weston, who's sitting beside me on the couch, a smile of admiration spreading over my face.

"You did it," I say, leaning over to press a kiss to his lips. "You solved the mystery."

"*We* solved it," Weston murmurs, brushing a lock of hair off my cheek and kissing me back. "I might be dead right now if it weren't for you."

"About that…" I smirk, holding up the paper. "There's nothing in here about Marcus pulling a gun on you and wrestling your leg off."

Weston tilts his head thoughtfully. "Well, I don't think my dad wanted *The Rockford Chronicle* to sound like a potentially life-threatening place to work. Might scare away new hires."

I laugh, folding the newspaper in half and studying the two mugshots at the top of the article. Montgomery, with his wrinkled brow and flat line of a mouth; Marcus, with his whole life ahead of him, now shadowed by a reputation he'll never be able to escape.

"I don't feel bad for him," I say decisively.

"Which one?"

"Both of them. But especially Marcus." I toss the paper onto the coffee table. "What sort of legal consequences is he going to face?"

Weston shrugs. "He made things more complicated by threatening me at gunpoint. Plus, he's guilty of more than just forgery. He's also facing charges of defamation, filing a false police report, blackmail, obstruction of justice, malicious persecution… He got a lot done for a guy who was too lazy to make his own coffee."

I stifle a smirk. "And Montgomery?"

"Up to ten years in prison. Maybe more because he tried to frame Boone for the arson." Weston shakes his head. "I want to believe the police would've gotten to the bottom of all this if we hadn't intervened… but I'm glad we did. A guy like Boone couldn't afford the fancy lawyers Montgomery had in his pocket. And I know he's messed up in the past, but you can't judge people based on what they look like on the outside."

I nod slowly, tracing my fingertips over the back of his hand. "That's very true. And I'm sure Mr. Boone will be grateful to see his name cleared in the paper—to see the sheriff calling him an 'innocent man.'"

A little smile tugs at Weston's mouth, and he sighs out a

breath he seems to have been holding for a long time. "Now what? Life goes back to being boring again?"

I laugh, smacking him playfully. "I *like* boring. Boring doesn't get you killed."

"That's why it's so boring." Weston reaches over, snatches the still-unsolved Rubik's Cube from the coffee table, and begins fidgeting with it. Blue and orange are the only two sides yet to be put in their proper places. "You know, a position is open at the *Chronicle* now. We could really use a new writer."

I roll my eyes, tipping my head against the back of the couch. "I told you, I'm no good at writing about local events."

"You wouldn't have to write about local events," Weston volleys back, spinning the cube at different angles. "You're good at other things. Like… giving people advice."

"Advice? On what?"

"Everything. Life, love, dating, marriage, that kinda stuff. People could write in to your column, and you'd pick the best questions and answer them." Weston shrugs. "I could totally get my dad on board with the idea. He needs something to appeal to the old ladies in our readership."

My eyebrows rise. "The old ladies?"

"Yeah, you're good with them," Weston says, nodding convincingly. "Look how much Mrs. Atwood loved you. It's because you're an old soul. Plus, you love bossing people around, telling them what they should and shouldn't do. You'd be great at giving life advice."

I narrow my eyes at him. "I'm sure there's a compliment in there somewhere."

Weston laughs, grabbing my hand and kissing my knuckles. "Think about it?"

I let him wait for a long moment before tipping my head indulgently. "I'll think about it. I *do* rather like telling people what they should do."

Weston seems satisfied that I've proven him right—again. He spins the Rubik's Cube one last time and stops, a smile dawning on his face. "Well, what do you know?" He tosses the cube into the air, catches it, and holds it up for me to see, a victorious twinkle in his eyes. "Solved it."

ACKNOWLEDGEMENTS

Confession time: when I finished writing *100 Days of Sunlight*, I had no idea just how much Tessa and Weston would steal my heart. I never could have imagined publishing my third book in this series and witnessing so much love, excitement, and support for these characters. So when it comes to the acknowledgements, my #1 biggest thanks goes to *you*, beautiful reader, for bringing this book into your life and following Tessa and Weston's journey this far. (Spoiler alert: it's not over yet!)

I want to give a huge thank you to my amazing mum and dad, for continuing to support my dreams and cheer me on. You both make the challenging days so much brighter just by being there for me. And of course, thank you to my sister Katie, for listening to the messy first draft of this short story collection and for encouraging me every step of the way.

So much gratitude to my amazing editor Jen, for always making the editing process way more fun than it has the right to be. Thank you for your dedication, encouragement, and—most of all—for the skink memes.

Thank you also to my dear friend Amy, for always keeping my spirits up and helping me to not take myself too seriously. And a big thank you to Brooke, for being such a wonderful, supportive friend and fellow indie author. I'm so blessed to have you both in my life!

And last but definitely not least, thank you to the entire Make Your Story Matter community for writing with me, supporting my dreams, and rooting for these characters since 2018. I wish I could hug each and every one of you.

Rock on,
Abbie

TESSA & WESTON'S PLAYLIST

———————————

Bridge Over Troubled Water · Simon and Garfunkel

You're Mine · Lola Marsh

I Just Love You · Roo Panes

You're All I Got · The Lumineers

Forever · Billy Raffoul

I'm With You · Vance Joy

Keep You Dry · Juke Ross

Heart In Two · Reuben And The Dark

In My Arms · Billy Raffoul

Overture · Sleeping At Last

Everything Is Possible Now · Clouds And Thorns

THE STORY'S NOT OVER YET!

Weston and Tessa will return in book four, the swoonworthy conclusion of the *100 Days of Sunlight* series. Scan the code below to stay updated on the release of their happily-ever-after!

You can find other bonus goodies like aesthetic boards, playlists, author Q&A and more at www.100DaysOfSunlight.com

ALSO BY ABBIE EMMONS

100 Days of Sunlight series:

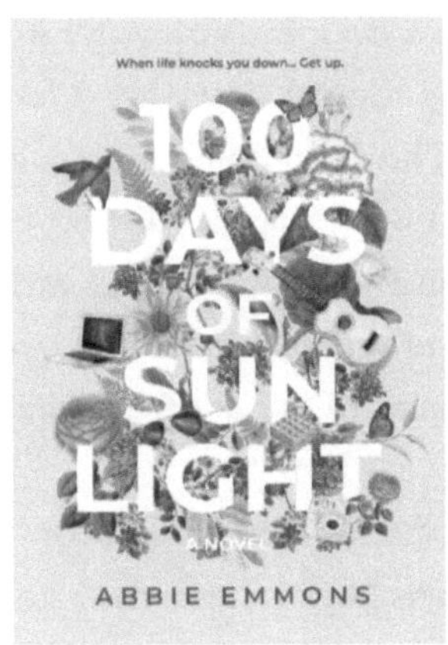

The Otherworld series:

ABOUT THE AUTHOR

Abbie Emmons has been writing stories ever since she could hold a pencil. What started out as an intrinsic love for story-telling has turned into her lifelong passion. There's nothing Abbie likes better than writing stories that are both heartrending and humorous, with a touch of cute romance and a poignant streak of truth running through them.

For over six years, Emmons has been sharing her wisdom on her YouTube channel, where she teaches writers how to make their stories matter by harnessing the power and psychology of storytelling to transform their ideas into masterpieces. When she's not writing or dreaming up new stories, you can find her binge-watching BBC dramas in her cozy Vermont home with a cup of tea.

youtube.com/abbieemmons

facebook.com/abbieeofficial

@makeyourstorymatter